THE HELION BAND

By AJ Mason

2022

Butterworth Books is a different breed of publishing house. It's a home for Indies, for independent authors who take great pride in their work and produce top quality books for readers who deserve the best. Professional editing, professional cover design, professional proof reading, professional book production—you get the idea. As Individual as the Indie authors we're proud to work with, we're Butterworths and we're *different*.

Authors currently publishing with us:

E.V. Bancroft
Valden Bush
Michelle Grubb
Helena Harte
Lee Haven
Karen Klyne
AJ Mason
Ally McGuire
James Merrick
Robyn Nyx
Simon Smalley

For more information visit www.butterworthbooks.co.uk

This trade paperback is published by Butterworth Books, UK

Cataloging information
ISBN: 9781915009173
Credits
Editor: Nicci Robinson
Cover Design: Nicci Robinson
Illustration: "Rose" by KC Lylark
Production Design: Global Wordsmiths

Acknowledgements

This is my first novel, and so I have inevitably got a rather long list of people to thank.

Nicci and Victoria at Global Wordsmiths for seeing the story inside me, patiently listening to my plot ideas, and teaching me how to bring the words in my head to the page. And also, for Nicci painstakingly editing my manuscript and helping me see and learn from my many mistakes.

My long-suffering family who have supported me on every step of this amazing journey.

My wonderful critical friends in the WOW and Swallows writing groups for all their good humour and encouragement.

Margaret Burris for finding all the errors and typos that I couldn't see anymore.

KC and Nicci for bringing the cover image in my head to life.

And last, but certainly not least, my darling, Lee, for her unwavering love and support, and for never ceasing to believe in me, even when I did.

Dedication

For my mum, Jill

For nurturing my love of books
and opening my eyes to other
worlds and other seas.

PROLOGUE

Year 202,055GT

"THE QUEEN IS DEAD! The queen is dead!"

Rose lifted her head, unsure of what she'd heard. She listened intently, but it was silent outside. She must have imagined it. She twisted her wrist in the dim light to better see the intricate patterns on the surface of her new bracelet, intrigued by their strangeness. She couldn't remember ever seeing them before, not in vids or on the jewellery and clothing worn by some of the more exotic visitors to the ship. There were more shouts and a terrible high-pitched wailing sent shivers down her spine. Doors slammed further up the corridor, accompanied by shouts for the household to rouse themselves.

Rose stiffened. They'd come to find her soon. Penthe had said she could keep the bracelet, that it was worthless junk, but the housekeepers might have different ideas. She needed to hide the small treasure and keep it safe from prying eyes. She pondered a good place to stash it in her tiny cotroom and her fingers strayed to her wrist but found only bare skin where there'd been cool metal seconds before. She looked down, turning her arm this way and that, but it was gone. Sweat broke out on her forehead. She scanned the floor and under the cotbed. Surely, she'd have felt it slip off. She willed it to appear again as mysteriously as it had disappeared.

Her left hand spasmed, pins and needles bursting in the tips of her rigid fingers. Strange, silvered symbols appeared on her forearm, popping up across the surface of her skin, as if gasping for air. They quickly slithered together, melded into a band, and began to languidly swim in a narrow stream that ringed her lower arm. A pleasant tingling sensation accompanied their actions, before her hand relaxed and returned to her control. Fear gripped her. She traced the pattern frantically with her eyes and fingers, desperately searching for something, anything, that might return the bracelet to its physical form. She pressed on the strange markings, now as much part of her skin as the small pale moles surrounding them, again and again, and became aware of a sudden, intolerable ache behind her eyes.

Footsteps approached, and her name was called by more than one panicked voice. She yanked down her tunic sleeve, ripping the seam a little in her hurry.

"Rose! What are you doing still sitting in here?" A chubby maid threw open the door, cheeks puffing from her exertions. "Go to your mistress immediately. She's having one of her fits. Get going before it gets worse, girl!"

Though her feet still throbbed from the long evening, Rose made her way quickly to the royal quarters. Any further delay would only result in punishment. There was a skittish excitement in the air; young voices babbled and choked off laughter. There was also a tangible fear. A couple of older women, once of the late queen's household, sat on a couch consoling each other. As was the custom they'd torn their clothes, and scratch marks were visible on their faces. Both looked up as she passed, trepidation in their eyes. There was no guaranteed role for them in the new household. The new queen, Penthesilea, would pick and choose the best and discard the rest to more menial tasks around the ship. They had always treated Rose haughtily, but she felt pity for them now. While her job felt unbearable, at least she had one. They might end up in the ship's laundry or worse, their devoted service forgotten.

She hurried on to Penthe's quarters and found it in a state of chaos, with her mistress hollering furiously at some unfortunate in the distance. In the Princess' reception room, the rest of the household milled around, unsure of what to do next. Rose could see triumphant looks on some faces, their ambitions at last realised. On other, perhaps wiser faces there was only a tired resignation. It had been a long, arduous journey with their young charge. Rose tried not to make eye contact with any of them, dreading being sent to the inner rooms to face Penthe's wrath. One of the senior housekeepers strode across the room. Acid bile rose in her throat at the look of grim determination on her face.

"Thank gods you're here, girl. Get in there and sort it out." She grabbed Rose and propelled her roughly towards the door.

Sort what out? Rose wanted to ask her. You mean distract her? Divert her ire from the rest of you? There was no point in arguing though. She couldn't evade the chaos that faced her in the next room.

As soon as Rose entered, Penthe's demeanour changed. Her screams and wild movements were replaced by an icy stare that made Rose's blood run cold. Penthe was far easier to predict when she was shouting.

"So, you finally deigned to turn up and serve me, girl."

Rose kept her eyes trained on the floor, maintaining a well-practised subservience. "Apologies for my tardiness, ma'am. It won't happen again."

Penthe walked over, pulled Rose's chin up, and slapped her face, hard. Anticipating the violence, she'd subtly adjusted her feet to take the blow but still struggled to stay upright. The room swam as she fought back the tears. No matter how many times this happened, it never got easier.

"I didn't ask for a fucking apology. Actually, I don't remember asking you to speak at all in my presence."

Out of the corner of her eye, Rose observed with weary detachment that the few maids that remained had started to slide out of the room. Cowards, all of them. She hated every single one of them. They were abandoning her, happy to have Penthe's wrath directed at her rather than them. Not for the first time she wished she had the strength to tell them exactly what she thought of them.

"Look at me, girl."

Rose lifted her eyes. Her mistress's eyes were wild with excitement, tears running down her face. Penthe paced the room, seemingly incapable of standing still, and her hands danced jerkily in the air to an unheard beat. Was this grief or happiness? Rose had never seen her behave like this before. As if in answer to her unspoken question, Penthe burst into speech.

"The queen is dead! The queen is dead!" Penthe's voice was high pitched, a perfect parody of those now hiding next door. "They think I don't hear, but I do." She smiled widely. "I see everything too. She's dead. All this is mine now."

Penthe snatched up a beautifully decorated antique vase from a nearby table and tossed it up in the air as if it was a toy.

"Please, ma'am. Calm yourself, please." She ran her hands though her hair. Why did she care? She should just let Penthe make a fool of herself. Penthe danced on the spot and tried unsuccessfully to balance the vase on her chin.

"Allow me." Rose couldn't bear to see anyone in this state, even

Penthe. She took hold of her arm and plucked the priceless artefact deftly from her hand. Penthe immediately ground to a stop, her arms slowly returning to her sides.

"Yes, your mother is dead, Penthe. You're our queen now. Queen Penthesilea of the House of Aximendes." She looked for some sign of understanding in her maddened, darting eyes. The mantle of duty and the weight of expectation were all Penthe's now. Everyone was watching; there would be nowhere to hide.

The last of Penthe's muscle tics eased, and her eyes finally focused properly.

She cocked her head to one side and looked at Rose with childlike wonder. "I'm the queen, Rose." Her eyes turned towards the door. "I'm their queen."

Rose's pulse pounded in her chest, hopeful the bout of mania was over. It wasn't the first time she had seen Penthe in such a state. The last time had been a summons, out of the blue, to assist her mother in welcoming the ambassador from a small itinerant mercantile community they needed to do business with. Given no time to revise the necessary diplomatic protocols involved in dealing with an insectile species, the young Princess had succumbed almost immediately. Rose had spent an intense thirty minutes talking calmly to her, before Penthe had calmed and left for the meeting abruptly without pausing to thank her.

She reached out tentatively for Penthe's hand. To her amazement, Penthe allowed her to guide her with no argument over to a couch next to the wall. The tears dried on Penthe's cheeks, but she was silent now, seemingly lost in her thoughts, and her eyes stared into the distance at an unseen horizon.

Rose joined her. She tried to sit as far away as possible but shuddered inside. Her stomach churning as she turned over one option after another, desperately trying to work out the best thing to do next.

"Everything is going to be okay, Penthe. I'll get the ship's doctor; she'll look after you."

Penthe's body went rigid. She jumped to her feet, her face suffused with anger and fists clenched, and loomed over Rose.

"I'm your queen! I do not need looking after."

Rose ducked under her arm, desperate to gain a safe distance. "I'm very sorry, ma'am. I didn't mean…"She edged backwards, her legs no longer feeling like they entirely belonged to her as Penthe advanced menacingly. She could call out for help, but no one would come. They never had before.

"I know exactly what you meant. You think I'm not capable, not strong enough to be queen. Just like my mother."

The first punch landed in her stomach. It took Rose's breath away and she doubled over, retching. The second one connected with the side of her jaw. Disorientated, her vision blurred, and the ground rose to meet her. Her mouth filled with the metallic tang of blood as her head hit the carpet. Surely someone would come in, someone would save her. She prayed to the gods for help.

"I'm going to kill you." Penthe's tone was conversational, matter of fact. "I should've done it a long time ago. I always knew you were working for my mother. Undermining me and spying on me. You still are, aren't you?"

Rose curled up into a ball and wrapped her arms around her head as Penthe aimed a flurry of kicks at her. A kick to her back made her scream out loud in agony. But still no help came. This would be the day that she died, and no one cared enough to try to prevent its inevitability. What had she done to deserve this?

"Yes, I think it's time to kill you. Now, where did I put my gun?" she asked, her voice strangely calm.

Rose watched as Penthe strode towards her dressing room. She willed herself to get up, but her body refused to respond. Every part of her was on fire. Her wrist, where the strange bracelet had melted into it, was hot and uncomfortable and the throbbing pain returned to her head. Her pulse hammered harder and harder behind her eyes, in sync with her terrified screams inside. The pain reached a crescendo, and she clutched her head, fearing it would explode. Her nose started to ache, and blood began to drip from it onto the soft, white rug. At the same, the pain started to ease slightly. But it was too late, Penthe had returned. Defeated, Rose closed her eyes and waited for the end.

"All right, bitch, where are you?"

Rose opened her eyes. Penthe was scanning the room, a confused, irritated expression on her face. She walked over to the bathroom door on the other side of the room, only a few metres away from Rose and peered inside.

"It's no good hiding. You're only making it worse. Show yourself immediately." Penthe's voice crackled with frustration.

Dizzily, Rose watched her walk into the bathroom. What was she talking about? She was in plain view. Quivering with faint hope, Rose tried again to get up. This time she managed to get to her knees, but one of her feet treacherously brushed the vase that had been left lying on the floor. It rolled into the leg of the couch and clinked against it.

Penthe strode back in the room, waving her gun. Rose put her hands up in a futile attempt to protect herself, but once again, Penthe stared right through her.

"Must've been my imagination."

It finally dawned on Rose that Penthe couldn't see her. Spots marred her vision, and she fought to stay calm. She held her hands up, looked down at herself, and pinched her skin. Everything was normal except Penthe couldn't see her. As if to refute her, Penthe walked towards her, towards the vase. Frozen to the spot, Rose held her breath and closed her eyes. She felt the draught of Penthe's breath as she passed, inches from her face. Rose was sure that her heart could be heard, it was pounding so hard.

Penthe sniffed the air like a hunting beast. "I can smell the little bitch. She can't have got far." She picked up the vase and slammed it back down on the table. A hairline crack zigzagged down its length. She stalked over to the bed and peered underneath into the shadows.

With Penthe's back turned, she shuffled back as quietly as possible and squeezed herself tightly in a corner. Penthe straightened and yelled for her housekeeper. Rose instinctively held her breath again but as she entered, the housekeeper showed no sign of seeing her either. She pulled up short at the sight of the pistol Penthe thrust at her.

"Where is she?" She punctuated each word with a jab of the pistol toward the housekeeper. "Don't look at me with that dumb expression, woman. You know who I mean. She couldn't have got out of here without you all seeing."

The housekeeper protested her innocence in vain. Penthe hit her across the face with the pistol, and a thin jet of blood flew from the housekeeper's nose. Rose winced and tongued the cut in her mouth from Penthe's attack.

Penthe dragged the housekeeper to each of the anterooms, as if she might be able to find Rose where she had not. When she pushed the woman roughly into the reception room, Rose managed a slow, painful ascent to her feet. Trembling, she edged closer to the door.

"Don't lie to me! She's not in my rooms, and there's only one way out. So, which one of you is hiding the traitorous bitch? Tell me now, or I'll have you all flogged until you scream for mercy."

The servants screamed their innocence, but Penthe was having none of it and crashing, splintering noises suggested furniture was being thrown. Rose waited patiently, not quite trusting her newfound invisibility. After a few minutes, it became clear that Penthe, while not entirely convinced that her household were not conspiring against her, was no longer willing to delay in her search.

"I want her found. Go through the ship. Leave no room, no cupboard, refuse bin, or bilge tank unsearched. If you want to live to see another day in my service, you'll find the bitch, and find her soon!"

The venom in Penthe's voice made Rose shudder inside. She listened to the servants running out into the far corridor, shouting her name. Penthe followed, her dark imprecations fading along with their cries, until there was only silence. Only then did she risk peeking through the doorway.

The room was empty except for a single guard standing to attention by the door to the corridor with a bored expression. One of the ornately carved tables was overturned and a broken chair was lying nearby. She winced at the irreparable damage that had been done to both. She'd often traced her fingers over the beautifully embroidered upholstery of the chair while polishing and dusting it. She would never own such an item, not only because of its value, but because every such chair was utterly unique and priceless. That Penthe had reduced it to firewood without a second thought made her want to scream and cry in equal measure.

Taking a deep breath, she considered her options. Staying was out of the question, but while the reception room was richly carpeted, the corridor beyond wasn't. Its bare floor would betray her escape.

Rose retreated into Penthe's dressing room and took her shoes off. Out of habit, she placed them neatly under one of the side tables. Would they be visible now? She had no idea. She looked down at the enigmatic markings on her arm, the only visible sign of the bracelet. It might have been worthless to Penthe, but it had somehow saved her life. How and why, she had no idea, but now was not the time to ask questions. She made a silent invocation to the gods and crept slowly through into the reception room. The guard coughed as Rose walked past her, making her heart jump. She held her breath and looked out into the corridor. Voices shouted in the distance, but they were only coming from one direction. Freedom beckoned in the other, and she didn't hesitate.

CHAPTER ONE

Five years later.

DREM, THE PLANET GLAVIN'S largest city, wasn't a place where it paid to be distracted. It was a bustling metropolis that never slept. Its buildings towered up into the sky, gesturing defiantly at the rest of the galaxy. The maelstrom of sights, sounds, and smells of millions of people living cheek by jowl bewildered most visitors. On the upper floors, the mega-rich fought ruthlessly with each other for capital and influence, while maintaining an air of urbane indifference. At ground level the battles were the same, but there was no veneer of politeness. The poorer denizens spent every day trying to navigate the taut surfaces of survival and ambition. Those that failed disappeared forever, without being mourned.

Unimpressed by the arrival of yet another anonymous soul drawn to its bright lights, the city had offered no respect or comfort. Instead, in the two cycles Rose had been here, it had pushed her around and tested her to near destruction. She still didn't feel in tune with its frenetic rhythm.

On her way back from the space port, the ageing transport tube broke down yet again, six stops short of her station. Swept out of the exit by the impatient crowds, Rose didn't hang around. Small time crooks from across the city would be converging like vultures on the milling, confused crowd. Left dizzy and cold from being pushed and jostled from every side, she looked for somewhere safe to take stock and recognised the rusting doors behind her as the entrance to the Central Hall. She'd only been here the other week showing Vash around. She pulled the door open and stepped inside.

Drem had started as a small trading settlement, and it was possible to still find its remnants. The Central Hall was where the merchants had fought with each other for the best resources, sometimes to the death. She was struck as always by the pervasive smell of damp and decay. Ageing glow lamps, the colour of burnt umber, dimly illuminated endless dusty surfaces, and scratched plastiglas cases reverently guarded unreadable yellowing leaves of paper. Vash had screwed her face up at the dust and the smell, but Rose drew comfort from the sense of small-town community that resonated deep within its walls. It reminded her of home, of the sense of togetherness she still mourned.

Today it was enlivened further by an invasion of school children. They ran around shrieking and laughing, their teacher vainly trying to get their attention, and Rose laughed with them. The innocence of their explorations lifted her spirits and gave her the strength to leave the hall and continue towards home.

There was no innocence in the boy that stood in front of Rose now, less than a klick or so from her apartment, holding a homemade blade to her stomach. It was her own fault she'd been lost in her thoughts. "Fishing for stars," her mother used to call it. He wasn't wearing shoes, although it was cold and wet, revealing the striped webbing between his toes that marked him as a Loric. Rose surmised that although he was probably physically about eight cycles old, in street age he was nearer fifty-five. She also knew him. "Harris?"

He peered more closely at her. His dark eyes flickered across her face, partially hidden by the cloth wound around his head. He made a quick series of hand jive movements to his partners in crime hidden in the shadows and tucked his crude plastiknife away. The skin on her forearm had barely tingled, thank the gods. Perhaps, in its own mysterious way, the strange band-like tattoo of symbols had known before her that she was in no real danger. Rose always tried her best to ignore it. Beyond an empirical knowledge that it reacted when she was in danger, she hadn't worked out a way to control its actions, and she was happiest when it was doing nothing at all.

"Fates, I'm sorry, Rose. Was in such a rush coming back from the action at the tube I didn't realise it was you. You gotta keep your wits about you, mind. You looked way too easy." Harris pulled down his mask, revealing golden stripes across his puckered cheeks, and a not particularly remorseful grin. He lowered his hands to his sides, relaxed and ready, but his gaze continued to dart about. Unlike her, he remained alert to the dangers of Drem.

They'd first met when he'd tried in vain to shelter in the sexden one particularly cold night. Drem was hard on its street dwellers. Rose had been distressed too often, returning each morning to her small apartment, by the sight of lifeless faces lying in the gutter. Wanting for once to make a difference, she'd snuck out from behind the reception and bought a big bowl of steaming noodles from a nearby vendor. The boy was where she expected to find him, huddled by the building's heating vent trying to warm himself. He'd looked at her outstretched hand as if it was an alien object, but eventually snatched the bowl from her. Watching with dark distrustful eyes, he'd inhaled the noodles. Neither spoke. There wasn't anything worth saying.

The next morning, Rose had found a tiny bunch of drooping flowers tied with plastic cord waiting for her at the sexden's reception. He'd probably stolen them, but she was still touched by the gesture. They weren't exactly friends, neither was that naive, but she kept an eye out for him and offered small assistance when she could. In return, he had offered advice on places to avoid and, rather ironically in the circumstances, ways to make herself safer.

"I thought you were going to give up all of this?"

He probably had no intention of doing so but a part of her enjoyed making him squirm a little for giving her such a shock.

"I will do, Rose, promise. Just not today, got to pay some bar bills, see. Remember now, no daydreaming. Keep safe!" Harris winked and ran off into the market crowds. His gang flowed out of the shadows and joined him, laughing and shouting.

Rose couldn't help but smile as well. At least he was honest, and the gods knew she needed something to lighten her mood today. Saying goodbye to Vash earlier had been as hard as ever.

They'd met at one of the port bars. Sent by her boss to pick up a package from a merchant who was late, she'd been sipping on her second citriflush when Vash had sat next to her and said hello. Her easy smile had disarmed Rose, and she'd shyly accepted the offer of another drink. They'd started talking and somehow never stopped. In the weeks that had followed, the handsome privateer had courted her; she'd brought flowers or some small gift from one of her trips off-system every time she visited. Rose couldn't help being drawn into the ancient dance, telling herself that she could, and would, move on before things got too serious. Being in a relationship was a risk she didn't need to take.

But she hadn't moved on. Vash had become a fixture in her life, and

Rose still had no idea of where they were going. And it was those thoughts that had filled her head until the run in with Harris. *So stupid.* Her blood ran cold at how close she had come to injury or worse. But this dissociation was fast becoming the norm. Increasingly, Rose found herself in a kind of weird limbo, going through the motions until Vash strode back in through the door so she could start living again. Vash showed no sign of letting her into her own life. She always came to find Rose, not the other way around. That had been okay at first, but gradually, as her own feelings deepened for Vash, it had started to matter. But it was foolhardy to think of making a home with Vash when the threat of Penthe was ever present. The events of the past few years, fleeing in panic from system to system, had taught her to be cautious. A few months after going on the run, she had spotted the first of Penthe's spies, disguised as a trader. It was a dark truth that only an Akmonian could spot another Akmonian in a crowd. She was asking casual questions, showing an image of Rose and spreading lies. Rose was a wanted criminal, with a reward on her head. She had stolen an item from the Royal family itself, a treason like no other. It could only be the bracelet; Rose had taken nothing else. For a moment she had considered giving herself up. Let them try to remove it, she would get on with her life. But Rose knew that path would only lead to death. Penthe would not forgive and forget. So she had fled once again. So far, she'd always managed to stay one step ahead—thanks to the band somehow knowing Penthe was close and alerting Rose to the danger, giving her time to escape. But everywhere she looked, she saw other couples building lives together and yearned to be like them.

Vash seemed to be serious about the relationship and to really care about Rose, despite the difficulties that dogged their time together. Rose's dark scars persisted in clouding their time with each other, and Vash's continued patience only made it worse. She could still remember the anxious anticipation, every ill-disguised flinch of those early days. It had been months before they'd lain together. Vash hadn't pushed, which added to the confusion. There was no doubt that Vash could have anyone she wanted in her bed. Rose caught the admiring looks from others when they were out. If Vash noticed the attention, she gave no sign. But were there other women in other cities? Perhaps that was why Vash was so patient with her. Even when they had finally made love, and Rose should've been basking happily in the afterglow, she'd not been able to prevent herself trembling in anticipation that Vash might want more. There was a part of her which had curled in a tight ball and hidden away deep inside. Vash's tenderness had slowly drawn it back out into the light. However, she couldn't seem to stop shaking a little inside every time Vash got physically close or showed any sign of irritation. She feared Vash was growing weary of constantly having to second guess her reactions.

That was probably the answer. Maybe Vash was worried that Rose would be shocked and alarmed by the rough life of a space trader. She closed her eyes briefly. What was she doing? At this rate, she'd end up with another knife in her back.

She walked on quickly into the depths of the market and was instantly enveloped by a heady atmosphere of scents. Perfumes, exotic dishes, sweets, and spices from across the galaxy suffused together creating a smell that she would still taste hours later. This was one of her favourite places, and for a moment, she was able to put aside all thoughts of Vash. One of her favourite vendors waved frantically in greeting, and she weaved her way through to him.

"My beautiful Rose, I've been looking everywhere for you. I've had a fresh consignment of the finest cheese. Cloned Friesians as well, none of your agrilab grown stuff. See, I have the paperwork. Would you like a taste? This is only for the connoisseur." His eyes twinkled.

She smiled at the compliment and accepted the sample. Rose was always an eager customer. The cheese was deliciously creamy to touch and taste, and she inhaled the divine smell, closing her eyes with pleasure. After she'd enjoyed the obligatory haggle and agreed on the price, they shook hands and he parcelled it up. Walking on, she smiled at the thought of the dish that she would prepare the next time Vash had furlough.

On the far edge of the market, she caught sight of a cushion. One of the better hardware sellers had hung it from the roof of their stall where its quality wouldn't be missed by the passing crowds. Nothing was wasted in Drem; the cloth used for the cover had probably once adorned a room at the top of one of the towers. However, it wasn't the quality of the material that attracted Rose, it was the pattern. It reminded her of something, somewhere. She chewed her lip as the hopeful stall holder sidled closer.

Ice ran down her spine. Penthe had one like it in her reception room. She motioned to the owner that she wasn't interested, pulled her scarf tighter around her face, and marched on, staring at the ground.

Only when she was clear of the stalls did she pause on a quiet corner. Every day she stopped in an effort to see the sky between the great towers before she went inside. She could only see a small patch at best, but the sight of the clouds or stars was a release from the sharp corners of the city. More than once, she had caught a glimpse of Glavin's twin moons, Hypnos and Thanatos, passing overhead at their zenith. She had stood there, drinking in the wonder while the rest of the city bustled past, too busy to care. However, on this occasion, the shadow of a city car dropping clients off at a penthouse high above obscured most of the view. She stepped back sadly and promptly bumped into a kidbin being pushed by a large matronbot. The cover was opaque, obscuring the child or perhaps children within. The bot stopped, patiently waiting for her to move and Rose instinctively held a hand up in apology, though the bot had more sensors than sentience. Face burning with embarrassment, she hurried on to the tower block where she rented a small third floor habroom. She was working in the bar of a fun palace nearby. Her boss had let her know when it had become available, enabling her to beat the rest of the crowd in the race for a bit of private space. She suspected that he might have done so in hope of future favours but so far, he hadn't called them in.

The entrance was only a few feet away when she felt the burning sensation in her arm again, growing stronger this time. A quick look around confirmed that she was in no immediate physical danger. No one was close so she pulled up her sleeve slightly. A dim glow emanated from between the bangles she was wearing. Danger: clear and present danger. From where? *Penthe*. Rose clutched at her stomach, nearly dropping her parcel. She glanced around one more time before running for the entrance hall and the stairs to her apartment. She ignored the happy cries of her neighbour's children, inviting her to join their game, and slammed the door and locked it.

This can't be happening. Not now, not after so long. Her heart pounded as she quickly snatched the strings of the louvred windows and blocked out the city. She sat on the edge of her bed and slowly pulled her sleeve up. In the darkness, the light was clear to see, throwing writhing shadows into the corners of the room. She removed her bangles one by one. The action left her feeling strangely naked, her arm cool and bare. A stream of symbols glowed brightly. Embedded in her skin, the oily metal flowed and swirled across her wrist. As always, it looked alive, like an alien symbiotic sentience creating complex fluid patterns in an attempt to communicate. Rose didn't speak its language but couldn't take her eyes from it. Entranced by its sinuous movement, she fell into and through the silvery river, and the voices in her head shrieked as the outside world disappeared.

Hysterical laughter in the distance started to intrude, and it took a moment to realise she was the source. She couldn't get enough oxygen into her lungs and desperately tried to focus on the coolness of her breath as it passed through the tip of her nose. To her relief, the voices faded. The connection to the real world was slowly restored, and she could breathe again.

The flow of symbols still glowed and danced, apparently impervious to her distress. It felt cool to the touch despite its movement. She had experienced this too many times though to doubt its meaning. Whenever such a frenzy of activity had happened before, it had proved to be a timely warning of Penthe's arrival in the locality. The band was somehow particularly sensitive to the Akmonian queen's presence. Did it want to return to her ownership or was it just a reaction to Rose's own unfettered fear of her pursuer? Whatever its motivations, she had to take it seriously. It'd been so very long this time, though. How was this fair? She'd put down roots in Drem, become part of the community, and found Vash. Rose looked down at her hands, shaking uncontrollably, and let her tears rain down onto them. She only had one choice, but that didn't make it any less painful.

CHAPTER TWO

"I CAN ONLY ASSUME the stars and planets cried in despair when you were born, you stupid woman." Queen Penthesilea glared at the woman kneeling in front of her. It was at times like these that the crown of the House of Aximendes weighed most heavily upon her head. "Whoever seeded you was a moron, and your mother must have been an idiot to breed with him."

Ypoploi Tedros stayed silent, though she rocked slightly in the face of her queen's wrath. Penthe stared up at the ornately decorated ceiling of her official reception. What would her mother have done? The late queen would probably have clicked her fingers and had the junior officer killed where she knelt. No doubt she would have been praised effusively by her fawning advisors for her strong leadership. Penthe shuddered inwardly. People talked behind her back about her short temper but had conveniently forgotten the blood-soaked time of her mother's leadership. Only recently she'd been gifted a new record of the House, brought up to date by the Guild of Historians. It spoke of consolidation and stability. They should have tried living with the old bitch. No, there were better ways to deal with this situation than ruining yet another priceless twistrug.

"Show me the readings again. I want to see the timestamps for each of the sensor scans. Why I'm having to deal with this at all is beyond belief." She drummed her fingers while she waited. The whole situation was both confusing and frustrating. This ship had been designed quite deliberately, anticipating her eventual ascent to the throne. The Aximendes VI was a thing of terrible beauty. Experts had likened it to a coleoidea, found commonly on water worlds. If only they knew how accurate they were. As a child often left to amuse herself, she'd watched screens avidly and had happened on an old docvid about these creatures. Despite the graininess of the restored file, she'd been entranced by their mobility and the way they hunted using nerve endings on the ends of their tentacles to detect their prey. There was no hiding from them in the darkest depths of the ocean, just as there was no hiding from her. Rose would soon learn that fact.

"Ma'am."

Archiploi Volos, her chief of staff, ran up and handed over the data sheets, keeping her eyes firmly fixed on the floor. Penthe scanned down them slowly and clenched her teeth. Nothing made any sense. According to these readings, the sensors hadn't detected the system defence drone until it was far too late. Which meant that either they had malfunctioned, or they had not been programmed properly by their operators.

Her mother had shown no interest in engineering and had ordered her to work with ship builders on the Aximendes VI. Penthe assumed the old hag saw it as an opportunity to side-line her away from more important House matters. However, Penthe had known exactly what she wanted and instructed the builders to construct a ship sporting long grasping limbs with the latest in sensor technology at the end of each. On its own, each limb was capable of scanning for objects over five lightyears away. Working together, they could construct a detailed picture of an object that more conventional ships couldn't do at even half the distance. The Aximendes VI swam the inky blackness between the stars searching out its prey, exactly like its watery counterparts, always able to maintain the advantage of surprise.

Her mother had dismissed the new ship with a disdainful flick of her wrist. Even though she'd expected such a response, Penthe had still been hurt by the lukewarm reaction. Only the knowledge of its capability—new offensive powers which she would gain the most benefit from—had kept her spirits afloat.

"Well, what is your explanation for this?" She scrunched the readings into tight balls and threw them at the head of the quivering officer. "These readings do not lie, Ypoploi Tedros. So, again, what is the explanation for this incompetence? Incompetence so great that some might call it treason." Penthe tried to control her tone, but her pulse was rising.

What particularly irked her was that her strategy had been so simple. Diligent enquiries had finally revealed that Rose had been found passage on a merchant ship bound for the RH15 system, but there were several inhabited planets and the vessel had stopped at all of them. Worse still, the merchants were enemies of the House of Aximendes with powerful allies of their own, so no amount of bribery or coercion could extract where Rose had disembarked. Penthe had planned to keep her fleet on the edge of the system while undercover intelligence officers posing as traders discovered her precise location. Then the Aximendes VI would steam in for a quick snatch and grab. The system boasted little else to entice her, and she didn't intend to get embroiled in an unnecessary conflict when a far bigger prize was on offer.

"Ma'am, it is evident that the defence drone was able to communicate before we destroyed it. I would suggest—"

"You'd suggest?" Penthe threw back her head and laughed. "I ordered, explicitly, that our sensors were to be used with the widest parameters possible. They should have been capable of picking up a space dust at three lightyears. Yet this drone remained undetected! You offer no explanation for why my orders were disobeyed, no rational excuse for why our smooth progress has now been impeded, and yet still you *dare* to suggest."

Against the far wall, bunched close to the exit, her advisors stood silent. None of them were stupid enough to offer any opinions or speak up for the hapless junior officer. Penthe leaned back, crossed her arms, and surveyed them contemptuously. None of them had the training or the breeding to sit in her chair, but some of them were ambitious and would try to take her throne at the first sign of weakness.

Unfortunately for them, her upbringing had not encouraged any to develop. Her mother, the vindictive old crone, had arranged for her to spend a season in another house. What was considered a privilege to be condemned to a period of servitude was a hellish finishing school for young royals. Her mother had allowed a minor house, eager to curry favour, to have the honour of Penthe's placement. From the moment she had arrived, she scrubbed floors, carried her mistress' train, and ate what scraps were left over from her table. Penthe had cried herself to sleep on the odd occasions she'd been allowed any. Her mistakes had been dealt with harshly but not until she returned home and discovered that the young princess sent in exchange had been sent back in a body bag had she realised how lucky she'd been.

She'd lain awake for hours, shaken at the thoughts of what the girl must have endured. Fearful of her mother's wrath, she'd publicly maintained an indifferent attitude to the girl's fate. In private, and for the first time, she'd questioned the conservative customs that her family and community clung to. That girl might have grown up to become a great leader, an asset to her House. Why did one mistake rob them of her potential? What did it prove?

Now she was queen, the one wielding all that power and awe. She had promised herself that she would bring change, but it had proved hard. Leniency and mercy were interpreted as weakness by those under her rule. An iron fist was not just expected, it was respected, especially by those who would never have to make those life and death decisions themselves. She swallowed and bile burned her throat.

Penthe leant down and pulled the officer up by the hair, until her pale, sweaty face was level with her own. "Well, I *suggest* that you track down the ingrate who did not program the sensors correctly."

Tedros nodded, eyes wide.

"I want them delivered to the T-suite within the next hour. When they've finished explaining exactly and in minute detail *why* they felt the need to disobey me, I want them ejected from the nearest airlock."

Tedros blinked as spittle from Penthe's mouth sprayed their face. She let the officer go, sat back and deliberately, carefully rearranged her gown. Her advisors remained silent, most now staring at the floor. The iron fist had been wielded.

"Hopefully those final few seconds of life will afford them the clarity of thought they were missing when at their post. Let the message go out: I will brook no more failure." Unable to hold in her frustration any longer, she lashed out with her foot and connected with Tedros' head. She cried out and Penthe smiled. Why should she be the only one with an aching head? "And don't bother coming back before this is done, Ypoploi Tedros, or you'll be the one taking a walk in the vacuum."

Tedros nodded, as did everyone else. A couple were taking notes, the gods knew why.

"Oh, just get out of here." Penthe reached for her goblet and threw the contents over the woman.

The officer backed away on her knees, kras dripping from her hair before she turned and fled from the room. She ran as if her life depended on it, which of course it did. Some of the advisors were fidgeting now, trying to catch her eye. She was in no mood for their reports or their excuses. "Leave me. I need to consider this matter further." She waved them all away.

Only once the last one had scuttled out of the room did Penthe rise and walk over to the exquisitely carved ivory desk, a gift from one of their subject systems. Her head still ached. She scratched at her head; the crown was making her scalp itch more than ever today. She wore it to impress, but there was nothing practical about its design, much like all the other ornate trappings that littered the reception area. The wealth in this single room alone could have funded a small orbital, but she hated every single highly polished and embellished bit of it.

Anything that had been gifted to Penthe had been placed into storage. Not a single trinket, picture, or trophy of war remained in her quarters, though her mother had been dead over five cycles. It hadn't gone unnoticed, and it had caused confusion and increasing dismay among her household and perhaps beyond. No one dared to say anything to her face of course, but the expectation was deafening.

Not that she dared reveal why. After all, Rose had taken with her the very thing that the fortunes of this House rested on. How could she call herself queen when she had allowed it to be lost? Every time she donned the crown, she felt like an imposter, a disgrace to her royal line. Until she retrieved what she had lost so carelessly, she merely occupied this ceremonial space and didn't deserve to call it her own. She let out a deep breath and removed the crown, carefully placing it back on its dais next to the desk.

A portrait of her mother hung on the wall. Placed where she was forced to see it, in her periphery. The ugly hag had sat for days for the artist. He'd been considered the best in his academy and been well rewarded for his efforts. Penthe couldn't fault his skill with the brush. He had somehow managed to capture the soul of the woman as well as her appearance. The cold, ruthless expression in her eyes, the judgmental set of her jaw. It was all there, damn him.

Her mother had insisted on hanging the portrait in this room, aware of its psychological effect on her visitors and subjects. She'd been so happy with the artist, an ambitious digital painter from the Xteltn system naively hoping for her patronage, that she had decided not to kill him. Instead, she had wiped his memory using drugs, and sent him back to his home planet with her agents. Penthe had never been able to look at those piercing eyes long. She could feel them, boring holes in her head. She fought the fierce urge to tear it down, to rip up everything in the room and throw it in a rubbish chute. Instead, she opened a drawer, fished out the silk cloth she kept in there for precisely this purpose, and carefully draped it over the frame.

Free of her mother's judgmental gaze, some of the tension flowed out of her body. It was time to take stock of the situation. She activated the gleaming, bejewelled console on the desk. It lifted and started to spring into life as she sank into the command chair. Servos whined quietly as the supple, hand-sewn tanskin adjusted itself perfectly to the shape of her back. Fates, what had she done to deserve this? Her head wanted to explode with the voices inside. They either shouted at her to do more, better and faster or spitefully hissed that she wasn't up to the job and never would be. That last voice was always the loudest.

The display on the console did nothing to improve her temper. They were still ten lightyears from the RH15 system, but the authorities there were forewarned, thanks to that damned defence drone. Penthe chewed her lip. Nothing this backwater wielded could overpower the Aximendes VI, but now she'd have to waste valuable time subduing them. Tasting iron, she wiped her mouth with her sleeve, indifferent to the stain of blood left on the expensive cloth.

She rested her hands on the smooth, cold ivory arms of the chair and noted that her nails were perfectly polished and smooth. They didn't look like the hands of a murderer. Shouldn't a murderer's hands be rough and hard-bitten, not soft and pampered like hers? Her mother's hands had been soft and manicured as well. She could still feel them scratching her face, squeezing her throat. She could hear her crisp cruel words, *Ugly little bitch. Spoilt, ugly little bitch, ruining my life.* Pressure built behind her eyes, and she closed them in desperation. She pinched the top of her hand hard and focused on the intense pain caused by her long nails sinking into the flesh. Slowly the pressure receded, and the voice retreated with it, becoming a distant whisper. She let out a long breath and savoured the release for a few moments.

The console display was still there when she opened her eyes again. The situation hadn't changed, but her resolve had returned. She would own this room. She would be the queen she was destined to be. She had nothing to lose and everything to gain.

CHAPTER THREE

VASH'S SCHEDULE HAD BEEN a hectic one lately. In the first few months, they'd been together for at least a week at a time, but that had reduced to a couple of days at most now, and Rose often found herself looking at the door, hoping that Vash would walk through it. Vash didn't talk much about her work, batting away any questions with a smile and a quick change of subject. However, it was clear she was swamped at present. She was flush with sysgeld and had sported a new pair of expensive boots when she'd last visited. The rich brown tanskin that Vash always favoured smelled wonderful. After Rose had admired them, Vash had pulled out a pair of delicate gold filigree earrings and beamed with pleasure when Rose modelled them. As usual, Rose had kept her real thoughts to herself, scared of appearing clingy. Yes, she loved the jewellery, but she would have welcomed a few more days with Vash.

Parting at the entrance to the port transport tube earlier, Vash had mentioned something about difficult repairs and a tight deadline. So, it was only after hours of agonising that Rose finally tried to make contact. She had to flee Drem, but she couldn't leave without talking to Vash.

"Hey, lovely. Did I forget something?" Vash's face, peering out from the small vidscreen, had smears of some dark substance on it.

"Oh no, no. It's just that…the thing is, I really need to see you. To talk to you."

"But I only saw you this morning."

Rose's face flushed. How could she explain over the phone? It was just impossible. Penthe would have her spies scanning all the open channels, searching for any clue as to her whereabouts. She shouldn't have made the call in the first place. "I know, but I just need to talk to you. I didn't know then."

"Didn't know what?"

"I can't say—I mean, I can't talk about it on this line." Rose chewed on her lip.

"Well, I'm kinda busy here—"

"Please, Vash. I need to see you." Rose clamped a hand over her mouth, shocked at her own effrontery. She tried to calm herself again. "I can't explain, but I really need to see you in person." Her hands were shaking badly now, and tears weren't going to be far behind.

Vash stared, deep concern etched in her expression. "Okay. I need to make some kit safe this end, but I'll be with you as soon as I can."

Rose looked up at the plastitiled ceiling with utter relief. Tears flooded down her cheeks unchecked, and Vash's voice receded for a few moments.

"Sorry, I'm so useless. What did you say?" She wiped the back of her hand across her eyes.

Vash pushed back a stray hair from her sweaty brow. "Look, I can see you're really upset, but just try to relax now. I won't be long. Whatever this is, we'll get it sorted out. Just hang in there. Promise?"

"I promise, and thanks… Thank you so much."

Vash smiled, put her fingers to her lips and then to the surface of her vidscreen, leaving a small smear. "See you soon, gorgeous." The screen went blank.

Rose rested her head in her palms. She'd never deliberately lied to Vash, but she would have to again before the night was over. Just thinking about the deception made her shudder. This was all so unfair. Drem was the fourth city in the third system that she'd tried to hide in. After five cycles, she'd dared to hope that she'd finally thrown Penthe off her trail. The gods knew that she'd never have taken such a risk with Vash otherwise. She was so tired of running, of being afraid and skulking in the shadows. The precious time she spent with Vash let her forget all of that. Now she'd have to step back into the dark embrace of those fears again and make a life in another strange place more remote than this.

Three hours later, the apartment was in darkness, the air inside hot and still. Tightly closed blinds blocked out the pulsing neon lights outside, and the only sound was the excited chatter of the children on the landing outside, playing one of their games. The loud thud of her own pulse beat out the rhythm of her anxiety, its tempo rising and falling. The band had settled a little, but her arm was still alive with its movement. Rose had put her coat back on, worried that in the darkness the glow would be visible to Vash through her thin shirt.

Footsteps echoed on the concrete stairwell. Someone was taking two steps at a time, a favourite habit of Vash's, but Rose stayed silent, needing to be sure. The knock on the door was firm and shadows appeared in the crack of light at the bottom. Rose stood, heart thumping, and crept over to the door on bare feet, careful not to make any noise. She hadn't been able to afford an apartment with Safevid. Now she rued both her finances and complacency as she was forced to put her face close to the surface of the door to see who it was. As she pressed her eye to the peephole, there was a bang on the door, harder this time, and she jumped.

"Rose, are you in there? It's Vash."

It sounded like Vash, but paranoia drove her to look through the peephole to check anyway. Vash stood, hands on hips and a tense expression on her face. Rose carefully released the door locks and opened it a crack. She stepped back to keep out of sight.

Vash pushed the door open and came in. Stark white light from the stairwell flooded in and forced Rose to shield her eyes but not before she'd seen the children staring at her. What did they see? Their friend, Rosie, standing barefoot and wild-haired? Would this be how they remembered her when she was gone? She yearned to shelter in the darkness again.

"You okay, Rose? Why haven't you got the lights on?"

Vash's voice, though not loud, reverberated around the room. Rose pressed one finger to her lips and motioned frantically to her to close the door. Vash did as instructed, and they were both plunged into deep gloom again. Vash crossed the room. There was a quiet click and a dim circle of light spread outwards from a glow lamp, throwing up deep shadows in the corners.

"That's better. It's not good for anyone to hang around in the gloom like this."

Vash sat on a threadbare seat next to the table and after a pause, raised her eyebrow. "Aren't you going to sit down?"

Legs on autopilot, Rose sat in the other chair. Avoiding Vash's questioning gaze, she fussed instead with the sleeves of her coat, anxiety gnawing at her stomach. *Where to begin?*

Vash cleared her throat. "So, how are you, gorgeous? I've been worried since you called me." She took Rose's hand.

Rose looked down at Vash's fingers lightly tracing circles over the back of her hand, barely registering her words. Vash's touch was so comforting, her fingers brushing her skin with a gentle kindness she didn't deserve.

She pulled her hand away. Vash looked up at her, a familiar expression of confused pain on her face. Rose slid her hand back, but the damage was done. Perhaps it was time to get this over with. "I've got to leave Drem. I have to leave the system." There it was, she'd said it. She couldn't bring herself to look up, and Vash didn't respond. Laughter came from the stairwell where the children had returned to their game.

"Leave? I only just got here."

Vash's jocular tone didn't fool Rose for a minute. She yanked her sleeves down again and didn't answer. What more was there to say? Nothing would make the situation better. Vash moved from her chair and crouched down next to her. Her cologne filled the air, the gentle spices evoking such wonderful memories. Fates, why was this so difficult? Perhaps she should have just left a message. Rose wrapped her arms around herself and stared at the ceiling, tears pricking at her eyes.

"Please talk to me, Rose. I can't bear to see you like this." Vash said softly. "Is it something I've done? I'd never mean to hurt you but—"

"No, it's nothing to do with you." Rose looked down in horror at Vash's honest face and shook her head. "You haven't done anything, believe me." A tear tumbled down her cheek.

"So, tell me what's upset you so much that you want to just pack up and leave." Vash wiped the tear gently away. "Is it your boss at that bloody sexden? Or that shifty Harris lad? I can sort it out, whatever it is."

Rose smiled despite herself. It warmed her heart when Vash got protective. She reached out and buried her fingers in Vash's hair. "I wish it was that simple, handsome. Even rough, tough Captain Munro won't be able to sort this one out."

Vash stood, her face flushing red in the light of the glow lamp. "I care about you, and I can see you are upset, but…" She walked towards the window and tugged aside the blind at one corner. "Maybe this is a big thing, but please don't make fun of me."

Fates, how could she have been so clumsy? "I know how much you care, Vash, and that's why I asked you here. I couldn't bear the thought of leaving without telling you."

Vash didn't turn around, but she let the blind go and it flapped back into place. To Rose's chagrin, happy as she was that Vash was listening again, she was more relieved that the blind was closed again.

"Well, you should also know I don't do mysteries, Rose. I want to help you, but you have to talk to me." Vash waited.

Rose bit her lip. This went against all her rules. Rules that had kept her safe so far. "Are you sure?"

"Please, tell me."

The pleading tone of Vash's voice made her heart ache, and her head pounded as her anxiety threatened to explode. The band was also growing steadily more active, reacting to her rising emotions. She swallowed and tried to keep her voice calm. "I'm an Akmonian." The words span languidly in the dust motes between them. With each passing second, the beat behind her eyes grew faster and harder. Vash turned slowly, her face paler in the gloom, and her expression unreadable.

"So, you're an Akmonian." She stepped forward, back into the circle of light.

Vash leaned over Rose and studied her face, scanning it intently for something Rose couldn't guess at, but the intensity of her examination gave her goosebumps. Finally, Vash stepped back into the edge of the glow from the lamp.

"Yep, I thought so. Try again, Rose. You've got green eyes, remember?" She crossed her arms, stony-faced.

She leant back in the chair and suppressed a highly inappropriate desire to giggle. All this terrible anxiety and Vash didn't believe her anyway. Oh, well, time for the next big reveal. She crooked a finger, inviting Vash to lean in. She frowned but came closer. Rose closed her eyes and concentrated for a moment before she slowly opened them again. "It's true that I do sometimes have green eyes, but I was born with these." They were so close that she could see her gold irises reflected in Vash's eyes.

"Oh gods!" Vash pulled the other chair over and sank into it. "A fucking Ak." Vash stared as she chewed on her bottom lip.

Rose waited. The words were aggressive, but she'd heard worse. Still, she tensed instinctively, anticipating violence. If she'd misjudged Vash, she was going to find herself in detention quickly. What she would give now for more time.

"Have you seen the news vids? About that Ak ship?" Vash fiddled with one ear lobe.

Rose hadn't, but she could guess what they were saying. "Yes. That's why I must leave. I think that ship's here looking for me." She prayed Vash wouldn't ask the obvious.

"Why would they be after you?"

No, the gods had obviously gone on vacation. Vash was silent and still, waiting for an explanation. Rose stroked her own arm, feeling the band swirling slowly under her fingers. Well, she'd come this far. "How much do you know about Akmonian ships and how we live?"

"Warrior civilisation, spread across the galaxy. When they turn up uninvited, they usually raze everything to the ground." Vash gave her a hard stare.

She blinked nervously. Though the reputation of her people wasn't entirely exaggerated, the myths surrounding their life made her sigh inside. The House of Aximendes proudly maintained an active fighting force, but the bulk of its fortune was made through trade, not plunder. "That's fair comment. I rather hope that you've seen a different side to what you think you know about Akmonians in me?" She took the faint blush on Vash's face as a positive acknowledgement. "Well, every Akmonian House has its own queen, a basilinna. She's the supreme leader of the House and its fleet."

"Yeah, I know that. I still don't understand where you come in."

"I worked in the household of Queen Penthesilea of the House of Aximendes. She mistreated me, beat me up. A lot. It got so bad that I had to run away."

Vash's expression softened a little. "I suppose I'd suspected that something had happened in the past. I hoped you'd tell me about it eventually."

"And given your reaction to me being Akmonian, now you know why I put that off for so long. I could've made something up but that wouldn't have felt right." She looked at her feet.

"Being someone's punchbag, that's just fucking…fucking awful." Vash sat forward again. "I understand why you left, but why is she looking for you?"

Rose considered her options. She longed to tell Vash everything, but she needed more time. How could she explain about the band when she didn't fully understand it herself? And there was the small matter of ownership. In the last system, Penthe had spread a story that she'd stolen it. Vash probably wouldn't believe that, but what if she did? No, it was best to take the easier route for now. "Akmonians bring shame if they ever leave their House. I only knew of one person who left, and we were told never to speak of her again."

"Why do people leave? Apart from trying to get away from psychopathic queens?"

"Sometimes they meet someone off-ship and elope. Others commit crimes against the House and are exiled. My House usually just executed those people to discourage others."

"They sound like a lovely family; I wish I could meet them."

Rose bridled at Vash's tone. "A queen has a lot of responsibilities. They must maintain the fortunes of the House and keep everyone happy. They're deposed and killed or sent into exile if they don't to live up to expectations." Who was she kidding? Painful memories flooded back. Watching, with the rest of the household, as an officer was executed. There had been no way of knowing if the alleged crime was just the product of royal paranoia, but Penthe's destructive distress back in her quarters had been real enough. "We weren't encouraged to talk about such things."

"You do surprise me." Vash raised an eyebrow and laughed. "Okay, I get not many of you leave. But you haven't said they hunt them down when they go. So again, why?"

Rose had always been such a terrible liar. *Just look her in the eye.* "I can only think it's because Penthesilea isn't well mentally. That was a big part of why she hurt me. She treated me as a possession, something to kick around and abuse. I think she believes I'm just a piece of property to be retrieved. We're not dealing with a rational person, believe me." She watched Vash's reaction, and prayed she'd got away with bending the truth.

"Yeah, that makes sense. She sounds deranged. You were lucky to get away." Vash frowned. "How has she tracked you anyway? Do you have a tracking device inside you or something? I've heard some strange things about Akmonians over the years."

Rose choked off a laugh. "No, no tracking device. The great houses have contacts in all the systems, a network of spies they use to get the upper hand when trading or…" She didn't want to think of the other activities that Akmonian's were renowned for. She felt a renewed tingling on her arm. No, no tracking device, just a strange alien band that lives inside of me. In the beginning she had worried that it was somehow betraying her location. She had quickly dismissed the idea, Penthe wouldn't have risked using the spy network, revealing the secrets of the Royal House, if there had been a quicker more discreet way.

Vash was looking at her. She had been silent for too long. "Yes, you're right, I was very lucky to get away."

Vash nodded, then looked quizzical. "Actually, come to think of it, how did—"

Vash's comms unit pinged loudly, startling them both. She muttered darkly as the text scrolled down, then let out a low whistle. "Well, that's not something you see every day." She stuffed the unit back into her trouser pocket. "I'm so sorry, gorgeous, but we're going to have to wrap this up. I have to get going."

Rose's heart sank at the words. So, this was goodbye. She gulped and choked back tears.

Vash put both her hands on her shoulders and smiled. "Sorry, that didn't come out right. What I meant was, *we* have to get going." She got to her feet and looked around the room. "You might want to pack a few things. I'm not sure how long you'll be away."

Her stomach clenched. Vash still didn't seem to understand. What did she have to say to make herself clear? "Vash, I can't come with you. You'd be in as much danger as me, and I can't bear the thought of you getting hurt. I have to leave."

Vash's expression changed abruptly, and her nostrils flared with anger. Rose licked her lips nervously as Vash gestured towards the door.

"Can you hear that, Rose?"

Rose listened, her knuckles white on the arm of the chair from gripping it so tightly. The children's voices were coming now from the landing above, and she could hear light footsteps running up and down. "I don't underst—"

"I'll make it really simple for you. I don't care that you are an Ak. You're just Rose to me. But your Queen Insanity and her ships have entered this system." Vash tapped at her comms unit. "That message was from Central Command. They've just received intelligence that she's been tearing up half the galaxy looking for something, and they've recalled my ship for immediate military service."

"I know, but—"

"We both know that something is you, Rose…and we both know that if she can't find you, she'll wreak havoc here as well."

Vash was right of course. Penthe would stop at nothing to find her.

Before she could speak, Vash stepped forward and thumped her fist on the table.

"Those kids outside that you love so much, they're going to die. That nice grocer who gets your favourite cheese, he's dead as well." Vash pressed her palm to her forehead. "To be brutally honest, it's not looking good for me either, unless I run with you. And no, before you ask, that isn't something I'm willing to do."

Tremors ran through her. She'd never seen Vash like this. Her arm was burning. How long would it be before something happened? How much worse was this going to get? With a whimper, she fruitlessly tried to burrow backwards out of her chair and held up a hand in defence as Vash moved closer.

"And if that's all okay with you, Rose, you're not the woman I thought you were. Just fuck off. I'll do my best to clear up the stinking bilgeslime that you've left us all in!" Her eyes bulged with anger.

Rose's chair tipped and dumped her on the floor. One of her fingernails broke as she tried to drag herself away. "I'm sorry. I don't want people to die, Vash. That's why I'm leaving. She'll follow me and leave you all alone." The argument was pathetic. "Please, Vash, don't!" She lifted her arm in defence.

Vash pulled up, as if Rose had landed a blow. She stood still for a few seconds, staring at the wall behind Rose. Then, breathing heavily, she hunkered down.

"No, you're running away because you're afraid. I get that, but this bitch is going to keep on looking for you. She'll continue to kill or maim anyone that gets in the way of finding you." Vash ran her fingers through her hair. "So, I have one simple question, Rose. Are you just going to let her do that, again and again, or are you going to stand and face her?"

Everything Vash said was the truth. Rose was spineless, and she hadn't wanted to admit it. Tears ran down her face, and she made no attempt to stop them. "I'm not brave like you, Vash. I can't fight back," she whispered, shivering uncontrollably. "You're all better off without me."

"I think it takes a lot of bravery to say that out loud."

There was sincerity in Vash's eyes. "I'm just a coward, aren't I?"

"No, you aren't. You're scared out of your skin." Vash sighed. The last vestiges of anger drained from her face and were replaced by weariness. "And I shouldn't have shouted like that, I'm sorry."

Vash stood and reached out. She gently pulled Rose to her feet, her hand warm and comforting.

"You really feel strongly about this, don't you?" Rose continued to tremble. Vash's anger had shaken her more deeply than she'd anticipated. She dealt with aggressive customers all the time, but the flash fire of Vash's temper had triggered long-buried memories of Penthe at her worst. Some part of her yearned for refuge, for time to recover.

Vash cupped her face. "I know it all feels impossible, but that's why you have me. You won't have to face her alone. Believe me, this Penthe is going to seriously regret the day she picked on my girlfriend." She smiled encouragingly. "So?"

Rose's legs refused to stop shaking and the room was blurred. Only Vash's face, calm and steady, stayed in focus. She concentrated on it and drew on its strength. She hadn't felt like this since the day she escaped from Penthe. That had been the right thing to do. She needed to trust that this was too. Somehow, with Vash, she thought it was. The band had calmed again too. Did it agree? "I'm coming. You're right. If I'm going to die at Penthe's hands, I don't want to gift her my back for a bullet."

"We'll make sure it doesn't come to that." Vash winked. "But I know what you mean. Now, get some stuff together. The briefing is in a couple of hours."

Vash wrapped her in a fierce hug and kissed her deeply. Lifted onto her toes in Vash's strong, capable arms, she didn't want to be anywhere else.

CHAPTER FOUR

THE AXIMENDES VI AND its small auxiliary fleet swept through the outer reaches of the system and began its braking procedure. Penthe sensed the atmosphere on the ship change and harden as the crew prepared for the business to come. Her people walked faster down the corridors, orders were crisper, and backs were straighter. Their pride in their performance matched hers. They weren't just the best: they were invincible when they worked together.

In contrast, her private quarters felt positively funereal. Her servants were gripped by a tiresome notion that only by working both feverishly and without extraneous sound could they be of service to her. However, all the constant ministrations, the soft tread, the hushed voices set her nerves on edge. She'd got rid of some of the older housekeepers, hoping fresh blood would encourage change. She'd spoken to them about the need for effectiveness, not slavish attention. But they simply reverted to type. Imbeciles.

"You. Yes, you. I don't want my cloak hung there. In fact, I didn't ask for it to be moved. Put it back in the wardrobe." She clenched her jaw when the attendant stopped mid-stride and looked at her uncertainly, "Put. It. Back. Oh, for the gods' sake, clear the room! I'll call you if I need anything."

In a few moments the reception was empty, and she could breathe again. She walked over to the nearby wall and pulled back the deep velvety drapes hanging there. The large portscreen they disguised offered a real-space view. Although the ship was still cruising at over five lightyears, the distant stars only crept past. Her thoughts returned to Rose, and she tightened her fists. They were so close now to finding her. Nose pressed to the screen's surface, icy cold despite the warmth of the room, she closed her eyes and tried to recall those last images of her. *What do you look like now, Rose? What does my band look like? Has it changed you?*

"Your majesty?"

"Nova!" She spun around, her heart racing. "What are you doing in my quarters? I gave orders not to be disturbed."

Anthypoploi Ariti, one of her guards, bowed deeply, "My sincere apologies, ma'am, but you asked to be told when the prisoner was ready to talk."

How long had she been there? She waved the junior officer back to a more comfortable distance. "Consider me told. And next time, ask to be admitted or I'll put you to work cleaning the bilges."

Ariti blanched, backing away hurriedly.

"And tell the housekeepers that I'll be going to the T-Brig immediately."

Ariti left and started to shout at someone in the main reception room, apparently taking out her anger and resentment on someone lower down the food chain. The bullied become bullies. Penthe herself was proof enough of this. *Will any of this ever change?* She considered this for a moment, the familiar shades of shame and sadness fighting for supremacy inside her but dismissed it. Not now, there was work to be done. There would be time enough to improve once this was all over.

The T-Brig was in a remote corner of the ship near the stern. Few of the crew ever went near it or wanted to. Mothers frightened their children with tales of what went on within and what might happen to them if they didn't behave.

Penthe was obliged by her high office to be a regular visitor. A queen had to be seen to be leading from the front, afraid of no one and nothing. She had all too vivid memories of the first time she'd entered the area. She'd lost control of herself, torn between vomiting or fainting, and in the end doing both. Nothing her anxious attendants had told her could have prepared her for the dreadful sensory overload. The visceral suffering had robbed her of sleep for several nights…as had the pain from the beating her mother had given her once news of Penthe's embarrassing behaviour had reached her ears. Now, she reflected with a slight shudder, she barely registered any of it. Somehow, that was worse.

She strode into the stark white cell, its foul scents barely disguised by an acrid smell of cleaning fluid. The prisoner was braced to the metal frame in the centre of the room, his body bruised and bloodied, hung limp in the restraints. Drip lines ran to his arms, providing just enough fluids and drugs to deny him the sanctuary of oblivion.

The tortured man wasn't the first to come looking for vengeance, and he wouldn't be the last. After all, perhaps half the galaxy had a reason to see her dead. Luckily, this would-be assassin had been found stowed away in the food stores. After a brief interrogation he would ordinarily have been ejected from the nearest airlock. However, when shown the stills this one had reacted. Only a surprised blink to be sure, but that was enough. Rather stupidly, he'd refused to talk.

Penthe glanced at Kelefstis Hasapi, the burly warrior responsible for the interrogation. Hasapi nodded and moved aside. The captive was ready to talk. Penthe walked around the rig carefully and stopped where the man could see her through his swollen, bloodshot eyes. Penthe dug her fingers deep into his dislocated shoulder to get his attention. "Sabato, isn't it? Or do you prefer to be called Sab? My kelefstis tells me you have something to say?"

The man wheezed, and his eyes flicked from side to side as if he was fitting. Perhaps he was.

Hasapi poked him in the ribs with a pair of pointed pliers. "The queen asked you a question. Show some respect."

Penthe waved her back and leaned in closer, ignoring the stench of urine and excrement. She looked directly into his battered face and smiled. "Just tell me where she is, Sab, and I'll release you from all of this. You have my word."

The prisoner opened his mouth, but all that emerged was a husky dry whisper. Fates, this was so very boring. "Moisten his mouth. I can't hear what he's saying."

Hasapi roughly worked a filthy cloth around and into the prisoner's mouth. Red water dripped and pooled on the tiled floor.

"I swore I'd kill you for what you did to my cousin. I've been waiting ten cycles to get to you in person, bitch." The prisoner strained at his harness. He sucked in his cheeks as he tried to use the precious moisture in his mouth to spit at Penthe, but what little saliva emerged just bubbled and slid pathetically down his chin.

Penthe raised her eyebrow. Such spirit at this stage was laudable, if misguided.

Hasapi sprang forward before Penthe could speak and punched him hard across the face with the pliers. He choked and teeth flew from his mouth. Penthe didn't bother to move. Instead, her eyes strayed to the doorway to appreciate the toned biceps of the warrior on guard there.

"May the gods forgive me…she's on the fourth planet, Glavin, in the city of Drem," the captive whispered before he coughed violently, and more blood hit the tiles as he fought for breath. "You're out of luck, you bitch. She isn't alone; she's with Munro. You'll have to kill her to get to your woman. She's one of the best…saved my life once." His rose-tinted tears dripped onto the floor and created ripples in the fluids already pooled there. "I don't know what your woman has done, but Vash will never let you take her. " His head drooped, all his energy apparently spent.

Penthe's heart raced. This was priceless information indeed. Now they knew the planet, the city, and even the name of a local contact. There was no way that Rose could evade capture this time. Hasapi stared, and Penthe's heart sank at the warrior's hungry expectation. This man had committed the ultimate crime of plotting against the Crown. There was only one path open now, however much Penthe might admire his bravery. Penthe unsheathed the ceremonial knife from her waist belt. At least she would do him the honour of using her own weapon. She lifted the prisoner's head by his ear. "Thank you for the information." She smiled at the man's defiant glare. "Never let it be said that I break my word."

Penthe slid the knife across his exposed throat in one swift motion, let go, and took a step back as blood and gore gushed out across the floor. In truth, she had done the man a favour by sparing him a lingering, painful death in the vacuum.

Penthe turned sharply to Hasapi, who was smiling broadly and nodding her approval. She had an urge to run her through with the knife as well. "Clean this up and take out the trash."

Archiploi Volos, her Chief of Staff, walked through the door. She paused briefly when she saw the man hanging dead, then came smartly to attention. "Ma'am, you're needed in your quarters. We're approaching the first inhabited planet."

The journey back to her quarters through the endless sterile corridors took forever. They passed through several checkpoints, but she ignored the guards, lost in anxious contemplation. Rose was with another woman, which conjured up unpleasant images in her mind. It didn't seem either possible or indeed probable that Rose had found any non-Akmonian woman who was truly attractive. She was obviously with this Munro only because of coercion or perhaps simple convenience. Still, it wasn't a pleasant thought and quite robbed her of the elation of having gained the intelligence in the first place. She was glad when she reached the comfort of her rooms.

She snapped her fingers at her servants to get her refreshments and sat at her desk. A holographic video feed of the Command Hub appeared in front of her. The senior officers were gathered, ready to report. Archiploi Volos sood at the front, having made her way there after fetching Penthe.

"Update, please." Penthe drummed her fingers on the arm of her chair.

"The planet is only lightly inhabited, ma'am. Our reconnaissance ships have encountered no resistance. It appears to be acting solely as a source of food for the system. The large agrifarm stations are manned mainly by bots, with only a token organic presence." Volos exuded calm competency.

Penthe gave a curt nod. It was time to go to work. "Very well, everyone. A well organised and thorough trawl-and-purge will serve to impress upon the more heavily inhabited planets the futility of any resistance. It will also be an effective training exercise for our newest recruits. I expect to see order and excellence. Go to it!"

Penthe watched as they dispersed swiftly towards their tactical teams. One recently promoted antiploi looked a little uncertain. She was about to instruct Volos to replace her when the officer peeled off and started to issue instructions briskly to her team. Penthe chewed her lip and reached for her tablet to make a note of her name.

One of the housekeepers brought her some kras and a selection of sweets. She was ravenous. Fates, this was turning into a long day. She leaned back in her chair and listened as orders streamed out in all directions from the stations. Numbers appeared in the display, indicating the drop carriers powering up in their bays, with heavily armed ground troops boarding them. Menacing black attack drones had already departed, dropping down towards the planet. The unmanned vessels were used as the vanguard of any attack to minimise troop losses. Their armament included guided missiles and long-range lasers, all controlled from dedicated stations in the Hub. She had argued with her mother over their procurement. It had been their final disagreement.

The attack force moved into its pre-programmed formations and swept towards the habitation units identified by the reconnaissance team. One large continent encircled the entire planet, which was, no doubt, the reason it had been turned over to agriculture. Lakes of fresh water dotted the fertile surface and farms had been placed strategically near them. However, this also left them conveniently isolated and vulnerable.

As Penthe watched intently, the display had changed to show a three-dimensional tactical view of the planet. Scattered green numbers, which indicated enemy buildings, started slowly to wink out, one by one. Larger red squares joined the silver drone symbols, showing the carriers landing behind them. Data next to them indicated their capabilities and the number of troops contained in each carrier. All of them were filled to capacity. Her warriors were trained to land fast and in overwhelming numbers. As they engaged the pitiful defences, small windows in the holographic display appeared, and their headsets returned live streams of what was happening down below. Images of burning buildings and agricultural equipment from across the planet, along with the occasional blackened body spread prone in front of them, seared her mind. Aware that her staff were watching, Penthe didn't look away for a moment. She took a long draft of her kras.

The engagement took less than fifteen minutes. As the last of the carriers started the climb back to the ship, she finally allowed herself a smile and swept her hair back from her brow. It had been a while since the Aximendes VI had been forced to demonstrate its power, but it had done so well. There had been death, but it had been kept to a minimum. Penthe clapped her hands, and Volos turned to the camera.

"Please pass on my personal congratulations to the training corps, Volos. I'm pleased with the performance of our brave Naftoi warriors today."

Volos nodded, eyes burning bright with evident pleasure and pride. "I shall pass on your message, ma'am."

"Well, I'll leave you to clean up. I'm going to see Antiploi Sakas. Please brief me when you have a full inventory." Penthe terminated the feed without waiting for a reply. She got up and stretched her back to release the last of the tension.

The planet and its few inhabitants had stood no chance. However, the speed in which it had been overrun would soon get back to the authorities which ran this system, not least because she would provide full vid recordings to them within the next hour. She chuckled and popped one of the sweets into her mouth. She needed them to realise that any resistance would not only be futile, but possibly catastrophic for their settlements and citizens. However, on the off chance that they didn't get the message, she wanted to discuss the next moves with the commander of the Black Team, Sakas.

Sakas' office was located close to her quarters. Team members personally guarded the corridors which surrounded it and accompanied her wherever she went. They were handpicked from the ranks, chosen for their intelligence and tenacity. She didn't just want a bunch of muscled goons protecting her, she wanted them to be actively working on her behalf.

The commander's office was spartan: a place of work, not ceremony. A gun rack in the corner housed several plasma autoloads and a battle suit hung in its fixings alongside. It was battered from frequent use, though its metal surface still shone from hours of spit and polish. The only decoration on the wall was the Black Team pennant, a black claw on a red background, which glowed proudly above the desk.

Penthe walked in without announcing herself. She sat down on the hard, functional seat in front of the desk and crossed her legs. "You've seen the latest intelligence, Sakas?"

Sakas was a small battle-hardened woman with intense eyes who didn't waste words. "I've instructed our intelligence team to hack the system's registration bank and get the details of any women called Vash Munro, ma'am. They'll report back within the hour."

Penthe smiled. As usual, Sakas had pre-empted her first order. "Any information about the city, Drem?"

"Inhabited by millions. Total chaos. No order or discipline to the habitations. There appear to be no reliable maps or plans, ma'am, and it wouldn't be advisable to go in without precise intelligence. We'd succeed in the end, but we might incur heavy losses. I wouldn't recommend it, ma'am."

Penthe grimaced at the harsh appraisal but had to agree. While she didn't flinch from the thought of sacrificing troops, the loss of significant numbers would weaken her position politically. Many a basilinna had been killed for failing their Houses through weak stratagem. She rose from the seat. "You're correct, Sakas, as always. I appreciate your candour. We'll wait until your team report back. Hopefully, they'll help us pinpoint the exact location. I don't want to linger in this backwater for any longer than I have to." She paused at the door. "Oh, and when you have the report, bring it directly to my personal quarters. I wish to discuss these matters with you further."

Sakas acknowledged the coded message with a small smile. They'd discuss the report, but Penthe had other needs of her tonight. Personal needs.

CHAPTER FIVE

AN UNMANNED PODCAR TOOK them to the space port. With time pressing, Vash had decided to splash out on the more expensive transport option, unwilling to endure a crowded train again. The inside was too warm and smelt stale. Faux skin-tanned seats worn down to the thread beneath meant she felt every bump and hole on the metal roadway. The plastiglas surface in front of them, protecting the electronic brain controlling the car, was covered with scratches. Someone had painstakingly etched a heart with the letter J in the middle. Seeing that Vash was staring out the window, Rose reached out and traced its rough surface with a shaking finger. Who was J, and who had loved them enough to go to that effort? Would Vash ever carve a heart like that for her? Vash shifted on her seat, and she pulled her hand back self-consciously. Their future was too uncertain for that sort of romantic nonsense.

She was, despite her best efforts, still trembling inside from their earlier confrontation. The anger and menace displayed by Vash had brought back unwanted memories of Penthe. True, everything seemed okay with Vash now. So why couldn't she rid her mind of the image of her advancing, her eyes bulging with fury?

Vash turned from the window and smiled. She took Rose's hand, and her expression changed to one of concern. "Hey, you're shaking. What's going on? I thought we were okay?"

She worried at one of her nails and picked at the quick. She was unsure of how to explain herself. What if she made Vash angry again?

As if reading her thoughts, Vash put her arm around her shoulders and pulled her closer. "I really upset you back there, didn't I?"

"No…well, okay, yes. Oh, what I mean is that you were right to be angry with me. I was being selfish. It's just that I've never seen you like that before. It was…scary." She pulled harder at the quick.

Vash flushed. "I'm sorry you had to see that. I don't regret what I said, but I don't like that I frightened you."

She didn't know what to say and her silence spoke volumes. Vash pulled away, a dejected look on her face.

"It never gets any easier does it, Rose? I'm starting to understand why things have been so difficult for us. This Penthe woman really got to—" Vash stopped and stared at her, eyes wide with shock. "Fates, you're afraid because I reminded you of her, aren't you?"

Rose looked at her finger; it was starting to bleed slightly now. "I'm sorry, it's really difficult to explain," she said. She put the finger in her mouth and sucked gently on it to clean it.

"Not as sorry as I am. We've never really argued, have we? I just wanted things to be different with you, but I guess I'm never gonna change."

Vash's honesty cut Rose to the bone, and she searched for the right words to say in reply. "Vash, you've been wonderful. I never imagined I would find someone who cares for me like you do."

"But my bad temper took you back somewhere so terrible, you're still shaking now." Vash looked down at her lap. "Not exactly something to be proud of, is it? I'm so sorry."

Rose desperately didn't want to tell Vash the truth. She didn't want to remember, and she didn't want to have to say the words out loud. All this time, she'd tried so hard to just let herself be enveloped and protected by Vash's love. The reality was that none of it had gone away. Now here was Vash, blaming herself when she was another victim of Penthe's violence. She deserved better. Rose wrapped her arms around herself, a pathetic shield against what she had to say. "I didn't properly explain why I ran away."

Vash nodded. "You don't have to tell me anything until you're ready."

"I think I need to…that is, I have to. You deserve the truth, Vash." Rose's cheeks burned. She found a loose thread on her trousers to pick at.

"Well, we've got a little while until we get to the port if you want to chat."

"There are seven great Akmonian houses, of which the House of Aximendes is the greatest. Each house controls its own territory and is ruled by a queen, a basilinna. Everyone is sworn to serve their house. I was born into one of the servant classes." Rose pointed at her leg. "Do you remember asking me where I got the little abstract tattoo on my calf done? It's not a tattoo, it's a metric marking I got when I came of age. With the right instruments, you could discover the name of my mother, my date of birth, and my designation."

Vash scratched her nose and looked down at her feet. Was she thinking about all the times she had traced her fingers over the marking in ignorance? Rose yearned for when things had been so much simpler. "My mum wanted the best for me. She taught me my letters and basic maths. I shadowed her everywhere when I was old enough and learned at her feet. Eventually, I attracted the attention of the head housekeeper, and I was assigned to serve the Crown Princess. My family were so… proud." The final words filled her throat, each one more difficult to extract than the last.

"I mean it, Rose. If this is too difficult, we can leave it for later." Vash touched her hand.

The gentleness of Vash's voice made things worse. Rose gulped and pushed back her tears. "No, I need to tell you. I'm just not sure how." Her heart slowed a little again as Vash's fingers drew endless soft circles on her arm, and she tried again. "You see, I thought I'd landed the best job in the world, but it was a nightmare. Penthe was—is—really damaged. Her mother, the old queen, treated her badly. She really hurt her." Her face tingled. She was speaking too fast but didn't dare stop. "I couldn't say or do anything to stop it, so I just tried to do my best to look after her. We grew closer, and she seemed to appreciate my company. I thought she was being kind. One evening we…"

Vash put her arm around her shoulder again. "Hey, deep breaths, lovely. It's okay, just take your time."

Rose shut her eyes and could see it all so clearly. "Penthe came back late. She was limping and holding herself. She was in a lot of pain. I helped her undress, and I could see the bruises beginning to form over her ribs, adding another rainbow layer to the ones already there. She'd obviously taken another beating. I told her to lie on the bed while I applied some balm." Penthe's pale skin had been crisscrossed with red, weeping weals. The smell of the balm filled her nose. "She just looked at me and…well, we were in each other's arms. I'd never, you know, but she seemed to know what she was doing. I spent the night in her bed. It was wonderful."

Hearing nothing but her own heart pounding, Rose looked at Vash cautiously. She was pulling at her lip and staring into empty space. Rose couldn't read anything from her expression. Was she angry? Disappointed? She wished Vash would say something, even if she was just going to shout. This silence was awful. "It was only the next day when the enormity of what we'd done struck us both. Penthe was very quiet and wouldn't talk to me, and I kept my distance. And the following day, she changed completely." Her pulse raced as if she were back there again. "As soon as I arrived on duty, she hit me really hard and made my nose bleed." For a moment, a phantom metallic tang of blood filled her mouth again. "She said I was late, though I wasn't. All day, she shouted at me, hit out at me for no reason, and I couldn't get away." Fear enveloped Rose again, and she hunched over as if she were waiting for the next blow. "No one helped. They'd seen it all before. I wish they'd told me, but I was so new, you see. There's a strict hierarchy among the servants, and I was the one breaking the rules. I suppose they thought I deserved what I got." She shook her head at her own stupidity. "But that wasn't the worst of it, that came later, when we were alone. She…"

Her throat constricted and made it hard to breath. Her brain refused to supply the words that should follow. She couldn't think them, let alone say them aloud. She rocked back and forth, trying desperately not to let the images in her mind take her over. How many times she had sat in the apartment and let them envelop her? How many times had Vash reached for her in innocence, only for her to flinch and draw back? Penthe hadn't just punished her, she'd punished those who wanted to care for her. It was a wonder that Vash had stayed with her this long.

The air in the shuttle grew heavier. Rain was falling now, and the city swam past beyond the windows. Rose looked to see Vash clenching and unclenching her free hand. It was anger then. Anger at what Rose's past had inflicted on the present, on her as a person. She'd known this was the risk, and perhaps it was better this way. She might as well get the rest over with and they could go their separate ways at the port. She would face Penthe another day. "I never told anyone about that. No one would have believed me and even if they had, they wouldn't have gone against their queen. I didn't tell my own mother. I was so ashamed." The inside of the cab swam, and she grasped Vash's arm, desperate for some response. "I was supposed to be the pride of the family, Vash. My mother went without things, fought for me to get into the household. How could I get it so wrong? I dishonoured my family and let them down so badly. Oh, please, Vash, say something!"

For a moment Vash just stared out the window before she covered Rose's hand again with her own. She squeezed gently and finally looked around. Her eyes were bloodshot, and her mouth trembled.

"I can't begin to imagine how hard it was for you to tell me all of that." Vash pulled her arm out from behind Rose and cupped her face. "I just wish I'd known sooner." Her voice cracked. "But you'd better believe this, I don't give a bilgesucker's ass what your family may or may not think. I don't care about some outdated hierarchy or stupid honour system. If that monster was here now…" Vash's face was pinched, and she took a couple of deep breaths. "Sorry, I'm trying so hard not to get angry again. Look, I can't take away what she did, but I won't have you feeling bad or blaming yourself." Vash stroked her face tenderly. "All you did was try to show her some kindness, Rose, some simple love. I'm just so very sorry."

A wonderful weightlessness engulfed Rose. Dizzy with the speed at which her view of the past had been turned on its head, Rose opened her mouth to argue. She shut it again. She didn't care anymore. The only thing that mattered was that Vash wasn't angry at her. "Oh, Vash, all those times…I so wanted more, but I got scared. I knew I was hurting you, but I didn't know how to stop myself. I've been so worried you'd leave."

"I'm not going anywhere. So, you can stop that worrying right now."

Vash slung her arm back around her shoulder and the strength and warmth of her ignited a bright light deep within Rose's core. It drove those terrible dark images back into the shadows again and she started to relax. She snuggled in.

"No one is going to hurt you ever again."

Bringing her fingers to her own face, Rose wasn't surprised to feel wetness there, though she couldn't stop smiling. The future was scary and uncertain. She was safe here in the back of the podcar. She wished she could stay there forever.

CHAPTER SIX

PENTHE WAS GLAD TO reach the calm of her quarters again and wearily allowed her maids to fuss over her. They guided her into a warm bath, cleansed and massaged her skin with expensive oils. As the tensions of the day slipped out of her muscles Penthe reflected, not for the first time, how good Rose had always been at this. No one had come close to replacing her. Did she miss her? Penthe tried to dismiss the idea, disturbed by its implications, but she couldn't shrug it off.

In those days she'd often taken her baths alone, reluctant to expose her bruised and battered body to her servants. Most of her household had long since succumbed to the embarrassed silence that surrounded each event. They avoided her and looked away, perhaps not wanting to confront the abuse she was receiving. Rose was different. Rose had stepped forward and looked her in the eye with concern. How shocked she'd been when Rose walked in, unasked, and began to bathe and soothe with her words and gentle attention. She should've ordered her out. But too shocked at her brazenness and exhausted from the latest confrontation with her mother, she hadn't been able to think clearly.

She'd never experienced such kindness before. It had intrigued her, but afterwards she had tossed and turned in bed, worrying that it was just another trick, another trap laid by her bitch mother to test her mettle. When nothing happened and no comment was made and nobody appeared to care, she'd decided to play along. Penthe had, albeit cautiously, allowed Rose to look after her from that point. She'd listened patiently to her innocent prattling about her family and worked on looking like she cared, rewarding her with smiles she'd practised in the mirror in private. She rubbed at the back of her neck. She'd been such a fool.

"Get me out of here." She grimaced and hissed as they lifted her from the bath, pinching her skin with their clumsy hands. It took an age for her hair to be brushed and pinned up. At last, having been dressed in a real silk chemise, she brusquely dismissed her maids for the night. She ambled over to her bed, sunk her toes deep into the warm tread of the woven woollen twistrug and hummed happily. Peace at last.

The covers had been pulled back ready. A gold platter of fresh fruit was on the nightstand next to a crystal flagon of kras and two goblets. Perched on the corner of the bed, she poured some of the dark sweet liquid into one of the goblets. Each one was hand carved from a single ruby. She held it up against the soft light of her bedside lamp and admired how the contents emanated like glowing embers from within. She'd brought these into the House coffers herself. Their previous owner had tried to defraud the House and had no further need of them now. They really were exquisite.

She moved an enamelled box onto her lap and looked at the jewels in it. Only the royal signet remained on her finger, always worn. It was a constant reminder of both her duty and her past mistake. Surrounding the dark blue sapphire was a twisted band of platinum: an oblique clue to the band, her family's greatest secret.

Penthe traced the design with the tip of her finger. It was her mother's fault. She should have told her about it. She'd only found out about its existence when she'd taken a routine debriefing of her mother's closest advisors in the T-Brig. She'd punished their treasonous negligence by having them all executed. As they had died, screaming faces frozen and bloodied in the vacuum, she'd fervently wished she'd been throwing her mother out of the airlock instead. When Penthe had innocently pointed out the band in the treasury only a couple of cycles before, her mother hadn't taken the opportunity to explain. Instead, the old hag had flown into a furious temper and kicked her around the room until she'd passed out. Everything related to the Rose situation was her mother's fault. It was her mother's head housekeeper who had recommended Rose for the household. That stupid woman was now just another piece of flotsam floating somewhere in deep space. Good riddance.

She took a sip and savoured it, rolling the sweet velvety taste around her mouth. The past often seemed like a dream now, a little like love and romance. One of her tutors had given her a book which described it, but it had struck her as rather abstract until she met Rose. Lying there night after night, with Rose tenderly soothing her skin, she'd considered that the feelings washing over her might well be this *love* thing.

If that was the case, it had proved very dangerous. She'd lost control of herself and given in to its siren call. She'd never make that mistake again. It was a weakness unbecoming of a queen, and it was a good thing that she'd soon put it right. She closed the box but barely resisted the temptation to throw it across the room. The platter rattled as she slammed it back down on the stand instead.

She took another gulp and willed the liquid's warmth to relax her. That was the only trouble with raking up these memories, they brought back the stress of the situation she now faced, the consequences of her actions all those cycles before.

Almost immediately after they had lain together, the doubts began to creep in. She had stayed awake into the early hours, her mind a maelstrom, sure it was another test. Had Rose been planted by her mother to expose her vulnerabilities? Penthe had been determined not to fail when she was so close to the throne. Looking at Rose the next day had caused her discomfort and embarrassment. So, she'd ignored her while she was thinking over the best thing to do next. Finally, she'd made a decision, and it had been the right one—to correct the mistake before things went any further.

Rose's face as she had repeatedly hit and shouted at her the next day had been tough to look at, but Penthe had started to feel better straight away. Back in control again. She was sure that Rose understood, really, it was the way of things. Certainly, the rest of the household had since none of them had dared to make any attempt to intercede on her behalf. Rose had let them all down.

She could be certain none of this was about lingering feelings of *love* towards Rose. Having run over the events once again, she was sure of that. Rose had embarrassed her, undermined her by running away, and betrayed her by stealing the band.

No, this was just about getting her rightful property back, and she would bring a fugitive to justice. It was the correct course of action. Sakas had told her so. There would be risks: the nature of the band necessitated caution. However, if Rose resisted, Sakas had promised to step in and do what was necessary. There was no need for Penthe to get her hands dirty with such petty things. Contented, she filled the other goblet generously and waited for her lover to arrive.

The next morning, Penthe woke early. She lay still, eyes resolutely shut. She was in no hurry to rise after such a busy night. Instead, she focused on dozily enjoying the comforting warmth of her bedclothes. Unfortunately,

Sakas was still lying beside her, preventing her from spreading out as she wanted. Moreover, her musky scent, so arousing hours before, now pervaded her space. It overpowered Penthe's own favourite blend of floral notes, which she preferred to smell coming from the sheets.

Intimacy made her skin itch slightly. She'd always been choosy about who she allowed to stay the night. Sakas was being afforded that privilege at present but only on certain occasions, usually on nights when Penthe was enjoying herself so much that she let down her guard. Such weak decisions always came back to haunt her the next day. Would she ever learn? Hopefully Sakas would rise soon of her own volition and be gone. The earlier the better really, though no doubt the household would be twittering later. They wouldn't gossip further afield though: loose tongues were removed from their owners around here. She couldn't summon the energy yet to wake her and order her to be gone, but she would have to do so soon.

Penthe reluctantly opened her eyes to slits and let some of the dim light of the chamber in. The glow lamps around the walls were timed to provide a staged solrise. Establishing a steady diurnal routine, matching the galactic standard model, through the maintenance of an artificial day and night was essential to the good mental and physical health of everyone, especially on a large ship such as hers. At the same time, Sakas stirred and there was a faint buzzing sound nearby. Sakas sat up immediately, transitioning from sleep to awake in a rather impressive instant, and studied the display on her wristband.

"I must beg leave to go, ma'am. We're receiving intelligence from our informants of fleet movements deeper in the system."

She nodded indifferently and waved languorously toward the door. "You'll no doubt let me know what is going on when you have more information, Sakas."

Sakas jumped out of the bed and pulled on her crumpled fatigues. She bowed abruptly and jogged out the door. Didn't she feel pain? Surely her back must be sore after last night, where Penthe's whip had raised welts. She sighed and rolled back over to where Sakas had lain and luxuriated in the warm spot left behind.

When she next stirred, the lights in the room were brighter, and she could hear distant voices arguing in the room outside. Those bloody housekeepers, did they have nothing better to do? She sat over the side of the bed, wiped the sleep from her eyes and looked at the small console on her bedside table. Her stomach was telling her it was time for some breakfast, and there was a message from Sakas requesting to report to her urgently. She barked out for her servants, and they bustled in. Within the hour she was bathed, dressed, and ravenous.

Penthe strolled out into her reception room and wasn't surprised to see Sakas standing to attention at her desk. She waved her over and invited her to join her for some food. Sakas waited until she was seated, then perched on the chair opposite and ignored the laden table. As usual there was a rich selection of breads, fruit, and meats. Penthe snapped her fingers and a maid hurried over to pour her a goblet of freshly squeezed juice. Sakas pursed her lips. Really, she was so impatient, she must learn to wait. Penthe took a long leisurely drink, slowly put the goblet back down and dabbed at the corners of her mouth with a napkin. "So, what news now, Antiploi Sakas?"

"According to our agents, ma'am, the authorities have called all the system-based privateers in for a briefing. None of my people could get into the meeting itself but from the activity around the military port, it's clear that they're gearing up for some form of action."

How predictable. She rolled her eyes and reached for some fruit. The pears looked particularly appealing this morning, and she bit deep into the flesh of one, savouring the sweetness of the juice that trickled down her chin.

"Hmm, you should really try some of this fruit, you know. We salvaged some of the crop from that agriplanet. It's of the highest quality."

Sakas' face was stony, the barest hint of irritability in her eyes. Penthe would have to do something about that. Sakas helped herself to a small apple but didn't eat it. Instead, she rolled it in her palms like a ball. Penthe took another sip. "Where do our strategists think that they will try to engage us?"

Sakas frowned. "Our models predict that they will look to engage us before we reach the inner planets. They have very limited resources, so I don't expect them to pose much of a problem, ma'am."

"Your agents have done well, Antiploi Sakas. Nevertheless, I wish every precaution to be taken. I'll be in the Hub in ninety minutes. I'll expect a full battle plan, with contingencies, to be ready for me when I do."

Sakas nodded and turned to leave.

"Antiploi Sakas," Penthe called out to her just as she had exited onto the corridor. Sakas returned to the doorway. "Your performance continues to please me. Keep it up."

Sakas lowered her eyes as her cheeks flushed slightly pink. She turned and was gone.

Penthe took another pear and stroked its skin as she wandered over to her desk. The eyes were watching her again. The silk scarf had been removed, but she knew she'd find it back in the drawer. She should demand an explanation, shout, and scream at the housekeepers, but something always held her back. The action felt less an act of insubordination and more like a subtle distress call. They revered her mother, and so should she as their queen. She didn't, but neither did she feel that she was the true bearer of the Crown. So, she kept silent.

"You wanted all of this, Penthesilea. Remember?" Her mother's voice rose from the background murmur in her head, and her scornful laughter rang out so loudly that Penthe dug her nails into her palms to stop herself from looking to see if anyone else could hear. *Yes, because I thought I would have everything, that I would have power over everything, like you always did, Mother. I thought I would be in control, not lose what I had left of my privacy and have every part of my life observed and judged. Every. Single. Day.*

A polite cough at her doorway signalled the first meeting of the day. Her advisors would be lining up outside, shuffling their feet and avoiding each other's eyes. They'd sit around and offer their daily reports. She'd listen, someone would get shouted at, and it would be time for lunch.

She reached for another pear. They could wait. Nothing ever changed in this dreadful limbo of almost-queen. The only thing that kept her going was the band and the power it represented. Own it, and everything would change. She would be the true queen of the Aximendes. And not just the House; she would use it to change the course of her entire people. Nothing and nobody would stand in her way once she bore the band.

She tore into the fruit with her nails, ripped it apart, and let the mess fall onto the twistrug below. Someone else would clean it up, they always did. "Come."

CHAPTER SEVEN

As soon as Rose and Vash turned the corner, the man waiting outside the battered entrance to the vacuum tube stopped kicking at the dented metal and started towards them. She touched Vash's arm and got a small nod in reply. So, this was Alvin. Vash hadn't talked about him much, and she'd imagined some muscled, efficient, pens-in-pocket, engineering type much like she saw sometimes on the daytime vids in the sexden. He was short and fat, with long greasy hair, and wore an overall that was begging for a wash or three. How much more she had got wrong?

"Let me handle this," Vash said under her breath.

She needn't have worried. Alvin ignored Rose altogether. He pulled out a grimy rag and hawked noisily into it. "Took your time, Vash. Been here a while waiting. Was a bit worried. Was gonna go to the meet alone, represent you, like."

"I didn't know you cared so much, Alvin. I'll make a note for the future." Vash coolly faced her chief engineer down.

Alvin tried to match her stare, small dark eyes burning behind thick glasses, but after a few moments, he looked away. Rose wasn't fooled for a moment. He oozed ambition, and it was clear that if Vash had missed the deadline, he would have bad mouthed her to Central without a second thought.

"This is Rose. She's going to be joining us, Alvin." Vash walked up the corridor. "Have you heard anything on the grapevine about the plans?"

Rose quickly followed her, but Alvin stood stock still for a moment, apparently processing the news. When he did catch them up, he was breathing heavily. He overtook and put his hand out to block Vash's path.

"What do you mean she's coming with us? Why didn't you ask me about that?"

Vash pushed him aside and kept walking. "Last time I looked, Alvin, I was the captain of the Bellerophon. Do you know any different?"

Rose kept quiet, careful to keep her expression neutral. Vash needed to deal with this in her own way. For a second it didn't seem that Alvin wasn't going to follow them but after a pause, he ran to catch up.

"Nothing concrete on the grapevine. Lots of chatter about seeing them off like we did last time, but I don't see anyone volunteering to lead the charge."

"Yeah, well, there are enough wise heads around to see the folly in going down that path. Thanks for keeping your ear to the ground, Alvin."

They hurried to the briefing, traversing a maze of corridors that went on forever. Vash had explained to Rose that Central Port was the largest in the system, capable of docking over a hundred ships. Apparently when she'd been a kid, this had been her favourite playground. Toting toy guns, she'd amused herself pretending to defend it dock by dock while her dad did his deals. No invaders stood a chance against "Vash Munro, Space Hero." Other crews knew her dad and played along, hiding behind crates and playing dead. Vash's love for her dad had bled through every word. She rarely spoke directly about him but, treading these same corridors, Rose wished more than ever that she'd met him.

Nearing the large hangar that was being used by Central Command for the briefing, the hum of voices grew louder. As they walked in, she got a sense of just how many privateers there were. Hundreds were milling around, talking and exchanging news. Most were humanoid, but there were the unmistakable armoured exoskeletons of the insectoid Optroids, and in one corner, three self-contained floating chambers provided safe environment for their fragile Fyella captains. However, despite the diversity, they obviously held at least one thing in common. Regardless of their opinions on the current situation, none were prepared to miss what Central Command had to say.

Alvin waved to a couple of people and made as if to join them.

Vash tapped him on the shoulder. "Don't go far. We may need to move fast. And no need to go gossiping about Rose, okay?"

He rolled his eyes but nodded.

Rose wasn't sorry to see him go. "I'm sorry, Vash."

"What for?" Vash looked genuinely confused.

"Causing you all this hassle with Alvin. I hadn't realised he'd be so upset."

Vash laughed. "Rose, Alvin gets upset if I don't stock his favourite caffrush to drink when we're on a long run. He's like a spoilt child.

However, he's also a great engineer so I just have to manage him carefully." She patted Rose on the shoulder. "Don't worry about him, all right?"

Before Rose could reply, Vash came to an abrupt halt and craned her neck. Taking hold of Rose's hand, she led them though the throng. With the crowds blocking her vision, Rose couldn't see where they were going. Then, as the people thinned, a small group of military officers stood in their path. The sight of their uniforms sent her pulse racing, and the skin on her arm started to prickle. What was Vash doing?

The oldest of them broke off from talking and enveloped her in a tight bear hug. "Good to see you, Vash Munro. Are you ready for a little fighting?"

Vash smiled. "I'll do my best, Vice Admiral."

Vice Admiral? Rose froze on the spot. Had Vash lost her mind?

"Please, I think of you as family, Vash, just call me Curtis." He clapped Vash on the back and turned to the officers with him. "This is old Munro's girl. He was a bloody good captain, and she's followed in his stead. Who's your friend, Vash?"

He looked Rose up and down, his expression not unfriendly. Rose just about managed a smile in return, although her stomach churned painfully. The prickling sensation grew stronger, and she willed herself to remain calm.

"This is Rose. I hope you don't mind me bringing her along. She's visiting from Pernick, and I wanted to show her around the Bellerophon."

"Not at all, Vash. You know I don't stand on ceremony. At a time like this, everyone's needed to lend a helping hand. Nice to meet you, Rose."

Curtis held out his hand and Rose shook it, praying that he wouldn't notice how much she was shaking. Her heart pounded, and she struggled to fight the impulse to simply run.

Vash, on the other hand, seemed completely relaxed. "I'd better leave you to it, Curtis. I can see that you're busy."

He waved her away affectionately and turned back to his officers. As soon as they were far enough away, Rose whispered in Vash's ear, "Are you mad? Why did you bring me here?"

"Perfect camouflage, don't you think? No one will ever expect to find you here." Vash turned to another captain, who'd waved at them. "Hey, good to see you again."

Rose reflected on what Vash had said. It was so typical of her, always intelligently impulsive. Rose admired her thought process but that didn't reduce the anxiety gnawing at her stomach. Only as they moved further away from the military personnel and back into the anonymity of the civilian crowds did she relax slightly, and the band calmed too.

They made their way through the crowds, with many of the captains and officers greeting Vash. It was clear she was well known and well-liked. Some tipped their caps, others waved and shouted to her.

Vash was scanning the crowd, frowning slightly. "What's the matter?"

"Nothing, I was just hoping to see Sab here. I haven't heard from him for a while." Vash scratched her head.

"Who?" Rose asked.

"An old friend, we go back a long way. He likes to say I saved his life, but anybody would've done the same. He's second officer on another ship now, but I can't see his captain either, which is weird." Vash shrugged. "I'll ask Alvin when we get back to the ship. As you saw, he usually knows all the gossip. Oh, here we go."

"Everyone, please!" A commander used the hangar's communication system to bring the meeting to order. "I appreciate that you're all eager to hear what's going on and what we plan to do next. Listen carefully, and I'll put you all in the picture. After I've outlined the situation as we know it, there will be plenty of opportunity for you to ask questions."

The crowd fell silent and moved forward as one towards a large holographic display that had sprung up behind the commander. It showed the system with all its planets, moons, and orbitals. In one corner, a red triangle could clearly be seen orbiting a small planet.

The commander cleared his throat. "The Akmonian ship, confirmed as the Aximendes VI, went into orbit with its service fleet a short time ago around the planet designated AR2. It's primarily used for agriculture. There are some citizens living planetside, but the bulk of the work is done by agribots." He looked across the crowd. "We didn't have time to evacuate any of our citizens. Akmonian drop-ships entered the planet's atmosphere ten hours ago. What you're about to see is footage sent to us by Queen Penthesilea of the House of Aximendes. Please be warned, what you are about to see is extremely disturbing."

Rose started at Penthe's name. A holoscreen flickered into life behind the commander, and she watched with the rest of the crowd in horror the scenes of destruction and devastation that unfolded as the planet was razed by Penthe's forces. The room went deathly silent, with only the occasional gasp, click, or hiss as another blackened corpse came into focus. Acid bile filled her mouth, and she turned to bury her face into Vash's chest, unable to watch any more.

"What we gonna do about it?" A shout went up from the back as the hologram faded from view.

More voices joined in, anger spreading through the crowd like wildfire. Two of the Optroids drew themselves up to their full height, antenna waving and beaks clacking noisily.

The commander put his hands up. "The harsh reality is that we were not able to do anything for that planet. No, listen to me, please." He waited for the crowd to settle down. "If we'd wasted resources trying to stop that attack, we'd have been leaving millions more of our citizens vulnerable. That's why we've decided instead to form a defensive line at this point." He indicated a point in the system roughly a third of the way from its centre, on a direct line between the Aximendes VI and the most heavily inhabited inner planets and hubs. "We'll place our best ships here. We believe we have the firepower to hurt them badly and make them turn back."

"And what if we don't?" someone to the left of Vash yelled out. "What'll we do then?"

Mutterings around them indicated he wasn't the only one worried about the consequences of defeat.

The commander's face was stern. "Have no doubt, we have to turn the Akmonians back here. Our computer models indicate that we've a fair chance of doing that. If we don't succeed, we have contingency plans to evacuate as many citizens as possible to the nearest friendly system. However, that's a risk we only intend to take as a last resort." He scanned the crowd, obviously trying to catch the eye of as many of the men and women as he could. "For a long time, I've had the honour of working with many of you here. We've defended our communities from a variety of threats and made this system a safe place for our families to live. I know that we can do it again. This is the biggest threat that we've ever faced, but I believe that, if we work together, we can overcome it."

Feet shuffled and embarrassed coughing filled the room. Rose looked down at the floor, her heart thumping. She still had it in her power to stop all of this. All that she needed to do was put her hand up, tell them the truth, and surrender to her fate. Tears pricked at the back of her eyes, and her head weighed heavy with shame at her own cowardice.

Vash took her hand, and Rose felt strength in the firm hold.

"I'm with you, commander," a young jock said. "These Akmonians think they rule the galaxy. They picked on the wrong system this time."

His youthful bravado was picked up by the crowd, who stamped their feet, beat their armour, or floated higher with approval. The commander visibly relaxed. He waved his hands again to get their attention.

"Now, listen. The plans and co-ordinates for your ships are being beamed to them. Get back to your vessels and start making your final preparations. We'll be leaving in four hours."

The crowd around them drifted apart slowly, voices excited with anticipation. Rose looked around for the exit, still unable to stop herself trembling. She fought the desire to flee, knowing it would draw unwanted attention.

Vash seemed to read her mind. "Just give me a couple of seconds. I need to check on something." She quickly walked over to another captain.

He listened, face sombre, and took Vash's outstretched hand and covered it with his own.

She walked back, expressionless. "Sorry, another good friend. I'm not sure when I'll see him next. Shall we get back?"

Rose nodded, unable to trust her voice. All these people were putting everything on the line because of her.

"Alvin!" Vash waited until he looked up from his hushed conversation and acknowledged her. "Let's get back and see what they have planned for us."

They walked out of the hangar together. Would she ever see any of those present ever again?

CHAPTER EIGHT

The walk back from the briefing wasn't pleasant. Rose's nerves had scarcely settled by the time they reached the vacuum tube leading to the Bellerophon. Alvin continued to ignore her, and Vash responded by doggedly engaging him in small talk, the sole purpose of which appeared to be to goad him. She meant well, but the rising tension between them only exacerbated Rose's stress levels. Her head was pounding by the time they turned the last corner to see a fresh pile of crates next to the entrance, a port tech sat on the edge of one looking bored.

"Looks like that shipment of engine parts," Alvin said grumpily. "Thought you were gonna get them diverted to the Bond. We need them in secure storage until we get back."

"Yeah, well, they obviously didn't get the message." Vash sighed heavily. She turned to Rose. "Listen, why don't you go ahead, while Alvin and I deal with this?"

The tension in the air could have been cut with a laser, so Rose nodded and walked straight through into the tube. It was extremely functional and the air, pumped in from both ends, had a chemical aroma. Industrial wall lamps flooded the scuffed metal walls and floor with a harsh white light. The interior of the Bellerophon was tantalisingly out of sight at the far end, hidden by an opaque privacy screen the colour of the pollution haze that hung over Drem on a hot summer's day. As she approached it, her excitement grew at what lay beyond and dampened the bubbling pools of acid in her stomach. The more reticent Vash had been about her ship, the more Rose had yearned to see it. As she finally stepped through the main hatch into the dimly lit space beyond, her senses were on high alert.

She knew quite a lot about space travel. She'd been born and raised on a spaceship, and she had also seen the inside of others while working for Penthe. More recently, she'd experienced travelling on different carriers and merchant vessels as she'd fled from system to system.

But none of that prepared her for the Bellerophon.

Firstly, it was smaller than any ship she had been on. She found herself in a claustrophobic entrance space crowded with boxes piled up haphazardly. Most of the ship was probably storage space, given that was Vash's business. But it was so cramped and cluttered that her chest started to tighten slightly, as it did when she was on a crowded transport tube. There were three dimly lit narrow corridors visible through hatches leading off the space but no real clues as to where they led.

She could hear Vash and Alvin talking with the tech back on the corridor, so Rose stood still and focused on calming herself and getting orientated. The last thing she wanted was to reveal how out of her depth she felt and give grumpy Alvin more ammunition.

Spots blinked in her vision. She stepped to one side to try and take everything in, only to trip over the corner of one of the boxes. She reached out to save herself and ended up with sticky brown greasy goo on her palm. She grimaced and held her hand as far from her body as she could. Stars, the Bellerophon was a lot dirtier than any space vehicle she'd ever been on as well. A rag hung from one of the boxes. She grabbed it and wiped the smelly gunk off as best she could. Every inch of wall and floor was covered with something: electronics, tools, and assorted stuff. Wires hung randomly and pipes appeared from all surfaces, in all sizes and materials. One narrow pipe in the ceiling started to hiss violently and some kind of gas or perhaps steam escaped. Rose shrank back, alarmed in case it was toxic, and nearly jumped out of her skin when a cheerful voice spoke behind her.

"Hi there, you must be Rose. It's lovely to meet you at last."

A small metal ball with blue light beams bursting at intervals from its surface was hovering in mid-air. Rose instinctively reached out to touch it.

"That tickles!" The ball danced out of her reach. "Oh my, what is happening here?" The ball moved swiftly over to the pipe. "Naughty little pressure leak." The hissing subsided, and the gas cloud slowly disappeared. "That's no way to welcome a visitor." The ball bounced up and down a few times as if doing a victory dance, before returning to float in front of her. "Oh, you must think I have no manners. I've not introduced myself properly. I'm Bel."

Rose smiled. Bel reminded her of one of her cousins: a fussy, houseproud woman who nevertheless had a warm heart. The memory was comforting and some of the tension drained from her. "It's good to meet you, Bel. Vash asked me to come on board and go to her cabin, but I have no idea where I'm going."

"Well, isn't that just typical of her? Follow me; it isn't far."

Rose followed Bel as it led her through some hatches. At each one, it stopped and reminded her to mind her head. Finally, they reached a hatch that led off the corridor into a small room. It didn't take much to see that it was Vash's private area. It was just as messy as the rest of the ship, but there were some personal touches. She caught sight of a 3-D image and gasped. It was of her, smiling and leaning against the window of their favourite restaurant. Rose remembered Vash taking it. She'd grouched at having to pose in the cold. Vash had placed it above the foot of her cotbed, right next to a picture of an older man that Rose assumed was her father. When she woke in the morning, it would be the first thing she saw. Rose blinked back tears. All the time she'd worried about Vash wanting her in her life, and here was a screen of her in the most private place in Vash's world.

"Yes, the captain must love you a lot. She asked me to tidy up before you got here. She's never done that before. Not even when she picked up that woman on…oh, I'm sure you don't want to hear about that."

Rose turned around and looked at the ball, surprised at the level of empathy that it showed. Was that really Bel, the artificial intelligence that ran the ship? It didn't seem possible that such a small thing could house the processors needed to run a ship and maintain such a high level of sentience.

"I appear to have confused you, Rose. Please accept my apologies, I should have explained. This is merely a service bot I keep for when we have visitors. I have noticed that humanoids seem to prefer the personal touch. The truth is I'm all around you, in everything you see. I am the ship."

"How do you know what I'm thinking? Can you read minds?" Rose blurted. She froze inside and tried to put any thoughts about the band out of her head. Although the Aximendes VI had computers, it had no advanced AI, because they were viewed with suspicion. Her people preferred their machines not to think outside their boxes. She supposed some of the ships she'd been on might have had them; she'd certainly encountered Avatoids acting as passenger assistants but nothing as independent as Bel seemed to be.

"Oh, no. How terribly invasive that would be. No, Rose, I have simply been programmed to observe and learn. I enjoy learning; I spend most of my free time studying."

"Free time?" Rose frowned.

"Oh, I get a few nano seconds here and there." Bel chuckled. "Now, unless you need anything else, I'll leave you in peace. If you want me, just say my name."

The bot shot up to the ceiling and disappeared into a small hole that Rose hadn't previously spotted. She took a deep breath, thankful to be alone again to process everything that had happened. She splayed her fingers across the cover as she sat, savouring the familiarity of the soft fabric. Never had an ordinary microfibre blanket felt so good. Her head and arms were leaden, and the adrenaline that had got her this far had finally run out. She desperately wanted to sleep, but at the same time her mind was running hot trying to process everything.

She rested her head, comforted by the scent of Vash on the pillow, and pondered the best thing to do. She wanted to help. *No, I want to survive.* Her pesky moral compass wasn't going to let her kid herself. Okay, she wanted to survive. There was no shame in that, and she wanted Vash to survive as well. But how could she really help? She was no warrior. All she'd proved best at was surviving and running. She'd done that for cycles, thinking her way out of tight corners. On the other hand, she already knew one thing that no one else did. She slid her fingers up her sleeve and ran them over the markings, dormant for the moment. Perhaps the best way she could help was by finding out more about the band. So far, she'd not discovered anything. She'd risked showing it to a couple of people once, but they'd just admired her "tribal markings." She sat up and swung her legs back over the edge of the cotbed.

"Bel? Are you there?" Rose chewed her lip, feeling faintly ridiculous as she called out to the empty room.

"Yes, Rose. How can I help?"

The bot didn't reappear, and Bel's voice came from thin air. Had she ever been alone? She pulled her knees up and hugged herself. This was definitely going to take a while to get used to. "You said that you're good at observing. What are you seeing now?" she said.

"I can see that you are very tired," Bel said after a slight pause. "However, you're clearly fighting sleep, though it would be beneficial to you. The ship's sensors tell me your heart rate is elevated above normal levels. From this I surmise that you are worrying about something. Is there anything I can do to assist you with this? Would you like some herbal tea? A little cheese, perhaps?"

Bel sounded genuinely concerned. Was that all part of her programming? Still, the suggestion of cheese made Rose smile. "Vash told you about that, did she? Well, I'm okay for something to eat and drink right now but..." How far could she trust this AI? What if she reported this back to Vash? Rose's stomach sank as she weighed up the possible consequences, but whatever way she looked at the problem, she only had one choice. She needed more information, and it wasn't like she was going to be able to hide anything from Bel while she was onboard. "I wonder, do you have any archive footage of the Akmonian Queen Penthesilea, House of Aximendes?"

"Allow me a moment to consult my databanks…I do have some footage taken some time ago. It was recorded during a Galactic Council reconciliation meeting between the Akmonians and a group of their victims. Would you like me to display it?"

Rose uncurled and leaned forward. Her throat became unbearably dry. "Yes, please, Bel, put the footage up for me."

A screen appeared in front of her, projected holographically from somewhere on the desk. It flickered into life to show a group of citizens and officials decked in uniforms or ceremonial garb walking towards the camera. Penthe strode along in the middle. She was older, but her proud face was still uncompromising and beautiful. She talked to officials walking beside her, nodding and looking slightly bored. Then she looked straight at the lens: straight at Rose. Hypnotised, Rose reached out to touch the screen. The film ended abruptly, and the screen disappeared.

Rose shook her head as if waking from a dream. How, after all these cycles, could this woman still hold such sway over her? She felt a whirlpool of awe and fear threatening to take her under, back to that dark place within herself. She bent over, shaking and afraid she would faint.

"You are clearly distressed, Rose. Should I contact Vash and ask her to come to the cabin?"

"No! No, please don't, Bel. I'm fine, really." Rose tried to still her shaking hands. "Bel, can you consult your databanks for information about the Akmonian family that Queen Penthesilea is part of. Specifically, records of any special artefacts that they have in their possession?"

In the distance there were clanking noises, muffled voices. It sounded like Vash and Alvin were aboard now.

"My local databanks record that the House of Aximendes is recognised as one of the richest families in the galaxy. Their wealth has been gained largely through the illegal trading practices and 'trawling.'"

"Trawling?"

"The Galactic Council defines trawling as the practice of attacking and plundering in their entirety: ships, orbitals, or planets vastly inferior to yourself."

"Oh, right." Rose was sorry she'd asked. "Please, go on."

"The early history of the House and its rise to power isn't well documented. Some historians have commented on a sudden change in its fortunes about two hundred and fifty cycles ago."

Rose did some quick calculations and figured that would date to about ten generations before Penthe.

"During this time, they were able to manoeuvre from a position as a minor house to one of the senior houses in the larger community. This seems to have come after a short alliance with another merchant house of a different species, which became extinct a few standard cycles after. The fortunes of the House improved considerably after this time; however, the extent of their physical holdings is not explicitly recorded in the data I have accessed so far."

Rose was grateful for the distraction of Bel's exposition. It was strange yet fascinating to hear the history of her community recounted in this way. Rose swallowed hard. She was about to take a risk, but there was no other way to get the information that she needed.

"I need your help, Bel, but I need to you to keep it secret from Vash. Are you able to do that?"

Rose looked down at her feet while Bel considered the question. She told herself it was to protect Vash that she didn't tell her everything, but deep down, it was about protecting herself as well. At some point, she had stopped trusting as she once had. Bel obviously had some form of ethical programming built in. *Shame I don't.* Perhaps she should ask Bel to forget the request.

"Vash ordered me to treat you as part of the crew. She informed me that you were important to her and that I was to assist you while on board and ensure your needs were met."

Rose's heart skipped. She was so important to Vash that she'd given her own ship a direct order to look after her. No, there was no way that Bel would betray her captain and Rose had no right asking her to. She put her head in her hands and waited for Bel's outrage.

"There is no reason why she should know anything you tell me in confidence unless it directly compromises her safety or the security of this ship. In that event, I would have to inform her immediately."

Rose looked up slowly, not sure whether to be relieved or aghast that Bel had just granted her permission to deceive Vash. She clenched her fists. If she was going to do this, she had to do it the right way. Vash deserved that much.

"I don't think what I'm going to ask is going to do that, Bel. I think it's going to help her, but I don't want to trouble her with it right now. However, I understand that if it does now or in the future, you must do the right thing and protect Vash and this ship."

"I agree to assist you, Rose." Bel said.

The calm measured response was reassuring. Taking a deep breath, Rose pulled up her sleeve, parted the bangles, and held out her arm so that the markings could be clearly seen. "Bel, can you take a visual record of these markings and see if you can match them to anything recorded in your local databanks or any other data you have access to?"

"Detailed recording has begun. Please hold your arm still, Rose."

After a few seconds, Bel told Rose to relax. She lowered her arm and pulled her sleeve back down. There was no way she could relax though, not now.

"What you have asked for will take some time, Rose. I'll inform you as soon as I have any information. Your chamomile tea is now ready."

A small ancillary bot tray glided in the door bearing a simple pot of steaming fragrant tea and a mug. Rose sat and prayed she'd done the right thing.

CHAPTER NINE

THE SOFTLY LIT COMMAND table dominated the darkened space with a holographic display of the system floating ghostlike above it. Tactical stations ringed the table, each tasked with a different part of the vessel's offensive and defensive capabilities, both human and machine. Pale faces could just be made out in the gloom, eyes reflecting a kaleidoscope of colours from the consoles they were trained on. Uniforms flitted through the shadows, accompanied by whispering and the rustling of papers.

To an outsider it probably looked busy, almost chaotic. However, Penthe regarded it simply as part of a far larger machine, the Aximendes VI itself. If the great Sol-10 engines of the ship were its beating heart, the command hub was its brain. She had only to give direction and human synapses would pass her orders swiftly to the body and soul of her great ship. *This* was why she wanted the throne, why she'd endured everything her mother had thrown at her. Standing here at the centre of the action was like being a god. She breathed in deeply and drew herself up tall before advancing to the table.

The plans her senior officers had drawn up were superimposed on the table's tactical display for her to scan. Above her, modelled predictions of the battle ahead played out on an endless aerial loop. The tactical computers showed they were always victorious, but only idiots trusted their predictions without further consideration. Their results always missed a vital variable: the chaos of the battle itself. The more variables involved in a fight, whether living, machine, or simply environment, the greater risk of the unexpected happening. The battle computers were powerful but not omniscient.

The tactics were competent but uninspiring, and her mood plummeted. The battle ahead was far more complex than the attack on the agriplanet. Open space battles were rarely fought because so few of their variables were fixed, but her senior officers should have been capable of putting together something better than this. Her euphoria dissipated, replaced by a familiar frustration, and she rued choosing them for their loyalty rather than their flare. They were always far too cautious and lacked the imagination which naturally came with her higher breeding. Her head started to ache slightly as she mulled over how to put right their mistakes.

"We appear to be assuming that our superior firepower will just win the day, Archiploi Volos. What if they have a hidden weapon our spies don't know about? What if one of their ships slips through that first wave of our defence? We intend to win, not simply minimise our losses!" She didn't bother looking up. The silence in the room was proof of their undivided attention. "I've spoken before about the dangers of becoming complacent. We must assume that our previous strategies have been studied by our enemies. This plan is barely adequate, no more."

"As always, you bring much needed wisdom to the command table, ma'am. What should we change?" Archiploi Volos's back was ramrod straight, her gaze fixed on a point above Penthe's head.

Penthe's headache intensified at her Archiploi's oily sycophantic tone. She choked down a sudden urge to slap her face. Really, did she have to do everything herself? "I should've thought it was obvious: inject some contingency or add a little of the unexpected. Dare to show some imagination perhaps. May the gods be thanked I asked to see this before the action started. Now, how about this?" Penthe slipped on a tac-glove and used her finger on the table to drag a group of fighters out of their proposed defensive position in front of the Aximendes VI. As she moved them, a contrail of blue light formed and followed a path that took them out well beyond some nearby planets and back again, to come in behind the enemy forces. Above them, the modelling smoothly adjusted to accommodate the change.

"I want these ships to maintain strict stealth mode until the last moment. If they attack at maximum speed, the enemy warships will have no time to react. Once they're removed, we'll be able to mop up the rest of the enemy fleet at our leisure. The system will be ours, and perhaps without some of the losses that might result if we're too predictable."

"It's a magnificent strategy, your majesty." The face of the antiploi in charge of the ship's defences flushed slightly. "However, it will remove vital units tasked with protecting us. Is that too great a risk?"

"Our queen knows what she is doing. Do not presume to question her," Sakas said.

Penthe glanced at her and recognised a fellow huntress in the fiery light of her eyes, eager for the kill. She shared her frustration. How she wanted to shake and kick some sense into her officers. However, she also needed to keep them working for her willingly as well as obediently. That was something Sakas would never understand. There was valuable experience among them that would take too much time to replace. "Thank you, Sakas, but all viewpoints can be aired at this table."

Sakas' cheeks burned red, but she stayed quiet.

Penthe turned to the officer. "I agree that there is a degree of risk. Only the foolhardy would deny it, and I'm sure you would agree that nobody around this table is a fool."

The officer bowed. "My apologies, ma'am, if I—"

"Enough." Penthe was weary of all the tiresome politics. It was time to conclude this pointless discussion. After all, she was the only one present who had a vote. "I'm confident that the remaining forces will be sufficient, provided that their training has been carried out effectively."

The officer, a veteran of hundreds of battles, saluted, her face expressionless. "Ma'am, I am sure of the abilities of our pilots. They'll not let us down." She looked around the table, as if daring anyone to disagree.

Now she needed to be the magnanimous god. *Smile, Penthe, smile.* "Very well. I have the greatest confidence in you. I'm sure that this sorry business will be over very soon. Antiploi Sakas, please accompany me back to my quarters. I have wish of your counsel regarding the most efficient way to capitalise on our impending victory."

She swept out of the hub in silence with Sakas a few steps behind. The commander was always mindful to avoid familiarity with her in public. They walked back to her quarters in silence, and as they strode through the reception into her private rooms, she waved at her servants to leave immediately. Only when the door closed did she begin to laugh. Sakas hesitated, shook her head, and joined in just as loudly.

"Oh, ma'am, the look on their faces. They're so sure of themselves but so devoid of imagination. Never would they have suggested such a flanking strategy. It is a masterful move on your part." She put her hands on her hips, her face lit by excitement. "You are truly our greatest queen. Songs will surely be written about this day."

Penthe held her stomach, still gasping for breath. "Songs will be written, eh? I like the sound of that, Sakas. I think I'll hold you to that one."

Sakas' words danced in her mind, and she imagined her troops and families across the fleet singing her name in praise. What would you say to that, Mother? Elated, she sank down on to a sofa and patted the seat next to her. "Now, we have a little time to spare before the games begin. Perhaps we can start working on some verses to these songs of yours."

Sakas sat down, her face flushed. "As you wish, ma'am. I live to serve."

Headache forgotten and replaced by a deeper ache lower down, Penthe traced the contours of Sakas' bulging biceps with her finger. "I'm sure you do, Sakas. I wouldn't expect anything else." Sakas' eyes darkened with lust as she leaned in to kiss her deeply.

Two hours later, Penthe sat alone at her command desk waiting for the battle to begin. She might be a god in the command hub, but right now she was just a spare part in the great machine, waiting for the call to battle. She yawned and arched her back to ease the tension in her muscles. Sakas had long gone to check on the latest intelligence and make sure her team were prepared to go to work as soon as the battle was completed. She must have covert agents in the enemy fleet as well as on the home planets of the system. There was no way that Sakas could have collected the intelligence she had without having people on the ground. Even now, they were probably inveigling their way into the heart of proceedings by any means necessary. Penthe could have asked for the details, but she preferred to keep their distasteful, but necessary, activities at arm's length. There was no honour in spying or treachery.

Were they putting their lives, their souls, on the line out of loyalty to her mother or to Penthe? She picked at a tiny piece of gold leaf that had come free on a nail. Did one's subjects follow blindly, or did they truly appreciate leadership? Of course, in practical terms it made little difference, but it would've been nice to know that she inspired loyalty. From the way some people spoke of her mother, it seemed that she'd led by consent rather than fear. They still sang about her victories, the glory she brought to the House, and their pride in serving her. All Penthe could remember was the fear and it chilled her thinking of it now. Yes, she would reward Sakas' team when they returned. Let the word get around that she was generous to those that were loyal to her.

She leaned back in her command chair, focused on the cool of the tanskin against her bare legs and closed her eyes. The room was blissfully quiet, giving her a chance to calm her thoughts and quiet the maelstrom deep inside. Unless she summoned them, none of her household would disturb her. They were all confined to their own quarters while the ship was at battle stations. She'd made it clear that the last thing their supreme leader needed at this time was their endless, mindless attention. The inevitable looks of disappointment on their faces had been more than compensated for by their absence.

The ship started its final manoeuvres a few minutes later. Despite the immense size of the vessel, she still felt the floor tremble as its retro engines fired. Desperate for the something to do, she walked over to the portscreen on the wall and pulled back the heavy cloth that hid it from view. Distant stars were wheeling slightly as the Aximendes VI banked and hit by a tinge of nausea, she had to stop looking at them. The face of a nearby planet was lit by the system's sol. The star itself was obscured by one of the ship's grasping limbs, a hazy corona down one of the edges the only clue to its position. She stood for a moment, entranced by the beauty of the light bathing the hull.

Penthe couldn't see the enemy ships. They were still hundreds of thousands of miles away. The tactical computers were lining the Aximendes VI up in the optimal position to rain death upon the pitiful fleet that was racing out to meet them. It would be a slaughter of course; it always was. She had long since stopped counting the numbers that died at her hands in these battles. She felt no connection anymore to the individual. Distance numbed the mind to such things. How must it have felt, eons before, when her ancestors battled in person on the same piece of earth? To hear weapons clashing, feel the hot breath of the other, and smell the sweat and blood. Death could be inches away, not thousands of kilometres. The idea terrified and excited her in equal measure.

Her reverie was interrupted by muffled booms that signalled the batteries were testing their guns. After a few seconds they ceased, their crews apparently content that all was well. Penthe pulled the cloth back into place and walked slowly back to her desk where she could monitor proceedings on the tactical display transmitted directly to it. The metrics coming in from their long-range scanners caught her eye. The composition of the enemy fleet was exactly as Sakas had reported, with only three battleships of any worth. Gods, that woman was a witch with a coven of Hekate's spies at her disposal. Penthe shivered, glad that Sakas worked for and not against her.

Ripples raced across the surface of her kras when the central hangar doors opened. Just as the liquid settled, the goblet rattled briefly again on its platinum tray. She checked the display. Yes, her special squadron was departing from the rear of the ship to start their long flanking move. The fools would never see them coming. Penthe had always wanted to try such a tactic. But only now, emboldened by Sakas' faith and her own desperation to get this charade over as quickly as possible, had she dared to try. What would the ship's official bard write after this? *Our queen, brave and brilliant, scintillating in looks and execution.* Penthe giggled and took a sip of her kras, savouring its rich undertones.

"So pleased with yourself, aren't you?"

Penthe stiffened and acid bile replaced the taste of alcohol in her mouth. The voice issued from the console speakers.

"None of this would be necessary if it hadn't been for your stupidity, your pathetic weakness. You aren't fit to sit on my throne."

"Please, Mother, enough. It wasn't my fault. You should've told me about the band." Penthe turned and stared defiantly up at the portrait of her mother. The eyes didn't flinch; they just stared coldly back.

"If you hadn't debased yourself with that woman and kept her in your service when you should have killed her, she would never have seen the band in the first place."

Her mother's voice was overlaid now with the voice of others, getting louder and louder.

"Whore! Whore!"

"Majesty? Are you there? Ma'am? Can you hear me?"

Penthe started. The voice was very real and coming in on the priority channel. With a shaky hand she reached out for the comms switch. "Yes, what is it?"

"We're in position, ma'am. Units are deployed. Do you wish us to proceed or wait for you?"

Penthe looked up again at the portrait, her mother's eyes positively glinting with hate. "Proceed as planned, Archiploi Volos. I'll join you in the hub presently." They were loyal to her. They had to be. Sakas might inspire to an extent, but this ship fought for its queen.

"And I'm queen now, Mother." Penthe threw the silk scarf over the portrait before she left the room.

CHAPTER TEN

After Bel departed, Rose set to work stowing away her meagre belongings. While Vash's cabin wasn't large, she soon discovered that it boasted an impressive amount of storage. Even the cotbed lifted to reveal a deep well, where Vash appeared to keep a mixture of heavy-duty work gear and fitness equipment. There was a gelech set with a customised bat, and she made a mental note to ask Vash about that later.

After half an hour, Vash popped her head through the door. She was smiling, but Rose could see worry lines deepening around her eyes.

"Sorry for leaving you. Everything okay?"

"Yes, of course. Bel took great care of me." Rose walked over and kissed Vash on the tip of her nose. "You don't have to worry about me, honestly."

The lines softened, and Vash's shoulders relaxed a bit. "Well, hopefully it won't be much longer." She sighed and ran her hands through her hair. "We have a tech coming on board to check over our systems and make sure everything is up to scratch."

"I am not sure why my systems require such a check." Bel's disapproving voice interrupted them.

Vash shrugged. "I told them that everything's okay, Bel. But they don't know how efficient you are."

Bel made an electronic noise that sounded like a snort of derision.

"As I say, Bel keeps our systems in good order, so he won't be here long. I'm going to try and keep him up on the bridge, but you should stay down here. We don't need more people than necessary knowing you're onboard. When he disembarks, I'll get Bel to tell you straight away."

"Sounds a good plan." Rose pressed one finger against Vash's lips. "Now, captain, get back to your bridge and stop fretting about me, all right?"

Vash pulled her closer and kissed her, long and hard. Then she was gone, running back up the corridor.

Rose dropped her brave face and closed her eyes. What would she do if the tech did come down here? A vortex of conflicting outcomes threatened to fill her head. She gazed around the cabin, desperate for something to do to keep her mind occupied. Finally, she rummaged in her belongings for her electrocomb. She ran it slowly through her hair, letting it gently untangle the knots. The simple act comforted and calmed her, easing the knots of anxiety in her brain as well. She kept going until Bel coughed.

"Rose, Vash asked me to tell you that the technician has disembarked."

"Thanks, Bel." Rose put down the electrocomb and took a deep breath. It was time to leave her refuge.

She made her way quietly back to entrance hatch and craned her neck around the privacy screen to double check no one was lurking in the tube. Satisfied there was no one there, she considered her options and chose the corridor going in the opposite direction. It brought her to the bridge hatch, which was wide open. Now, she wasn't sure how to proceed. Did she have to ask permission to enter? She didn't want to cause more trouble with Alvin. She stood, frozen in place by her indecision.

Rose could just see the ship's engineer hunched over his console in a corner. The space was largely in darkness. Light from the main screen and the other technical displays provided dim illumination and one cool white tunnel of light shone directly down on to a grubby, torn notebook which was constantly being flicked back and forth. His nails were blackened and cracked and made her wonder how often he showered. Every now and then, he spoke into his mouthbead, which looked to be held together by brown industrial tape. He mumbled softly as his fingers moved again, dancing to the distant tune in his ears.

In contrast, Vash sat languidly in her command chair, one leg slung over an arm. She'd rolled her T-shirt sleeves up. Rose's stomach flipped at the sight of her toned upper arms. Her eyes adjusted a bit more; the co-pilot's seat was filled with a mountain of snacks. Rose smiled broadly as Vash reached across to grab a handful of something luridly purple and green and munched on it. She burped loudly and thumped her chest. Rose clamped her hands over her mouth to hold back the laughter.

Vash narrowed her eyes and looked over towards Alvin. Apparently satisfied that he was immersed in his work, she reached into her jacket and pulled out a small black box. She opened the lid and looked at the contents. Intrigued, Rose stepped through the hatch to get closer and see the contents. As she did so, her foot caught on the edge of a metal box. She stood on one foot and swore under her breath. Luckily, neither Vash nor Alvin seemed to have heard. Vash continued to look at the box as she rubbed the tip of one ear.

"Have you injured yourself, Rose?" Bel's voice boomed out.

Alvin turned around immediately and yanked off his headset. Vash snapped the box shut and stuffed it into a pocket before she stood.

"You okay, lovely? I didn't know you were there." Vash raised her eyebrow.

"Yeah, fine, just being clumsy. I'm sorry if I've disturbed you both." Rose could feel herself blushing under Vash's intense stare.

"Of course not. I should've come to find you. Do you want a proper look around?" Vash hurriedly cleared the co-pilot seat and tossed the snacks haphazardly into an old tanskin kit bag she had next to her chair. "Sorry, we don't often have company." Vash whipped around at the low growl from Alvin's corner of the bridge. "Sorry, Alvin? I didn't catch that."

"You know how I feel, Vash." Alvin didn't turn around, but the back of his neck was slowly turning brick red.

"Yes, you've made your opinion abundantly clear more than once. And again, I'm the captain of this ship and the matter is closed, Alvin."

Vash's tone was icy calm and though she wasn't the target, Rose still felt frozen with fear as the atmosphere thickened around her.

"Yeah, okay," Alvin mumbled, still looking down at his console.

"Sorry? I didn't hear you clearly, Alvin."

Vash was obviously determined to stamp her authority on the situation. Rose tried to stand as still as possible, not liking the aggressive atmosphere. Just how heated had the earlier discussions got? Alvin obviously wasn't happy about her being aboard, but he hadn't said anything to her face.

He shook his head slightly. "Yes, captain."

"Excellent." Vash smiled in his direction before she waved Rose over. "Now, why don't you try this for size."

Rose lowered herself gingerly into the chair. Like the rest of the furniture on the bridge of the Bellerophon, it looked as if it had been bought long ago or thrown out of a junk yard. However, it turned out to be a good fit. Decades of use had softened the lab-grown tanskin and she sank into it, loving how comfortable it felt.

Vash stood back and looked at her critically. "Not bad. Just a few adjustments."

She walked around the back, and with a high-pitched squeal, the chair jerked roughly downwards until her feet were on the floor. Vash swore softly under her breath, and there was a jolt as if she had kicked something. The chair tightened around Rose's body rather more than she would have liked.

"Got to be sure it fits you properly. It could get a bit bumpy later and if you get thrown around, you'll get bruised all over. Now let's look at the harness."

Vash threw the straps over her shoulder and came back around the front. She fastened them to the fixings between Rose's legs, and her fingers brushed against the inside of her thighs. Did her fingers really need to be exactly there? When Vash straightened up to pull hard at the straps, she smirked slightly.

"Okay, how's that? It has to be really tight, I'm afraid." Vash's eyes twinkled.

Well, two could play this game. "This doesn't feel right, Vash." Rose pointed one of her shoulder straps.

When Vash leaned in to look more closely, Rose grabbed the back of her head and pulled her in for a deep kiss. She broke off and gave Vash her sweetest smile. "Yes, you know that feels a lot better now."

Vash's eyes widened, and she wagged her finger at Rose. "I can see it's going to be interesting having you on the bridge."

For the next twenty minutes, Vash talked to her about the controls on the chair, the console, and what the displays she could see were showing. She didn't seem to spare one single technical detail and although Rose tried desperately to keep up, she struggled. She brushed her hair back from her face and puffed out her cheeks.

Vash smiled. "Sorry, Rose. I forget how complicated all this sounds. Look, I don't really expect you to have to use any of this. If for any reason I'm incapacitated, Bel will take over all the important functions. If she needs you to do anything, she'll explain it all."

"I agree, Rose. Do not overly concern yourself with trying to remember anything, Vash usually doesn't," Bel said.

Rose grinned at the outraged look on Vash's face.

"Remind me again why I don't just disconnect your higher functions, Bel?" Vash's eyes narrowed.

"Because you enjoy my witty banter on long journeys."

"Yeah, well, I might be reconsidering. Now get back to helping Alvin, you reprobate."

Bel went silent but, judging by the twinkle in Vash's eye, it was obvious that she had great affection for her AI. However, something that Vash had said clawed madly at Rose's brain. *If for any reason I'm incapacitated.* Rose hadn't really considered that possibility. This had all seemed such an adventure, but if things went wrong, Vash might get injured or killed. They *all* could get injured or killed. An icy lump settled in the pit of her stomach as she began to dwell on what she'd pulled them all into.

"Hey, I'm not going to take any stupid risks." Vash touched her hand to Rose's cheek gently. "I have my orders and we have a job to do, but once it's done, I'm going to get us to safety. I really don't want to die today, okay?" Vash kissed Rose's nose.

She nodded and forced a smile, but she couldn't let go of a terrible foreboding that everything was going to go wrong.

Later, Vash asked her to tuck herself away in the cabin again while some more military techs visited the ship. She was sat on the cotbed, trying to remember some of what she had been shown, when Vash appeared at the hatch.

"Hey, beautiful. Did you enjoy your first proper foray onto the bridge?"

Vash's tone was light, but Rose could see the strain in her eyes. She smiled back to reassure her. "It was…interesting. I had no idea what you did was so complex."

"Well, Bel wasn't completely lying when she said that I get a lot of help, and Alvin takes care of all the hard engineering, of course. I just get to fly her, really."

Vash stepped into the room and sat down on the cotbed next to her. Rose put her hand on Vash's shoulder and pulled her in closer. Vash made out like she was tough but sometimes she just wanted a cuddle. They sat in comfortable silence for a while with Vash resting her head against Rose's chest while she stroked her hair.

"So, you going to tell me what's really going on?" Rose squeezed Vash's arm.

Vash sighed deeply. She straightened up, moving a little way to the side and drew her knees up to her chest.

"Can't keep any secrets from you, can I?" Vash nibbled on a thumbnail.

"Thing is, I'm a bit worried."

"Anything I can help with?"

"I'm not really sure about these orders. Alvin thinks it's great, the system fleet going all guns blazing up against your old ship. I just think we're going to take a hammering."

Rose let out a deep breath, relieved to hear Vash express the same misgivings she had herself. The successes of the House of Aximendes were celebrated with stories and songs. She'd heard so many times of other systems and communities who had suffered terrible losses because of their futile resistance. "Why didn't you say anything at the briefing?"

"There was no point really. Some of the wiser heads there know the score of course, but it is what it is. There are enough hawks in charge that surrender was never going to be on the table." Vash frowned.

"You do realise what the Aximendes VI is capable of? What Penthe is capable of?"

"Yeah, but I couldn't exactly tell them that my girlfriend is an Akmonian and has the inside line on the situation, could I?"

But you wanted to… Rose could only imagine how conflicted Vash must feel. It broke her heart a little. "I'm sorry I've put you in this position."

Vash shook her head. "I made my choice back in Drem, Rose. Nothing has changed."

"But these are your people, I'm just—"

"Just what, Rose?" Vash leant forward and stared into her eyes. She kissed her, and her warm lips lingered for a moment before she pulled away. "Does that help answer your question?"

Rose tried to smile, but her stomach quivered. "A little, I suppose, but the fact remains we're in great danger. Penthe might be insane, but she is also queen. The crew will die for her if that is what it takes."

Vash banged her head lightly back against the wall. "Stars, this is such a mess. I half wanted to make a run for it, but I can't do it, Rose. I can't leave these people."

"And I care too much about you to ask that. Do you want me to surrender to your authorities? I'm prepared to do so, you know." Rose flushed, not quite able to believe she'd just said that, but for the first time it seemed the right option.

Vash looked sideways at her, one eyebrow raised. "You really mean that, don't you? You'd surrender to that lunatic to save me, to save us."

She looked up at the ceiling and Rose could see the corner of her eyes glistening. "Yes, I would. You mean that much to me, Vash. This system and its people have come to mean that much to me."

Vash sniffed and fiercely wiped her eyes. "Well, that isn't going to happen. Not now, not ever. Over my dead body." She sighed heavily. "Though maybe I shouldn't say that." She thumped her knee. "You said you wanted to help?"

"Yes, of course, but I'm not a pilot or an engineer. I can make a good caffrush, as you know."

Vash snorted. "I'd love to see you with a wrench in your hand."

Rose wasn't having that. "Hey, I might be able to show you a thing or two if you did. I'm not completely useless, you know. I did manage to fend for myself in Drem before you turned up."

"Oh, Rose, I'm sorry." Vash didn't look particularly apologetic. "But there's something I think you might be able to help with. Something you have a proven track record of being good at."

She moved around, sat cross-legged, and faced Vash. "What do you mean?"

"Well, to put it bluntly, you're very good at getting away from trouble. Now don't get upset with me—"

"I only did what I had to, Vash." She wrapped her arms around herself and stared defiantly at Vash.

"Yes, I know. The thing is…you did it really well. You have a gift for staying alive."

Rose had to admit Vash was right. There had been several occasions when she had to think on her feet, like the time when she stowed away in a cargo ship's kitchen dumper and stank of rotten food for three days after. "Okay, let's say you might be right, I still don't see how that helps."

"Well, I want to have a plan in hand in case everything goes wrong," Vash whispered.

Rose looked over towards the door half expecting to see Alvin appear. "You don't want Alvin to know?"

"Stars, no, he's just looking for an excuse to bad-mouth me with Central and improve his own situation." Vash's face flushed slightly, but she seemed to check herself. "Sorry, I know I shouldn't be afraid of the little shit, but he's got some influential friends back at base. It just isn't worth the risk."

"So, you want my help to put together a plan B. What about Bel?"

"What about me?"

Bel's voice whispered in the air just to the left of her head and Rose jerked around. Of course, there was nothing there, but she heard a quiet giggle.

Vash grinned. "Bel works for me. Besides, I asked her to rerun Central Command's battle plans and model them. She wasn't impressed either."

"I predict a thirty percent chance of success based on our current strategy. As I've no wish to become a piece of floating space junk, I fully approve of Vash's decision to put a back-up plan in place."

Rose laughed at Bel's frankness. She could see why she and Vash worked so well together. Vash got off the cotbed and moved over to her desk.

"Bel, will you put up a holo of the system, please?" A slowly rotating hologram of the RH15 system appeared above the desk. "Add in both fleets."

Two sets of coloured symbols appeared. Rose had no problem making out the Aximendes VI; it was the largest ship symbol in the display, a bright red star moving inexorably towards the central planets. Smaller red symbols could just be seen on the far side of the outer planets, probably representing auxiliary vehicles. Rose's heart sank. Penthe must be feeling supremely confident to have brought them into the system as well. Usually they were left far behind, catching up to re-provision the capital ship after a battle. "What's this symbol here, Bel? A planet?" Rose pointed at a small circle.

"Yes, it's a small mining planet. MR3."

"They're run by a private company in collaboration with the system authorities. They share the profits from the operation." Vash raised an eyebrow. "Why are you asking, Rose?"

"Are there many people working down there?" Rose concentrated on the position of the planet in relation to the Aximendes VI.

"It is very lightly inhabited, Rose. Current records show sixteen open mines currently, all manned by solo engineers who operate mining bots."

Vash eyes narrowed. "Are you thinking—"

"You'll have to sort out the details with Bel, but if you're looking for somewhere to hide in a hurry, that might be perfect."

Vash threw her arms around her. "Genius. You know, Bel, I think we might just survive today, after all."

Cradled in Vash's arms, Rose tried to smile, but she couldn't take her eyes off the red star of the Aximendes VI moving towards them. Plan B or not, they were going to need a twist in space and time to make it out of this alive.

CHAPTER ELEVEN

THEY SPENT ABOUT AN hour with Bel firming up the backup plan. Vash went back to the bridge to make sure everything was going smoothly. Rose tried to get some rest, but her brain was too busy. She gave up and tidied the room, if only to take her mind off her increasing nausea.

Vash had shown her more spaces in the cabin, some of which were very cleverly hidden away. She hadn't tried to hide anything, making Rose feel at home. Most of the gaps were filled haphazardly with Vash's clothing and junk. Rose managed to condense the contents of three into one, just by folding things properly.

Eager to get on her way with Vash, she'd brought very little. Rose tried to judge if she had brought enough. Enough for what though? A single battle or another cycle or so on the run? She'd locked the door to her apartment carefully but would probably never see it again. Her vision blurring dangerously, Rose hurriedly closed the drawers.

"We're thirty minutes out from the designated rendezvous point," Vash's voice came over on the comms.

Rose left the hatch and headed to the bridge. Vash strapped her tightly into the co-pilot's chair, with no games this time, and asked Bel to close the internal hatches.

As they all shut, clunking and rattling with an ominous finality, a heavy silence fell on the Bridge. Alvin stopped flicking back and forth through his notebook. He sat with his arms crossed and leaned back in his chair. His eyes were closed, but Rose couldn't make out if he was asleep or just studiously ignoring her. He hadn't acknowledged her presence at all, which made her nerves jangle even more.

"Bel, what's our ETA?" Vash asked.

Her fingers rested lightly on a control pad on the arm of her chair. The identical controls on Rose's seat were covered with a clear plastic lid, presumably to prevent Rose sending them into hyperdrive or something by mistake.

"What's ETA?" Rose asked.

"Estimated time of arrival," Bel said.

Of course. She'd heard it being used by officers on the Aximendes VI.

"And it's twelve minutes, thirty-two seconds and counting." Bel's jocular tone had disappeared, replaced by cool precision.

Vash looked sideways at Rose. "Would you like to see what we're up against?"

"Won't we see it on the view screen?" The large display in front of them was covered with strange groups of numbers and symbols.

Vash chuckled. "That screen can show a vid feed but in battle I'll be using a HTAC. It gives me greater clarity. The big screen will just be supplying essential data instead. It's better than seeing blurred images."

"HTAC?" she asked. Why did pilots have to use all this jargon?

"You ever worn a vid helmet? They based those on HTAC."

Rose nodded. The sexden she worked in had a few. They served as cheap thrills for the customers who couldn't afford the services of real people. She'd tried it out once to understand what it offered. She'd only lasted a minute, fighting claustrophobia and a need to shower.

"It's kind of like that but with a live feed. It's easier if I show you." Vash popped part of her harness and leaned over.

She lifted the guard on Rose's arm controls and quickly punched a couple of buttons. A loud whirring sound preceded movement from the back of the seat. Arms swung over either side of Rose and presented a helmet with a clear visor. It lowered very carefully, no doubt using sensors to position itself over her head. It was weird having a machine do all this for her. Even with the integrated cameras maintaining a view of the bridge, her claustrophobia was growing, and she hoped this wouldn't take long. As soon as it was positioned, Vash pressed some more buttons and the scene in front of her eyes changed. The bridge disappeared, and it was as if she was hanging in space. Claustrophobia was replaced with vertigo, and she flailed wildly as she tried to steady herself.

"Easy, Rose. I'm coming."

Vash's voice came from by her side, as if she was beside her in space. Her hands were gently lowered and inserted into some soft gloves. "Just breathe in and out. It always feels a bit weird at first. Just keep looking at the stars ahead, straight ahead."

Rose fixed her gaze on a group of stars in the distance, and her heart rate started to settle. Slowly she risked turning her head. Another ship was moving to the starboard side of the Bellerophon.

"That's a mate of mine, Stefan. Good captain," Vash said. "But if you want to see the good ship Aximendes VI, turn your head a little to the left. See that glint over there? Raise your right index finger and touch it."

Her right index finger, transformed by the HTAC into cross hairs, hovered over the distant reddish glint. Rose touched it and immediately shot forward, the Aximendes VI racing towards her, growing bigger until it blocked her view of the stars. Was she going to slam into it? Her stomach clenched violently as she came to sudden halt, and she fought to hold on to the few snacks she'd been able to eat in the cabin. Fates, look at it now. The enormous vessel towered over her, its huge limbs stretching out around her. The gaping maw between them was closed for now and a pinprick of light at the centre of great interlocking teeth was the only clue to the docking areas within. Squadrons of fighters and carrier ships would be ready to join the battle ahead. Each limb housed hundreds of people. A community, a family, all working together for the good of the ship and the House.

A terrible yearning to be part of that whole again hit her. She tried to hold back the tears, to hide them from Vash and Alvin, but one broke loose and trickled down her cheek. Once upon a time, that ship had been her world. Now it was closed to her, and her future lay elsewhere. Where could she call home now? "How do I get back, Vash? How do I disengage the HTAC?"

"You finished already?"

Vash sounded surprised. She'd obviously assumed that Rose would want to spend longer exploring. "I've seen enough, thank you."

"See that green symbol in the top left-hand corner of your display. Touch that."

Rose did as she was told and was relieved to feel the HTAC lift from her head. Leads snaked away from the gloves and retreated underneath the seat. She pulled them off gently.

"Just pop them in that open drawer on the right-hand side of your chair." Vash pointed. "So, what did you think?"

Was this some kind of test? "It looked very…impressive."

"It's nothing our fleet can't deal with. We just need to follow our orders," Alvin said. "They might think they're the rulers of the universe, but we're more than a match."

"Thanks for the pep talk, Alvin. Have you visually checked the shield generators?" Vash rolled her eyes at Rose, safe in the knowledge that Alvin couldn't see from his angle.

"Only about ten times, Vash."

"Well, can you check again, please? I don't want to chance being on the end of a freak shot."

Alvin sighed but stayed silent and popped his harness. He clumped out of the bridge. Vash looked at her and winked conspiratorially.

"Five minutes from rendezvous, Vash. All combat systems are online," Bel said.

Vash put one finger to her lips while she reached into her jacket pocket and pulled out the same little black box Rose had seen her coveting earlier.

"A gift from Central Command," she whispered.

As Vash opened the box, Rose peered inside at the two syringes and two capsules.

"Something to help me during the fight."

She'd heard talk in the bars from young jocks boasting about the drugs that heightened reaction times in their staged space fights. They got their drugs from the black market. Vash had been given the official military version.

"When I ask, will you inject me with the antidote?" Vash held up the syringe with a green band.

Rose nodded. She had no intention of leaving Vash on cloud nine for too long. "Vash, what are the capsules?"

Vash's face tightened. She didn't answer at first but held one of the capsules up.

"Suicide drugs. If we get captured, we're supposed to take them."

"There are only two…"

"I didn't tell anyone about you, did I? And I told Alvin to keep his mouth shut too. So, you and Alvin get the pills. I've got my gun."

"Vash." Rose tried to grab the box.

Vash moved it quickly out of reach. "Look, it's not like we're going to need them, Rose. I'll get us to safety as soon as I can, I promise."

"All up and running, captain, just as they were thirty minutes ago," Alvin said as he stomped back onto the bridge. "All right if I return to my seat now?"

His tone still bordered on insubordinate, and Rose's stomach tensed in anticipation of a reaction. However, Vash just gave him a thumbs up.

"Good work, Alvin. Yes, get strapped in. We're nearly there."

Rose sank back into her own seat, deeply disturbed by the capsules. Did Vash really intend to shoot her own brains out to avoid capture? Just thinking about it sent an icy chill down her spine. She knew the reputation of her people, of course. She'd been brought up to celebrate their dominance. They were the natural leaders, born to rule over the weak and unworthy. That also meant she'd never had to face up to what it felt like to be on the other side. Rose had never seen what happened to prisoners. She'd never needed to, and it wasn't considered a polite topic of conversation. She shuddered at the knowledge that, for Vash and her people, the thought of being captured by Akmonians was worse than death itself.

She reflected on her earlier yearning to be with her people again. Her cheeks grew hot as the maelstrom of conflicting thoughts increased. Memories of her own family, her loving childhood, and the close sense of community swam through her mind. Her mother had owned little of tangible value, but they had never gone without. When times were tough, like when her mother had lost a baby, the House had made sure that they were both cared for. Those weren't the actions of monsters.

No, they weren't all bad people, and she longed to tell Alvin that. But it was naive to think he would listen. Just as she'd never believe that there weren't creatures living in the depths of the ship's bilges, feeding on the raw sewage with great glassy, sightless eyes. For Alvin, and perhaps for Vash, Akmonians were the creatures of nightmares. Something to frighten little children with stories about. Misbehave and the Akmonians will come for you.

Now they had.

She was trapped. She couldn't go home but couldn't reveal herself either. Imprisonment and likely death lay in either direction. No, all she could do now was keep on as she was, relying on her own moral compass, her instincts, and perhaps on the band. All she could do was hope that one day she would find acceptance, and safety, and a place to call home again.

"You sure you still want to stay up with me? Last chance to go back to the cabin," Vash said.

Rose shook her head. She didn't feel particularly comfortable on the bridge, but at least she was with Vash. "I'll stay."

Vash passed over a headset. "Plug this in on the arm of your chair. Yeah, just there."

Rose clicked it into place. The plastic was worn and scratched the back of her ear slightly.

"I'm going to put a tactical display up on the screen, so you can see what's happening. This'll let you hear what I'm saying to Bel and Alvin, and you can talk to me if you have to." Vash lowered her voice. "I might not reply though, at least not straight away. I reckon that once I use my little helper, I might not be a great conversationalist."

She smiled, but Rose didn't smile back. Mouth dry, she quickly patted her chest pocket again, checking for the antidote. Vash flicked a glance towards Alvin before she jabbed the syringe straight into her thigh. A quick punch to the button on the arm of the chair and her HTAC deployed, motors grinding as it swung over and onto her head. Shutters clunked noisily down into place around them and removed any views of outside. Her pulse rose steadily, and she hated that she couldn't see Vash's face.

The main screen sprang into life. Scores of blue symbols were scattered around the Bellerophon. Behind them, three big squares indicated the battleships were ready to bring their larger artillery to bear. In front, moving inexorably towards them was a single red star: the Aximendes VI.

"Let's go to work, shall we?"

Rose grimaced, hating how the drugs had already changed Vash. It reminded her too much of Penthe when she'd drunk too much kras, and how the laughter was always followed by a black mood. One of the things she loved about Vash was that she never drank alcohol.

"1.5 AU, Vash," Alvin said. "Do you want me to light up the missiles?"

"Not yet, Alvin, just a little longer. I don't want any false positives. You're strapped in tight? I don't want any accidents when the party starts."

"Aye, boss."

"Bel, everything looking okay your end?"

"All systems are optimal, captain."

"1.4…1.3…1.2…1.1," Bel slowly counted down.

With each report, the thumping of Rose's heart grew louder.

"Missiles sniffing hard now, Vash. They are locking on their targets." There was a slight edge to Alvin's voice.

"Light 'em up, Alvin."

"All targets acquired and confirmed, captain. Fire when ready."

"Missiles fired."

On the screen, five small markers flew from the ship towards the Aximendes VI. Only as they fired did it finally dawn on her that the great ship was now in danger, and she was sitting on one of the ships responsible. *Gods, what am I doing? Trying to kill my own family?* She watched the path of the missiles and held her breath, willing them to miss or malfunction. Vash and Alvin groaned in unison as one of them disappeared, and she leaned forward hopefully. The rest of the symbols continued onwards though and made contact. Sets of unintelligible figures appeared on the side screens.

"How did we do, Bel?"

"One missile lost to enemy defence fire. The four others made contact. One gun turret destroyed, significant damage to another. Minor damage caused to port engine."

Rose stared numbly at the screen and tried to make sense of it all. People had died, only on military areas of the ship to be sure but still, her people. Penthe no longer had to lie about Rose. She really was a traitor now. She covered her face, unwilling to watch.

"We have incoming, Vash," Bel said calmly.

Rose looked up. A swarm of tiny triangular symbols were issuing from the Aximendes VI. Penthe was unleashing her fighters. Fates, it was all happening so fast.

"Alvin, let's get some more power online. Warm up the guns," Vash said.

"Aye, Vash."

"Bel, I want regular updates on our shields."

Rose didn't understand how Vash could sound excited and not alarmed. Two of the enemy fighters peeled off and made straight for them. Vash banked the ship sharply to port. At the same time, a series of loud and fast drumbeats echoed around her as Vash fired at the fighters. The noise of the guns bypassed her ears and went straight to the pit of her stomach. One of the attackers disappeared from the screen.

"Up the universe!" Vash yelled, and Alvin joined in with a raucous cheer.

Rose looked in shock at the empty space where the symbol had been. Had that been a life reduced to a symbol that no longer existed? There was no time to mourn. The other ship moved towards them rapidly. Something launched from it, and the Bellerophon took evasive action.

"Hold on, Rose. It's gonna get bumpy."

There was a loud bang and the screen flickered.

"Damage report, Bel."

"Direct hit to starboard hull. We've lost the starboard gun. Partial damage to starboard engine, and ten percent loss to performance. Shields down to seventy percent."

Vash swore inventively, but there were already two more enemy ships swooping in to join the fight. Worse still, Rose could see that friendly symbols were starting to wink out all around them.

"Central Command to attack fleet. Situation update, please," a stern voice cut in from the comms.

"Bellerophon to Central Command, Green," Alvin said.

Answers were coming in thick and fast from others. "Ignis to Central Command, Status Orange. Damage to port engine…Telephus to Central Command. Status Orange. No, No…Status Red. Hel—"

Harsh static replaced the last voice. Was that one of Vash's friends, Stefan even? Rose immediately regretted the thought.

"We're getting fucking slaughtered," Vash said.

Rose's harness just about held her in her seat as Vash manoeuvred the ship more and more violently.

"Come on, Alvin, you've got to give me more here!" Vash yelled.

Rose was hypnotised by the symbols dancing on the screen, and her heart thumped in her throat. There was no way out of this. Everywhere she looked enemy fighters were flitting around like demented solflies. Her head was starting to ache appallingly. An enemy ship approached on a collision course with the Bellerophon. She turned to Vash; words trapped in her mouth.

Everything changed.

She was hanging in space, and the Bellerophon was moving serenely away. She could see it weaving like the Floris dancers who paraded through Drem every cycle during the Festival of the Moons, with silvery chaff ejecting from its belly. That attracted the attention of an incoming missile, which was fooled and exploded harmlessly. As it did, she felt the floor shake under her feet. What floor? What about Vash? And as she made the mental connection, she was back on the bridge as if she'd never left. She looked at Vash, still engrossed in the dog fight.

Rose double checked her own HTAC, but it hadn't deployed. *What just happened?* The headache was still there and getting a little worse. She'd panicked. She'd wanted to run. And then she was outside the ship. Her arm twitched of its own accord, and she pulled up her sleeve slightly. The band was on the march, the strange symbols pulsing and throbbing. How stressed had she been not to notice?

"Everything okay?" Vash asked.

"Yeah, I'm fine." The last thing she wanted was Vash being distracted by her. All their lives right now depended on her staying focused. "Just tell me if there's anything I can do to help."

"Shields at fifty percent," Bel said calmly.

Rose kept an eye on the band's markings as her stress levels started to rise, and her head pulsed in time with their flow. *Get me out of here!* Even before the thought had passed through her mind, the bridge disappeared and was replaced with stars. The battle was raging around her, munition and lasers flying in all directions, distant ships moving to a vicious beat. This time she fought to keep calm and stay in the moment. The Aximendes VI was visible in the distance now, and space opened up in front of it as the friendly forces were driven back. *Take me back.* The centre of her forehead throbbed in answer.

"Vash?"

"What's up, Rose? Bit busy at the moment."

"I'm looking at the display. Why don't you fly towards the Aximendes VI? There's a clear path now."

Alvin snorted. "Cause we don't want to die even quicker, girl."

"Just shut it. Rose, Alvin's right, we can't outgun her."

"Yes, but this is a small ship. You might just go under the radar. Their batteries will be mainly targeting the big battleships, won't they?"

Vash went silent, obviously weighing the options. Rose admired the way she could apparently do that while throwing the ship from side to side to evade attack. Whatever those military drugs were, they were doing a good job.

"What do you think, Bel? How does the idea compute?"

"I've modelled Rose's proposal. There are many variables but—"

"Yeah, I agree. Alvin, I want the lot now. Divert everything we can afford from life support to the engines and the front shields."

Rose was thrust back into her seat as Vash pushed the engines to their maximum. On the display she could see that they were leaving the main fight behind and approaching the Aximendes VI rapidly. She closed her eyes and prayed to any gods still remotely interested in her.

They were rocked by what felt like turbulence, and Rose's stomach churned queasily again as Vash weaved the ship in all directions.

"Hm, think they might have noticed us. How are the shields?"

"Shields at thirty percent, Vash. We've lost communications with Central Command, but the pressure hull is still fully intact."

"Come on, just a little further, my beautiful, just a little further."

Rose risked opening her eyes a little. They were on top of the Aximendes VI, probably flying past one of her vast limbs.

The turbulence ceased, leaving just the gradually receding scream of the engines as Vash throttled them back to safer levels.

"We've made it. You're right, Rose, their gunnery crews didn't notice us until we were too close. They didn't have time to calibrate their guns properly. We've cleared their firing space." Vash raised one fist.

Rose wasn't fooled. That had been too close.

"They might still turn around, Vash," Alvin said.

"Oh, come on, Alvin, admit it. Rose was right. They won't bother with us for a while. Plenty of time to fix a few things around her. Bel?"

"Shields at fifteen percent. We're badly damaged, Vash."

Rose smelled burning and the others sniffed too. Vash smacked a button on her seat. The HTAC disengaged and she jumped up, overbalanced, and fell back.

"Hang on." Rose reached over and jabbed the antidote in. Almost immediately the wired look in Vash's eyes receded. She tried standing again, and this time kept her balance.

Vash winked at Rose. "Alvin, check your screens. Where's the fire?"

Alvin was struggling with his harness, beating at the clips with his fists. "You mean, where are the *fires*? You take the one in storage two, and I'll tackle the one near the port engine. Bel can handle the others."

"Can I help?" Rose was bewildered at the speed of events.

"Stay here, Rose, I mean it. If either of us get hurt, we'll need you and Bel to take over." Vash flashed a quick smile at her, and then they were gone.

Rose undid her own harness. She stood, glad to have a few moments to compose herself again. The Aximendes VI continued its course, seemingly content for now to ignore them. Had they really managed to escape?

On the main screen, a new squadron of enemy fighter symbols appeared from nowhere. They made straight for the three battleships. She watched, horrified, as one of the battleship symbols winked out of existence. Another started to move erratically, and it appeared to collide with the third which had kept close quarters. The symbol for one flickered and disappeared. The other one kept going, but its virtual path was now highly erratic.

"Vash! Vash!" Rose tore off the headset and screamed into the mouthpiece.

Moments later, Vash ran onto the bridge. Rose pointed shakily at the screen, unable to get the words out.

"There has been a significant development, Vash," Bel said.

"Show me, Bel."

A new display appeared on the main screen: a re-run of what she'd just seen. Alvin stepped onto the bridge with an irritated look on his face. Before he could speak, Vash held up her hand for silence. He peered past her and looked at the screen. His face turned white.

"No. My uncle is on that ship, Vash. We've got to go and help." He ran to his console and started punching buttons.

Vash looked desperately at her, and she swallowed, unable to think of anything to say. His anguish had been hers only minutes before.

"We can't do anything, Alvin."

"We have to do something," he said.

Vash put her hand on his shoulder. "Alvin." Vash's voice was softer than Rose had ever heard before. "We're too badly damaged."

Alvin spun and ripped Vash's hand away, his neck and cheeks flushing red. "This is all her fault."

He pointed a quivering finger at her, and she shrank back from him. The band was still active. Would it take matters into its own hands?

"If she wasn't here, you'd take the risk. You wouldn't just leave them to die."

"Alvin, look around you. If I take us back into the fight, the ship will fall apart. Come on, Alvin."

Rose stepped back as he pushed past Vash and advanced on her, his face twisted with anger and eyes burning with hate. She fought not to give in to her fear, but her temples throbbed dangerously.

"You should never have come aboard. You ain't one of us. You've made her a coward."

For a second, she thought he was going to hit her, and she raised her arms, but he turned and ran from the bridge.

Vash stood stock still, a stunned expression on her face. Rose lowered her arms and hugged herself, her legs not quite feeling like her own. The pain in her head was receding, but her heart still ached.

"Rose, it'll be okay. He's just really upset." Vash stepped towards her.

"But he's right, isn't he? If I wasn't here, if I'd given myself up, all those people wouldn't be dead." She reached out to steady herself on the edge of the hatch. How could a heart hurt so much?

"You aren't responsible for Penthe's actions, Rose. You aren't responsible for the bad strategy of our rear echelon idiots." Vash held her arms out. "And you are definitely not responsible for me. I told you not to run. I told you not to give yourself up. So, if anyone killed them, it was me."

"I've dealt with the remaining fires, Vash. However, we're being passively scanned," Bel said after a few moments of silence.

"Who by?"

"It's originating from the Aximendes VI."

Vash sighed and ran her hands through her hair. "Time for the last roll of the ship." She smiled at Rose. "Initiate our plan please, Bel. Dead beast. Dead beast. Dead beast."

The ship's engines surged. A short burst of power was turning them in the direction of that nearby planet. After a couple of seconds, the engines powered down. The side thrusters fired randomly and sent the ship into a slow tumble. Everything went silent and the main lights went out. Emergency lamps bathed the deck in green, and the instruments swam in her vision.

Vash's teeth glowed eerily in the dark. "We'd better dig some thermals out for you," she said.

Rose followed her out of the hatch, her legs on autopilot while her mind reran the destruction of the ships. How many more would have to die before this was over?

CHAPTER TWELVE

Penthe stood at the head of the command table and scowled as her great ship swept forward imperiously. The enemy were bravely standing their ground and fighting despite the overwhelming odds. The shields of the Aximendes VI were easily able to deflect their warships' pitiful long-range armaments with ease, but smaller fighters continued to buzz, and harass, and inflict irritating levels of damage to her squadrons. Even as she watched, another two of her ships were disabled and forced to retreat. She slapped her hand on the command table, making Archiploi Volos jump.

"Enough, it's time to finish this. Where are my fighters?"

"The squadron is coming into position, ma'am. So far they've not encountered any defences."

Volos irritably waved away another officer who was trying to get her attention.

"Order them to maintain their speed. They aren't to waste a single missile. I want all of those battleships destroyed." She watched transfixed as the fighters closed on the rear of the enemy battle group, and her knuckles turned white as she gripped the edge of the table. *Imagine the panic going through the minds of the enemy commanders.* Screaming orders, trying to reposition shields and batteries to protect their lumbering ships. They'd never stood a chance against her superior strategy.

The first battleship took five missiles straight to its engines, as the squadron executed a tight roll away from its defensive weapons. She'd ordered that the squadron be equipped with the latest, expensive model of missile despite the objections of her cautious procurement officers. Whatever shields the enemy had deployed were no match for them, and she raised a fist in triumph. *See, I am the leader this House needs, Mother!* The battleship listed heavily to one side; its manoeuvring ability fatally compromised. It drunkenly moved towards one of the other battleships that had kept close quarters. That ship tried to steer away from its wounded partner but there wasn't time. It took the impact squarely midships and was nearly sliced in two. Powerful explosions broke out all along its hull as it tumbled out of control. The crew around her broke into raucous cheers, but she imagined bodies being thrown and broken against bulkheads on each ship, and her stomach roiled. She shook her head to rid herself of such stupid sentimentality. They would have done the same to her ship, to her people.

Volos shouted for everyone to get back to work as the squadron came back in for the kill. This time their missiles were aimed at the third battleship. One of the missiles must have hit its armoury because it exploded, filling a real time display in front of her with gold and red light of such intensity that shadows were thrown across the room and she was forced to shield her eyes. The debris tumbled away, metal and flesh thrown out in all directions, with some of it hitting the first ship. Unbelievably, it was still moving under its own power, turning, and trying to run for safety.

She grabbed Volos' collar. "Order them to go around again. I want that one as well."

"They're out of missiles, ma'am. I've ordered them to return to the ship."

Penthe growled with frustration but there was nothing she could do. She thumped her fists down. "Let's take care of the rest. What are you waiting for?" She turned away from the table and something caught her eye on the tactical display. "What's that ship doing there? How did it get behind us?"

"We're tracking it, ma'am. It poses no risk as it has taken significant damage. As soon as we have dealt with their fighters, we'll send a couple of ships to destroy it."

Penthe nodded. "I'm going back to my rooms. Let me know when they contact us with their terms of surrender."

Back in her quarters, she shouted for a bath to wash away the stresses of battle. She luxuriated in the creamy vanilla foam as her handmaidens massaged her shoulders with soft sponges, and the tension slipped away.

"See who it is," she said when a knock sounded at the door. She flicked some of the foam at the nearest maid, who got up from her knees and opened the door a crack.

"It's Antiploi Sakas, ma'am. Shall I tell her to come back later?"

Penthe pulled herself up. "No, I want to hear what she has to say. Leave us, all of you."

Sakas came in, bowed, and perched on the edge of the tub. Her usually sombre face was lit up.

"Well? I take it that smile means we've received their full surrender?"

"Total surrender confirmed five minutes ago. All their remaining ships are rendezvousing at agreed co-ordinates. We will take their crews hostage, subject to the return of our property. Their government representatives wish to meet with us as soon as possible to start that process."

"Were there any ships left?" Penthe breathed deep, flushed with victory.

"A few, my queen, but only a few. Our fighters will be drinking into the early hours; they've had a good day among the stars."

Penthe beckoned for a tablet to be brought to her. She punched up the display, which confirmed Sakas' report. "What happened with the pathetic little ship that got past our battery?"

Sakas frowned. "Oh, yes. I saw that in the reports. The damage must have been terminal. Not long after you left the hub, it started to drift without power. Our sensors detected that life support systems were not in operation. If anyone was still alive, they're certainly not now. Archiploi Volos and I didn't deem it worth wasting missiles on. It will be destroyed when it falls into the well of one of the nearby planets."

Penthe lay back in the tub and allowed a wave of elation to finally wash through her body. This ship—her ship—was invincible. "Send my congratulations to the gun crews. They did good work protecting the ship. It won't be forgotten."

"I'll make sure they're told personally, ma'am. I'm sure they'll be honoured to be praised." Sakas stood and bowed.

"Where are you going, Sakas?" Penthe smiled and arched her eyebrow. "You promised me a song."

Sakas knelt by her side. She picked up a sponge and ran it slowly down over Penthe's breasts, igniting sweet fires.

"I will sing sweetly for you, my queen."

She shut her eyes contentedly and slid further down into her bath, as Sakas' husky voice soothed away the blood-ridden visions in her head.

***

Penthe rose from her desk and walked over to the sofa. She relaxed back and looked at the ceiling. After a minute, she sat up, returned to her desk, and drummed her fingers on the surface. Stars, this was boring. Boring and irritating. She was particularly irritated by her staff officers, who milled around talking in soft voices. Why did they persist in whispering? How many times must she tell them it was rude? When this was all over, she was going to show them what happened to obtuse people.

"How long before they arrive? Why *am* I having to wait?"

Archiploi Volos stiffened. "I'll check immediately, ma'am."

She turned and spoke softly into her communicator. A distant tinny voice answered straight away.

"It seems that they had difficulty finding transport, ma'am. They're just docking now, and I've instructed my officers to bring them here with no further delay."

Penthe sighed. She had to respect conventions and meet with these local people face to face, but it was all so very tedious.

The door to the throne room opened, and a junior officer in the Black Team announced the delegation, a mixture of military officers and civilians. All of them looked tired. Volos led them towards her, and she drew herself up to her full height. As befitting of someone of royal birth, and at nearly seven feet tall, she towered over her staff and everyone else in the room. She was dressed in her full royal regalia complete with her ice white crown, palladium tipped crystal horns sweeping out past her cheeks, a deliberate choice to intimidate their "visitors."

But why weren't they bowing? She raised an eyebrow at Volos, who looked embarrassed. Really, the arrogance of these people knew no limits. Her pulse pounded behind her eyes, and she fought to keep her voice calm. "Ambassadors, you took your time. Perhaps you don't appreciate the gravity of your situation."

The delegation stopped talking and looked at her. One or two of them had the decency to blush. She waved at the seats that had been prepared for them.

"I would have asked you to sit and join me in a light repast. However, as you didn't have the courtesy to arrive promptly, I will no longer be offering you any of my extremely valuable time." She walked over to the table, laden with fruit and drink, and picked up a goblet of kras. She sipped on it and scanned their ruddy, fat faces, so coarse in comparison to the pale, fine boned elegance of the Akmonians. "I'm not interested in whatever pitiful offer of treaty you've brought with you. I'm only interested in one thing, and that is the return of my rightful property." She threw the goblet to the floor and advanced on the group. They huddled together, seeking safety in numbers. Fates, they were pathetic. "You have one standard day to locate and return my property. If you fail to do so, I'll throw the hostages from the nearest airlock. You'll have another half standard day before we ransack the nearest residential planet and enslave its inhabitants."

Each of the fat fools looked satisfactorily horrified. "Every time you fail to meet a deadline, the penalty will worsen. It is entirely up to you how many citizens you wish to lose." She raised a finger when one of them tried to speak. "Archiploi Volos will give you all the details you need regarding my property. Now, I have important business to attend to."

With a wave at Volos to carry on, she swept out of the room. She was boiling inside. Sakas waited at the door, and they walked down the corridor towards her personal quarters. "Antiploi Sakas, I wish you to take personal command. I know I can trust you in this matter."

"I assumed that would be the case, ma'am. I've prepared my ship and will go back with the ambassadors. They'll do nothing without my knowledge, of that you can be assured."

Penthe touched her shoulder, genuinely grateful and already a little calmer inside. Sakas' practicality was such a boon at times like this. "I know you won't fail me."

They reached the entrance to her quarters. Seeing they were quite alone, she grasped the back of Sakas' neck and kissed her fiercely. When she pulled back, the fire and naked desire was clear in Sakas' eyes. "Come back soon, Antiploi Sakas."

"I will do my best, my queen." Sakas walked away, her head held high.

A few hours later, working at her private desk, Penthe was alerted to an incoming message from Sakas. She quickly dismissed her maids and asked the console to display the video as a hologram. Sakas appeared before her, a flickering ghost. Constant tics present in her movements and speech betrayed the distance between them.

"Ma'am, I must furnish you with an update on progress."

"Is this link secure?" The last thing Penthe wanted was the system authorities knowing her plans.

"Fully encrypted, and I also scanned the room for devices before I started transmitting."

Penthe relaxed and settled back in her chair. "Still, you've taken your time. It has been over a quarter of a day, Sakas. I've grown impatient for news."

Sakas looked apologetic. "These idiots are so slow, and there's so much bureaucracy. Even now they don't appear to comprehend the peril they're in."

Penthe sighed. That would change shortly if she didn't get what she wanted.

"However, I've finally got some useful information. Munro was on one of the ships that attacked us, and it hasn't returned to dock. There are conflicting reports about how many people were on board. All agree that her chief engineer was present, but I've had reliable eyewitness reports that another woman was seen with her at the briefing. An argument was later overheard regarding another woman being on board, between Munro and her engineer. My agents have also located the apartment belonging to the traitor in the city. It's empty and neighbours report she left about a day ago."

Penthe felt the blood draining from her face. Another woman? It must be Rose, but how could she have ended up in the midst of the battle itself? How was that possible? Her hands flew to her throat as it started to constrict.

"Do you believe the ship to be destroyed, Sakas? Is my property lost?"

"At present that is…however…"

The audio drifted in and out, and she leaned in closer trying to hear Sakas, but the image only faltered and disappeared completely. She flung open the door. "Get me a technician. I need a technician immediately."

Her household scattered in all directions and a senior technician appeared at the door moments later, puffing and red faced. She bowed low.

"Ma'am, I'm at your service."

"I was talking with Antiploi Sakas via a comms link. It failed, and it must be restored immediately. Immediately, do you understand?"

The technician hurried to the console to interrogate the system. She murmured under her breath as she scrolled through a myriad of strange looking screens. After an eternity, she turned around.

"I've located the problem, ma'am. A solspot in the system has interfered with our communications. It should be clearing momentarily." She made a few more taps on the screens. "Yes, I think I can restore the connection now."

Sakas appeared again, her image stronger now. "Ma'am? Are you there?"

"Yes, Sakas, but wait." Penthe pointed at the door. "Get out. Tell your line officer you may have two extra hours' leave for your prompt service."

The grateful technician didn't linger.

As soon as the door closed behind her, she turned back to Sakas. "Is my property lost or not?"

Sakas shook her head. "I cannot confirm that yet, ma'am. The ship in question is on their lists as missing rather than destroyed. I've sent my team the reports to cross-reference with our battle sets. I'm confident we'll have an answer within a couple of hours."

She growled with impatience. "I must know, Sakas."

Sakas held her hands up. "I understand, ma'am. As soon as I have any more information, I'll let you know immediately."

"Is there anything I can do at this end to speed up the process? Do you have enough resources?" Penthe chewed her lip. All the trappings of power and she was still utterly impotent when it mattered.

"I have what I need and what I trust. Please be patient, ma'am. We'll know soon enough."

She punched a button to end the link. Saka disappeared in a blink, leaving her alone in the empty room. She leaned forward, and let her tears slide down her face and onto the thick rug beneath. The pinprick stains gently spread and darkened its sumptuous colours.

To have been so close only to fail. She couldn't bear it. If Rose was lost to the vacuum of space, this system would pay. They would all pay. She stared at her trembling hands and tried desperately to ignore the smug, hurtful voices inside her head.

CHAPTER THIRTEEN

Rose wrapped her arms tighter around herself as she sat in a cryofood unit at the rear of the ship. She wore several layers of clothing and heavy oil wool blankets that they'd put inside the storage space ahead of time, but her hands were icy cold despite her gloves.

Vash looked at her and shook her head. She pulled the thick cloth wrapped around her face open wider and yanked down her portable oxygen mask. "I'm starting to think that death is preferable to losing my fingers and toes, Rose."

Clouds of vapour exploded into the air between them, though Rose could hardly hear her. "You don't mean that."

Vash raised her eyebrow. "What?"

With the mask in place, Vash obviously couldn't make out a word she was saying. She fumbled to close the valve on the tank before she lowered it. Vash had assured her that the tanks held a minimum of eight hours of gas, but four had already passed. It still intrigued her that Vash had them onboard at all. They were military quality, not retail, and must have cost a great deal of sysgeld. Had she pulled this sort of stunt before? "I said, you don't mean that. Besides, it's not like you came up with a better idea." She pulled it back on and opened the valve again, careful to keep the flow to a minimum.

Vash sighed heavily and wiped away the frost that had formed on her eyelashes before she pulled her own mask back up. From beneath a mountain of grey blankets in the corner, Alvin grunted but didn't look up. He hadn't spoken a word to either of them since his outburst but had allowed himself to be pulled into the unit.

"I think the plan is working, Vash. The Aximendes VI is moving away from us towards the central planets, and they've stopped scanning us," Bel said softly.

Vash clapped her hands together and sent a flurry of white cloud into the cold air. She tugged her mask down again. "Thank the gods for that. I say we keep up this charade for another fifteen minutes, then use the side docking jets to adjust our course towards MR3."

"Agreed, captain. I will restore life support in ten minutes."

"Moving where, captain? Where can we hold our heads up ever again?"

Rose looked over at Alvin, who looked at them both with puffy, reddened eyes. He straightened up and some of the blankets covering his head fell away.

He yanked his mask down, wiped his beard with his sleeve, and spat on the floor. "There ain't nowhere for cowards to lay their heads."

"Play another tune, Alvin. We're alive and that means we get to fight another day. We aren't *going* anywhere. We're going to fix Bel and then we're going to kick some Ak ass."

Alvin's sullen expression suggested he wasn't persuaded. He repositioned his mask, growled something under his breath, and pulled his blankets tighter around himself.

The constant antipathy between the two of them was getting to her but she had no idea how to fix it. She shuffled across the floor to Vash, needing the comfort of her strong arms to chase away the nagging doubts still filling her head.

Vash frowned at Alvin. She spread open some of her blankets to make room and put her arm around Rose as she snuggled in. "Good idea. We'll both feel a bit warmer this way."

Rose tried to rest her head against Vash's shoulder, but her muscles were so tense, she might as well have been carved out of wood. Rose reproached herself for not noticing how stressed Vash was. At least this close, she didn't have to remove her mask to be understood. "I looked at what's on this planet. Like you said, it's all industrial mining. Not a lot of people, but a good chance we will find tools and materials to repair Bel."

"Yeah, I've been here a few times on business. To the port, anyway. The miners can be a bit surly, but they're straight enough. Besides, they'll have been watching what was going on." Vash rested her chin lightly on top of Rose's head, her warmth thawing her frosted scalp. "I reckon they'll be keen to help us get on our way, if only to avoid drawing attention to themselves."

"How bad is the damage?" Rose whispered, fearing both the answer and the possibility of another argument between Vash and Alvin. Vash pulled her in a little closer, and she wished she hadn't asked.

"Won't know until I get her on the ground. The main thing is that our comms unit was damaged, so we can't call for help," Vash said. "Bel has pinpointed some other electrical and hydraulic issues, and I still don't really know how the hull has held up. We took a bit of a pounding when we swung by the Aximendes VI."

Vash fell quiet. Concerned, Rose snuggled in closer. "I'm glad I'm here with you." She looked over at Alvin, still huddled under his blankets. "I know we're still in big trouble, but the weird thing is that I feel safe all the time we're together."

"You know the weird thing, Rose?" Vash asked, sounding serious. "I always feel in real trouble when you're with me." She chuckled.

"You're awful." Rose pulled away and punched Vash's arm.

Alvin moved under his blankets but made no comment.

Vash closed her eyes in mock pain and clutched at her arm. "Hey, try not to damage the bodywork. I might need this later."

Rose shook her head. Where had she found this woman? She took a long pull on the oxygen, then tugged Vash's mask down and kissed her deeply, savouring the heat in her lips. She never tired of their taste.

As they pulled apart, Vash opened her eyes and grinned. "I wouldn't want you anywhere else, Rose. We make a good team."

Six hours later, the Bellerophon was on the far side of the planet. They'd moved at the ship's slowest speed, not wanting to bring any attention to themselves. Rose watched the monitors as the ship descended through the atmosphere. There was a flash of light from a landing site. An almost invisible door had opened in the steep escarpment on one side, and someone stepped out, their face obscured by a large fur-lined hood. She leaned closer, transfixed. They were still several kilometres above, descending slowly through the cloud cover, but the screens were able to show them the landing site in detail. The ship's sensors recorded a brisk wind speed and flecks of snow were driving across the zoomed picture. The stranger below bent over and rocked violently back and forth as they hugged themselves.

Coughing? Her anxiety was momentarily forgotten. It was a harsh environment for the physically fit, let alone someone with damaged lungs. They pulled something from their pocket and popped it into their mouth. A light-coloured tube with a faint glowing light at one end. A leafroll? She sat back with a small gasp. She hadn't seen one of those in a while. Only the occasional visiting merchant on the Aximendes VI had sported one, and she'd never seen a lit leafroll in Drem. City ordinances had driven them underground to exclusive clubs and sexdens. Not that the city council cared about the health of its citizens. What it feared was the fire risk to an increasingly congested conurbation. But the coughing made more sense now.

The stranger's face lifted to the sky. Their hood tumbled backwards to reveal a bearded man. His eyes stared straight into the camera, and her mouth went dry. He'd obviously heard their engines for the first time. She glanced quickly sideways at Vash to see if she'd also spotted him.

"Yeah, we've got company. Alvin, any more life signs down there?" Vash didn't seem overly concerned.

"Only the one, Vash. Mind you, our sensors won't go that far underground: too much granite in the rock," Alvin said.

Rose looked at him, hunched over his console. He was keeping his own counsel but had been willing enough to help get the ship on the ground. Perhaps self-preservation had outweighed his moral objections for now. She couldn't get the image of him advancing on her out of her mind though. She instinctively held her breath every time he spoke, waiting for another explosion.

"Yeah, but these mines are usually one-man operations. Keeps the costs down. Records show he's the sole digger. Prepare for landing, Bel."

There was a deep grinding noise. She looked at the displays to see if something was wrong with the ship. She surreptitiously checked her seat harness was locked in place, and her stomach churned uncomfortably. Another metallic, grinding mechanical noise came from beneath them, culminating in a loud thunk.

"Landing gear successfully deployed, Vash," Bel said.

"Thought you were going to say a part of the hull had just fallen off, Bel." Vash looked over and winked at her.

"The hull remains intact, captain…for now."

Bel was obviously not in the mood to banter. The ground came up fast, and the picture from the cameras disappeared behind the cloud of grey gritty dirt thrown up by the landing thrusters. A spine-jarring jolt that made Rose's teeth click announced that the ship had landed, and she was glad for the snugness of the straps holding her in.

Vash released herself with a quick punch to her midriff and stood up.

She stretched her hands above her head and groaned. "Fates, my back." She scratched her ear. "Guess I'd better go and talk to the welcome party."

"Do you want me to come with you?" Rose expected the answer would be no but needed to offer.

"No. Best that I go and greet the locals alone. My ship, my responsibility." Vash grabbed her jacket and slung it over her shoulder. "Alvin, lock the hatch after me, will you? Any trouble, just get Bel out of here, okay?"

Alvin nodded. "Yes, captain."

"Are you sure it wouldn't be better if we all went?" Rose didn't want Vash going out there on her own. She might get injured or worse, and it left her with Alvin. She reached for her own harness release, but Vash stepped in front of her and pressed her hand over it.

"There isn't going to be a problem, okay? I know these miners. It's a hard job, and it breeds hard people. But I've worked around hard asses all my life. I know how to talk to them." She gave Rose a peck on the forehead. "I'll be back soon. Promise me you won't disembark until I ask?"

Rose's throat tightened, and she could feel tears wanting to come, but she needed to be strong for Vash. "I promise." Her voice didn't sound like her own.

Vash straightened up, smiled warmly down at her, and ran through the hatch. Alvin sat down heavily in Vash's seat and punched his security code into her console. He brought the video feeds up on the main screen and motioned to Rose to put her headset on. She didn't like him sitting there, where Vash should be, but she kept quiet not wanting to invite his wrath further.

She adjusted the headset. Vash hummed a tuneless sound as she walked away from the ship. More snow was coming down and it swirled all around her. She'd put on a bulky thermal overcoat, and the steam from her breath rose briefly before it was swept away in the strong breeze.

"Lovely day for it, isn't it?" Vash said. "Remind me to come back here for my holidays."

Rose yearned to be there with her, by her side. She pressed her fist to her mouth. Oh, why had she promised?

"She'll be fine."

Alvin's voice startled her. His face was expressionless, but his tone wasn't unfriendly. Of course, how many times had he sat here guarding the ship while Vash stepped off to complete a deal. Rose hated him for being so matter of fact about Vash putting herself in danger. Nevertheless, she turned back to the main screen feeling a little calmer.

Vash was wearing a headvid and, from its feed, she got a better look at the miner, who was perched on an old piece of piping just outside the door. As Vash got closer, he stood and the snow that had settled on his hood slid to the ground. One of his sleeves hung empty and limp at his side.

Vash's right hand slid down and rested on the bulge of her gun, nestled in her coat pocket. It was such a casual move. Did Vash know she was doing it?

"I'm Vash Munro, captain of the Bellerophon." Vash stopped at a polite distance.

"Jakub Wolcuk." He looked Vash up and down. "You ain't from the company," he said, his voice deep and gravelly.

"No, I'm not, Jakub. I'm part of the emergency fleet that were fighting the Akmonians."

"I wouldn't know 'bout that. I've been busy with a new seam. Big fight, was it?"

He sounded completely disinterested and Rose could quite believe that he had no idea what had been happening. Were these miners so out of touch with the rest of the system?

"Pretty big, yeah. My ship took some damage. I'm hoping to fix her up here."

"I should tell the company really. They might not like it, you being here without their authorisation." Jakub scratched his beard.

Caution and fear tightened around Rose's chest. This was the crunch point for them all.

"Do you have to? I'd prefer to stay under the horizon if possible. I'm a bit worried those Aks might come after us," Vash said, her voice even.

Jakub pursed his lips, as if weighing up his options. Vash's hand slipped into her pocket.

"No need to get that gun out. I ain't gonna to turn you in." Jakub rubbed his hand on the front of his stained jacket and held it out. "I knew someone who got killed by those Aks. Long time ago, but they're nasty bastards. Their enemies are my friends."

Vash grasped his outstretched hand with both of hers. "Thanks, Jakub.

I really appreciate it. Are you the only one here?"

Alvin let out a deep breath next to Rose, as if he was just as relieved as she was.

Jakub waved an arm in the direction of a couple of low-level buildings. "Just the beasts over there for company up top and five company bots below, but they won't bother you."

"Well, there are three of us. I promise we won't interrupt you operation, and we'll be on our way as soon as we can."

Jakub laughed and revealed three gold teeth. "It doesn't make any difference to me. It'll be nice to have company." He leaned over. "Don't s'pose you got any orbon in that space crate of yours? They search us for drugs and such before they shuttle us in, and I confess I'm missing the taste."

Vash laughed. She turned her head around, her head vid offering a clear view of the Bellerophon for the first time. The ship had taken quite a lot of damage. To the untrained eye, it looked as if parts of the hull were hanging off.

"Hey, Alvin. You still got that bottle of '24 hidden under your bunk?" Vash asked.

Alvin groaned and put his head in his hands. "How the hole does she know about that?"

"I can't think who told her," Bel said.

Alvin looked up and grumbled. "If this was my ship—"

"Thankfully it isn't, Alvin, it's mine," Vash said. "Now, we can discuss why you've brought alcohol onto my ship, or you can unlock the hatch, bring that flask out, and join us over in Jakub's habpod. Which is it going to be?"

"On my way, captain." Alvin glanced over at Rose. "You'd better come too."

Stepping out of the ship lifted her spirits immediately. Drem's air could be drunk from a glass on a bad day and the ship's air was recycled. Breathing this clean air was wonderful, though it was wickedly cold. She took careful shallow breaths until her lungs didn't feel like they were being seared with fire. She'd put the heavy padded clothing she'd worn in the storage compartment back on and was glad for the protection it gave her. The sol inching slowly over the mountains wasn't as bright as on Glavin and offered little warmth. The planet was certainly no paradise. There was no vegetation to be seen in any direction, only bare rock. If it hadn't had minerals to mine, it was probable that no one would have bothered coming here at all.

"You going to stand there all day or are you going to come and meet Jakub?"

Vash's voice interrupted her reverie. Alvin had already reached them and was holding out the large flask of orbon. Vash waved at her, and she scampered to catch up as they trudged over to the nearest habpod.

Once inside with the door firmly sealed shut, Jakub thumbed a couple of buttons on the wall, and warmth flooded the room from vents in the ceiling. He rooted in a cupboard and came up with some plasticups. Alvin poured a generous amount into his and Jakub's. Vash rested a hand on the top of hers and shook her head.

"I, for one, am always glad for a sip of the gods' nectar." Alvin raised his mug and took a mouthful. He swirled it around his mouth before swallowing, eyes shut with obvious pleasure. He poured a little into another mug and held it out to Rose. "Here you go. I guess I owe you some thanks for helping save us and all with your ideas." He took another quick swig, his face flushed.

Rose couldn't help a small smile. Perhaps adversity was bringing them together at last. Vash raised her eyebrows when Rose sniffed the liquid. She avoided orbon as a rule, preferring the richness of kras, but didn't want to spoil the moment. She risked a tentative sip and gasped when the fiery liquid hit the back of her throat. Alvin snorted and Vash patted her on the back.

"We don't get many sophisticated ladies out here," Jakub said.

Rose turned to see him looking shyly at her. He'd taken his thick jacket off and thrown it over the back of a chair. The boiler suit underneath looked equally well lived in, all sweat stains and oil trails. Vash was right about this being a hard life, but she liked his big, honest face. "I'm very pleased to meet you, Jakub. Do you own all of this?"

He chuckled. "Nah, I just work for the company. I'm a journeyman, so I just go from job to job. It suits me and the wife. She gets the sysgeld, and I get the peace and quiet."

"The old ones are still the best, huh, Jakub?" Vash rolled her eyes. "Bet you don't have a wife, old timer."

"Sure, I do. Three actually, one in every spaceport I've worked. That's another reason I keep on the move."

They all laughed.

Alvin threw back the last of his drink. "Well, I'd better be getting back to the ship. Those electronics won't fix themselves."

"Yes, same here," Vash said. "I want to take a closer look at the hull. Are you coming, Rose, or would you like to stay here in the warm?" Vash zipped her coat up.

"I'll stay here…if that's okay with Jakub?"

He nodded. "It'll be nice to have some company. The bots aren't very talkative."

Vash smiled and unsealed the door. She grimaced at the cold that poured in, pulled her hood up, and strode out. Alvin followed her and shut the door behind them. Rose went to sit down, but Jakub put one hand up to stop her and quickly wiped the chair and the table over before gesturing to her to sit.

"You'll have to excuse the mess. I try to keep things clean, but I've let it slip recently 'cause of work."

"I'm not that picky, Jakub, honestly."

"Well, you seem like a real lady to me. Your woman there though, she's definitely a worker. She's got dirt under her fingernails. You don't seem that type to me."

"I'm not afraid of hard work, and I'm not sure she's *my woman*, Jakub. Vash is a very independent spirit." Rose bridled at the suggestion.

"That's not how I see it. The way she looks at you seems to me she won't be running anywhere soon." He scratched his chest. "Mind, if you start having a domestic, you'll have to go. I come here to get away from all that."

Rose slapped him on the leg, and he put his hand up in mock terror.

"I ain't done nothing wrong."

Her gaze was drawn to his empty sleeve. To her shame, he caught her looking and picked at the sleeve to pull it out a bit.

"I lost it in some machinery a while back. The accident stopped me working in space. No need to moan though, it could've killed me."

Rose blushed and shook her head. "Don't you miss working in space?"

He shrugged. "I miss working on the orbital gangs. It was wild fun at times. Mind, I don't think my wife misses me chasing all the skirt," he said and winked.

"Vash is right, you're an old fraud. I bet you've seen a few things in your time and been to some interesting places." Rose took another small sip of her orbon, feeling her muscles unknot. Having such a normal, everyday conversation was the perfect antidote to the stresses of the past few days.

"Yep, I seen all sorts. I like the quiet life now though, and I like looking after my family. I work in a mine like this for three months at a time. It makes me twice as much as I'd earn in the fabplants back home."

"Where is home?" Rose asked.

"I was raised on Huvet, but I've lived the past twenty cycles on Glavin. I met my wife there when I was learning my trade. She swept me off my feet."

His face softened as he remembered, and Rose looked away so that he wouldn't see the sadness on her face. He had somewhere to call home, where people were waiting for him. She had Vash of course, but that didn't make her own lack of somewhere tangible to call home any less easy to bear.

"Anyhow, I should probably be getting on with my chores, " Jakub said.

He ran his hand through his thinning hair, his sleeve falling back, revealing a chunky wristband. He held it out for her when she asked.

"That's a company shackle. The thing tells them when I'm working and when I ain't. I don't usually do long stints, it's too humid down there. But I hit a rich seam today, and that might mean a bonus." He smoothed the fraying sleeve back over the band. "Now, I'd better get those guardbeasts fed. You can come along if you like."

Swaddled up again, she followed him outside to a cage where three enormous guardbeasts stood on their hind legs, pawing at the bars. She'd never seen such shaggy animals before. They looked friendly enough, but Jakub grabbed her arm to stop her putting her fingers through the bars.

"Ah, no, not pets, Rose. These are working guardbeasts. They'd rip your fingers off as soon as look at you."

She shivered inside at how badly injured she could have been. She needed to stay focused. He went around the back of the enclosure and pulled a big sack out of a bin there. His bicep bulged with the effort of lugging it back. He unlocked a small hatch in the fence and balanced it on the edge before he tipped it forward and poured the dried food into the trough below it. Another trough had a constant flow of water running through it, perhaps to stop it freezing. If so, it was also heated slightly for the same reason, because steam rose in delicate tendrils from it. The guardbeasts wrestled with each other to feed, although Jakub had provided plenty for them all. Behind them was a very basic shelter. The floor was bare metal with no comforts of any kind.

"They breed them specially. They've got lots of snowhound in them, that much I do know. They wouldn't survive here otherwise. I'm guessing there's a bit of attack DNA in there as well." Jakub stood next to her, hand in his pocket.

"Do they ever come out?" They looked so cuddly, she really wanted to stroke them and bury her fingers in their thick fur. But knowing that they were bred purely to kill made her slightly nauseous. How could anyone do that to an animal?

"I usually let them out when I go below. They guard the place for me and the company. They're trained to come back in here when a buzzer on their collar sounds. Although I always double check on the monitor before I come out."

That wasn't so bad. They weren't cooped up all the time in this cramped space. She didn't like the idea of anything being confined. She'd hated Penthe keeping a caged songbird in her rooms. It'd been a gift, but Penthe quickly bored of it. To her chagrin, she had no idea what had happened to the poor creature.

"Vash doesn't look very happy."

Jakub was looking towards the Bellerophon, and she followed his gaze. Through the light blizzard, Vash could be seen stomping her way steadily along its length. Every now and again she paused, hands on hips, and looked up at the sky shaking her head. Rose frowned, and her pulse rose. Something was very wrong. "I should go and see what's going on."

"Well, remember, I'm here to help as much as I can. We'll get that ship of yours patched up in no time."

Rose stood on her toes and gave him a peck on the cheek. "You're a good man, Jakub."

He blushed and smiled. As he ran for the warmth of the cabin, Rose hurried back towards the ship, her heart starting to pound again. The cheerful conversation in the habpod was long ago now, its false aura of comfort replaced by the harsh biting reality of the predicament she was in.

CHAPTER FOURTEEN

THE YOUNG WOMAN SAT in the corner of Penthe's sitting room embroidering. She appeared to be oblivious to her surroundings as she concentrated on the fine stitching. Penthe watched her toil with the needle, unable to focus on her own work. She was supposed to be checking over the House finances, signing off on various purchases they intended to make at their next stop. How anyone could expect her to do something so trivial at a time like this, escaped her. Penthe turned her signet ring back and forth and looked over again. She didn't remember seeing this maid before but with the chaos of the past few days, that wasn't a surprise. Perhaps the woman had been given this monotonous task to acclimatise her to the royal presence as well as to keep her from under the feet of the senior housekeepers. Certainly, judging by the soft sighs she was making, it wasn't because of her needlework skills. Penthe remembered her own attempts at learning the craft as a young girl. Her mother had taken one look at the handkerchief, which had taken her three weeks to complete, and torn it to shreds in front of her. She'd laughed, and everyone else in the room had laughed with her. The memory made her eyes grow hot.

"You were terrible at embroidery. Like everything else you did." The familiar voice cackled in her head.

Penthe closed her eyes, needing to centre herself again, but heard a sharp intake of breath. Alarmed, she opened them and looked around. Had someone else heard the words? The would-be seamstress raised a finger to her mouth and sucked on its tip. From beneath a curl of fly-away hair that had escaped her uniform cap, she glanced at Penthe, an anxious expression on her face. Penthe pretended to be absorbed in her papers. Apparently reassured, she returned to her task, the tip of her tongue poking out slightly as she lost herself again in the work. Penthe shook her head. This one really wasn't going to last long.

She looked down for the hundredth time at her wristband. There was still no news from Sakas. She hadn't reported in for hours now. Penthe twisted the signet ring again and ignored how sore her finger was becoming. Sakas must know what turmoil she was in. Her upset stomach had put paid to breakfast and probably would do the same to lunch. Tapping one polished nail idly on the tiny display, she considered contacting her. Would that show weakness? Yes, patience was key. Sakas must not think that her queen was hostage to anxiety. She'd seen her looking out of the corner of her eye as Penthe had raged at yet another incompetent member of her staff. Sakas had said nothing, but a subtle negativity had flickered across her eyes, Penthe was sure of it.

"Stars!" Penthe kicked out at the footstool in front of her and knocked it over. The reception room outside, humming with activity, went silent. After a slight pause, one of the senior housekeepers came bustling in, her eyebrows raised. Penthe shook her head, and she turned to go.

"Ma'am?"

The maid had a quiet voice. Rose had always spoken softly too.

The housekeeper froze on the spot and glared at her junior. "Mind your place and get on with your work."

The young woman shrank back and lowered her flushed face to the embroidery again.

Penthe's jaw started to ache from the effort of staying silent. Normally, she did not like to interfere in such matters. But something about the housekeeper's righteous tone had disturbed her. It sounded a little too much like her mother's voice. Enough. "Yes, girl, what is it?" she asked.

The maid looked shyly over at her. "Ma'am, I was wondering if you'd like me to straighten the stool, ma'am?"

Penthe felt sure that every ear in the room beyond was straining to hear what would happen next. "That would please me." Penthe took great pleasure in the look of shock on the older woman's face.

The maid got to her feet and, like a timid mouse, scampered across. She picked up the stool and replaced it carefully in front of Penthe again. Eyes still to the floor, she turned, rushed back to her corner, and snatched up her work again.

The housekeeper snorted, whether with disapproval or disbelief Penthe couldn't tell. Penthe shot her a warning look, and she strode from the room, back ramrod straight.

"Bloody woman." Penthe pulled a face and stood. Who was in charge around here anyway? She walked to the console on the wall and coldly issued the order. Then she sat again, satisfaction warming her within. The insubordinate cretin would not find scrubbing floors in the ship's galleys as comfortable a life.

The maid hadn't made another sound, but her mouth twitched upwards into the hint of a smile. So, she had a bit of spirit. Interesting.

Her wristband buzzed fiercely. Excited, she snatched up her tablet from the side table, but her heart sank immediately. It was just another plea for an extension from the system representatives. Idiots. Did they think she had got this far by showing clemency? She debated ordering a missile strike on their remaining battleship. It might sharpen their resolve in finding Rose. She called up Archiploi Volos, and the woman's face appeared almost instantly. "I'm tired of these pathetic messages. I'm of a mind to remind them of the precariousness of their situation. Perhaps we could destroy that remaining battleship. Thoughts?"

"They are indeed irritating, ma'am, however I wonder if a flyby of their main space port might be enough at this time. If the situation escalates, we could demonstrate our superior firepower."

Volos was right, but it didn't help Penthe's mood. She needed to do something, anything. She let out a loud breath. "Order a flyby, but I want several missiles to be fired as well. I want them scared out of their wits, understand? If I must wait, they have to suffer." She slammed the tablet down and leaned back. She shut her eyes and tried to centre herself again, to slow the storms raging inside her mind. A quiet sound tickled her ears, and she opened her eyes slowly. The young maid was humming softly as she worked, her fingers moving in time to the gentle melody. Penthe was sure she didn't even know she was doing it. It was an old tune, sung by children all over the ship. Rose had hummed it while she worked too, while she tended to the bruises and cuts on Penthe's body, as if the sound itself would soothe and heal. Sometimes, it almost felt like it had.

Penthe swallowed and wiped the moisture from her eyes.

"You were always weak!"

Her mother's voice was clear in her ear, and it took all her will power not to turn around and confront the phantom. Penthe could feel her breathe on her neck, hot and harsh.

"A stupid girl hums a childish tune, and you cry? You disgust me!"

"Go away," she hissed quietly.

The humming stopped and the maid looked up, confusion in her eyes.

She clapped her hand over her mouth, suddenly aware of what she had unconsciously been doing. She stood, smoothed down her tunic and curtseyed, then moved towards the door.

"Stop." Penthe's voice sounded shrill even to her, and she cleared her throat. "Stop right there. I didn't give you permission to leave."

The maid paused, her eyes fixed on the floor.

"Get with your work as before and sing. It pleases your queen."

The maid looked up and smiled, and Penthe's heart missed a beat. She waved her back to her corner and picked up the tablet, pretending to be busy.

"Always so weak!" The voice didn't hide its disdain.

***

The room was in darkness, but Penthe didn't remember turning out the lights. She stood in the gloom and tried to gather her thoughts. Her legs didn't seem to belong to her.

"Oh, gods…help me."

The voice nearby was familiar and strange all at the same time. Whoever had spoken was sobbing, hitching their breath. Penthe looked around slowly, the whole room swimming, and tried to identify where the person was and if they were real. She made out a shape on the floor, their shoulders heaving.

"What's the matter? What's happened."

The shape stopped moving abruptly. "No…no."

Utterly bewildered, Penthe stumbled over and switched on a table light. Its soft glow threw shadows across the room and dimly illuminated a girl curled up on the ground. Penthe didn't recognise her. She was badly injured, blood pouring from her mouth, and one of her legs was bent in an unnatural position. She took a step towards her, still not able to understand what she was doing there, but the girl held out a trembling hand, as if warding her off.

She knelt anyway and wiped some of the blood from the girl's face, revealing her features. A cold finger of fear slid like a dagger into her own chest. Memories blossomed: the new maid, humming as she embroidered. The other servants had come and gone as the evening waned. Penthe had asked for the girl to stay to help her get ready for bed and she'd seen the raised eyebrows, but she hadn't cared. Something about the girl was comforting, and she was their queen, and she was stressed. Stars, why shouldn't she have some pleasure. She clamped her hand across her mouth, chilled to the core. What had she done?

The maid began to contort wildly, the whites of her eyes visible as her head twitched violently, and she gasped for breath.

"No, no. Don't do that." She tried to hold her arms, to stop her moving somehow. Blood flew up into her face, and the girl became still. Penthe wasn't sure she was breathing any more. "Somebody. I need help in here," Penthe screamed at the top of her voice. She shouted again and finally heard feet running towards them. The door burst open, and two of her personal guard came to her side.

"Let us take care of this, ma'am." The older guard gently pulled her to one side.

Penthe caught the looks passing between them, but she had nothing to offer in defence. Trembling with shame, she got up and retreated to her bed. More guards appeared, two with a stretcher. They all looked momentarily horrified and one gasped out loud before she realised Penthe was there. There was a breathing tube in the maid's mouth now, but Penthe hadn't seen that happening. The stretcher was lifted, heavy with its limp cargo, and left the room. The last guard, the one that had spoken to her, looked back once, her expression unreadable as she closed the door quietly.

In the dreadful silence, more of the evening came to her. Someone had taught the girl how to give a good massage. Yes, she remembered that clearly now. Those lovely small strong hands had kneaded all the aches and strains out of her muscles. She'd slid back and forth until the storms in Penthe's head had dissipated, and she'd come to a calm place within herself. After that, there was nothing. No memories at all.

But something had happened. Something had definitely happened. Penthe sat on the edge of the bed and clutched a glass of water in her shaking hands. Now the lights were on properly, she could see the room was in disarray, chairs and tables tipped over. Blood stains marred the rug by her bed. The floor was strewn with objects and ripped pieces of clothing.

"Attend to me, Rose. You should have ears only for your queen, your ever merciful queen. After all, here I am, ready to forgive you and take you back."

Penthe could hear herself, but this wasn't a memory from cycles before. She'd been talking to Rose only hours ago. At least she thought she'd been. The rational part of her knew that she'd hallucinated again, that Rose had never been there. In the moment, it always felt so real. She dropped the glass, drew her knees up, and rocked back and forth. She was losing her mind. She'd brutally attacked an innocent maid and didn't remember doing it.

She shook her head, unwilling to accept that conclusion. It was the stress; it was always the stress. She just needed to get the band back to have full control of her destiny. All these strange…incidents would cease. She lay back and closed her eyes and willed herself to stop shaking. There would be time enough in the morning to clear up the misunderstanding. The girl was in the best hands now, she'd recover in time, and Penthe could sort out what to do with her. Yes, the best thing would be for her to leave her household. She probably wouldn't want to stay, and Penthe had plenty of contacts. She'd find the girl a good position in another household and make sure she was provided for. Penthe tried to comfort herself with expansive thoughts of all the ways she would recompense her.

The door burst open again. She sat up, annoyed, and was about to shout at whoever it was that had dared to intrude, but it was Archiploi Volos. Penthe waved for her to come forward. "What is it now, Volos? Can't it wait? It's been a very difficult evening."

Volos picked her way across the room and picked up a chair leg that was lying on the floor. She held it by her side and stared at Penthe stony-faced. "She's my niece, ma'am."

Penthe hadn't known. She cringed. It certainly made things a little more complicated. Still, it was best to brazen it out for now. "Who was… oh, you mean that new girl that kept me company this evening. Oh yes, I remember my mother signing the breeding permit now. Well, it was a terrible accident, of course, all very regrettable, but she's receiving the best of care. I'm going to be checking on her in person shortly."

"You won't see her again, ma'am."

Her face twisted strangely and whilst Penthe instinctively bristled at her tone, there was something about her demeanour that demanded caution. "Have you been drinking orbon, archiploi? Of course, I'll see her again. I'll see whoever I like whenever I like." Penthe kept her voice even and matter of fact.

"You won't see her ever again because you'll be dead. She's lying in the sickbay fighting for her life. The doctors say her chances aren't good, not after the beating you gave her. You broke half the bones in her body." She stood staring menacingly at Penthe, her free hand clenching and unclenching in an aggressive rhythm.

Penthe slowly swung her legs around onto the floor and stood up. She stretched, and yawned, and leaned casually against one of the bed posts. She discreetly depressed the switch hidden in its ornate carving. Where were her guards? "You'll remember to address me with the due respect at all times. As for your niece, I didn't *beat* anyone." Penthe willed the guards to arrive. "She seemed to have the wrong idea about why I'd asked for her personally. I was forced to rebuke her for being so forward. I hadn't anticipated that she would get so upset and start hurting herself. I tried to help—"

Before she could finish, Volos charged forward and clubbed her viciously across the head with the end of the leg and sent her sprawling to the floor, dazed. As Penthe tried to get back up on her knees, Volos picked up a small iron table that was lying on its side. Penthe held up a hand as she advanced with it.

"You sick bitch. All she ever wanted to do was serve in your household. How dare you suggest she was a…a slut? There's only one deranged slut around here and I'm looking at her. You don't deserve to wear the crown, let alone be addressed as queen."

Volos swung her arm high above her head aiming to bring down the table on Penthe's head. *Let it come.* She waited for the death blow. Instead, the woman's mouth opened in shock and a red patch spread rapidly across her chest. She swayed a little and burped wetly. Blood poured from her mouth as she brought her hand up.

"She's a good girl."

The dying woman toppled forward, pinning Penthe to the ground with her body. Writhing underneath the dead weight and struggling vainly to escape, Penthe retched violently.

Someone dragged the lifeless body off her. The taller of her two guards held out her hand and pulled Penthe to her feet. She stumbled back to the bed and sat down heavily. She couldn't breathe. Where had the oxygen in the room gone? Her eyes fixed on the blood smears across her shaking arms, and she fought back the scream filling her throat.

The guards waited while she calmed down slightly. Eventually, she wiped at her mouth. "Fates, you took your time. She almost killed me."

They shuffled their feet and didn't meet her questioning gaze. "She took advantage of a shift change. It won't happen again, your majesty."

"No, it will not. I'll discuss this further with Antiploi Sakas on her return. Now get the housekeepers in here. Tell my maids to attend me at once. I require a bath; I stink of this treacherous bitch."

As she turned towards the bathroom, another guard ran in. She pulled up short at the sight of the mess and looked at Penthe with a shocked expression.

"What is it?" Penthe's nose filled with the smell of blood. She bent over, nausea overwhelming her again.

"Antiploi Sakas is on the line, ma'am. She says she has important news."

Penthe threw up all over the guard's shoes. She stumbled from the room and prayed that Sakas had some good news.

CHAPTER FIFTEEN

As Rose neared the stern of the Bellerophon, Vash kicked a piece of engine housing that was half hanging off. It fell to the ground, scorched and deeply scored from laser fire. Vash swore loudly and kicked out at it again.

"Hey, anything I can help with?" She rubbed the back of her neck, already wanting to be anywhere but here. Seeing Vash lash out, if just against an inanimate object, reminded her of Penthe's rages. Her hands were already starting to tremble. Vash had never struck her, and she was sure she never would, but she readied herself anyway and shifted on her feet.

Vash spun around, hands on her hips. Her face was flushed, probably as much from temper as from the cold. "I don't suppose you have a spare spaceship hanging around in your back pocket, do you? This heap of junk isn't going to be flying us home anytime." She clenched and unclenched her fists before abruptly turning back and poking at another section of the engine housing. "I don't know where to start, Rose. Look at this bloody mess." She picked up the fallen plate and threw it to one side.

Rose moved cautiously closer, still maintaining a safe distance. The band was sluggishly moving on her arm. She needed to take the heat out of the situation if she could, for both their sakes. "Well, at least the locals are friendly, Vash. Jakub seems really keen to assist."

"Yeah, true. I prayed we'd find someone who'd turn a blind eye. We'll need all the help we can get. Nova! Look at that." Vash scratched the back of her head and swore again softly. She backed towards Rose, who stepped back automatically.

"I think he's quite shy. He showed me the guardbeasts. They live in a kennel out the back, and the water's heated to stop it freezing." Rose wittered, unsure of what else to do. Vash turned and looked over her shoulder. She must have seen something in the way Rose was standing because she turned and held out her palms.

"Oh, Rose. I'm so sorry." She stepped forward. "How could I be so thoughtless?" She smacked her palm against her forehead. "After everything you've told me."

Rose quickly closed the distance between them and slipped her hands around Vash's waist. "Hey, handsome, I'm still here, aren't I? Don't go hitting yourself like that. We need that brain of yours in working order."

Vash sniffed. "Not sure I have one sometimes."

"Don't be silly. It's going to be okay."

Vash gazed pensively back along the length of the ship. "I wish I was so sure."

Rose gently stroked her back, feeling the knots bunched there, and considered her words. She shared Vash's misgivings. The Bellerophon was a mess, and Penthe might find them any time. But saying it out loud wouldn't help. She squared her shoulders and held Vash's gaze. "Listen, we just need to take this one step at a time. We landed safely, and we've found a safe base for the next couple of days. Now, we need to start patching Bel up."

Vash didn't reply, but she let out a deep breath. Her shoulders gradually subsided under Rose's fingers as they continued to draw circles, and she lowered her face until she nestled in Rose's neck, her warm breath on her skin. Rose was in the habit of doing the same when she needed comfort. Something about the scent of Vash's skin helped in those moments, but this was the first time Vash had done it. Touched by the almost childlike gesture, Rose blinked to rid her eyes of the moisture that gathered there.

Slowly, Vash's breathing returned to normal. She pulled back and looked at Rose sheepishly. "Yeah, you're right. Sorry about all the melodrama. It's just that I was hoping the damage wouldn't be quite so extensive." Vash chewed her lip. "On the plus side, it's mostly on one side and it's labour-intensive work, not technical. Bel and Alvin are already working on the electronics. If Jakub helps with the hull damage, we should be able to get out of here in a few days."

"See? You're already talking more sense."

There was a cough behind them.

Jakub walked slowly towards them, worrying at his beard. "Sorry to interrupt, captain. I wanted to let you know that I'm going back below now for another shift. I wouldn't normally go back so quick, but I'll be back topside in about eight hours."

Vash looked confused. “Well, okay, thanks for telling us. Rose said you wanted to help, but we can be doing some of the prep work on the hull, minor stuff, if you’re busy.”

Jakub’s face fell. “Didn’t Rose tell you?”

She blushed with embarrassment. “I’m so sorry, Vash, I completely forgot to say. We must stay in the ship while Jakub is below. That’s why he is pulling a double shift.” She smiled weakly at them both. “Right, Jakub?”

Jakub nodded and looked at Vash. “I figured I could be working while you guys rested and planned, and I’d join you for a bit when you woke. I don’t need much sleep.”

“Why? What’s the problem with being out here?” Vash asked, eyes widening. “What have I missed? Bel reckoned the biggest danger was getting blown over.”

He held up his hands. “You didn’t miss anything. It’s just the company insists that the guardbeasts are freed while I’m in the mine, in case of unwanted visitors. You’re very much wanted, obviously, but the bosses monitor everything that happens here.” He tugged at his beard. “You can’t be out here when those guardbeasts are free, captain. It’s too dangerous.”

Vash covered her face and groaned. “Stars, what else can go wrong?”

“I’ll be able to help out during my rest periods. I’m sure that—”

Vash turned and punched the hull. She bent over and held her fist with her other hand. “Fucking bilgesuckers! That really, really hurt.”

Rose went to her aid. “The ship was always going to win that fight, wasn’t it? Let me see.”

She shakily slipped off the glove. Vash’s knuckles were already swelling. The metal had torn the fabric and scratched across the top of the hand. A nasty bruise was welling up, and blood was seeping from one end of the scratch. Why had Vash done that?

“Make a fist.”

Vash slowly clenched her hand, wincing with pain as she did so.

“Well, I can’t see any major damage, but Bel will need to check it out.” She shoved the glove in her pocket. There was no way it was going to go on again.

Jakub looked shocked.

“Sorry about all this, Jakub. You get below, and I’ll get Vash inside. Will you give us a signal when the guardbeasts are released?”

Jakub nodded and started to walk away.

"Jakub," Vash called after him.

Jakub turned, an anxious look on his face.

"I just want to…well, sorry for being so stupid. I do appreciate everything you're doing for us," Vash said.

Jakub's face relaxed, and he smiled warmly. "I'll be back soon. Promise." He smacked his forehead. "I forgot to give you this." He fished a small plastic box out of a pocket and tossed it to Rose. "One-way signal. If you have any serious problems up here, press the button and I'll come back up. Just don't go out of the ship, okay? Remember, those guardbeasts look cuddly, but they'll rip you apart."

Once they were back inside the main hatch, Vash activated the locking mechanism. She'd tried to make light of her injured hand on the way back but grimaced every time she flexed it.

"I think we should get your hand fixed up before we do anything else." Rose could see blood seeping through the bandage.

"I need to talk to Alvin and let him know what's happening." Vash pushed a stray hair back from her forehead.

Rose walked up to Vash, spun her around, and pushed her in the direction of her cabin. "Don't argue with me, Vash Munro. That hand needs cleaning and bandaging. If you get an infection, you won't be doing any work at all."

Vash tried to turn back, but Rose stood her ground, arms crossed.

"Bel, will you do a scan of Vash's hand when she gets to the cabin? I want to make sure nothing is broken."

"Of course, Rose. I shall examine it thoroughly," Bel said.

Vash looked at her for a moment and shook her head. "Okay, I give in. I suppose you want to see the sickbay."

"You have one?" She couldn't believe a ship of this size had the room.

"We do." Vash walked on up the corridor and stopped by a long cupboard set flush into the wall. With a flourish, she flung open the door. A landslide of medical supplies fell at her feet. "Welcome to the Bellerophon Medical Bay." She gestured cheerfully at the contents of the cupboard. "You'll find everything you need in there. Somewhere."

Rose peered into the cavernous depths of the cupboard. Vash wasn't wrong; there was a mountain of supplies in there. Well, more like a landslide now. She could see bandages, painkillers, drug filled hyposprays and quickneedles, and what looked like a miniature scanner. Just how rough did Vash's work get?

"Very impressive, captain." How could anyone live with such a mess? "Why don't you go to the cabin and talk to Alvin and Bel from there? I'll get what I need and follow you."

Vash patted her on the shoulder and cried out with pain, clutching at her bad hand.

She shook her head in mock despair. "Cabin, now. The doctor will be along on her rounds in five minutes."

It was more like ten minutes by the time she got to the cabin. She'd spent most of it trying to get the spilled boxes and packets back into the cupboard. In the end she'd given up, thrown everything in and quickly shut the door.

Vash was lying on the cotbed, her eyes closed and lips slightly open.

"Hey, sleepy head." Rose sat down carefully next to her and poked her in the ribs. "No snoozing before you're patched up. What did Bel say?"

"Bel said that the injuries were superficial, and her captain is very lucky." Bel's tone was prim.

Vash opened one eye. "Normally I'd complain about the abuse, but I guess I deserve it this time." She propped herself up and put her hand onto a pillow for Rose to look at. "I was an idiot, wasn't I?"

"Yes, but I still love you." Rose cleaned Vash's swollen hand carefully. "I'm going to put something onto this cut that'll sting. Ready?" She didn't wait for an answer before applying the cleaning fluid liberally and was rewarded with a sharp hissing noise from Vash.

"You sure you know what you're doing? It hurts more now than it did before."

"For a tough woman, you spend a lot of time complaining, darling." Rose didn't bother looking up. She broke out a sterile bandage and set to work wrapping her hand up carefully. She needed to make sure Vash could still freely move it so she could use it the next day.

Vash looked down and nodded. "I take it back." She flexed her hand. "Do you want to sign on as Ship's Doctor?"

"I'm far too busy, I'm afraid. I have interests back in Drem." She winked. "But, yes, I think you'll be fit enough to play gelech again. I might even give you a game."

"Gelech? Oh, you found my old bat. Long time since I got on a court with anyone."

"Well, I have played a couple of games on my travels. I really like it."

Vash smiled. "I'm a terrible loser. You might regret you asked."

Rose poked her in the belly. "We'll see. But first, we need to get this hand fixed properly. Just one more thing." She held up a quickneedle.

Vash's face paled. "I don't do injections." She pushed herself further up the cotbed.

"You've got to do this one, Vash. That was rusty, dirty metal you decided to box with out there. I'm not taking any risks. Stop being such a baby."

Vash turned her head away and pulled up her sleeve. Rose chuckled. "This one doesn't go in the arm. Vash. It's not an inoculation."

Vash looked around, obviously hoping that she was joking. Seeing that she was serious, she grimaced. "Just get on with it." She lay down on her stomach and sighed heavily.

Rose laughed, tugged Vash's trousers down a bit and made short work of the injection. "There we are. All done. That wasn't so bad, was it?" Rose slapped her ass lightly. The reply was muffled by the pillow, but it didn't sound very positive. Rose started to tidy up all the supplies she'd scattered across the covers.

"Rose?"

She looked up in time to see Vash's brown eyes twinkling at her, before she found herself on her back looking up at her grinning face. "Hey, I thought you were tired?"

"Not *that* tired. Besides, you're sexy when you do medical stuff. Let me help tidy up." Vash made a sweeping movement with her forearm and sent everything tumbling onto the floor. "See, much better, isn't it?"

"How can you have so much energy—"

Vash's warm lips pressed against hers, cutting her off and a familiar tingling started deep in Rose's belly. She wrapped her arms around Vash and surrendered happily to her love.

CHAPTER SIXTEEN

Rose woke first. She didn't rush to move, enjoying the warmth and security of the moment. Vash always looked so relaxed when asleep, and she made the most adorable small, contented puffing noises. There was no need to drag her into the land of the living just yet. The day ahead was going to be hard.

"Bel?" she whispered, praying that the ship would get the hint. A small bot popped out of the corner of the cabin and hovered close to her ear.

"Yes?" Bel whispered back like a co-conspirator.

Rose suppressed a laugh. She was starting to like Bel more than most people she'd met. So many people wanted something from you. So many lied and told you it was for your own good. Bel was a good humoured, honest companion. "Can you show me how to use the shower?" She slid out from beneath the cover as quietly as she could.

Bel walked her through working the complicated set of pipes and valves. The water was piping hot, and Rose started to relax under the spray. She'd just rubbed some shampoo in her hair when it cut off.

"Sorry, Rose, time's up. We run a water poor regime when away from port, so you only get two minutes." Bel sounded suspiciously amused.

"Oh, come on, Bel. That's not fair. I can't go out like this; my hair's a foam ball."

Bel giggled. "Okay, but only two minutes more."

Back in the cabin, Rose rummaged through Vash's clothing until she found an old shirt and a pair of cargo pants that would fit her if she pinned the bottoms up. She rolled up her sleeves, determined to show Vash that she could help with the repairs.

Vash hadn't stirred, although she'd overbalanced trying to put the trousers on and had hopped awkwardly across the cabin. She really hated to be the one to wake her, but the clock was running down. She perched on the edge of the cot and gently shook Vash's shoulder. She groaned and opened one eye.

"Time to get up, handsome." Rose stroked a stray hair from Vash's forehead.

"You know, you're way too cheerful in the morning." Vash yawned and stretched her arms. "Still…" Vash reached out to pull her in.

"Oh no, you don't. I hate to break it to you, but your breath smells like something dragged out of the bilges. I love you, but not that much."

Vash pouted. "Is this the thanks a brave, fearless captain gets?"

"Oh, shut up and get in the shower. I might just consider kissing you afterwards, you hero." Rose gestured at the towel hanging on the back of the desk chair.

"You worked out how to use it? I was going to show you."

"Yeah, Bel explained. Although, if she'd told me about the two-minute rule before I got in, I might not have used so much shampoo."

"What two-minute rule?" Vash looked confused.

Rose groaned. "Really?"

Bel's giggle filled the room. "Oh, Rose, you should have seen your face."

"Vash, where did you find that AI? And how did it come to have such an evil sense of humour?" Rose couldn't believe she had fallen for the prank. Of course, there was plenty of water. Vash had shown her the controls for the reclamation tanks only yesterday.

Vash grinned. "I taught her all I know. Ain't that right, Bel?"

Bel giggled again, and Vash fell back clutching her stomach, tears running down her cheeks.

Rose shook her fist in their direction. "Right, well, while you two are having fun, I'm going to find something to eat. It's only half an hour before Jakub will be back topside."

Vash stopped laughing abruptly. "I'll be on the bridge in fifteen."

Rose stopped off at the galley for an energy bar and a beaker of water before wandering up to the bridge.

"Hi, Rose. Nice morning for it." Alvin waved at the screen which showed an expanse of glittering white. The storm had cleared, and the distant sol shone down on the snow and ice.

Rose smiled back. His eyes were a little bloodshot. Too much orbol, no doubt. "Morning. Vash won't be long."

Alvin snorted. "She's not an early riser, I should tell you about that time we were moored up at Kreflin Port. That'll make you laugh."

Rose sat down and listened as Alvin recounted a series of mishaps that had befallen Vash and himself over the cycles. Most were very funny, and her stomach soon ached from laughing, but she didn't drop her guard completely. Penthe's mood swings had taught her that such highs could turn in an instant to ugly lows. She was slightly relieved when, after ten minutes, Vash appeared in the hatch.

"Vash, why didn't you tell me that Alvin was such a good storyteller? He was just telling me about the time you fell into that crate of—"

"Yes, yes. Thanks, Alvin, I owe you one."

"Any time, captain." Alvin looked smug.

Vash pointed to the tablet in his hands. "Is that the list of jobs?"

He handed it over, and Vash scanned down it intently. "Any progress on the comms unit?" she asked.

"Bel has pinpointed the problem. I just need to ask Jakub if he has a part. I reckon he should have one somewhere, what with him having to maintain those mining bots."

"Good." Vash handed back the tablet. "As soon as we get his signal, I'm going to get to work on the repairs outside."

Rose leaned nonchalantly against the hatch, hands in her pockets. "Captain, what can I do?"

Vash ambled over and patted her on the head. "You keep the workers fed and watered. That's a very important job."

A very important job? Vash's patronising manner ignited a flame of outrage inside her. She pulled herself tall and glared at Vash. "I'm not useless, you know. I'm sure I can use a power laser or whatever as well as either of you."

Vash's mouth twitched. Enough! She narrowed her eyes, daring her to laugh. Vash swallowed hard.

"All right, all right. I'm sorry, I shouldn't have said that. You can shadow me. See how I do something before you have a go." Vash shrugged. "But it's going to be hard work, Rose, and there's no shame in being the support crew. Right now, I could honestly do with something to eat and drink. Bel, any chance of some breakfast?"

"Of course, Vash. I am always happy to be your 'support crew.' My highly engineered, state of the art processing units have been programmed especially for my role as ship's cook."

Vash threw her hands up. "Right, I give up. I'll make my own breakfast.

May the gods save me from the lot of you." She stomped out of the hatch, muttering under her breath.

***

The distant sol offered little warmth and Rose was glad for the thermal layers she wore under her coveralls. Wind whipped across the valley, grit and dust dancing along the surface. She'd never seen such a desolate place. It was so colourless. There was no vegetation, just rock and snow. The muted-coloured clothing they wore appeared radiant against the backdrop.

After scoffing three kinds of pastry and drinking what looked like a party flask of strong caffrush, Vash had declared herself ready to work. The buzzer had sounded fifteen minutes before, but when they stepped clear of the ship there was no sign of Jakub.

"Should we check on him?"

"If he has any sense, he'll get some shuteye before he joins us." Vash looked unconcerned. She hefted some bulky gear onto her shoulder. "Let's get going."

Rose picked up her own pack. It was heavy, but she made no complaint, determined to prove her stamina. "Yes, I can't wait to get on with the repairs."

They walked half the length of the ship to the first significantly damaged area. Vash assembled the high-powered laser gun and showed Rose how to prepare the area. She watched carefully as Vash applied the plastimetal and used the laser to seal the edges. Vash handed her the laser gun, held together with discoloured unitape, and Rose cleared her throat.

Vash glanced over. "Are you sure you haven't changed your mind? I could really do with another caffrush."

Rose gritted her teeth and inhaled deeply through her nose. With a grunt, she hefted the gun and stepped forward as Vash had done and carefully pulled down her visor. She pressed the control button on the side of the helmet and waited for the view to adjust to a bluish tint before activating the laser.

"Just go slowly, Rose. Let the laser do all the work. You saw how I did it." Vash kept a close watch. "Take your time…yeah, that's good."

Rose turned off the laser and pulled up her visor to take a closer look. She pumped her fist. It really wasn't bad. Not quite as smooth as the section that Vash had done, but it was good enough. "See, I told you I'd get the hang of it. I bet you can't do formal service."

Vash grinned. "That's very true, but I can offer a high-class service anytime." She wiggled her eyebrows.

"I fell right into that one." Rose rolled her eyes. "Anyway, shall I carry on?" She was about to pull down the visor when a flash caught her attention. Higher up the side of the hull, there was another small flash of yellow. "What's that? Is that a fire?" She pointed toward the area.

"What?" Vash squinted at where she was pointing, concern etched on her face. Then she relaxed again and chuckled. "No, that's our little helpers."

"Helpers?"

"Bel's fleet of service bots. They're tackling some of the work up there. We'll probably join them in a day or so."

Rose looked at the steep side of the hull. How on earth were they going to get up there?

"It's okay, you won't have to climb up." Vash picked up her pack and slung it over her shoulder as if it had a feather inside. "There's a service hatch up there. You're okay with heights, aren't you?"

Rose wasn't sure she was okay. Heights made her slightly dizzy. But this wasn't the time to make an issue of it. "Oh yeah, I'll be fine."

Vash smiled broadly and pointed to the gashed section of hull. "Good stuff. Well, you carry on sorting out that bit. I'll go and look at that dodgy looking section on the other side. Give me a shout if you are unsure about anything, okay?" She trudged off towards the end of the ship with a wave of her hand.

Rose turned back to the repair. Really this wasn't that different from those times she had applied ornate decorations of wax, oil, and gold leaf to Penthe's skin, before an important banquet. She just had to stay focused. She activated the visor and the laser and returned to the task, humming happily to herself.

She was so engrossed in the work that she didn't notice Jakub approaching. His shadow fell across the metal and startled, she swung around without thought. Jakub shouted and threw himself to the ground, just before the deadly laser beam would have hit him.

"Oh, Jakub. I'm so sorry." Rose hurriedly deactivated everything and flipped up her visor.

Jakub got to his feet and dusted off his overalls carefully. He'd grazed his cheek on the stony ground. "Not as sorry as me, miss. I thought you were going to fry me." He wiped his brow. "That's a dangerous tool you got there. I ain't sure you're safe enough to be left alone with it." He looked around, obviously searching for Vash.

Rose pinched her nose, her cheeks hot with shame. Vash needed all the help she could get, not more problems. Why did she have to go and mess things up? "Please don't tell Vash, Jakub." She reached out and touched his shoulder. "There's so much to do. I really want to show her I can help."

Jakub looked thoughtful, as if weighing up his options. "Well, I suppose." He scratched his beard. "But you've got to promise me you won't ever do that again."

"I won't. I've learned my lesson, honest."

He came closer to look at the repair and whistled loudly. "You've done a good job there, Rose. The company might have a job for you here if you're ever looking."

A happy glow washed through her. She carefully put the laser into its box and gave him a bear hug. Jakub was blushing deeply when she finally let go. "You're a good man, Jakub. I bet your wife misses you."

Jakub smiled broadly. "Not so much. Truth is, we've been separated a while. We met when we were young. It was love at first sight, but even love struggles when one of you is working for months off-world. We both tried, but it was for the best in the end. This way we stayed friends. If I die, she gets my pay out, and every sysgeld I can spare goes back to putting our son through school. No child of mine is ever going to wear a company shackle. My son is going to the Engineering Academy on Glavin this autumn."

"In Drem? That's where I live. You must let me know when he is coming. I can make sure he settles in okay." The well-meaning but absurd words slipped out. How could she promise such a thing when she would likely never go back to her old life?

Oblivious to her discomfort, Jakub beamed. "That'd be good of you. I must admit I'm worried about him in that big city. There're lots of ways to get lost and hurt."

"Who's getting lost and hurt?" Vash ambled up next to them. 'Hi, Jakub. You gonna join in the fun?"

Rose puffed out her chest. "Jakub says he might give me a job."

"You can take her off my hands any time, Jakub. But I warn you, she's very high maintenance—"

Vash ducked as Rose picked up a small rock and flung it at her. It bounced off the hull and landed with a puff of dirt at Jakub's feet.

"And she has violent tendencies, as you can see."

"Now, we're meant to be fixing this crate up, not damaging it further." With a twinkle in his eye, Jakub kicked the rock under the hull. "So, what can I do, captain?"

"Would you help Alvin? He's working on our comms unit and he's struggling a bit. I was hoping for another pair of eyes…"

"I could take him to Alvin, Vash. I was thinking we could both do with a drink."

"Well, if you're offering, I won't say no. You sure you won't feel demeaned?"

Rose stuck her nose in the air. "We workers have to support each other. Anyway, I'll expect you to make the drinks next time."

"That's me told. I'll carry on here."

As Rose walked away, she looked back for a moment. Vash put on the helmet and picked up the laser gun as if it weighed nothing. The pale sol beyond her created a halo and she looked for all the world like a god, clutching her weapon of office. Rose swallowed, entranced by the vision. The sol disappeared behind a cloud, and the wind gusted. She swallowed hard and turned reluctantly to follow Jakub, wiping at her eyes as if they had picked up a stray speck of dust.

CHAPTER SEVENTEEN

ROSE ALMOST CRIED WITH relief when Vash finally told her to pack up. The unrelenting cold had seeped through the layers she was wearing and chilled her to the bone. Every inch of her body was aching, but there was no way she was going to show it. One look at Vash's face told her that she was suffering just as much, if not more. There were dark shadows under her eyes, and she was favouring her injured hand again, trying to carry everything in the other one. When she made to grab for the tool bag with her bad hand, Rose stopped her and picked it up herself. "You've got enough to carry, Vash. I can manage this."

Vash frowned but stayed quiet. They didn't waste energy talking as they trudged back to the main hatch. The snow was falling again, a stiff breeze driving the cold white flakes into their faces, darts of pain on any unprotected patches of skin. Rose slipped on some ice and steadied herself against Vash. She made a mental note to ask Bel if there were any spikes for their boots on board.

Once inside, Vash activated the lock and dropped her bag onto the floor with a thud. Rose threw back her hood and sagged gratefully against the nearest wall, eyes closed. Only Vash's fingertips on her forehead, lightly brushing her hair from her face, stopped her from falling asleep where she was.

"Why don't you go grab a shower. I'm going to go and chat to the guys, but I'll join you soon, promise."

"You're sure I can't do anything more to help?" In truth, Rose couldn't wait to hit the cotbed.

Vash shook her head. "This time *I'm* not taking any argument. I won't be long, but I want to check how everything is going with the comms unit. I don't want the boys using it without me being there. We don't know who might be listening in."

It was a good point. Penthe's agents would be monitoring all comms traffic in the system. There was no point risking giving away their location until they were able to make an escape. Thank the stars Vash still had the sense to think straight.

Vash headed for the bridge and Rose walked unsteadily towards their cabin. Her feet were arguing with her back over what hurt most, and her face was sore from the biting cold. The sensible bit of her brain told her to get a shower, and the hot water eased some of the aches and pains. Bel kept her distance this time. The AI had obviously been keeping a close eye on them though. Every time Rose had returned to the ship for refreshments, there'd always been hot drinks and food ready to go in the galley.

She wrapped a plastitwist gown she'd found scrunched up and forgotten in the bottom of one of the drawers tightly around herself. Vash still hadn't appeared, so she walked back up the corridor to the galley to make a last hot drink for them both. As the machinery hissed and whirred to make two very frothy herbal hotshakes, she sat down on the floor and rested her chin on her knees.

She'd lost count of the number of small repairs she had done. At first, she'd been fascinated by all the different parts and pipes covering the outside of the ship, but as the hours had gone by, she'd stopped caring. All that mattered was the piece of metal in front of her and the ones still to be done. Rose hadn't felt this tired since leaving the Aximendes VI, and there was plenty more to do. She closed her eyes against the dazzling light in the galley and listened to her pulse beating in rhythm with the chugging snorting of the auto chef.

Heavy footsteps in the corridor outside woke her. The galley was in darkness, the gloom punctured only by the lights on the machinery. She willed her tired muscles to get up but stopped at Jakub's voice.

"You've got brains, girl."

"I do have a name, Jakub. You might try using it occasionally. I haven't been a girl for a long time." There was weary irritation in Vash's voice.

"Sorry, Vash, no offence meant. I just wanted to compliment you on how you've been handling all of this. You've got everyone working hard for you, and that's a rare gift."

The footsteps stopped just outside, and Rose stayed quiet. She didn't want to interrupt Jakub. Vash deserved a pat on the back after all her hard work, and she was glad Jakub had noticed.

"Sorry, Jakub, and thanks. I mean it, I appreciate that coming from you. I…oh, fates."

There was the hissing sound just outside the door and the soft thud of something coming to rest on the metal gangway. She strained to listen, unable to work out what was going on.

"Hey, what's up, Vash?" Jakub whispered.

There were a few sniffs, but no other sounds. Was Vash crying? She wanted to go to her, but she might not want her making a lot of fuss, especially in front of Jakub. Fates, what should she do?

"Sorry, Jakub. I don't usually make a fool of myself like this, promise." Vash's voice cracked and was replaced by quiet sobbing.

Rose hugged her knees tighter, frozen inside. Tears welled up at Vash's distress. She kicked herself now for staying hidden. She was eavesdropping and spying on her own girlfriend.

"It's been a long day for all of us," Jakub said quietly.

"I... it's like everyone is looking to me to keep them safe, to get them home. I don't know if I can do it."

"Will you take the advice of an old man? You're only human, Vash. It's good that you care so much, but you must allow yourself to be supported as well. Your Rose, now she's a real trier."

Rose blinked at the unexpected compliment. What had she done to deserve praise? She rubbed the back of her neck. She'd probably just slowed things down.

"You can't convince me that she usually spends her days wielding a laser, but she's doing it to support you. So, let her."

"Yeah, I know, I know. It's just the expectation. I'm so tired, Jakub. I don't know if I'm doing the right things or not."

She closed her eyes tightly, ashamed. She just taken for granted that, as captain, Vash knew what she was doing. Rose dug her nails into her palms. None of this would be happening if Vash hadn't tried to protect her.

"Well, you sounded pretty sensible to me back there. It makes sense to keep radio silence until we can get your ship off the ground again, and that Alvin... I can see he's a bit of a character." Jakub chuckled quietly.

"That's an understatement."

"I've worked with men like that myself. You've got to have eyes in the back of your head to stay on top of them, but you seem to know how to keep him on task."

There was a heavy sigh and the sound of a nose being noisily blown followed by a creak of tanskin and fabric that suggested Vash was getting back to her feet.

"That's better. I mean it, you're doing a good job, captain. I wish I worked for you myself." Jakub's rough voice was full of warmth. Rose wanted to run out and hug him for looking after Vash. Her cheeks started to burn. *Looking after Vash should be my job though.*

"Well, Mr Wolcuk, if you ever find yourself wanting to leave the mining business, you look me up."

Jakub laughed. "That's a deal. And, if you'll excuse me for saying, talk to Rose. She just wants to be there for you, I'm sure."

There was a pause and a heavy sigh. Rose strained her ears, listening for the reply.

"I'll think about it, Jakub. Thanks again though."

Rose stared at the wall opposite. What was there to think about?

"Okay. I'm going to get going down below for a few hours. I'll be back at first light."

A set of heavy footsteps walked away back up the corridor. Rose held her breath. Was Vash going to come into the galley? Vash muttered something and her footsteps followed Jakub's. Rose gave thanks to whatever gods were looking out for her.

Steam still rose from the drinks on the hotplate of the galley dispenser, and she snatched them up. She poked her head out long enough to confirm that the corridor was empty, then scuttled as fast as she could along to the cabin. She put the drinks on the desk and dove under the covers. No sooner had her head hit the pillow than she heard footsteps approaching. Rose closed her eyes and pretended to be asleep. Someone stepped through the hatch. There was a pause before the unmistakable sound of slurping. Rose opened her eyes and yawned theatrically. Vash stood by the desk, clutching the cup with both hands.

"I was starting to wonder when you were coming."

Vash looked over and smiled. Her eyes were still a bit puffy from where she'd been crying. "Yeah, sorry. I needed to make sure Alvin knew exactly what I wanted. You know what he can be like. He does good work, but he argues all the time. It's really tiring." She stared into the depths of the mug for moment before she put it down. "I'm going to take a quick shower."

"No problem, I'll keep the covers warm." This wasn't a good moment to probe. Perhaps a hot shower would be the best thing. They could talk properly afterwards, and Vash would share her concerns.

Five minutes later, Vash walked back in, towelling her wet hair. She rummaged in a drawer for a clean T-shirt and slid in next to Rose. She spooned her arms around her and gently kissed the back of her neck.

"Is everything okay? You seem very quiet." Rose waited patiently for Vash to open up to her. She stroked Vash's arm, hoping to soothe her, but felt her body tense slightly.

"Sorry, gorgeous, I'm really tired." Vash snuggled closer into the pillow. "Thanks for the caffrush. I needed that."

She fell silent and after a few minutes her breath evened out. *Why aren't you talking to me?* Her mind raced to find a reason why Vash would talk to Jakub and not her. Had she changed her mind? Was she thinking about contacting the authorities for help? Rose turned over and faced the wall. *Stop catastrophising!* But her brain wouldn't quiet. She went back over everything. A few centimetres separated them physically, but the metaphorical gulf was far wider. Tears trickled down her cheek, and she rubbed at her eyes angrily. Nova! The truth was that she could face Penthe, prison, or exile from everything she knew. She could deal with the worst that the universe wanted to throw at her, but only if Vash was by her side. There was no point denying that anymore. A small noise caught her attention. Vash was dreaming, her feet moving slightly under the covers. *Where are you, Vash? Am I there too?* Rose gritted her teeth and pulled her cover tighter. Whatever tomorrow might bring, she wasn't going to give up now. She owed that to both of them.

CHAPTER EIGHTEEN

PENTHE WAITED AT THE entrance to the hangar, drumming her nails on the door. Sakas had stayed online just long enough to inform her she was on her way back. Penthe had been initially annoyed at her reticence. Having reflected on it, however, it probably meant that Sakas had information she didn't wish to entrust to the comms systems, however secure. Surely this was what she'd been waiting for. Sakas had found Rose.

It was some hours after the attack in her quarters. She'd been bathed and attended to by medics, but her face was still tender and her mood as dark as the bruises that were slowly emerging. How dare that woman attack her. What was the universe coming to? As for those so-called guards. They'd be finding out how uncomfortable life could be when they were reassigned to the missile tube cleaning crews tomorrow.

The green light above the door winked on, indicating that the shuttle had successfully landed. A couple of minutes later, Sakas strode towards her across the hangar and the pressure door released.

"Ma'am, I have good news."

Her eyes were lit with excitement. Penthe's spirits lifted, but she put her finger to her lips. "Not here. Let's find somewhere more private, Antiploi Sakas."

They walked quickly to one of the hangar's storerooms, careful to secure the door. Sakas immediately tried to wrap her arms around her. Penthe stiffened at the unwanted familiarity. She pushed her away and crossed her arms. "You forget yourself, antiploi. What have you to report to me?"

Sakas blushed deeply and lowered her eyes. "Apologies, ma'am, I've missed you so much—"

Penthe brusquely lifted a hand. "Please, Sakas."

Sakas looked up, hurt in her eyes. Penthe sighed. She'd let her get too close, and it was affecting her judgment. She gestured for Sakas to speak.

"We've found the ship, ma'am."

You've found the band. The pent-up tension of the past hours flooded out of her. Sakas smiled uncertainly as Penthe blinked to clear her eyes of tears, unable to speak for a moment. Finally, Penthe got control of herself and beamed at her, the earlier misstep forgotten. "I knew you wouldn't let me down. Where is it? Where is my band?"

Sakas reached into her flight suit pouch and laid out a map on top of a cargo box. "We went over the data, both from their tracking systems and ours. It took some time but eventually we realised that the reason we hadn't captured the ship was because it had ended up outside the main battle area. We cross-checked our records and—"

"It was that ship, wasn't it?" Penthe banged her fist on the box. "The one *you* assured me was dead in the water?"

"Our data indicated that it was critically damaged, Penthe." Sakas blanched as Penthe narrowed her eyes. "I mean, *ma'am.* We detected no life support and our thermal sensors found nothing. We moved forward to consolidate our strategic position. There was no way—"

Penthe backhanded her hard, and her signet ring sliced Sakas' cheek open. "You told me it wasn't worth bothering about. What changed?"

A thin trail of blood trickled down Sakas' white face, and she looked down at her boots. "We returned to the post-battle data logs the system had recorded. It seems that a short time after we left the area, the ship powered up and made for this planet here. MR3. It's dotted with mining settlements and—"

"How could a ship full of dead people power up? You bloody imbecile." Penthe stared at the ceiling, her pulse pounding behind her eyes. She should have checked herself, known better than to trust anyone. She grabbed Sakas' head roughly with both hands. "Where is my property, antiploi? Last chance."

Sakas pointed frantically at one of the maps. "There, ma'am. We're sure it's there."

Penthe let her go and stared down at the map. "Sure? You were *sure* before."

"Our modelling indicates that it's the most likely location. With your permission I would like to send a fighter to overfly the area and confirm—"

"No."

Sakas looked confused. Penthe gritted her teeth. She was surrounded by morons, Sakas included. "You aren't going to send a fighter. You're going to fly the fighter yourself. Go and find my property, Sakas. And if it isn't there, don't bother coming back." Without waiting for a reply, she unlocked and wrenched the door open.

As she strode through the corridors, she sensed again a subtle change in the atmosphere around her. She had felt it before, walking to the hangar, but hadn't been able to identify what was awry. But now her senses, driven by an inner rage, were alive to her surroundings. Yes, everyone was still formally greeting her as always, saluting or bowing as necessary. But it was their eyes. They wouldn't look her in the eye. Instead, their gaze slid over her shoulder or to the floor.

She slowed. Was this how it started, the beginning of the end of her rule? Not with mutinous words spoken aloud, but with the smallest subliminal signals that your authority was not absolute anymore. The respect was gone and replaced with what? Barely disguised disgust? Suppressed excitement at change to come?

She quickened her pace again, eager to get to the Command Hub. She had insisted on this meeting with her senior officers purely as a matter of routine. Volos had never seemed particularly popular to Penthe or effective. She'd only kept her in the post because she couldn't be bothered to find anyone else, and she'd considered her harmless. That had apparently been a mistake, and mistakes could cost a throne or even a life.

Penthe paused before the entrance to the Hub and chewed her lip. Sakas might have made a good replacement, but she was becoming a liability as well, perhaps a threat. The guards kept their eyes trained forward, but they were watching her every move. She had to get this right. She might only have one chance.

Her senior officers were gathered as before around the command table. The Hub itself was nearly empty. With the surrender of the system achieved, only a skeleton watch was necessary. She was glad for once that the audience would be small. She needed to play a careful hand. "Thank you for being so prompt. I expect you all know what happened earlier today."

There was a quiet shuffling of feet and a few muted sounds of acknowledgement around the table.

"I'm as disappointed as you all are that such a good officer has been lost." Penthe watched carefully for their reaction. A few backs straightened and more eyes met hers. They were apparently pleased to hear Volos' service being recognised. She'd been right to be cautious in her approach. "However, her death at the hands of my *loyal* guards, although regrettable, was necessary." She watched them again, hoping they had heard and understood her emphasis on the word loyal. A few heads stayed bowed though. Perhaps it was time to wake them up a bit. "I've asked the Black Team to carry out a full investigation. At present they believe her assassination attempt was driven by personal motives and that she was unfortunately not in possession of all her mental faculties at the time." It was time for the stick. "However, should it emerge that she had assistance from anyone, swift and severe action will be taken against those individuals."

To her amazement, her strong words, usually so effective at inspiring, had the opposite effect. Once again, all the heads hung low, studiously looking at the table. She took a step back. Their insolence was shockingly brazen. Surely, they understood that she couldn't allow any act of violence against her to go unpunished. What did they hope to achieve by this insubordination?

She cleared her throat, increasingly uneasy at the continued silence. Some of the officers carried small arms, as if a coup was being plotted. She glanced to the exit, unsure if she would make it.

"Permission to speak freely, ma'am."

The new young antiploi she'd noticed the other day looked up. The rest of the officers seemed to be holding their breath. Penthe waved her on, curious to know what the group's apparent spokesperson had to say.

"If, as you say, the Chief was mentally disturbed, does this mean there will be no further action taken against her family?"

Penthe considered this. It was true that usually the whole family would suffer for the mistakes of one. However, perhaps this time some magnanimity on her part might be a wiser course. "Correct. I've decided that, given the previous good record of this officer, no further action will be taken. I'll also ask that her body be returned to her family so that the proper ceremonies can be carried out, and her soul released."

The atmosphere around the table lightened considerably. Faces once again rose into the light and turned respectfully in her direction. Stars! Was giving the stupid woman's corpse some death rites all it took? If only all things in her life were this simple. Penthe choked back a groan and maintained an expression of matriarchal concern. "Which brings us now to the tricky question of who is ready to step up to the post of archiploi?"

Penthe watched with no little satisfaction at the subtle sideways glances around the table. Conspirators turned to competitors in an instant. It was all she could do not to smirk. This was more like it: a bit of old-fashioned divide and conquer. By the time she'd finished, the disloyal would be weeded out, demoted or worse. Those who stayed loyal would be rewarded handsomely. Perhaps this was an opportunity to build a new powerbase, perfectly timed with the resolution of the old problems that had been holding her back. She smiled broadly at her officers. When Sakas got back with Rose and the band, things would change.

As Penthe walked back to her quarters, everyone she met on the way back to her quarters looked her in the eye again. News clearly travelled fast on the Aximendes VI. Her own household were considerably more diligent to her needs. Her bedroom had been cleaned up thoroughly, and there was no visible evidence of the earlier unpleasantness. She sat in her private reception room, helping herself to some soft warm sweetcakes, fresh from the kitchens.

The open insubordination of her senior officers still played on her mind. Yes, they'd come around but only after considerable compromise on her part. Their complete lack of concern for her personal safety particularly worried her. She needed an ally fast, someone to help her shore up her authority. Sakas was the obvious choice but only if she returned triumphant. Perhaps she'd been too hasty in sending her away. She had no idea how long it would be before she heard from her.

As if in answer, her wristband alerted her to an incoming signal from Sakas requesting a real-time video link-up. Penthe moved to her private desk and waved for everyone to leave the room. She pulled out a bejewelled vid helmet from a drawer and positioned it over her head, careful not to catch her hair in the platinum filigree which entwined around the eyepieces before forming a triumphant arch above her head. It was such a ridiculous design, but she enjoyed the wide-eyed looks she got when she wore it. She worked the controls and the room gradually disappeared to be replaced by the view through Sakas' eyes. "This is the mine you spoke of?"

From a quick glance at the fighter plane's instruments, she could see Sakas was currently maintaining a high-altitude position above the location. Cameras on board her ship beamed back highly detailed pictures of the surface below, which appeared in the corner of Penthe's visual display.

"Yes, ma'am. You see the two spaceships?"

The feed showed two ships on the ground. Smooth sleek lines of one contrasted with the battered hull of the other. The damaged ship also sported several weapon systems, according to the data coming through with the pictures.

"I believe that the older, damaged ship is the Bellerophon, ma'am. It matches the description that we have."

"What of the other ship?" She ground her teeth. Did Munro have allies assisting her? If so, she would have to send Sakas reinforcements quickly. They could escape from under their noses at any time.

"I'm not sure, ma'am. It could be a ship from the mining company. My team are checking the logo on its wings. If it is, it must have arrived unannounced. I can't see Munro calling for any help, unless in extremis. It might be in her interest, but it would attract too much attention."

Penthe leaned back. This made the situation more interesting. "Is there any sign of my property?"

"Not at the moment. I can only detect one female life sign clearly, and the comms coming from her indicate it's Munro."

So, Munro was down there. Sakas' intelligence had been correct. Penthe was sure that she wouldn't have abandoned Rose. If Munro's late friend was to be believed, that would be very out of character. She considered her options, feeling energised. If the other ship was from the mining company, it could help. Perhaps they would flush Rose out from her hiding place. "Maintain your current position until the identity of that other ship is confirmed. If it is from the mining company and they discover my property, take immediate action to retrieve it. Otherwise, and unless Munro boards the ship herself, wait until they've left before you land and investigate yourself. Do you understand?"

"Yes, ma'am."

"Very well. Unless you think that the other ship has my property onboard, I don't expect to hear from you until you have retrieved it. Don't disappoint me, Sakas."

"I prom—"

Penthe severed the connection. She'd no interest in words, only results. Her own survival increasingly looked as if it depended on it.

CHAPTER NINETEEN

Rose was woken by Vash coming back from the shower. Her limbs were leaden and the skin on her face was tender.

"I'm going to head up to the bridge. Don't hurry, I need to work out the jobs before we head back outside." Vash's expression revealed nothing, but her eyes were tired. She turned and left the cabin.

Rose waited until the sound of her footsteps had gone before she got out of bed. Her head ached, and she needed something to drink. After stopping off at the head, she made her way to the galley. The machine prepared some ice-cold water and she gulped it down, feeling her head ease a little as she did so. She leaned against the counter and looked at the wall opposite, noticing for the first time an eclectic selection of memorabilia stuck on it. Vash appeared to have collected packing labels from her travels across the system. Some of them were from other nearby systems as well.

"They are fascinating, aren't they?"

Rose jumped, spilling some of the water onto the floor.

"Oh, I'm so sorry. I'll send a service bot down to clean that up," Bel said.

"No, I'll clean it up, Bel. Don't worry." Rose put the glass down, her hand trembling a little.

"Did I scare you? I didn't mean to."

"It's okay, Bel. I've just got a bad head this morning." Rose didn't want to admit that she still found the whole situation with Bel strange. Perhaps the AI had been correct, it was easier to address a physical object rather than an omniscient presence, however friendly that presence was. "Has Vash been collecting these for long?"

"Some were already here when I was installed. She told me they were memories. I explained that I kept a log of everything and everywhere we went, but she seemed to think this was better." Bel sounded confused.

Rose smiled. How could she explain the myriad of emotions evoked for Vash whenever she looked at this wall? At least Vash had something to look at. The further she got from home, the more she yearned for some sentimental items herself. She'd just packed the basics. Everything she'd collected in Drem had been left behind in the apartment, and it didn't seem likely she would ever get back there now.

"Sometimes memories are more than just timestamps, Bel. Objects like these can switch on emotions. They can take us back to a moment and let us feel it again."

"I see. That is very interesting, Rose. I have studied these objects for a long time, trying to fathom their secrets, but you are saying that only Vash would be able to unlock them?"

"Exactly. I'm sorry, Bel. Does Vash know that you've been trying to work them out?"

"No, I have not told her."

Was it her imagination or did Bel sound a little shy?

"I want to understand her better, so that I can optimise my performance."

Rose hid a smile. "Well, I think that would please her. I know it would please me."

"Actually, Rose. I do have something to tell you."

She raised an eyebrow. "What's that, Bel?"

"About the markings on your arm."

She froze, every part of her on high alert. "The markings?"

"Yes, you asked me to investigate their origins."

Stars, how could she have forgotten? It was an eternity ago that she had made the request. But she hadn't imagined getting the answer here, in a communal area of the ship where anyone could walk in. She edged over to the door and listened intently for the smallest sounds.

"It took me longer than I thought. I did not want to neglect my duties."

"Yes, I can appreciate that, Bel. Um, is there any way we could—"

"However, I think I now have the information that you wanted."

She reached out for the side of the hatchway, her legs threatening to give way.

"Are you okay, Rose? Do you want me to get Vash to assist you?"

"I'm fine, Bel. There's no need to call Vash." She prayed that Bel did as she asked. She needed time to process whatever information the AI had discovered before she spoke to anyone.

"The markings are in an extinct language. I found them recorded in only one place in the archives of the University of Drem. They were not identified, but the archives directed me to—"

"What are they, Bel?" She clapped a hand over her mouth. "I'm sorry, I didn't mean to interrupt. It's just that I have been wanting to know for so long, you see." Her hands were shaking again.

"I can see that you are eager to know more," Bel said. "They belong to an artifact called the Helion Band."

The Helion Band. She rolled the name around her brain, but it meant absolutely nothing to her. "I've never heard of it, Bel. Where's it from?"

"It has great antiquity. It was first recorded more than fifty thousand standard cycles ago. The extant records show that there were three in existence at that time. None have been seen for over half a millennia. They were believed destroyed."

Why would there be three of them? "Who made them, Bel, and for what purpose? Do the records show that?" She froze, ice encasing her spine. Why were most things created? To save or to kill.

"The architects were an elder civilisation known as the Nfex. The records indicate that they were created as a weapon of war. It may be a coincidence, but it is believed by academics that the Nfex suffered an extinction level event not long after."

She gasped out loud, unable to help herself. Slowly she extended her arm. The band, the Helion Band, was sluggishly moving. "Bel…" She didn't know how to ask the question that had started to plague her the most. "Is this Helion Band sentient?"

"It is unclear. The older records only contain sketchy details. More recent records contain more but researchers have faced a significant problem."

She swallowed, not sure she wanted to know. "What problem?"

"The Helion Band appears to have been designed to exist only in symbiosis with another life form. None of the life forms recorded in the past twenty-five thousand standard cycles, the period in which most of the information comes from, have survived the experience long enough to be able to provide detailed information about it."

Oh gods! She fell to her knees, retching violently.

"Are you sure you don't want me to call Vash?" Bel asked, her voice full of concern. "My scans show that it is in symbiosis with you. You could be in grave danger."

"How did they die, Bel?" Fates, what a wonderful gift Penthe had given her. She wished she could rip the band from her arm and fling it back at her.

"Records indicate that they either committed suicide or were destroyed by the band itself."

"Why did it destroy them?" Rose held her head in both hands, trying to stay calm.

"It doesn't appear to be a deliberate act, rather a by-product of its use as a weapon. Their nervous systems were either overwhelmed or they were physically destroyed along with their apparent target. Not all volunteered to join with it."

She rocked back and forth, unable to take all this in. A living, walking weapon of war. *Just point me and fire*. She giggled.

"What is funny, Rose?"

"Nothing, Bel." She took a deep breath and pulled herself together. She'd been lucky. Vash and the boys were obviously engrossed up on the bridge, but they could be along anytime. "Thank you for telling me all this. Do you need to inform Vash? I'd prefer to tell her myself." Tell her and get out of her life forever. There was no choice left now. Run and this thing might destroy her; stay and Penthe certainly would. But whatever happened, she wasn't going to allow Vash to be killed as well.

"If you intend to do so, I will not report it. However, I must now monitor you closely. I hope you understand my caution."

"I do, Bel. I understand completely." *Don't worry, Bel. I'll be out of your hair soon enough.* She climbed to her feet and looked at the band again. It was sentient, listening and learning from her all the time. As she watched, it returned to dormancy, looking for all the world like an exotic tattoo. *But you don't fool me anymore, band.* She had no intention of letting it get its way. There'd been enough death already. As for Penthe getting her hands on the band, Rose shuddered at the possible consequences.

She showered and dressed quickly. As she approached the bridge, she tried to rehearse how she would begin the conversation. There was no obvious way to break the news. Perhaps she should wait and make her escape as soon as they reached a port. But Bel wouldn't let her silence continue that long. She was on borrowed time now. As she neared the hatch, she heard shouts.

As soon as she stepped though, Vash turned. She looked alarmed and walked towards her, waving at her to leave.

"Go back to the cabin, Rose, please."

Vash's face was strange, she couldn't make out if she was worried or angry. "What's going on? Have you all started breakfast without me?" She smiled, hoping to lighten things, but Vash's expression was sober.

"Rose, we have a problem—a really big problem."

Jakub and Alvin stared at her, making her feel like a laboratory specimen. "Why are you all looking at me like that?" She stiffened. Perhaps her conversation with Bel had been overheard?

"Well, I can't speak for the others," Jakub said, "but I ain't ever harboured a real fugitive before."

She started to shake, understanding Vash's expression. "Vash?" Rose clutched her hands to her chest. Vash had decided to give her up.

"No! How could you think that?" Vash's eyes widened. "I asked for a comms test. The first thing we heard was a system-wide alert message with a description of you. They know that you're with me."

"I still can't believe you brought an Ak on the ship." Alvin's face was beet red with fury. "How do you know she wasn't signalling them? She could've been betraying us all that time."

Vash rounded on him in fury. "She helped saved your life, remember?" She punctuated each point with a sharp jab of her finger to his chest.

Alvin didn't budge. "Saved her own life more like. She doesn't care about you or me, Vash, she just doesn't want to face the music back home. Your Ak bitch could be a murderer for all we know."

Vash stared at him in disbelief, then flung back her head and laughed. "Make your mind up, Alvin. First, she's a spy, now she's a fugitive from Akmonian justice? Let's face it, you don't know bilgepiss.

She didn't need to hear any more. If she hadn't already got a good reason to leave, she did now. The corridor blurred as she ran down it. All she could see were the horrified expressions on their faces, the accusation in their eyes. She'd tried to warn Vash this was how it would be. The sooner she got out of their lives the better.

When she reached the main hatch, she squinted at the controls, desperately trying to remember what buttons Vash had used to open it. She tried pushing a few but only got orange error lights for her trouble. Frustrated, she punched the control panel and swore at it.

"Rose, is everything okay?" Bel said.

“Bel, open the main hatch for me, please. Now.”

“Cancel that order, Bel. I’ll take over now,” Vash said.

Rose swung around. Vash stood there, hands on hips, and Jakub strode down the corridor behind her. “You can’t keep me here. Open the hatch.”

Vash looked steadily at her. “Where are you going to go, Rose? We’re thousands of miles from anywhere.” She stepped forward and tried to take her arm, but Rose batted her hand away.

“It doesn’t matter. The main thing is I won’t be here, putting you all in danger.” Rose turned back to the controls and tried a few more combinations.

“Bel, override the controls, please. And keep the hatch locked until I give you a direct order.”

Rose felt Vash’s hand on her shoulder. Furious with the whole situation, she turned and pushed her away. “What do you want from me? You aren’t even talking to me anymore. I know you don’t want me here.”

Vash backed off slightly, looking confused. “What do you mean?”

“I heard you and Jakub talking. You’re right; you need to get the ship home, get Alvin home. Why didn’t you just tell me? I can hand myself in.”

“I want…”

Vash trailed off. Her face moved strangely, as if the words were turning inside her.

Rose shook her head. “See? Now, please open the hatch.” She turned her back to Vash, determined to wait as long as needed.

Vash stepped in front of her. “Okay, I don’t know what I want, Rose, but I can tell you what I need.”

She tried to push her out of the way again, but Vash stood firm.

“All I need right now is you. I really don’t care what anyone else thinks. If you leave, I might as well be dead as well.”

Rose wasn’t sure that she’d heard correctly. Judging by Vash’s expression, she couldn’t believe she’d said it either.

“Vash, will you feel the same when you’re ostracised by your whole community? When none of your friends will talk to you? When no one will give you any work?” Rose hated talking to her like this, but she needed to be honest. “Okay, we’d have each other, but I love you too much to see you suffer all of that.”

“You don’t know that’ll happen. I’m sure that when I explain…”

“You saw how Alvin reacted. People won’t want to know. I’m the enemy, and there are too many lives at stake."

"I wouldn't mind knowing," Jakub said quietly. "Seems to me that you might do me the courtesy of explaining before you walk off."

Rose threw her hands up in despair. "Why can't you both just let me go? What have I got to say?"

Jakub stepped forward and put his hand firmly on her shoulder. "I guess I can't believe the woman who offered to take care of my son and wanted to know those guardbeasts were well looked after is such a bad person. So, convince me, Rose. What have you done that's so bad you're on an Akmonian queen's most wanted list?"

She looked at the ground, unable to meet his eye. "Jakub, I haven't told Vash all of it. I'm shouting at her for keeping things from me, and all this time I've been holding back too. I'm not the paragon you think I am." Out of the corner of her eye, Vash stiffened.

"I don't reckon she's a killer, Vash. I've met a few, and she don't fit the mould." He pulled her chin up gently. "But I think it's time you came clean. We've got to know everything."

Rose didn't have the strength to argue anymore. Perhaps she deserved all of this. Telling the truth and watching Vash's love for her drain away, there was no greater punishment she could think of. She nodded. "I'll tell you everything. Then I'll leave."

CHAPTER TWENTY

THEY SAT AROUND THE scuffed table in Jakub's cabin, steaming flasks of caffrush in front of them. He'd suggested it as a neutral venue, and she'd agreed gladly, having no inclination to face any more hostility from Alvin. He was probably just as glad to see her off the ship. "I asked Bel to do something for me, Vash. I asked her to keep a secret."

Vash frowned. "Keep a secret? And she agreed?"

"Yes, but only on the condition that if anything occurred that endangered you or the ship, she would inform you immediately."

Vash raised an eyebrow. "Still, I'm not sure I'm keen on her going behind my back."

"Let her speak, Vash." Jakub lifted his mug of steaming caffrush. "After the events of this morning, it doesn't seem important."

"The thing is, I needed to know about this." Rose rolled up her sleeve to reveal the band. She was relieved it wasn't moving right now. There was no need to shock them more than she was going to anyway.

"Your tattoo?" Vash peered at it. "What's so special about that?"

"Well, I got it while I was on the Aximendes VI." How was she going to explain the symbiosis? It was impossible.

Vash scratched her head. "Is it the reason this Penthe woman is after you?" Her eyes grew wider. "Oh gods, it's a family marking. You're the real heir to the throne, and she's trying to kill you."

Jakub leaned forward intently. "Is that it, Rose? Just tell us, we'll do our best to protect you."

This was all going too fast, and in the wrong direction. "No, to all of that. Penthe gave it to me. It's just…I don't think she knew what it was."

Jakub was looking confused. She didn't blame him.

"I was putting away some of her jewellery in the treasury room." She remembered Penthe laughing at her after the banquet, the light of the gold and jewels playing across her face. "I saw this plain bracelet on a shelf, all covered in dust. She saw me looking and thought it was funny."

Surrounded by all of this, and all you're interested in is the ugliest thing in the room. Ugly, like you! Go on, have it. Penthe's voice was as clear as ever in her head.

"So, she gave a bracelet to you. What's that got to do with the tattoo?" Vash asked.

"The bracelet *is* the tattoo. I put it on when I was alone in my room, and it became the tattoo."

"Here, let me see." Jakub gently took her arm and ran his thumb over the skin. "Yeah, I can feel something under there, but nothing hard like a biomesh." He let her arm go again. "I've heard of some strange things, Rose, but this takes the quantum."

"The bracelet became part of you. That's a bit… I don't know what to believe, Rose." Vash pursed her lips.

"You don't have to take my word for it. Ask Bel when you get back. She researched it, and found that it's really old, and it's really called the Helion Band." She ran her hands through her hair. If they didn't understand this bit, how could she ever hope to explain the rest?

Jakub reached out for his flask, but his hand stopped in mid-air as a loud buzzing noise came from his jacket.

"What the…?" Jakub fished around and tugged out his communicator.

He read something on the screen, scratched his head and swore loudly. She watched him closely. Whatever it was, it was serious. He'd never sworn before.

"Well, things just got a lot more interesting. The company is sending a team out. It seems they've received a message that I've got unauthorised visitors on site, and they want to investigate," he said.

"What? We haven't finished the repair work. I can't take off with her in this state. I don't understand, Jakub. How do they know we are here?" Vash got to her feet, looking aghast.

Jakub threw his hands up and looked equally exasperated. "How do I know? This could cost me my job."

Rose banged her fist on the table. The last thing she wanted was for them to start arguing as well. Things were bad enough. "Can't you guess?"

They stared at her, apparently unable to grasp the obvious.

"It's Alvin," she said.

Running as fast as she could, she couldn't keep up with Vash. Fury had given her wings and by the time Rose reached the main hatch, she'd already disappeared inside. Terrified of what she would find, she followed the sound of angry shouts, and sprinted up the corridor to the Bridge.

Vash was looming over Alvin down in a corner and he looked terrified. He glanced towards her as she stepped through the hatch and held up his hands.

"Come on, Vash, you know I've done the right thing. When the authorities get here, they'll clear this whole mess up."

"You backstabbing bilgeslug. How dare you go against my orders?" Vash leaned closer and he squirmed, trying to dig his way out through the metal with his shoulders.

"She's an Ak, Vash. Maybe not a murderer or a spy, but definitely an Ak. We shouldn't be hiding her. I'm just doing my duty."

Rose winced in anticipation. He must be mad trying to be righteous about this. Vash looked at him coolly for a moment then punched him in the stomach. He doubled up and fell to the floor with a grunt.

"Doing your duty? You don't know the meaning of the word. I took you on when no other captain would touch you because of your drinking." She kneed him in the face, sending him flying back into the wall behind him with an audible crunch of compressed metal. "I gave you a chance, and this is how you repay me."

"Vash, please, this isn't right." Rose tried to get Vash's attention, but she ignored her.

Alvin struggled to his knees, blood and snot streaming from his nose. "I'm sorry, Vash, but I want my life back. You can live on the run, fucking your Ak whore, if you like. I ain't going anywhere."

He fell back with a high-pitched scream as Vash kicked him squarely in the balls.

She smiled as she gazed down at him. "You're right about one thing Alvin. You aren't going anywhere. Now, get up."

As he rolled on the ground clutching at his groin, she reached for her gun, clipped to the back of her chair.

"I said, get up. Get up, or I'll shoot you right here."

Rose stepped between Vash and Alvin. *Hey, gods…anyone? Could really do with help now.*

"Get out of my way, Rose. He's been asking for this for a long time." Vash's eyes were flinty.

"No, Vash, I won't. I won't let you kill another person because of me.

There's been too much death already." Rose swallowed hard and put her hand over the barrel of the gun. "Put the gun down, Vash, please."

Vash didn't seem to register what she was saying, the red mist of her rage too deep. As if in answer, Vash pushed her to one side. The band started to move on her arm. She tried to send a message in her mind. *I can handle this on my own.*

"I asked you to get out of the way, Rose. Alvin and I have pressing business to—"

Jakub's hand plucked the gun out of Vash's hands. The movement was so quick that she had no chance to respond. When she did turn to see where it had gone, Jakub's fist, still wrapped around the barrel of the gun, connected squarely with her face. She crumpled to the floor, her head slamming into a console as she fell.

"Sorry it took me so long, Rose." He looked down at Vash's prone body. "Looks like I was nearly too late."

Rose got down on her knees and cradled Vash's head. "I thought she was going to kill him."

"Yeah, thanks, Jakub. I owe you, buddy," Alvin said, his voice weak. "I'll buy you a drink when we get back to civilisation."

Jakub walked over to Alvin, who proffered a hand. "Alvin, I wouldn't drink with you if you were the last person in the universe." He swung the pistol butt across Alvin's head and knocked him out with one blow. "I'm sorry, Rose. I'm not a violent man usually, but the likes of him..."

All she could do was nod numbly. There were two bodies lying on the floor. Two people injured and unconscious, and she was to blame for all of it. What could she say? Nothing was okay anymore.

Jakub stuffed Vash's gun in his pocket. He crouched down and stroked her head. "I'm sorry, Vash, you'll have a real shiner. But better that than being a murderer."

He flipped her over and picked her up around the waist as if she weighed nothing. Rose followed him out of the bridge and down to their cabin. Carefully, almost reverently, he placed Vash on her cotbed.

"I'll leave you to take care of her. I'll sort out Alvin." He looked desolate.

She wrapped her arms around him. "Thank you, Jakub…for everything."

"You sure, Rose? I knocked your woman out. I don't think she's gonna want to talk to me for a while."

"You saved her life as well as Alvin's. She'll see that." Rose kissed his cheek. "I'll never forget what you did."

He blushed deep red and walked out of the cabin.

Turning back to the cotbed, she looked down at Vash. She looked peaceful, but there was a lump on her forehead and an angry patch on one cheek promised a nasty bruise to come. Rose fished around the drawers until she found a cloth. She ran cold water over it in the head and sat down on the edge of the cotbed. She pressed it gently to Vash's bruises, hoping that its cool surface might soothe the skin. Out of the corner of her eyes, a small bot moved in through the door.

"Bel?" Rose kept her voice low.

"Yes, Rose."

Bel sounded strange, and the hairs on Rose's neck stood up. She hadn't considered Bel in all of this. The AI's ethical protocols were probably being severely tested. Perhaps they were lucky that she hadn't already reacted. "Bel, I know this must all be very difficult for you."

"It is true that I'm extremely concerned for my captain's welfare, Rose."

"You know that I would not do anything to hurt Vash, don't you, Bel?"

"I know that she holds you in deep affection, Rose. However, it's also the case that she is currently unconscious, and you did nothing to prevent that. You also wear the band."

Rose took a deep breath. Her instincts were correct; Bel was very close to moving to defend her owner. She felt the familiar tingling sensation in her arm and clamped her hand over it. She couldn't do anything about the growing ache behind her eyes though. She tried to find the right words. "Did you see what happened prior to Vash being injured, Bel?"

"I see everything that happens on this ship, Rose. I can see you are now tending to her wounds."

"Do you understand what could have happened to her if she had killed Alvin?"

"There is a high probability that she would have been tried for murder and executed in line with the local justice systems. I am very confused by her reaction. All he did was disobey an order. He has done that before, many times."

Rose took a deep breath. How could an AI be expected to understand human emotions? Bel was a rational sentient being. Humans weren't. "That order was a very important one. He put the ship in danger, which made Vash angry. He also put me in danger. When a human gets as angry as Vash did, we do things we shouldn't. When Jakub hit Vash, he was trying to prevent that. Are you able to understand that?"

"I think I understand what you are saying, Rose. Mr Wolcuk intervened to protect us all and to protect Vash?"

She relaxed a little, hopeful the danger had passed now. She felt the pain in her head subside.

"However, Vash is still not conscious, and I remain concerned for her welfare. I also do not understand what Alvin is now doing in the cold storage unit. The ambient temperature will not be beneficial to his recovery."

So much for that hope. She felt Vash's pulse again. She showed no sign of coming around, and the lump on her forehead was getting larger by the second. "Bel, I need your help. Could you please check her vital signs?"

"I have been continuously monitoring them, Rose. At present everything is within acceptable norms."

In answer to her prayers, Vash's eyes started to flutter. Rose stroked her hand gently. "It's Rose. Everything is okay. Just take it easy."

Vash's eyes opened and looked at her. She tried to lift her head but groaned and lay back again. "My head is killing me. What happened?"

"Jakub hit you. He was worried you were going to do something stupid, as was I."

"Something stupid…oh, gods." Vash tried to lift herself up again, panic in her eyes.

Rose put a hand on her chest and pushed her back. "It's okay, you didn't kill Alvin. He's out cold too. Jakub put him in one of the cold storage rooms."

Vash closed her eyes, obviously relieved. Whatever red mist had descended back on the bridge had apparently dissipated. Tears emerged from the corner of her eyes, and Rose used the cloth to gently wipe them away. The service bot hovered closer.

"Captain, are you alright?" Bel asked.

"Bel? Yes, I'm fine."

"I am very concerned about your safety."

Vash put her hand to her forehead and winced. "I know you are, Bel, thank you."

"Bel has been worried about you, very worried." Rose tried her best to convey the situation to Vash. She wasn't sure she'd succeeded.

Vash opened her eyes and looked at her, one eyebrow raised. She grimaced and turned her head to look at the bot. "Bel, everything is okay now. I'm safe and in control again. Please return to your duties."

"I'm very glad to hear that, captain. I will return to my repair work."

The bot bounced a couple of times and shot out of the cabin.

Vash closed her eyes again and exhaled loudly. "I really wanted to kill him. He said some things about you…I can't repeat them. After everything I did for him, this is how he repaid me."

Rose didn't know what to say. Thanks for nearly killing someone for her. She was on the run from someone who embraced that sort of violence. The last thing she'd wanted was to spend the rest of her life with another woman who acted the same way. She glanced over at the image of herself hanging above the cot. She looked so carefree; that had been such a good day. How had it all got so complicated?

"I've frightened you, haven't I?"

"Yes, you have. Sorry, I can't deny that right now. I knew you were tough, but I never thought you'd be so violent towards another person. I asked you to stop and you didn't." The pressure behind her eyes grew, and she looked at the ceiling, blinking away the tears. If she saw Vash's face she might falter, and she needed to say this out loud. "I know I'm not perfect and the gods know I've let you down as well. But I'm not a violent person, you know that. I couldn't hurt a habroach. I'm just not sure right now where this leaves us."

"I'd never hurt you, Rose. You do know that, right?"

"I never thought Penthe would hurt me. And look where that got me."

"Please don't compare me to her. Never compare me to her."

Rose turned, unable to bear the pain in Vash's voice. Vash had propped herself up and tears slowly ran down her swollen, bruised face. She rubbed at her temple. Here she was, judging Vash, while harbouring a weapon of war in her own body. It made her shudder. *I'll never ever use it again.* Goosebumps ran up her arms. Had Vash made the same resolution? She guessed she had, perhaps many times. Vash had gone out on a limb for her, and it was time she stepped up to the mark. She sat beside her. "I know you'd never set out to harm me, Vash, but we both know that if I was in the wrong place…" She couldn't finish the sentence. Judging by Vash's horrified expression, she didn't need to. "But I think I know now why you insist on a dry ship, why you've never touched alcohol when you're with me, and why you've never taken me to any of your usual haunts. You were afraid of what I might see. The other Vash?"

Vash nodded and turned her head away. "When I'm with you, Rose, when I see how you are with people and how you view the world, it's such a good thing. I didn't want to lose it. I didn't want to lose you."

"I know, and it's the same for me. All these things you've done, and these changes we're both making. That's the difference right now. That's why I'm here, talking to you and not running for shelter with Jakub. You've changed me too."

Vash put her head in her hands and sighed deeply. "But you thought about running."

"I'm not going anywhere now." Rose ran her hand through Vash's hair. "You told me not so long ago that I had to stop running, that I had to face up to things. You've put everything on the line for me, and I'm going to do the same for you." Rose stroked her face, the truth of the words igniting a bright light inside she hadn't believed she'd get back after this morning. She was going to resist the band and help Vash resist her demons as well. "I'm not going to make you promise never to lose your temper again. No." Rose put her finger on Vash's lips. "I do want you to promise me one thing though."

"Anything, Rose."

"Talk to me. Tell me when things are going on in your head. Like last night."

Vash's face tightened, and she turned away.

Rose reached over and gently pulled her back. "I didn't mean to eavesdrop, and I'm truly sorry about that, but I don't understand why you didn't talk to me afterwards."

Vash looked up at the ceiling. "I guess I didn't want to worry you. Stars, I'm meant to be protecting you, not be protected by you."

Rose gently brushed a stray hair away from Vash's forehead. "You can't do all this on your own, Vash, no more than I can."

"I know, but…"

"We're a team, you said so yourself. So now, when you're down, you're going to lean on me. When you're feeling angry, you're going to find me by your side. I'm going to support you every way that I can."

"I don't deserve you," Vash whispered.

"That makes us equal." Rose kissed her forehead, her nose and finally found Vash's lips.

CHAPTER TWENTY-ONE

THEY LAY TOGETHER, JUST talking. Rose stroked Vash's back and held her close while she cried, remembering her dad. Her mum had died in childbirth. He had furiously resisted any efforts to take her from him and learned how to care for her himself, and she loved him for that. He'd taken her everywhere with him, and she'd played with discarded wrappers and flasks under bar stools in the same way other kids played with toys at home. Vash had listened to his banter and watched as he and his friends used their fists to sort out problems. In their world, loyalty was everything, and deals were done with the shake of a hand rather than a thumbscan on a tablet. As she'd got older, she'd been offered more and more alcohol herself and grown to enjoy the comfort of a glass of kras. One of her happiest memories was him carrying her around the bar, showing off her black eye after she'd got into her first fight and won.

Rose sighed. Parents should really have to take a test. Penthe's mother had only offered indifference at best, and at worst, cruelty and violence. Where had that come from? Penthe was probably just the latest in a long line of abused royal children. Images of her own mother flashed in her mind, tired after a long day's work in one of the ship's many fabricating plants but still reading Rose a bedtime story and stroking her head until she fell asleep. She'd died a month before Rose had made her escape, never knowing the truth of what her daughter had endured. It also meant she hadn't faced any retribution for her daughter's treason. In the face of Penthe's murderous fury, Rose might've chosen the nearest airlock if her mother had still been alive.

They were eventually interrupted by Bel, who let them know that Jakub was asking permission to come on board. Vash sent a message for him to meet them inside the main hatch. He shifted nervously from foot to foot, not looking either of them in the eye. After a few moments of silence, Vash reached out to shake his hand. He took it hesitantly, and she pulled him into a bearhug.

"Thank you, Jakub."

He pulled away and scanned her face. "I'm just sorry I hurt you."

The bruise on Vash's face was starting to come out in all the colours of the rainbow. Well, that would be around for a while. She'd suffered similar enough times herself to know.

"You did what you had to. I would've done the same in your shoes." Vash smiled warmly. "I'm glad you were such a good friend."

Jakub blushed and looked down at his shoes.

"Is there any news from your bosses?" Rose asked.

Jakub looked up and frowned. "Yes, there's a shuttle inbound now with two company officers coming to check out what is going on. They'll be here in an hour."

Vash pursed her lips. "Any ideas?"

Jakub looked sly. "How about we hide Rose in the mine?"

Vash fiddled with her ear. "Won't they want to go down there as well?"

"Perhaps. Although finding your ship here will be a big distraction. Besides, there are some smaller side tunnels with no built-in lighting that I'm sure will make a perfect hiding place." He looked at them both for approval.

Vash shrugged. "I can't think of anything else. What do you think, Rose?"

She nodded. "I think that makes sense. Just tell me what to do, Jakub."

"Grab your jacket and follow me."

After a brief hug from Vash, she followed Jakub over to the mine entrance. The metal door was set flush into the earth, paint peeling from its surface. Jakub yanked at the handle, and it swung open with a high whining creak. It was a surprisingly large area inside, with a lift shaft visible at the far end. Yellow glow lamps dimly lit the space, leaving dark shadows behind the large crates piled up against the wall.

He took her down in the mine lift, and she was glad of his company as it shuddered and swung on their descent.

"It's all in good working order, I promise," Jakub shouted over the din of the machinery.

The lift ground to a halt, revealing another large chamber with two tunnels leading from it. Jakub beckoned to her, and she followed him down one, already feeling the warmth and humidity. Eventually, about a hundred metres in, he stopped by a side tunnel. She peered into its gloom and just made out the outlines of two huge mining bots.

"Here, take this." He handed her a small earpiece. "It's one-way. Part of the kit I use when the cargo carrier comes to collect the ore. It connects to a local mesh, and from there by cable to the surface net. I'm gonna to give Vash the communicator to hide in her clothing so you can hear what's going on with her."

She put a hand on his arm. "Thanks, I really appreciate it."

"You sure you don't want a light wand?"

"There's no need if I'm near the entrance, and if I need to go deeper, I'm not afraid of the dark. It's not like I'll be down here long."

"True. Hopefully it'll all be over soon." He turned to walk back up the tunnel. "I'll be back as soon as I can."

Rose walked further into the tunnel, leaving the light behind. She carefully skirted the bots and sat down on the far side. The floor was rocky but covered with a fine sand. She fidgeted, trying in vain to find a comfortable spot. As the minutes passed, her back grew damp resting against the clammy uneven wall. False images of texture and movement filled the darkness. A constant leaden ache in her arms and legs reminded her of how long the day had been.

"Hey, gorgeous? Hope you're okay down there. Wish you could talk to me."

She started as Vash's crackly voice broke in.

"The company shuttle just arrived, and Jakub's gone to meet them. Here we go."

Her voice disappeared and was replaced by static again. Rose hugged her knees, the fatigue in her limbs replaced by the tingling of adrenaline.

"Captain Munro? Pleased to meet you. Miner Wolcuk has explained the situation to us."

"I'm so very pleased to meet you, Mr Tyler."

Rose stifled a laugh before remembering no one could hear her.

"Nick Tyler. Please call me Nick."

His voice was closer. How close was he prepared to get into Vash's space? Usually, unwelcome guests got a rude awakening, but Vash would have to hold her temper.

"Well, *Nick*, I'm really sorry that I had to make an unauthorised landing on your company's property. As you can see, it was an emergency."

"Yes, it's clear that you were lucky to be able to make it this far. This whole business with that Akmonian ship has been terrible."

Tyler made it sound as if the battle with the Aximendes VI was just a bad day at the office. She clenched her fists. All those deaths, and he was probably more interested in how it had interrupted the mining operations. She listened intently, worried that Vash might let her anger show, and was relieved when she stayed silent.

"I don't understand why Miner Wolcuk didn't contact us earlier, captain."

"I'm afraid that was down to me, Nick. I begged him not to. You see, I lost my chief engineer in a fire while we were fleeing for our lives. His death got to me. I was paranoid that the Akmonian ship might be listening in." Vash sniffed softly.

"Yes, I can see how that might have been of some concern. Please accept my sympathy, captain. I hadn't realised that you'd lost a crew member. Has Miner Wolcuk been assisting you with your repairs?"

"Yes, he's been invaluable—only when he isn't on shift, of course. He's a credit to your company, Nick."

Rose grinned at Vash's shameless attempt to get a good word in for Jakub.

"He's always been a good employee. Sometimes a little eccentric perhaps…"

Tyler was obviously squirming a little in the face of all these compliments for Jakub. Just how "eccentric" was Jakub in his dealings with head office?

"But I'm sure you don't want to stay here talking, Nick. Would you like to see my ship?"

"If you don't mind, Captain Munro. It's just so that I can give a full report to my superiors, you understand. I'm already sure that nothing is amiss now. My colleague is accompanying Miner Wolcuk down into the mine—"

"Down below? Why is that necessary?"

"Oh, we're just combining the visit with our routine inspection of the workings. It's nothing out of the ordinary."

An icy tendril wrapped around Rose's spine. Just what they hadn't wanted to happen. What if they were already heading her way?

"Of course, Nick, that makes complete sense. Let's go across to my ship. If there are any problems below, I'm sure your colleague will be in contact. I'll be interested to hear how the inspection goes."

Rose got the message loud and clear. Vash was going to keep to the agreed script but monitor the situation closely. It would also be easier to disable Tyler on board the Bellerophon if that was needed. She hoped that it wouldn't be.

There was the faint hum of distant machinery. The lift had been activated. She stood up and made her way back to the entrance of the tunnel. She held her breath and listened. The voices in the distance were steadily coming closer and closer. Nova! Jakub had left her in this tunnel because the two mining robots were parked in it. In his own strange way, he'd obviously thought they would provide some company. However, it was probably their very presence that was bringing the company man to this location. He'd want to inspect their property.

She reversed back into the darkness of the tunnel. She glanced down. Her footprints were clear in the light covering of grit and sand on the floor. They would lead anyone with half a brain to where she was hiding. *Think!* She pulled her jacket off and dragged it over the ground. She relaxed again as the scuffed sand obscured her marks.

As she continued backward, covering her trail, she tripped over the metal tread of a bot and fell heavily. Her shoulder smacked into the side of the machine, and the sharp impact drove the breath out of her body. She lay still for a few moments, stunned. Had she cried out? Her pulse was thumping so loudly in her head that she couldn't hear anything clearly. *Move, you idiot!* She forced herself back to her feet. Her shoulder screamed in pain, but there was no time to lose. She continued to back away down the tunnel, taking it more slowly. After about ten steps, she felt the air thicken slightly around her. The back of her head scraped painfully against the tunnel ceiling, so she ducked down further and further until she was crawling along dragging the jacket. Eventually her boots hit something behind, but the space was too narrow to turn in, so she lay down and put the jacket over her head. All she could do now was wait.

"Yes, the two spare boys are just down here, Mr Roberts. I gave them their annual maintenance a couple of weeks ago," Jakub said.

Rose didn't look up, horribly aware that her eyes would gleam brightly in any light from her hiding place. She concentrated on their voices, alert for the smallest change in tone.

"You have the logbooks, miner?" Roberts asked. "Please tell me we don't have to go back top for them."

"Of course not. They're right here in this box."

There were metallic noises: the sound of a lid being prised open? There was the faint sound of paper rustling.

"Yes, it all seems in order. Let's get out of here before any more of this filth gets on my suit."

"Of course, Mr Roberts. Follow me, please."

Rose was hit by a cramp in her leg. She squeezed her eyes shut, trying to block it out, but let out a small gasp as a second stronger wave hit.

"Did you hear something, miner?"

Please, please go away. I can't stay still much longer. Rose had only seconds left before she would have to move to ease the pain.

"No, nothing, Mr Roberts. Perhaps it was the rockface. It can creak a bit. Even experienced miners get spooked sometimes. There's nothing down there; it's a dead end."

"This whole mine is a dead end if you ask me. Let's go."

The sound of their boots faded. Unable to keep still a moment longer, she struggled around onto her back and flexed her foot. The cramp subsided and her whole body relaxed. Their voices were now just distant murmurs that slid over her sweaty body like a gentle breeze as the darkness took her totally.

"Rose? Rose?" Vash's voice echoed through the trees.

She was swinging peacefully in a hammock, looking at the dappled sollight on the skin of her legs. Looking up into the canopy, she delighted in the sight of brightly painted parbirds flying from tree to tree, their iridescent wings catching the light in a rainbow of colours. There was a small trakhener up there as well, its six limbs sturdy on a branch, eating leaves. She frowned. How had it got up there? She'd only ever seen them pulling old farm machinery in the children's books she'd read. It seemed so happy though, so there was no need to worry. She was more relaxed than she had been for a long time. Occasionally white petals rained down in a soft shower, gradually filling up the hammock around her.

"Rose? Where are you?"

She mused that it was a peculiar question. This wasn't a very big forest; she couldn't be hard to find. Vash's voice got steadily louder, making her ears hurt slightly and the trakhener reared up, frightened by the booming noise. It fell from the branch and plummeted towards her. She could clearly see the sweat patches on its neck, and its white teeth which grew larger and larger until they were all she could see—

"Rose? It's Vash. Can you talk?"

She blinked unsteadily into the white light shining into her eyes. "Vash?"

The light moved slightly to one side, and Vash's concerned face stared down at her.

"Let's get you out of here. Just stay still."

Rose felt strong arms lift her slightly and pull her gently back into a wider part of the tunnel. The pain from her shoulder was intense, and she bit her lip to keep from crying out. Just as a scream started to well up, she was lowered to the floor again, able to catch her breath. Jakub came into view, his eyes blinking nervously.

"Be careful with her shoulder, Vash. It doesn't look right."

"What do you mean? Hey, what happened?" Vash stroked her head, her face creased with worry.

"It's okay." Rose tried to sit up, but as soon as she put weight on it a bolt of pain shot through her. She fell back, hissing with pain. "Sort of. I had a quick fight with one of the robots, and I think it won on points."

Jakub knelt beside her and ran his hands over the joint. He moved the arm up slightly, manipulating the shoulder as he did so. "Well, you got lucky. I can't feel any skeletal damage. That won't stop it being painful for a while."

Vash let out a sigh of relief. "Thank the gods. I think we should get you topside as soon as possible. I want Bel to take a proper look at it."

"Can you help me up?" Rose didn't want to risk putting weight on the shoulder quite yet.

Vash and Jakub gently lifted her to her feet.

"Are you sure you're okay to walk?" Vash still looked concerned.

"Absolutely. It's my shoulder that took the hit, not my legs." Rose smiled to reassure her. "I just need my bed and a hot drink."

"Coming right up. Are you staying down here, Jakub?"

"Yes, the reps might have gone, but this thing is still recording my every move." He held up his wrist with a rueful expression. "These minerals won't mine themselves, you know, but they gave me an override code for the kennel, so you're safe to go back up without me."

"Let us know when you're finished, there'll be a large caffrush waiting for you." Vash lightly punched his arm.

How quickly the three of them had become firm friends. She couldn't imagine life without either of them now.

As they walked back to the lift, Vash filled her in on what she had missed. She'd shown Mr Tyler around the Bellerophon. As planned, she'd taken him to the cold storage area where they had left Alvin sedated and well wrapped up.

"I reckon I should get an award for my performance. I played the grieving colleague so well that the bilgeslime didn't go in. He peeked around the door and decided he was better off comforting me in my time of tragedy."

Vash laughed, and it lifted Rose's spirits to hear it. "How is Alvin?"

"Still sleeping it off. Jakub offered to keep him here when we go, but I don't want to make any more trouble for him."

"No, we mustn't. He's been so good to us, Vash." The idea of anything happening to Jakub made her stomach churn.

"Right, so I'm going to keep him sedated for now and put him back in his cabin where I can keep an eye on him. I'll offload him at the first orbital we find."

She stopped and looked at Vash. "You have it all planned, don't you?"

Vash blushed a little and looked away. "Yeah, well, I didn't want to bore you with the details. The way I see it, we can't hang around here. I can always find work with a ship this good."

She took her arm. "You'd do that for me. Give up your life in this system?"

"Yeah, I would. I didn't know for a while that was what I wanted. But, knowing you were down here, and that they might discover you and take you away…" Vash seemed to be engrossed in something invisible on the wall.

Rose kissed her on her cheek, and she blushed further. "You're wonderful, you know that? I've no right to expect any of this from you."

Vash shrugged. "You'd have done the same for me."

Would I? Would I have been so courageous? But that wasn't what Vash needed to hear. Instead, she pulled her face around and kissed her fiercely. When she pulled back, Vash was looking at her with a drunken, loved-up grin that made her heart stop for a beat.

"About that hot drink, Captain Munro?"

They rode the lift back to the surface in contented silence, staying close to each other in one corner. Vash pushed open the entrance door slightly and stepped out. Rose squinted at the bright light as it flooded in. "Five seconds, Vash. I need to adjust to the light a bit."

She stepped back, and that's when she sensed movement behind her. There was a sharp prick on the side of her neck and the ground came up to meet her.

Rose reached out to Vash, but she drifted farther away as billowing black clouds closed in and finally engulfed her and everything else in a deep, bottomless abyss.

CHAPTER TWENTY-TWO

Sakas made her descent to the planet as soon as the company shuttle departed and was over a hundred klicks away. Two life signs had made their way to the mine entrance as her ship dropped down through the atmosphere and its sensors showed no others on the surface. She swiftly landed and disembarked.

The surface of the mining planet was as unappealing as it had looked from space. Penthe wasn't surprised that only a handful of people had settled on it. Its surface, scraped back to bare rock, had been scoured by eons of incessant cold winds. The snow that covered large tracts of it now only made it seem more desolate. She was glad to be in the sumptuous warmth of her quarters, following Saka's progress remotely. Sakas' vital signs in one corner of the feed indicated that she was impervious to the conditions. Stars, was the woman a bot in disguise?

"I'm going to begin a full sweep of the area, ma'am."

"Remember, Antiploi Sakas, I want this extraction to be as clean as possible. You may use extreme prejudice but keep it to the minimum," Penthe said over their comms.

"I understand, ma'am."

The system authorities weren't in any position to retaliate effectively, but any firefight might result in injury to Sakas. That would necessitate the dispatch of additional troops and cause further delay or, worse still, some form of expensive negotiation with the mining company.

Sakas made her way to the Bellerophon first. The main hatch was open, but she drew her weapon before entering and exploring. She found a man in the cold storage unit, wrapped up securely. He was unconscious, but she bent over him and shifted swiftly. Penthe was in the middle of eating a snack, and her mouth filled with bile as the bones snapped, indicating Sakas had broken his neck.

"Was that really necessary, Antiploi Sakas?"

"I must prioritise securing the surface before going into the mine, ma'am," Sakas said.

Penthe sighed but said nothing more.

The habpods were deserted. Kennels housed guardbeasts, but they were locked up. She was mildly surprised that Sakas didn't kill them as well.

The feed degraded slightly when Sakas entered the mine, but Penthe still heard the lift ascending. Sakas hid behind the large crates, hunkered down in the shadows. Rose and Munro walked past, oblivious to her presence. As Munro pushed open the door, Sakas slipped out and behind Rose, swiftly administering a sedative using a hypospray Penthe had insisted she use, worried that Rose might try to injure herself in transit. In truth, she didn't want to risk Sakas finding out anything more about the band and further fuelling whatever ambitions she might have.

Rose fell to the floor incapacitated. Munro turned and saw Sakas for the first time. She started forward, reaching for her weapon, and stopped when Sakas raised her own gun.

"Nova! I'm putting my gun down. Just don't hurt her, please."

It was fascinating to finally see Vash Munro in the flesh. She wasn't as tall as Penthe had imagined. Though, she had to grudgingly admit, she was quite pleasing to look at even though she lacked the natural beauty of Akmonian breeding. Her dreadful rough voice though. A shudder ran though her. And she had no dress sense at all. Who'd wear those drab colours? She let out a slow breath. No, she couldn't see any reason why Rose had given her a second glance. It was obviously just a matter of convenience. Well, it was better it ended this way. Munro could go back to her own people, the degenerate adventurers that had colonised this system, and Rose would be coming home to answer to hers.

Penthe nibbled delicately on the tips of her nails. Sakas and Munro were well matched physically. This was going to be interesting.

"What do you want with us?" Vash put her weapon on the floor and booted it towards Sakas, who stood in the doorway, blocking the only way out.

"I'm here to collect the property of the House of Aximendes." Sakas kept her gun trained on Munro.

"Property?" Munro's face hardened, and she narrowed her eyes. "Her name is Rose, and I don't think she's going anywhere. Not if I've anything to do with it."

Sakas sighed. "That would be unfortunate. My queen's preference, against my advice, is for this transaction to be non-violent."

Penthe was amused to see Munro looking out of the corner of her eye for anything that might serve as a weapon.

"I would counsel you, Captain Munro, that it's highly unlikely you could get to any object nearby and remain alive," Sakas said.

Vash clenched her jaw and nodded.

"Good decision." Sakas pointed towards the mine lift. "Now, please walk away from the door and get into the cage."

"You won't harm her?"

"I'm simply here to take her back. Those are my orders."

Munro walked over to the gate of the cage and pulled it open. Sakas waved her inside and reached for the control hanging inside. With one sharp yank, she snapped the wire and slammed the gate shut.

"You shouldn't have touched her, Munro. She wasn't yours to have. We're not like your kind."

Penthe sat up, ice trickling down her spine. What was Sakas doing? Why wasn't she just wrapping this up? "Sakas?"

Sakas didn't answer. They had agreed not to communicate inside the mine so that she could stay focused, but Penthe was unconvinced that was the reason she remained silent.

"I love her. You obviously don't know anything about that, or you wouldn't be doing this."

"I'm simply following my orders. Our demands have been clearly communicated to and agreed by your system authorities. Once she's back on the Aximendes VI, they'll be given the hostages and we'll be on our way."

"Still doesn't make it right though. Look at her. Fates! How can you stand there and justify condemning her to death?" Vash grasped the bars of the cage.

Sakas put her hand up to the external controls.

"You don't understand. You're an outsider. It's better this way. Now please stand back, you don't want to be injured on your journey down." She pressed the down button, and the cage began to descend.

"Please, it doesn't have to be like this. We can give you protection. Don't do this. Don't take her."

Munro's face disappeared as Sakas turned back to the entrance. Penthe smiled. Rose was hers now, and Sakas had proved her worth once again.

***

Rose floated in a dark swirling mist. Its tendrils wrapped cold around her like rotten green-grey vines. There was a faint light above. She moved her arms and legs, but they refused to co-ordinate. She tried to swim up towards it, but the effort was too great. Exhausted, she gave up. Beneath her, thunder clouds roiled and rumbled, and sharp tongues of blue-white fire licked upwards. She railed against the mist, frightened that the lightning would strike her, but it was no use. The lightning fell short and eventually stopped. She let herself rest in the mist, and her breathing returned to normal.

Silver snowflakes rose towards her. They enveloped her and lit her surroundings. Some drifted closer and touched the mist, but it didn't give way. They tried again and again in vain. She was strangely comforted by their presence and reached out, but the mist closed around her hand and arm, an unwanted shield against...what? Who or what was friend or foe here? Thunder growled again, nearer this time. The light above grew steadily brighter, and the snowflakes sank away again. She squinted. The light felt too bright but when she closed her eyes, it broke through and she lifted her hands to shield herself.

The engines roared in her ears. The glare from the low sol was cut off as the cockpit roof descended and sealed. Her arms were by her side, secured to the arms of the seat. She was strapped into a two-person craft. A fighter? The red claw logo on the helmet in front of her was so familiar, but her brain was so fuzzy. Where had she seen it before? She fought to focus her thoughts, straining every mental sinew. *The Black Team*. The special guard of the House of Aximendes. As she remembered, the mist rose around her. She took in deep breaths, praying for a few more minutes of cognition.

A distant door burst open, light silhouetting a woman running towards them. She knew her. What was her name? She strained against the harness and beat her fists on her helmet. Vash, the woman she loved, coming to get her. Tears filled her eyes, and she opened her mouth to cheer. Then the ship lifted from the ground.

In the storm of dust and rocks, Vash fell backwards. She took an age to hit the ground, her head bouncing when she did. She lay motionless on the barren ground, cruelly unprotected against the debris hitting her. Rose raised a hand, some strange spark inside her head trying to override the muddled signals coming from her addled brain, but nothing happened.

The ship's nose tilted slowly as the pilot prepared to fire the main thrusters and take them out of the planet's atmosphere. Her view of the ground, of Vash, disappeared. She slumped back, crushed by despair and defeat. Vash could be dying or dead already. A terrible wail filled the cabin. It sounded like her, but she wasn't sure. Without bidding, her helmet banged back and forth against the headrest in a terrible dark rhythm. Her feet kicked out at the seat in front, keeping time.

"What's going on back there, woman?" A harsh voice came through the helmet's speakers. "Quieten down or I'll cut the oxygen feed to your mask."

"Please…please?" Rose tried to find some words, but her vocal cords were on strike. As the g-forces struck her, the mist swirled ominously around her legs, chilling her to the bone. Her body stilled as it rose higher, anaesthetic to both her mind and body.

"Just shut up and sit still. You'll have plenty of time..."

The voice became gradually more distant until it faded completely. Everything reduced to static, hissing snakes in her ears. The ship rolled sharply, and stars sparkled against the inky blackness. The glowing blue curvature of the planet came into view, the distant sol bursting over its edge. At any other time, it would have filled her with joy. Now she just stared at the vista and shivered. Soon she would dead and drifting in the vacuum.

The only heat left in her body was in her arm where her sleeve had been pulled back. The band throbbed and glowed, more alive than ever. Her skin marched to its beat, and there was a corresponding rhythm in her head, but no connection. No sense of power. The drugs were making sure of that. Did it know it was being returned to its rightful owner?

Exhausted, she closed her eyes and let the chemical tendrils drag her back into the mists again.

CHAPTER TWENTY-THREE

Penthe stood at the observation window watching Rose. Despite the soundproofing and one-way mirror, she'd stood like this for over an hour, her mind adrift in a maelstrom of thoughts. Her hands were wrapped around the top of the guard rail so tightly that her knuckles had gone white, and her eyes were gritty from staring for so long.

She was confused by her own reaction, having spent the last five cycles imagining and sometimes yearning for this moment, indulging fantasy after fantasy in her mind. In one scene she'd be the haughty monarch, sat languidly on her sumptuous throne as the guards dragged Rose in crying. In another, the compassionate mentor wanting to help but having to do the right thing. She'd toyed with the idea of presenting herself as the raging warrior, slapping Rose to the floor with distain before executing her in person. *You'd like that, wouldn't you, Mother?*

Instead, she found herself rooted to the ground with no clear idea of what to do next. One thing was certain, she didn't want to kill her anymore. She should kill her. It was the easiest, simplest route out of all of this. The problem was that every time she imagined ordering her execution, her guts churned, and goosebumps popped up on her skin. She'd spent the last couple of days delaying a decision, and now time had run out. She clutched her head, forced to bend over with the pain behind her eyes. The voices were loud again, admonishing her weakness. She needed to quieten them.

The door handle rattled behind her. She dropped her hands guiltily and straightened up, wincing as another thunderbolt shot through her skull. Sakas came into the room and stood at her side silently. Stars, the woman moved like a bloody cat.

"My people have just transmitted news from the system authorities. It seems our prisoner's *lover*," Sakas said, "is now under arrest and in detention at the Central port. She's charged with high treason and might be executed. They sent footage. Look, it's wonderful." Sakas pressed a tablet into Penthe's hand.

Penthe took it slowly, still unable to take her eyes off Rose, who sat motionless with her hands folded on the table in front of her, staring at the door. Stood in the darkness, Penthe could see every crease in her tunic, every hair on her head. She wasn't crying. She didn't look particularly upset at all. She'd been kept in a controlled coma for over two days while she was scanned and checked over. She'd eventually been slowly awakened and left in this room. Over six hours now without a single word. No sign that she had any idea of the mortal peril she was in. Somehow, Penthe needed to change that.

"Ma'am, I still don't understand why you haven't executed her," Sakas said.

Penthe sighed. They'd already had this conversation twice, and her excuses were starting to sound feeble to her own ears. "As I have already explained, Antiploi Sakas, I wish to interrogate the prisoner. She might have valuable intelligence to share from her time in exile."

Sakas huffed. "My agents gathered a great deal of information as we followed the fugitive, ma'am. I can't see how a mere servant could add to our knowledge."

"You forget, she wears the band. There is much she could tell us about the experience." Penthe looked at Rose's arm, but there was no sign of the band hidden away under the sleeve. She had examined it while Rose was still sedated, but the strange markings had given up none of their secrets.

Saka snorted. "Ma'am, from what you have told me, if she'd experienced anything she would have used it already. Or is there something you haven't told me?"

"No, there is nothing more to be told, Antiploi Sakas." Penthe had no intention of furnishing her with any more information. She already knew too much. Sakas' eyes had lit up hungrily, too hungrily, when she had revealed that the band was a formidable weapon. Ever since she had returned and handed Rose over, Sakas had kept her distance. The atmosphere on the ship remained muted despite Penthe's meeting with her officers, and she was starting to suspect that a coup was being planned. Was Sakas plotting her downfall? Whatever the truth, it would not be prudent to confide in her.

The true nature of the band was a closely guarded secret. The House archives were clear that it was a weapon of last resort, a danger to all on the field of battle. She might have to use it; there was no denying that. But after she had read its potted history of death and destruction, she'd lain awake for hours, chilled to the bone. The House of Aximendes had only tried to use it once. She supposed the attempt could be considered a success. Certainly, it had prevented any more insurrection in the target system. That it had done so using an immense solar flare, killing every living thing, including the Akmonian observers, and rendering all the planets uninhabitable for millennia to come, was more than unfortunate. The Aximendes II had only just escaped the conflagration, and the bearer had dropped dead on the spot. After that, the band had been locked away, known only to a chosen few at the centre of the Akmonian hegemony. It was the reason why her mother had got away with bullying every other Akmonian house and why they still deferred to Penthe in any meeting.

In the end, her curiosity and ambition had finally outweighed caution. Few people would ever be in the presence of a wearer of the band. There was a risk, but she'd taken steps to minimise it. Two armed guards had been posted in the cell with instructions to shoot if anything, *anything*, unusual occurred. Two more had been posted in the observation room with control over a remote laser mounted in the ceiling of the room. She had stayed in her quarters for a full day, twisting her ring back and forth, wondering if she'd doomed them all. Nothing had happened. If Rose had any control over the band, she hadn't revealed it.

Penthe turned her attention back to the tablet Sakas had given her. The video wasn't great quality, and the images jumped around the screen. It'd obviously been taken using a concealed camera. Munro was being dragged down a corridor by burly guards. She didn't resist, but they handled her roughly anyway. There were crowds of people on both sides, braying like animals. One man stepped forward and spat in her face and another kicked out at her legs. The guards did nothing to stop them. *And they call us savages.*

Sakas' smile was thin and cold. She smiled back and let out a deep breathe. Yes, this was exactly what she needed to bring Rose to her senses. After that, she'd feel more in control again.

As she turned to hand the tablet back, a cup smashed into the window. She recoiled into Sakas who was in turn pushed violently against the wall. She only took seconds to recover her composure and started to reach for her gun. Penthe stared in shock at Rose's face pressed up against the glass.

Her features wavered, dissolved in the rivers of water.

"I know you're there, Penthe. I'm not stupid. Why don't you talk to me in person?" Rose's nose was pressed up so hard against the window that she could see the tip of it turning white.

"I'll deal with her, ma'am." Sakas, white lipped and gun drawn, edged towards the door.

Penthe raised a trembling finger. "No, I'll deal with this myself. Go back to your office and wait for me there."

Sakas stopped, one eyebrow raised. "I don't understand—"

"That's an order, Antiploi Sakas." There was no time for this. "I said, I'll deal with her."

"I'll summon the guard," Sakas said.

"No. I wish to speak to her in private." She looked into Sakas' eyes, daring her to argue again. "If I require assistance, I'll call for it myself. Now, leave."

Sakas slammed the door behind her, and Penthe wiped the sweat from her brow. Yes, she'd have to deal with Sakas. Her insubordination wasn't just dangerous, it could be terminal. She used her personal code to switch off the vidrecording module. She also locked the door to the observation room as she left. Standing in the silence of the corridor, she adopted a detached expression before opening the door to the interrogation room.

Rose sat at the table for a moment as if nothing had happened. Then she rolled up her sleeves, slowly and deliberately. Penthe gasped at the sight of the band's sinuous glowing dance. If it hurt, Rose gave no sign. Her face remained composed. Still sporting green eyes, Penthe noted with disgust. Only spies and traitors chose to hide the beautiful, unique blue-gold eyes of an Akmonian. Well, that would change when the medics removed the offending gland. There was a pool of water under the mirrored window, and the cup lay dented and discarded in the middle of it. She would ignore that for now. "I think it's customary for the interrogator to dictate the pace of the interview." She sat down opposite Rose and crossed her legs. "Wouldn't you agree?"

Rose looked at her, and Penthe fought an urge to shy away from her piercing stare.

"Is this a typical interview? The queen herself doing the questioning?" Rose's upper lip started to curl into a sneer, but she seemed to catch herself and her expression returned to one of disinterest.

"I'd hoped we might keep this civil. We do know each—"

Rose flung back her head and laughed, a harsh cackle that bounced off the walls. "You drag me here to kill me, hurting and killing the people I love, and talk of keeping things civil?"

Penthe sat back, momentarily speechless. She stroked her throat, acutely aware of her heartbeat. Where had all this strength come from? Rose had always been so timid, so eager to please. This new Rose was far more intriguing, more attractive. She chided herself. *Remember the struggle to reach this point.* This wasn't the time to be weak, it was time to be queen. Whatever was going on with Rose, she needed to come to heel.

"I have something to show you, Rose, something I'm sure will interest you." Penthe slid the tablet across the table and activated the screen. As the vid ran, Rose's eyes didn't leave the screen, and light from the images played across her face. Penthe fancied she could almost taste her pain. It was exquisite. "So, you see, Rose, it isn't looking at all good for your *friend.* Poor dear. I don't think she'll be riding to your rescue any time soon. I understand she's going to be executed for treason. There'll be a trial of course, but she doesn't seem to have any friends left, does she?"

Rose didn't twitch a muscle, but her eyes darkened and narrowed slightly.

Good, she was getting the message. Penthe smoothed back her hair. "It's strange, but I was told not so long ago that Munro would never allow you to be captured. Of course, in hindsight, the man giving the advice wasn't the brightest star in the universe."

Still Rose just watched the screen in silence.

Enough! She swept the tablet onto the floor, where it fizzed and popped in protest. "Are you listening to me, Rose? She isn't coming for you. It's just you and me now." She slapped her palm down. "You'd do well to show me a little more respect."

Rose closed her eyes, as if in pain. Had she finally cut through her façade? But when she opened them again, she had simply discarded the last vestiges of her disguise. Her eyes blazed their true azure and gold, channelling an internal inferno so furious that Penthe flinched.

"Yes, I heard you, Penthe." Rose pushed herself to her feet and started to move around the table. "Now, you'll listen to me."

Hypnotised by the menace in those eyes and that voice as cold as ice, the hairs stood on the back of Penthe's neck. She started to move without a conscious decision. Her chair flew backwards, clattering as it hit the wall, but she didn't stop. There was an intensity in Rose's face that was truly terrifying. She looked in desperation to the observation window but remembered there was no one there. Why had she sent Sakas away? How could she have been so stupid, so arrogant? Her back was against the door now, and its cold chill bled through the thin cloth, matching the icy fear that held her in its grip.

"I don't care what you want, Penthe. I really don't. You've taken everything from me. My family, my dignity, and now, the woman I love."

Penthe tensed in anticipation.

"So, I suggest that you just get on and kill me. That's what you brought me back for isn't it, *my queen*. In fact, why don't you just go ahead and do it now." Rose gestured at Penthe's belt, turned away and knelt to the ground. With a strange ceremonial formality, she lifted her head and exposed her throat. "Whenever you're ready, ma'am."

Penthe looked down at her, the beautiful line of her neck and her proud stance. Her fingers brushed the crystal handle of the ceremonial knife on her belt and wrapped tentatively around it. The room blurred around the edges. Where had all the oxygen gone? The blade emerged slowly, its ornately engraved edge glinting in the harsh white light. She recalled all those times Rose had dressed her. She'd always left this knife until last, almost reverently attaching it to her belt. The knife that had been given to her by her mother, drawn specially from the House treasury for her use. The only gift she ever gave.

Penthe turned it one way and another and traced the lines of the decoration.

She held out her arm and dropped it. It spun away into the pool of water, small waves racing across the surface. She opened the door and gazed, unseeing, at the spartan corridor beyond. Behind her, there was no sound, no movement. With no words, no coherent thoughts left in her, she stepped through and closed the door behind her.

CHAPTER TWENTY-FOUR

For a while after the door clicked shut, Rose kept her chin raised. Her head throbbed painfully, though whether from adrenaline or the effects of the band she couldn't tell. All her muscles ached, fatigued now from hours spent living on her wits.

The lingering mists of confusion left by being deeply drugged had slowly given way to a simmering cauldron of angry bitterness inside. What did she have to live for now that Vash was gone? She'd lain in the medical bay and ignored everyone around her, determined to refuse to help with the simplest request. If they wanted her to sit, walk or shit, they'd have to make her. Her days of timid compliance were over.

She listened intently, trying to ignore the burning in her knees. The metal floor had shallow grooves in it, perhaps to make it easier to clean up any mess. It certainly made her position painful to maintain. There was only silence. No footsteps in the corridor or voices nearby. She still didn't dare move, not quite yet. She had risked too much already to fail now.

When they had first moved her in here, she'd been bewildered. Every part of her was on high alert, muscles tensed for violence. Yet, here she was, completely unharmed. What was Penthe up to? Rose had always assumed, darkly, that the easiest way to retrieve the band was just to kill its host and force it to return to its physical form. Was this just a perverse interlude before the inevitable?

However, with the drugs completely gone, her returning memories had offered a thin sliver of hope. The images of Vash being thrown to the ground as the fighter took off haunted her. The sight of her lying there, probably dead, was unbearable. She tried to push them away, but the pain left her on the edge of tears she didn't want to gift to those who observed her. However, a niggling doubt had crept in. Had Vash moved? Dirt and grit had flown in all directions in the deadly turbulence from the engines of Sakas' ship. Any movement could just have been Vash being blown around like everything else. But what if it was something more? The more she stretched and scoured her mind for answers, the hazier the images got. But that glimmer of another outcome lit a hot flame inside her. A flame that drove away the shadows of her own fears. Somehow, if Vash still lived, it wasn't so bad.

Desperate for answers, she'd reluctantly decided to see if the band could help. As soon as she'd woken, the sensation of her skin rippling and buzzing had returned. But she hadn't considered using it to save her life. She needed to know about Vash. So, she made a new vow to use it passively and as little as possible. The people on this ship were still her people. They weren't responsible for Penthe's actions any more than she was. The thought of them getting harmed because of the band made her flesh crawl. She sat quietly and sent it a firm mental invitation. *Show me what you can do to help me.* She hadn't had to wait long. To both her dismay and elation, it had responded willingly to her mental overtures, as if it had just been patiently waiting for her to see sense.

Firstly, it had alerted her to Penthe's arrival. Somewhat randomly, it had done so by flooding her mouth with a taste of rich spices. Without quite knowing how, she'd known immediately it was Penthe, confirmed by the whiff of her favourite scent which the band helpfully offered as an afterthought. She'd swallowed rapidly. What was she unleashing here? However, with nowhere else to turn, she'd quickly expressed a wish to see the queen and found herself in the darkened space, looking through the window at herself. Penthe was very still. The queen seemed to be deeply focused on her, and Rose's mind had raced again trying to work out what she was thinking.

She'd had an outrageous idea that left her momentarily breathless. Concentrating as hard as she could and diving deep inside herself, she'd tentatively communicated a desire to see Penthe's thoughts. She swam that endless silvery river at the centre of her consciousness, making the request repeatedly with different words and images, while the symbols and lights of the band washed around her, carrying her on the flood.

Just as she was on the brink of giving up, sure that she had reached the natural limits of the band's powers, or just hers, it had accepted her request. Penthe's consciousness, like a fractal flower with petals of thoughts, memories, and senses, had unfolded before her. She still had her eyes open, but the room had disappeared, replaced by a hazy doorway that she drifted though. Unfortunately, or perhaps fortunately, the union was brief. Almost immediately she was driven back by a terrible swirling darkness and strange howling shrieks that carried on the wind of Penthe's consciousness. The connection had slammed shut, but not before she had witnessed the vortex of rage and shame there, raw emotions so strong that even now their fading remnants scratched and mewed in Rose's mind still. The strength of the shame was confusing. Penthe had always seemed so confident, never one for self-reflection. Had she put on a facade while she wandered the internal storms of her madness alone? And it was madness, there could be no doubting that. No one could endure what was going on in her mind and not be driven insane by it. Whatever the truth, the veracity of the experience could not be denied. It had taken all of Rose's willpower to resist the urge to be sick in the aftermath, and she had reassessed the band's reluctance. It had perhaps tried to protect her, not hinder her.

Which left only one course of action: confronting Penthe in the flesh. In retrospect, throwing the cup to get her attention had been dangerously childish. Penthe hadn't been alone behind that window. Increasingly comfortable with the band, she sensed another enter the observation room. She didn't waste time investigating further but, whoever it was, their aura had definitely flared. The taste of cold hard metal had been overpowering, causing her teeth to spark painfully. But it had dissipated, and Penthe had come in alone. Somehow that had been apt. In a way they were both alone now, facing their inner demons. She struggled to bear the band, while Penthe struggled with her very mind. How could anyone else have joined them and understood, when so much had not been said?

She probed the observation room. It was still empty. There were no remote cameras visible either, but that didn't mean there weren't any. Still, she couldn't stay here forever. Wetting her lips, she relaxed her head and took a deep breath. There was still no sound, so she reached out for the edge of the table. Using it for support, she managed to get to her feet. Her knees were screaming at her now, and she staggered to the chair and slumped into it.

I have changed. She was no longer the scared young woman that Penthe played with at will. Yes, offering her throat had been a risk. But deep inside she'd known the bluff would work. Somewhere along the way she'd grown up, got some backbone, and Penthe obviously didn't expect that. If Penthe was still predictable, Rose no longer was.

Penthe had unwittingly told Rose all she needed to know when she showed her the footage. Watching Vash suffer at the hands of her own people had been sickening, but she was alive. Alive. She'd wanted to scream with relief, and she might have if Penthe hadn't gloated. Executed for treason? Penthe probably believed she'd dealt a knockout blow to her spirit when she'd really gifted her a reason to live. The fire inside Rose burnt brighter and hotter than ever.

She pulled herself upright in the chair despite the terrible leaden fatigue weighing her down. Using the band's powers drained her of energy. Perhaps it was because she still didn't know the exact ways she could and was still feeling her way around. She'd no time to lose though. From what she had seen and heard, Vash was in terrible danger.

Her inner eye opened the moment her eyelids dropped down. She sought that silver stream at the centre of her consciousness. As she did so, the skin on her forearm grew hotter. Each time she did it, the route was becoming easier to find. She was able now to identify some of the patterns as they swirled and flowed. She followed them as they moved and beckoned to her, immersed herself in the flow as it streamed through her mind and into a place that was outside space and time. At times she heard a voice behind the stream, but it was too indistinct to understand.

However, one thing Rose did understand now was how to make the request. The key was not to ask directly. Instead, she simply offered the band images of Vash, her feelings of love and concern for her. As she expressed her deep yearning, she sensed a subtle shift in her reality. She was there, stood in front of Vash in her cell.

Vash sat on a cot in a spartan white cell, head in her hands. Rose reached out to comfort her, but her hands passed through Vash as though she was mist. She berated herself for her stupidity. *I'm not really here, remember.*

"Vash, darling, what have they…what have I done to you?" She knelt in front of her, desperate to see her face.

Vash lifted her head and for one hopeful second, she thought that Vash had heard her, but it was a guard standing behind the barred door.

"Rules say we have to feed prisoners."

His expression suggested he didn't think much of the idea. He lifted a bowl containing grey lumps of something swimming in a greasy broth. He spat heavily into it. Twice.

"Hope you enjoy it."

The bowl slid through a hatch at the bottom of the door, helped on by his dirty boot. Vash sighed as he walked away. She wiped her hand across her face, still swollen and bruised from Jakub's fist, and there was now a nasty cut under one eye and some dried blood beneath one of her ears. Vash walked over to the bowl and stared at it. After a few seconds she went back to the cot and lay down on it, eyes closed.

Tears pricked at Rose's eyes. "Just hang on in there, Vash, just hang on." With the band now an eager helper, she willed herself through the cell door to orientate herself with the surrounds. It was at the end of a short corridor, one of a set of three cells. The guard had returned to his messy desk at the other end, in an alcove just before it turned a corner. He sat sprawled in a chair that was a size too small for him. His dirty shirt had sprung open, revealing a white hairy belly, and she recoiled with disgust. There was no one else.

Taking a deep, steadying breath, she took a shortcut. As she had hours before with Penthe, she strove to gain access to his mind. The distance made this so much harder, and a tickling sensation under her nostrils suggested that her nose had started to bleed with the effort. A taste of sour sweat and rancid grease filled her mouth. Rose bore down on the terrible nausea and redoubled her mental efforts. It would be such a wonderful thing if she could just see into his consciousness, she suggested in her mind. This time, the band understood quickly. Was it learning from her as well? Unlike Penthe's mind, there was nothing complex or scary beyond the doorway here, just an endless grey tundra of turgid boredom. His thoughts and emotions appeared as oily ponds and half-dead trees. She wasn't sure where to start but the band started to translate, overlaying objects with text. Probing gently forward with its help, Rose eventually found what she was looking for. A small tweak and it was done. The guard's eyes closed, and he started snoring loudly.

Manipulating the magnetic lock on Vash's cell door was much easier. It only took a few moments. However, she paused briefly, aware that the band had grown stronger. It was as if each well-meaning request was fuelling it within her. Its symbiosis with her consciousness had spread and woven into her neural pathways like some invasive vine. Each new request offered it fresh routes. For the moment, it seemed content to do her bidding, but its power pulsed at her core. Would there be a point when she became the tool, and the band dictated what she did?

Momentarily panicked, she weighed up her limited options. However, as she started to explore them, there was movement at the door. Vash's head appeared slowly and peeked out into the corridor. Seemingly satisfied, she stepped out and walked cautiously down to the guard's desk. She paused in front of him and examined him silently with a look of disgust on her face.

The sight of Vash, freed from that dreadful cell, removed any uncertainty. Whatever the consequences might be, right now her priority was getting Vash out of that awful place. She considered briefly finding her way into Vash's mind to communicate. The band could make it happen of course, but something inside shied away from such an intrusion into Vash's privacy. So, she quickly looked for another solution. The guard's console sprang into life. The taste of blood was stronger in her mouth now, and she prayed the gods would give her the strength to finish this.

HELLO VASH ROSE.

She watched Vash's face as she leaned in, eyes widening at the sight of the text.

NO TIME EXPLAIN BIG DANGER.

"Rose, is that you?" Vash touched the screen.

PLEASE DON'T BE SCARED

"Please don't be scared, she says." Vash swore softly and looked around as if hoping to see her.

ON AXIMENDES VI HAVE TO GET YOU OUT

"Well, I don't like to point out the obvious, my beautiful, but there are a shit load of guards and soldiers between me and the docks. Unless you can make me invisible, I don't see how I'm going to get there."

MAKE YOU INVISIBLE

Vash tensed. Rose swallowed hard, but there was no time to properly prepare her for what was going to happen next.

MIGHT MAKE YOU FEEL WEIRD

Every instinct told her she could do this. Somehow the band itself was egging her on, following her thought processes, the tendrils of the band sliding further into deepest parts of her consciousness. A strange stream of energy burst from her and crossed the time and space between them. Vash doubled up, grabbed the side of the table, and vomited explosively into the guard's lap. She panted hard. Mucus dripped unhindered from her nose as she clutched her gut. Rose held her breath. Was Vash hurt? After a few moments Vash straightened up slowly and wiped her face.

"See what you mean," she said weakly. "To be honest, weird doesn't really cover it."

Using the wall for support, she staggered around the corner and up to the exit door.

"Listen, I hope you're right, Rose, but if you aren't, thanks for trying. I mean it."

Tears rolled down her face as Vash listened for a few seconds before she pulled the door open. The corridor appeared to be empty. Vash didn't hesitate and made her way up it as quietly as she could. She rounded a corner, and a soldier came into view at the far end, marching towards her. Vash pulled up, but it was too late to go back. She splayed herself flat against the wall as he walked past her. He stopped at a door on the corner and let himself in. He whistled under his breath before the door shut.

"Nova!" Vash whispered. "What have you done, Rose?"

Celebrating, the dreadful pain in her head forgotten for the moment, she heard the trepidation in Vash's voice, and it cut her to the core. Vash wasn't elated, she was just scared. Scared of her and scared of the band. She shuddered. *What have I done? I have done what was needed, whatever the price. Vash is safe.* A terrible thunderbolt of pain shot through her head and chest in reply, and her left arm started to go numb. Her body was finally giving up on her. She couldn't judge her own actions; others would have to do that. Perhaps the galaxy would be a safer place. Yes, she'd used the band and broken the promise she'd made to herself, made to the universe; but she had done so out of love, and hopefully one day Vash would understand. An invisible fist was curling around her throat now, squeezing it and making each breath harder than the last. It was time to say goodbye. There was a control console a little way further down and she focused on it. The numbers disappeared.

GOT TO GO NO ENERGY BE SAFE ALWAYS LOVE YOU.

Vash walked up and put her hand over the text.

"Don't go, Rose. Please."

Rose pulled back into her physical body. She struggled to stay, screaming at the band for just a few more words, but she'd spent the last of her energy with that final message. Defeated, she allowed the band to take her back knowing she had no choice but to trust it and to hope that it had understood her frenzied communication about the need for Vash to remain invisible long enough to get safely to the docks. If Vash could just make it that far, she was wily enough to get hold of a ship.

Returned fully to her body, Rose opened her eyes and squinted in the harsh light of the cell. Her vision was streaked with red, and there was blood all over her hands. More had already dripped and pooled on the floor. Now darker clots joined the torrent from her nose and ears, splashing into the puddle below. *Be safe, my love.* Toppling forward, she fell into the welcoming arms of oblivion.

CHAPTER TWENTY-FIVE

The sollight streamed in from an open window, falling on Penthe as she sat and worked. She looked up and frowned, a sense of something out of place, but relaxed again. The breeze tugging at the loose cotton drapes was pleasantly warm on her skin. There was no sound in the room. Occasionally she heard voices outside the window, but they hadn't distracted her from her piece of embroidery a great deal. She frowned again and looked down what she was doing. When had she ever been able to embroider? But her fingers continued to move confidently across the cloth, adding more and more intricate detail. To what though?

There was a faint memory of working on this embroidery before. When had that been? Oh, yes, the night her mother had died. *When I murdered her*. She twisted around to see where the sibilant whisper had come from, but the room was still empty. Had she started this embroidery in mourning? A small noise came from behind, and she turned, straining her neck to look at the vidscreen by the door. It showed her sat in the same room, head bent over, and the tip of her tongue poking out with concentration. There was a lot of noise outside the window. Now movement, a face at the window. Penthe shouted at whoever it was to go away. The screen flickered and faded as Rose came into view, standing there looking sad. Penthe sniffed and wiped at her eyes.

She held the cloth out and examined what she was creating. Acid bile flooded her mouth, and she gagged. It was the face of her mother. One of the eyes winked at her, and the image's mouth opened, wider and wider. She dropped it, but it fell achingly slow to the floor and a foul stench emanated from the black maw. Blood dripped from the cloth onto the mosaic beneath her feet. The mosaic was an image of Rose, kneeling and offering her throat. It was covered now by an expanding pool of dark red blood, and a scream sounded out, getting louder and louder—

Penthe opened her eyes, the echo of her scream still ringing in her ears. She was stood in the centre of her reception room, alone. Was this real?

And how was she supposed to tell? A time display on the wall caught her attention, and the blinking numbers hypnotised her for a moment. Fates, she must have been in that room for hours. Of course, she'd been trapped in her mind. Perspiration from her brow dripped and stained the sleeve of her dress. It was so hot in here. What if she'd been wandering the ship in this state?

Her mother stared down at her from the wall, the portrait uncovered once again. Of course, it was the same image as on the embroidery. Penthe walked towards it, mutinous legs nearly giving way, and stood in the glare of the icy gaze. Her mind filled with the image of Rose knelt on the floor, throat offered.

"You got too close to her."

Her mother stood in front of her. The reality of her proud, haughty figure only betrayed by a faint haziness at the edges.

"She was kind to me, Mother, something that you wouldn't understand."

"Don't make excuses. Only the weak make excuses. You should've executed her for being so familiar.

Penthe sighed. "I didn't have the authority, Mother. Remember? Besides, I—"

"And now you hesitate to do the right thing. Instead, she is still alive, and you have failed to take back what she stole from us."

Penthe covered her mouth with her hand, afraid of the words trying to fight their way out. *I didn't want to admit to you or anyone, even to myself maybe, that I wanted to be loved.* It was the shameful truth. She'd never wanted to kill Rose; she had just been scared witless by what Rose had represented. Not some romantic notion of love, but the simple act of caring for another, a desire for them to be happy. Instead of embracing that, she'd driven her away, hurt and belittled her. It was little wonder that Rose had run. And not content with forcing her into exile, Penthe had chased her halfway across the galaxy, causing her still more pain. Penthe wrapped her hands around her head. *Rose, please forgive me.*

The phantom snorted. "To think I gave up my body and my looks to have you. I would've been better off terminating the pregnancy."

Penthe flinched. A life spent yearning for approval or at least for understanding, just to hear this. Even now, from beyond the grave, all her mother offered was harsh, uncompromising criticism. Tears filled her eyes, and she pinched the back of her hand viciously. The skin between her fingers turned a bluish white with the promise of a bad bruise later. *Don't cry. It will only be worse if she sees me crying.* She saw again the body bag containing the young princess, killed for failing or perhaps for just being too *familiar.*

"You always were such a disappointment, Penthesilea. Did you think I didn't know how you cried for that stupid girl? You never understood. Only the fittest survive." Her mother's phantom started to fade. "Until you learn to wield power properly, you'll never be a true queen, Penthesilea."

Her fingertips reached out, desperate to cling onto the phantom. "Help me, Mother. Help me lead this great House into a new golden age, to follow the example of our ancestors and be respected as traders, not reviled as murderers. Is it wrong to want to rule by the willing consent of our people and not through fear?"

The stony face looked down from the painting once again. A voice did answer, but it was quite different.

"I'm sorry, ma'am. I thought you were alone."

She spun and looked at the young maid who was stood in the doorway. The girl blanched immediately at Penthe's expression and bowed her head reverently. Penthe looked down at her, seeing another young girl fresh to service. Another life devoted to thankless servitude. She seemed to represent everything that was wrong, everything that had led her to this moment. "I'm alone, girl." *I have always been alone.* "What do you want?"

The maid kept her eyes lowered. "There's been a message, ma'am. The prisoner has been found injured in the interrogation—"

Penthe grabbed her shoulders with both hands, her heart threatening to burst from her chest. "Injured! Injured how?"

"I do not have any more detail, ma'am. I'm sor—"

The rest was lost as she pushed past her roughly. As she burst from her quarters, the other maids shouted excitedly, but their voices soon receded. The corridors were endless. She ignored the curious looks, her mind too full of dreadful images. Had Sakas returned? Had Rose hurt herself? White corridor after white corridor, her anxiety spiralled.

Sakas stood outside the entrance to the sickbay in conversation with the chief medical officer. She turned as Penthe strode up to them and immediately backed away.

"Is this your doing, Antiploi?" Penthe roughly pushed her against the wall, channelling all her fury to pin her there with one hand against her chest, the other unconsciously going to where her knife would have been if she had not left it with Rose.

Sakas put her hand over Penthe's, her eyes wide with shock. "I don't know what you're talking about. I've only just arrived myself."

The doctor moved closer. "If I might interrupt, ma'am, perhaps I could explain."

"So, explain!" There were spots dancing in her vision, and she was hotter than ever.

The doctor flushed but stood her ground. "The prisoner was found collapsed in the interrogation cell, ma'am. She'd haemorrhaged badly. We're not sure of the cause. There was no sign of external injury, and emergency scans have revealed no obvious internal cause. We've administered a transfusion and are keeping her under close observation."

She let go of Sakas and put a hand against the wall to steady herself.

"Will she be all right? She will recover?" She could do with a chair; her legs didn't seem to belong to her anymore. All those cycles rehearsing Rose's death and here she was, weak with relief that she was alive. Penthe swallowed a desire to laugh as her emotions warred for supremacy.

The doctor nodded. "She'll make a full recovery, ma'am. It's just a matter of time."

As her panic subsided, she became acutely aware of how she must look. *You always were such a disappointment, Penthesilea.* She hurriedly smoothed down her clothes and pushed her hair back from her face. Sakas moved away, a dark expression on her face. The doctor simply looked concerned, which was worse. "Take me to her immediately."

The doctor led the way to a small clean room, which smelled of acrid cleaning agents. At the foot of the medibed, she looked down at Rose. Her face was drawn and dark circles ringed her eyes. Lines ran into her arms and sensors on her head fed constant data to the display on the wall above her. The numbers meant nothing to Penthe, but to her relief they were all green.

The band pulsated on Rose's bare arm, beating out a rhythm that didn't quite correspond to the vital signs being displayed. Had Rose been exploring the band's powers, and this was the result? The archives told of how dangerous that could be. Many had apparently tried to harness its power, only to fail and pay with their lives. Sometimes their failure had cost others their lives as well. No queen for generations had dared be the direct keeper of the band. Icy fingers wrapped around her spine as she considered the ramifications of what Rose had done.

Rose's eyes fluttered open. She looked dazed when she glanced up at Penthe before scanning the room.

"Where am I?" she asked.

Sakas stood close by. "You are, only by the mercy of your queen, in the care of the ship's doctor. What happened to make you collapse?"

Rose looked from Sakas to Penthe and back to Sakas. "I don't know. I was sitting quietly and then…I woke up and I was in here."

Sakas snorted. "You expect us to believe you. You've been hiding poison so that you could escape justice, haven't you?"

She went to walk past, but Penthe put out a hand and stopped her. "Thank you, Antiploi Sakas."

Sakas looked up at her, then down at the hand on her arm. For a moment she looked as if she was going to say something but decided not to. Instead, she walked to the wall at the back of the room and leaned against it. Penthe could feel her gaze of harsh judgment burning into the back of her head.

"Rose, I think we both know what happened." She observed Rose's face carefully, looking for any sign of acknowledgment but she gave nothing away. "I know it was the band, Rose. I'm not stupid."

Sakas stirred and took a sudden intake of breath as she finally comprehended what was going on.

Rose stayed composed. "What if I said it was the band and that I was using it? What would you do, Penthe?"

"You'll address your queen correct—"

"Interrupt me once again, antiploi," Penthe turned and glared at Sakas, "and I'll have you thrown in the brig."

Sakas threw up her hands in frustration, her eyes angry slits, a further sign if one was needed that their uneasy alliance was in its final throes. The only action that might repair it was one Penthe wasn't prepared to entertain. Instead, she returned her focus to Rose. "If you'd used the band and succeeded where so many had failed, I'd be in awe of you." Rose blushed before she turned her face towards the wall.

"Queen Penthesilea in awe of me? That would be a first."

Penthe sat on the medibed next to her and took her hand. How warm it felt while Rose's face was still so deathly pale. Was this how it felt to be at one with the band? "Rose, tell me the truth."

Rose clenched and unclenched her jaw. "Yes, I've used the band or perhaps it used me. I don't really know, but whatever happened, it's part of me now whether I like it or not. If you want it, you'll have to kill me."

Penthe's chest tightened, and pins and needles travelled the length of her arms. Her vision narrowed, and she fought to stay present as the room within her mind beckoned again. There were two clear paths in front of her: a well-lit doorway leading to a blood-spattered corridor lined with portraits of her forebears, and a dimmer corridor, empty and unfamiliar. To follow the path ordained by others, she would have to kill the only person who had ever cared about her. With Rose by her side, the new future had a slim chance. Her mother dead, the only judgment that counted now was that of her people. Would they understand, or was the damage done over the past few generations too great? Rose was the key; she had the strength of purpose. But Rose had no reason to care, only reason to hate. Penthe stared at the numbers on the monitor, the neon lines flowing endlessly across its screen and wanted to scream for more time to decide, but there was no time left now. As she made the decision, the bands around her chest started to release and the pressure behind her eyes eased. "Rose. There's something I would like to ask you. Something I've no right to ask, but…" She looked into Rose's eyes, trying to communicate the sincerity of what she was about to say. "Will you consent to be my consort?" The words fell out into the space between them.

Rose's eyes widened.

"No!" Sakas' shriek made them both jump.

Penthe was tugged back from the medibed and thrown hard to the ground. Her elbow hit one of its struts with a sickening thud as she fell.

Sakas stood above her, face suffused with blood and fury. "You'd marry this slut? This traitor?"

Penthe grabbed for the edge of the medibed, dazed. "You…you forget yourself, Sakas. How dare you lay hands upon me."

Sakas laughed harshly. "You didn't say that the last time we fucked, *my queen*." She stalked away, spun around, and strode back, pointing her finger. "All the things I've done for you, all my service. Not once did I ever presume. Not once." She pressed her face close to Penthe's, her voice deadly calm. "Never though, did I imagine you would lower yourself to this, to her."

Sakas spat in Rose's direction, but she didn't flinch, and the sight gave Penthe renewed strength. Ignoring the pain in her arm, she pulled herself up tall. "You don't understand, Sakas." She shook her head. Sakas had never meant anything to her; she'd made it clear their tryst was a mere dalliance. "If she has control of the band, I must move immediately to protect this House and its fortunes." It sounded weak, but she couldn't bring herself to express the truth. She had hoped for more time to work on her new vision. Ironically, Sakas might still be part of it, if only she would listen.

"Kill her as she suggests and take back the band. A true queen would never lower herself in this way. How can you permit a mere servant to carry the band and walk at your side?"

"She is not a mere servant. She is the bearer of the band. She has survived symbiosis and managed to control it. That is a rare thing, and I can't ignore it, Sakas."

Sakas looked unconvinced. "If this puny woman can bear it, imagine what I could do with it for you. Make me your consort, and we will rule the galaxy. All will bow down to us."

Penthe glanced down at Rose. For the first time there was real understanding in her eyes. She smiled ruefully. "If only it was that simple, Sakas. However, the records make it clear that physical strength is no guarantee of success. Some of our greatest warriors have tried and failed in the past."

Rose winced. How much did she know about the band?

"What Rose has achieved is something so remarkable, it will probably not happen again in our lifetime. The truth is, I need her by my side if this House is to become the greatest that it can be." Penthe held out a hand to Sakas. "You have to trust me, even if you don't understand."

"What is there to understand? You're our queen. The highest office, the greatest privilege. All that is asked of you is that you serve us with honour. Where is the honour in this?" Sakas' eyes teared up.

Fates. What more could she say to make her comprehend? But before she could utter a word, Sakas drew her gun.

"No, Sakas, I forbid it." Penthe fought to keep her voice calm, though her insides were churning. The pulse on Sakas' neck came into sharp focus, her own heart only beating a fraction faster.

Sakas lowered the gun slightly. "Either you permit me to do what you are obviously not capable of doing, ma'am or…" She glared at Penthe, as if daring her to disagree, and her finger tightened on the trigger.

"Or what, Sakas?" Penthe knew, but she needed to hear it. The bond between them was stretched to its limit. Her very connection to this House was on the brink of snapping, and she didn't care anymore. Given the choice between her throne and Rose, only Rose and the simple love that she represented was worth having. That understanding unlocked a serenity within her that she'd believed she would never know. It was as if a light switched on inside her, driving all the darkness within back into the shadows, where it belonged. All the cycles of pain and expectation fell from her shoulders.

She gently put her hand over the cold, hard barrel of the gun and smiled. "You'll have to kill me first, Sakas."

Sakas didn't respond. She didn't need to, her stony expression said it all. She re-holstered her gun, turned, and walked out of the room. Penthe looked at the door. What would happen next, exile or death? Would she die on her way back to her quarters or before a council of her peers? Perhaps she would be permitted to kill herself, rather than wait to feel the shells ripping into her chest.

"Penthe? What just happened?"

Rose's voice brought her back. She turned back to her and looked at the woman who had been the cause of all of this. "I think I just signed my own death warrant, Rose." Rose's face changed. She couldn't work out what she was thinking, but it didn't matter anymore.

"I'm so sorry, Penthe. Well, I'm not sorry for what I've done, but I'm sorry for you. I only ever wanted you to be happy, you know," Rose said.

Penthe looked down to see Rose was squeezing her gently. This woman, who she'd abused in ways that no person should be abused, was holding her hand, and trying to comfort her. The room blurred as tears started to trickle down her face.

"Is there anything I can do? I mean, I can't accept your proposal, but I think you already knew that." Rose's voice was quiet, filled with compassion. "Still, I could perhaps do something to help."

"You mean, use the band? No, you mustn't do that. Not for me." And she meant it. She didn't want to be rescued. "It's all over now." She wiped at her eyes and took a deep breath. "Did you use the band to rescue

Munro?"

A flicker of uncertainty crossed Rose's face and she nodded. "I did. I think she's safe and that's enough. What happens to me doesn't matter now."

She envied the simple love in her voice. Rose had found what Penthe had searched for all her life without really knowing it. "You should try to rescue yourself now and get off this ship. It's going to become a very dangerous place in the next few hours. I wish I could help but in truth, you're better off keeping as far away from me as possible."

She walked to the door and glanced back to see Rose propped up awkwardly on one hand, face flushed with the effort.

"Penthe." Rose bowed her head. "My queen."

Penthe smiled, and her heart ached in an entirely new way than she was used to. She bowed back and walked out to face her people, her destiny.

CHAPTER TWENTY-SIX

Penthe had barely made it back to her quarters when she heard heavy boots pounding down the corridor. The door burst open, and Sakas entered, flanked by a group of senior officers. She ignored them for the moment and considered her former lover and ally. She guessed she was meant to be cowed, expected to beg for her life. Her pulse rose, it was true, but with anger rather than fear. She set her jaw and stared straight into Sakas' flushed, self-righteous face. She wasn't particularly surprised that after a few moments it was Sakas that gave way, her gaze sliding away towards the port window. Penthe held her destiny in her own hands. "It's customary to acknowledge your queen, Sakas, even if you *have* come to kill her."

The sight of Sakas' cheeks colouring made her want to laugh, but she held it in. The entourage looked a bit sheepish in the face of their queen's quiet dignity. Good. If she was going to die, it was vital they understood the import of what they were doing.

After a small hesitation, Sakas offered a desultory bow. "My queen, I'm here—"

"To kill me. Yes, I know. Do you mind if I sit down? I'd prefer to be comfortable while we discuss my imminent death."

She walked over to her desk, knowing their eyes were following her every move for any sign of her trying to protect herself. However, she had no intention of playing into their hands by reaching for any of the many weapons that were secreted in the furniture. Instead, she sat and casually crossed her legs. "What happens now? Will you execute me here or perhaps you'd like there to be a trial? I'm sure there's a precedent for that."

"Shut up," Sakas said.

Penthe smiled and didn't miss the look of discomfort on the faces of Sakas' co-conspirators. Sakas, either oblivious or past caring, tugged her gun from its holster. Pulse pounding in her throat, Penthe's focus was reduced to the small evil hole at the end of the barrel. Only cycles of training and a deep ingrained arrogance kept her back straight and her chin high. If she was to die today, she would do so with dignity. “Who will be our queen now, Sakas? You?” Penthe asked quietly.

“Queen? What do you mean?” Sakas’ brow furrowed, and her gun hand fell to her side.

“I’m sorry, I’d assumed you’d replace me after my death.” Penthe bit the inside of her mouth as the officers, in unison, found something extremely interesting to look at on the floor. She’d been right; Sakas wanted it all. “Am I wrong, *antiploi*?”

“What happens to the Crown, to this House, is no longer your business, Penthe.” Sakas raised her gun again.

Penthe noted the use of her name and not her title. She looked past Sakas at the officers standing by the door. “Thank you for coming. I ask, as senior officers of this great House, that you bear witness that I willingly relinquish the throne and all authority that comes with it. I’m no longer worthy of the crown. I place myself in your hands and accept the will of the people.” Her heart lightened as she spoke. If she couldn’t bring change, she didn’t want this anymore. Someone else could take on the burden.

The tip of Sakas’ gun quivered. “This is a trick, don’t be fooled. We know what we’ve come here to do,” she said.

Penthe ignored her and maintained eye contact with the others. “It’s been an honour and a privilege to serve you. I know I can trust you with the safekeeping of the House of Aximendes.” The pleasure of speaking the truth, with no pretence or augmentation, was wonderful. These women had only ever offered her loyal service. They had followed her and fought for her, despite her many failings. She had no reason to believe she was better than they were.

Sakas stepped close enough that she could feel the warmth of her breath. “What are you up to, Penthe?” she hissed in a low voice. She glanced back towards the officers. “There can be no question of her leaving this room alive. She’s a dangerous traitor.”

“I may have many personal shortcomings, but I’ve done nothing to endanger this House. My wish is simply to leave and live out the rest of my life in exile. That is surely punishment enough.” Penthe lowered her eyes. “I can only stand here and ask for your mercy.” She bowed deeply, as she had been taught, just as if she was a child. She allowed herself a brief ironic smile, knowing it could not be seen. This might be the only time she had got it right.

The officers murmured amongst themselves.

The most senior of them, Ploiarchos Agave, who'd served the House for many cycles, finally stepped forward. "Antiploi Sakas tells us that there is a person on board who was a former member of your household. This is the fugitive we've been pursuing?"

"Yes, a former servant." She held up a hand. "And yes, she is the reason we came to this system. The reason I put the lives onboard this ship at risk."

Agave's face remained expressionless. "You let it be known that she had committed a terrible crime. Yet Sakas tells us this woman apparently carries only a great treasure, albeit one that underpins the very fortunes of the House of Aximendes. That it was *given* to her by you. Is this correct?"

"Yes. I gave her the most precious thing this House possesses, a great weapon, and it is now symbiotic with her." Penthe's face grew hot. "I could try and excuse myself and say that I gifted it to her with no knowledge of what it really was. However, the fact remains that I willingly gave away something that never actually belonged to me, at great potential cost to this House. I'm the one that committed the crime."

In the silence that followed, Ploiarchos Agave looked back at her colleagues. They were all frowning, and she couldn't blame them.

Sakas waved the gun in Penthe's direction. "You see, she admits her treason."

Agave held up a hand. "But it is to her credit that she confesses so freely, Antiploi Sakas."

Sakas snorted, but she lowered the gun again.

"You have not always been the easiest queen to follow and obey," Agave said and her colleagues dumbly nodded their agreement. "And we can't ignore the peril you have placed this House in, through your thoughtless actions."

Penthe held her breath, sensing the blade of judgment hanging above her head.

"However, you've given us great victories and filled our treasury with sysgeld. This ship is testament to your commitment to the House. Moreover, it is clear that you understand the seriousness of your situation. If you had lied just now, I would have shot you where you stand. However, we heard the sincerity of your words."

Penthe lowered her head, unable to look the older woman in the eye.

Agave sighed. "We will show clemency and grant your unusual request. So, hear this, Queen Penthesilea. From this moment you are banished. You are stripped of all titles and honours. You may not seek shelter or succour from any member of this House. Any victories, treaties and conquests will be assigned to the House common. Your very name will be expunged from our records and may never be spoken again. This is the law of our people and will be carried out. Henceforth, you are truly nothing to us."

"Have you all gone mad? Exile is not enough, she is dangerous, she is a disgrace to the crown." Sakas lowered the gun and turned to them.

"Nevertheless, Antiploi Sakas, she was our queen. Where she failed, we must do better. *Whoever* leads us next must do better." Agave's lips were tight.

Sakas shook her head. "If you cowards won't do what's best for this House, I will."

Penthe stopped breathing. Was that Death in the shadows of the doorway?

"Stop right there," Agave yelled.

The officers had drawn their guns and pointed them at Sakas, not her. Sakas saw it too. She slowly holstered her gun and closed her eyes, as if in pain. When she reopened them, there was a black hatred burning in their depths.

"I won't let this rest, Penthe. These fools may have fallen for your pretty words, but I see the truth. Rest assured, there'll be no haven for you while I still draw breath." Sakas turned and stalked out of the room.

The officers put away their weapons, but Penthe didn't move. Her legs were so unsteady, she didn't think she could. She reached for words, some way to show gratitude, but before she could speak Agave raised a finger.

"Enough. You should pack some belongings. There's a small ship in hangar bay ten. You may take that. You have thirty minutes to leave. After that…"

The officer didn't have to spell it out. If she wasn't off the ship by then, they'd hunt her down. Her stomach clenched. She had a way out of sorts, but what about Rose? "I understand, but might I know what you intend to do with the prisoner, Ploiarchos Agave," she asked.

Agave raised an eyebrow. "You fear for her safety? Perhaps you are right to do so, but I promise that we will not be hasty in our decisions."

"Will you—"

Agave shook her head. "That is all I'm prepared to say on the matter. It is no longer your concern. You have twenty-nine minutes left, Penthesilea."

Twenty minutes later, she was on her way towards the hangar. She'd selected only the essentials, including some valuable pieces of jewellery that had been gifted to her personally over the cycles. Everything formally belonged to the House, but she didn't have the capacity to cope with the idea of complete destitution.

There were few faces on her journey. As if some invisible wall of excommunication travelled ahead of her, distant voices went silent, and doors clicked shut just as she reached them. Nobody greeted her or deigned to look at her. Before she wouldn't have cared, but now she wished just one person would acknowledge her existence instead of confirming how far she had fallen. Barely afloat in a mental morass of self-pity and anxiety, she didn't register the figure that had hurtled around a corner until they collided with her and threw her against the wall. She slid down it, momentarily winded.

Dazed, her spine screamed with pain. The stranger got back to her feet and stared at her. Something about her was familiar, but even as Penthe tried to organise her thoughts, recognition lit up the other woman's eyes. She was dragged up by her hair, and her head slammed against the wall. Spots appeared in her vision.

"You bitch! Where is she? Tell me where she is."

Vash Munro. With belated understanding came the realisation of what terrible danger she was in. No amount of sweet talking would save her from Munro's wrath. Bands of steel wrapped around her chest.

"I said, where is she?" Munro's voice was menacing and low. She slapped Penthe's face hard with the back of her hand.

Her vision narrowed again, and a stream of liquid tickled the side of her nose as it made its way down her cheek. She'd bottled up her emotions as best she could while confronting Sakas, but now something inside her exploded, white hot. She kneed Munro's groin with all the force she could muster and smiled grimly when she hissed and stepped back, slightly bent over. Penthe followed up quickly with a blow to her exposed jaw. Munro reeled across the corridor and fell to her knees.

Penthe wiped her face and looked down at her. She really didn't have the time for this. Munro tried to get up, and Penthe booted her in the chest, putting her on her back again.

Astoundingly, Munro made as if to get up again. "This isn't going to get either of us anywhere, Munro."

"When I want advice from a psycho, I'll ask." Vash spat out a dark glob of blood and got to her feet.

"Look, I'm not trying to get in your way, Munro." Penthe stepped away and left the path clear for Munro to continue down the corridor. There was confusion in her face.

"Why should I trust you?"

"You shouldn't, no more than I should trust you. However, neither of us has much choice anymore." She pointed up the corridor. "Rose is in the main medical bay, two junctions down this corridor, left and then the next right. There are signs from there. Now, if you'll excuse me, I have business elsewhere."

She picked up her belongings and started to move in the opposite direction, towards her waiting plane. She heard Munro scramble to her feet.

"Seems to me you're in a hurry to get to the hangars. Now, why would the great Queen Penthesilea be fleeing her own ship?" Munro asked.

Penthe stopped. "Queen Penthesilea wouldn't, but I no longer wear the crown."

"Bit too heavy, was it?"

"Heavier than you or anyone else could ever know. But I'm nobody now. I have no crown, no ship, no kin, and no home." Her back stiffened as she spoke the words out loud. The first time she'd acknowledged the enormity of what she'd done. *Yes, you have no one now, Penthesilea. They're better off without you.* Her mother's voice, as vindictive as ever, was tinged with triumph.

"I should kill you for what you did to Rose," Munro said.

Penthe dropped her bags and spread her arms out, her back still to Munro. Any fighting spirit left in her evaporated in the cold light of the corridor. What value did her life have now? Yes, she'd escaped execution, but wasn't exile just an agonisingly slow death by a thousand rejections. Perhaps Munro was doing her a favour. "What's stopping you, Vash Munro? I'm not armed. You're the one with the knife at your side."

All she could hear now was Munro's breathing behind her. In her mind's eye, she saw the captain's hand drop to her side, and her fingers lightly brush over the hilt of the knife there. Only a few hours earlier she'd done the same with Rose. Now, she silently petitioned the gods to guide Munro's hand and put an end to it here and now.

"No, that's too easy. This galaxy is a hard place for a nobody. I'll let the gods decide your fate."

She waited until Munro's footsteps receded into the distance behind her. The noises of the ship—her ship—returned. That gentle hum, occasional clinks, and low rumble that she had spent all her time listening to and never really hearing. Now she'd never hear it again. Ignoring the tears running down her face, she clutched her belongings and walked toward her future beyond.

CHAPTER TWENTY-SEVEN

THE SOUNDS OF THE ship were a distance hum in the medical bay. Rose wished that she had the strength to use the band, but every time she tried to make a connection, the pressure in her head was unbearable. Clearly, her energy levels needed longer to recharge.

Every sense in her body was shouting danger, not from Penthe but from Penthe's enemies. The comfort of their unexpected reconciliation, albeit strange, had swiftly been replaced by the fear that it had made things worse not better. They were both in peril now. The expression on Sakas' face when Penthe had shown leniency had been a shock. Disgust, she'd expected, but not the deep rage and distress that went with it. It was clear Sakas had got too close to Penthe, like a moth to a flame, and now buzzed with angry pain. Would she feel the same if Vash ever betrayed her in the same way? Just brushing against that idea made her want to curl up, but she was halted by the lines in her arms and hands.

It was time to go. She began to gently pull the needles from her arm. The door opened, and the doctor walked in. There was no way to hide what she'd been attempting to do, so she didn't bother trying. However, the doctor put her fingers to her lips. She returned to the door and twisted the lock.

"I see that you're keen to discharge yourself. You do understand you're still a prisoner?" She sat down on the end of the medibed and folded her arms. Her eyes weren't unfriendly though.

"I know. You'd better call the guards to take me back to the detention cells. As soon as you're gone, I'm going to try to escape." Rose looked her straight in the eye.

The doctor sighed and looked up at the ceiling. "I heard about you from a friend of mine. She knew your mother and followed your progress." She chewed her lip. "What I'm about to say could get me executed, you understand?"

Rose nodded. The doctor was taking a risk by not calling the guards.

"Not long ago, a young woman was brought into the med-bay. She was in a terrible state. She'd been badly injured and had internal bleeding. We had to operate for three hours to save her life. She hasn't spoken a word since she woke up, not to me or any of my staff. She spends a lot of time crying."

A heavy silence hung between them for a little while.

"She was a maid in the queen's service, just as you were once. I understand she was found in the queen's bedroom." The doctor's hands twisted together. "During my tenure, there have been three others with similar injuries. One nearly died."

What could she say? This conversation exposed the stinking canker at the heart of her community. The doctor, sworn to ease suffering, had kept quiet when confronted with the terrible injuries inflicted by no reason by her queen. She had just patched them up and sent them back. She no doubt had excellent medical skills, but how could she look at herself in a mirror? It was as if everyone on the Aximendes VI had taken a collective oath to turn the other way, to swallow any guilt they felt. In favour of… what? Some twisted sense of tradition and honour. She had been a little different, but not much. She sang the same songs, was ingrained with the same culture. Fates, if she hadn't run, but stayed and told the truth of what had been going on, perhaps she could have saved those that followed her from the pain and suffering. Well, that was going to change, starting now. "I escaped from Penthe, otherwise I might have ended up in your care too. She was being abused and belittled by her mother, the late queen. She'd already been driven to some kind of psychosis by the time I entered her household. As well as hiding her injuries, I watched her suffer from hallucinations and terrible mood swings; she probably still does. I tried to be…kind, to help. She abused, assaulted and nearly killed me, convinced I was a spy sent by her mother."

The doctor looked at her wide-eyed, but she was in no mood to be merciful. It was time for the truth. "All Penthesilea has done is become a mirror image of her mother, and we all let that happen. We are all responsible."

The doctor winced and closed her eyes for a few seconds. She took a deep breath. "I understand what you're saying, but it's difficult. I was brought up to obey without questioning. The queen leads. She knows what is best for us, and we must all follow for the good of the House."

"So was I. But the fact is that because nobody intervened. Penthe never got the help she needed, and innocents have suffered because of that. This wall of silence has to be torn down."

The doctor stared at the floor for a while. When she finally looked up, she looked older somehow, and she didn't seem able to meet Rose's gaze. Instead, she got to her feet and gently finished removing the canula. "Thank you for your honesty. I will think over what you've said. I hope you don't think too badly of me, of your people."

"I don't, and I never will. I can still remember the life I had before I joined her household, the joy and love I experienced." Rose's throat was thick with emotion. "All I ask is that you not judge Penthe harshly either. She's a victim too."

The doctor nodded thoughtfully. There wasn't any point pushing the point. She was intelligent enough to carry on thinking about it. Maybe this would be the start of a change, but such change would not come easily. A loud pinging noise interrupted them, and the doctor pulled a thin tablet from her coat pocket. She frowned.

"I have orders to make you ready to be returned to detention. The guards will be here in five minutes." She swung her arm and slammed the device against the metal edge of the medibed. It fizzed and a smell of burning electronics filled the air. "Unfortunately, my tablet appears to have malfunctioned."

It was Rose's turn to be wide-eyed as the doctor unlocked the door and dragged in a medichair that was outside the door.

Twenty minutes later, she was nearly at the hangars. The doctor had brought her halfway, wheeling her briskly through the only security checkpoint they encountered. She'd kept her eyes down, maintaining the deceit of being the doctor's prisoner. But the guards ignored them both completely, more intent on the animated chatter coming from their comms. From what she'd caught, a coup was underway. The corridors were eerily quiet and deserted, everyone seemingly hiding from the oncoming political storm. A junction later, the doctor halted and unfastened Rose's cuffs.

"Keep going that way. Take a left at the second junction and a right at the next. You should recognise where you are when you get closer."

"I can't—"

The doctor had held up her hand to stop Rose thanking her. "No, please don't. I don't think I can deal with being thanked for treason, sorry." She ran her hands through her hair distractedly. "Now, I need to get back. It's about to get interesting around here and not in a good way."

She nodded. It was time to get off this ship somehow. With a final wave, the doctor disappeared back the way they had come. Rose continued as instructed, moving cautiously through the first intersection, straining her ears for any sound. Luckily, the footsteps approaching from around the next corner were clearly audible in the strange silence.

She turned around, desperately looking for somewhere to hide. Backing slowly up, she tried the door handles on either side, but they were all locked. The last one gave, but the door didn't open fully. She squeezed in as much as she could, ignoring the flaring pain in her shoulder, and held her breath. Her head started to throb, matching her racing pulse. Perhaps the band was coming back online again, but it was too late. The footsteps slowed and stopped.

"I can see you hiding there. Come out and show yourself."

That voice...it couldn't be. She stepped out, her hand to her mouth.

"Rose, is that you?" Vash moved forward uncertainly.

The corridor closed in, and she reached out, desperately wanting to believe this wasn't just a hallucination. "Are you real?" she asked.

Vash grinned. "I hope so, gorgeous."

They met, all hands, kisses, and tears. Vash gathered her up in her strong arms and swung her around wildly.

"Careful, I'm getting dizzy." But she didn't care really. Nothing mattered now. Everything was going to be all right now Vash was here and with that simple thought, a great weight lifted from her.

Vash set her down gently and stared, blinking as if she were taking photographs. "Are you okay? Did they hurt you?"

"I'm fine. You're the one who looks like she's been in the wars." She stepped back and studied her. She had an angry red mark on one side of her jaw, and her clothes were ripped. "We should go looking for some new clothes soon though."

"I might have had a little chat with your queen." Vash flushed.

"Penthe." Rose's mouth was hanging open, but she couldn't help it.

"Yeah, the nutty one herself. Turns out she was taking her leave as well. Sounds like there's been a mutiny or something. I did think about…" Vash looked away, seemingly embarrassed.

It didn't take a genius to guess what she had been going to say. "Killing her? But you didn't, did you?" She scanned Vash's face looking for the answer. She had no idea why it mattered so much, but she didn't want Vash to have Penthe's blood on her hands.

Vash shook her head. "No, I didn't. I wanted to, but I thought, what would Rose do? So, I let her go." Vash tugged at her earlobe, obviously still amazed at her own actions. "I think you've turned me into a pacifist or something." She looked worried at the thought.

Rose kissed her softly. "I love you." She wrapped her arms around her and breathed in her scent. "I'm so lucky to have you in my life."

Vash rested her chin on her head, "I think I'm the lucky one, Rose. The luckiest woman in the universe."

"Well, perhaps we can argue more about that when we are safely off this ship." Rose looked up the corridor the way Vash had come. "Let's get going, shall we?"

CHAPTER TWENTY-EIGHT

THE SHIP WAITED IN the deserted hangar, as Penthe had been promised. She climbed aboard and sensed, rather than saw, the eyes watching her every move. However, she'd no intention of reneging on her side of the deal. Her heart was riven with deep cracks of grief, but there was no future for her on this ship now.

The craft was cramped but well provisioned. A cursory examination revealed it to be stocked with plenty of food and fuel, at least enough to ensure that she could leave the system. She smiled ruefully at the efficiency of her senior officers. A gleam of metal caught her eye. A small pistol had been left on the navigation console. She ran her finger down the smooth cold surface of the barrel and closed her hand around the stock. It only shook a little as she held it to her forehead. "Bang."

There was no movement outside, which was disappointing. She put the gun back down, hands steady again. If they'd left it there to tempt her, they were naive. She might no longer wear the crown, but she had been bred a queen, and she intended to die as one. Suicide was a dishonourable death, an Akmonian faced their enemies.

Once the ship cleared the outer hull of the Aximendes VI, she banked steeply to see her great ship one last time. It was strange, but all the times she had gone on diplomatic trips, she'd never really taken the time to admire and fully appreciated its beauty. Pride welled inside her. There was no other ship like it in the galaxy. With or without her, it would serve the House well for decades to come. Perhaps it was the one great thing she had contributed to the family fortunes. She scrubbed at the moisture on her cheeks. Tears were no help to her now.

The more pressing question was, where to go now? She had been so focused on getting off the ship, she hadn't had time to give much thought to the future. The House of Aximendes had contacts across the galaxy. But she couldn't expect a warm welcome from the many of them. Others would perhaps give her shelter for a price. As news got out of her downfall and subsequent exile, she'd become the target for the multitude who held a grudge against her or the House. Anyone harbouring her would risk their own person and their property. The gold and jewels she had packed wouldn't be enough to pay for any lengthy protection she was sure. She'd have to think of what other skills she could offer.

The alternative was to simply go her own way, though that would be more complicated. There would be the radical changes needed to her looks to ensure her safety for starters. That would heavily deplete her capital as the costs would include a commitment to discretion on the part of any black clinic. All that, and she'd still be left having to make a life and a living in a strange community.

Her head ached with the stress of thinking through the unpleasant options open to her, not noticing the blinking light on the console until the last moment. Another craft, screaming out from the Aximendes VI, swept dangerously close to hers. Her craft rocked violently in the backdraft and threw her to one side. Swearing under her breath, she dragged herself back into the command seat. The vessel wasn't showing on her main sensors, its approach had only been picked up by the collision module, which explained how its departure had gone unnoticed and unchallenged by the Aximendes VI. It must have disabled its transponders or have a cloaking shield. She squinted at the screen, then sat back in shock. It was the Bellerophon. She recognised it from the images she had seen from Sakas' ship. Munro was leaving and judging by the insane speed she was pushing her ship to, she must have Rose safely with her. Adrenaline pumped through her veins, and she smiled, a smile that felt good and real for the first time in a long time.

It was also a timely reminder that she was still a little too close to the Aximendes VI herself to be dawdling like this. Chastened, Penthe backed off until the great ship was no bigger than a thumbnail on the screen. She pulled up some navigational maps to consult, trying to decide on an initial vector when her systems alerted her to another ship leaving the Aximendes VI. The identity of this one was broadcast in the clear to her console and elation evaporated and was replaced with cold dread. Sakas' personal attack ship was emerging from beneath one of the great limbs, gaining speed and heading towards her. There was no time to flee, and no way to outrun it in this little pleasure craft. She waited for the inevitable act of final retribution to play out.

But Sakas' ship banked sharply and accelerated away, totally ignoring her. Furthermore, the Aximendes VI itself started to manoeuvre delicately in space, its great engines firing up and eventually sending it slowly on its way after the smaller ship. She laughed, a little too loudly, and fought to calm herself. An interrogation of the navigation console revealed where they were going. Relief once again turned to icy shock and horror. Sakas was following Rose and Munro. Penthe frantically consulted the navigation computer to work out where they were all headed. That mining planet was still the closest habitable world, and all parties appeared to be travelling in that direction.

Penthe slumped in the command chair and stared at the screens. Only minutes ago, she'd been celebrating an unlikely victory for the good guys. She should have known better. Sakas would never just let the band go. Head in hands, she agonised over the best thing to do. If she interfered, she'd probably just end up in a hole in a ground herself or floating frozen in space. Anyone sensible and sane would ignore what they had just seen and go on their way.

"It's a good job I'm neither," Penthe muttered and punched in the co-ordinates for the planet.

***

As soon as the Bellerophon dropped her landing gear, Jakub appeared on the monitors running towards them. He stopped at a safe distance and bounced on his feet, waving frantically.

Vash powered down the engines and fiddled with some buttons on her console. A faint grinding noise from behind them indicated the main hatch was opening.

"Shall we go?" Vash glanced at her with tired eyes.

The new bruising from her brief fight with Penthe was coming out, adding another layer to the violent rainbow decorating her skin and swelling on the right side of her face. Rose touched her arm. For the first time in days, she finally felt safe, a word that somehow had come to mean just being with Vash. "I still can't believe you came back for me." How could she really convey how much that meant? How much feeling safe meant? She held Vash's gaze, who flushed red and found something important to look at on her console.

"Maybe next time you could give me a bit more lead time on psychopathic royal types trying to kidnap you?"

"I'll try and remember that, I promise." Rose grabbed her hand and held it tight. "I really love you. You know that, right? What you've done for me…I can't put it into words."

Vash finally looked up and her grin widened. "Yeah, I really love you too." She scratched the back of her neck for a moment. "You can't go telling everyone though. I've got a reputation to maintain."

Rose laughed. Some things never changed, and Vash's terrible self-deprecating humour was one of them.

"What reputation, captain?" Bel asked.

"Never you mind." Vash winked at Rose. "You just go back to going over the systems. We both know those military techs couldn't find their way around a service duct."

"I love you, Bel." She poked her tongue out at Vash and blew a kiss into the air.

Vash grimaced. "Yeah, well. I don't believe I thanked you properly, Bel, for everything you did while I was in custody."

"I only did what I considered to be my duty, captain. You know, those techs were quite uncouth. One of them suggested switching off my personality chip."

"Oh, the horror." Vash smirked.

Rose elbowed her sharply. "That's terrible. But I don't understand, what did you do?"

"I am sure I don't know. I did suggest that he might benefit from a shower. The captain has always been a stickler for good hyg—"

"I think Rose is asking what work you did, Bel." Vash rolled her eyes.

"Oh, that. I have been working in my spare time to expand my capabilities. Specifically, my deception and defence functionalities, which I consider adequate at best."

Vash smiled proudly. "I've encouraged Bel to appropriate any code she thinks necessary while we're on our travels. She's picked up some very useful stuff over time, even while we were parked in the military docks."

"Their security was quite lax. I found some very good code that enabled me to override our transponder and remove or replace our identity. It is unfortunately quite illegal in most of the systems we might visit."

"A device of last resort only, Bel. I explained that." Vash took on an air of innocence.

"So, that's how you got aboard the Aximendes VI. I had wondered." Rose grinned. "Bel, where is that lovely silver bot of yours?"

There was a faint metallic clattering and a whoosh, and the bot shot out of a pipe in the corner of the bridge. It floated gently down until it was in front of her. She leaned forward and gave its warm metal surface a kiss. "Thank you, Bel, for helping to rescue me."

"Oh, my…" Bel spun and wobbled erratically before it shot off back into the pipe.

"Stop distracting my AI, please." Vash laughed

"I just wanted to show Bel my appreciation."

"Well, I love you too, Rose," Bel said. "I was extremely concerned for your welfare when you were aboard that nasty ship. I spoke to its computer—"

"You did what?" Vash's eyes widened.

"Really, it wasn't in my class. A very basic model, barely any sentience at all. From the little I gleaned, that ship was not a happy place to be."

"You and I are going to have a serious talk, Bel. Really serious." Vash put her hands on her hips.

"Hadn't we better go before Jakub breaks the door down?" The last thing Rose wanted to do was talk about what had happened on the Aximendes VI. It was all too raw.

Vash nodded. "Later, Bel." She stretched and headed out of the hatch.

As she followed at a more leisurely pace, Rose looked down at her arm. The patterns were calm and more importantly, they were starting to make more sense to her. Her brain was offering translations for the whirls and colours. Whatever this thing was, it was gradually becoming part of her, and she felt more in control with every passing hour.

Vash and Jakub were chatting when she arrived.

Jakub swept her up into a crushing bear hug. "I thought I'd never see you again, young lady. I thought I'd lost your grace from my life forever."

She could see tears forming in his eyes, and there was a lump in her throat too. In the space of a couple of days she'd come to love this man as if he was family. "Whatever happened, Jakub, you'd never have lost me, and you never will." She kissed his stubbly cheek. "Now, would you mind putting me down before I pass out."

He lowered her carefully back to the floor. "Come to my habpod, both of you. I've got some food waiting. I think we've got a lot of catching up to do."

Her stomach growled approvingly at the mention of food. The lines in the sickbay had kept her alive, no more.

"Lead on, Jakub, I could do with something to eat." Vash slapped him on the back.

They trudged to his shack. The wind was as cold as ever, threatening to strip the skin off her face, and she was glad to be in the warmth again. He'd moved the old, battered table to the middle and found an old cloth from somewhere to throw over it. It was overflowing with little dishes of meats and fruits and their smells filled the air.

"Jakub. Have you got any supplies left in your stores?" She couldn't believe the size of the feast he'd laid on for them.

"Don't worry, I got some extra stuff from the military before they left. I think they felt sorry for me. When I got your tight-band comms, I knew you'd both be ready for a good meal." He waved his hand at the table like the puffed-up owner of one of the expensive eateries in Drem that Vash had taken her to once.

The large protein stick Vash chomped on rendered her response largely unintelligible. She swallowed and wiped her mouth with the back of her hand before trying again. "You weren't wrong, Jakub. I was ready for this."

Rose sat down and grabbed a piece of fruit. She took a bite and luxuriated in the taste of its sweet soft flesh as the juices dribbled down her chin.

Jakub wandered over to the small stove in the corner and started fussing over a small boiler. "I'll make some hot drinks while you two demolish the food. I want to hear everything, all the adventures you have been having while I have been stuck down—"

The harsh roar of landing thrusters nearby stopped Jakub in his tracks. Rose was hit by a wave of fear and looked at Vash. She'd frozen too, another stick paused halfway to her mouth.

"More visitors? I don't remember the company saying they were sending anyone." Jakub walked towards the door.

"I don't think it's your company, Jakub," Vash pushed past him and opened the door just enough for her to look over to where the sound was coming from. Turning around she looked at Rose and nodded.

"Do you remember that badass woman who kidnapped Rose before? Well, it looks like she's still got business with us." Vash patted her pockets frantically. "Nova! I've left my guns on the ship."

Jakub put his hand firmly on her shoulder. "I'll talk to her, Vash. I'll persuade her to give up this pursuit." He shook his head when Vash opened her mouth to protest. "I'm not stupid. While I'm talking, take Rose into the mine. Hide yourselves where Rose hid before. I'll find you there."

Vash looked at him and a message passed between them that Rose didn't quite catch.

Vash reached out and shook his hand. "Don't take too long, Jakub. I really want that drink and a proper chat." She opened the door for him, and he walked out without looking back.

Rose's head began to ache again, and she felt the insistent motion of the band on her arm. "We shouldn't let him go out there alone, Vash. Sakas isn't one for talking about things." She wanted answers, but Vash stood stock still, her head tipped to one side as if she was listening for something outside.

"He's a big boy, he can look after himself. We need to get into the mine." She opened the door again. "Soon as you're outside, run for the mine entrance. Whatever happens, don't stop."

Rose nodded. Her heart pounded in her chest as she waited for the signal to go. Vash glanced in the direction of Sakas' ship again and waved her on.

The mine entrance was close by but as she ran, it seemed to be miles away. Jakub strode towards the ship. The hatch lowered and Sakas emerged. He stopped and raised his hand in greeting.

Sakas' face looked grim, and she reached for her gun. Time slowed; Jakub's hand hung in the clean air, Sakas' gun unholstered and lifted in one smooth motion. The crack of the shot cut through the thin air, and Jakub slowly started to topple sideways. "No!" she screamed.

Vash grabbed her and tugged her forward. Time abruptly returned to its usual beat. "Keep running. Just keep going."

"But Jakub?" Rose couldn't bear the thought of leaving him lying there.

"He knew what he was doing. Don't let him die for nothing, Rose, please."

Rose looked back towards Jakub. Sakas hadn't even stopped walking.

She'd holstered her gun and was coming towards them now, her pace quickening and a broad smile on her face. Jakub lay on the ground motionless. There was no more time to think. She ran for the mine.

CHAPTER TWENTY-NINE

THE LIFT WAS JUST starting its descent when the mine door opened with an unmistakable rusty squeal. As the floor slid out of sight, Sakas' shiny black boots appeared, and she braced for gunshots or some attempt to stop the lift.

"There's nowhere to run, Rose. You won't get away."

Vash pulled her close, and she was grateful for her firm embrace, but her insides churned.

"Don't worry, we're not beaten yet, gorgeous." Vash kissed the top of her head.

"She's right. Where are we going to go? There's only one way in and out of here."

"Let's see what we can find down here. There might be something I can use as a weapon."

The lift ground to a halt.

"Hold the door open." Vash dashed over to the wall and kicked at the side of a rotting plastimetal crate that had been abandoned there. Its sides soon gave way under her heavy boots, and she tore at them, freeing two shards. She ran back and jammed one into the gate mechanism, and the other into the floor runners. The door tried to close again, but couldn't, and it grunted and groaned as if in pain.

"We might not be able to get out, but she can't get down here either. Hopefully she'll just give it up." Vash wiped the sweat from her brow. She glanced over. "I hate to ask, but I don't suppose…"

Rose didn't share Vash's hopes. Sakas would never give up. She touched her forearm. Yes, the band was eager to help. Too eager for her liking. "I could use it, but after what happened on the Aximendes VI, I'm a bit afraid to."

Vash nodded. "I only got to feel its power for an hour or so and that was enough." She took Rose's hand and squeezed it. "Forget I asked. You're right to be cautious with that thing."

She relaxed a little, but how long would it be before Vash asked again? She'd seen an iota of its capability and so had no real fear. Rose knew how powerful it really was. She shuddered, knowing it was just waiting for her to give in. She was determined to resist if she could for both their sakes. *If I don't use it, I can't kill with it.* The strange mantra repeated in her mind.

"What do we do now?" Nothing had changed since she was last down here. It was hot, humid, and dimly lit. Her shirt was already growing damp on her back.

"First things first, we need to recce the tunnels. I'm hoping that Jakub left some supplies down here somewhere." Vash chewed her lip and scanned their surroundings. "You take the left tunnel, and I'll take the right. Search for five minutes and meet back here."

At the thought of them splitting up, Rose started to shake. "I don't think I want to go anywhere on my own. I don't think I can."

Vash wrapped her arms back around her, concern etched on her face.

"I'm not going anywhere. It'll take a little longer, but we could explore together. That sound better?" She lifted Rose's chin and looked hopefully at her.

"Much better. Thanks, Vash. I'm sorry for being—"

Vash put one finger over her lips. "No apologies. It's been a hole of a day."

They checked out the left-hand tunnel first. It curved and started to narrow considerably after about two hundred metres. There was a stack of crates against one wall. Vash ran over and tore at the lids with excitement, but all that was inside was some small plastimetal parts, probably spares for the robots. Vash swore and threw one of them across the tunnel.

"Hey." Rose touched her arm. "There's still the other tunnel, why don't we go back?"

Vash looked at the ceiling and puffed out her cheeks. "Yeah, sorry. I was just really hopeful there for a minute." She looked back the way they had come. "You're right. Let's check the other tunnel. Jakub must keep some tools down here somewhere."

The brighter lights of the lift junction dazzled Rose's eyes as they walked back towards them. The lift still hadn't moved, and she sighed inwardly with relief. They turned into the other tunnel and started trudging down it. One of the huge robots was parked to one side, standing silent guard over the mine.

"I wondered when you'd turn up."

Rose nearly jumped out of her skin at the voice. They turned slowly. Sakas stood in the lift junction, her gun aimed steadily at them.

"Nova! Where did you come from?" Vash's voice cracked slightly.

Sakas smiled. "Yes, I would have preferred to use the lift. It's fortunate that there's an emergency ladder on the shaft wall."

Vash slapped her forehead and looked apologetically at Rose. "How could I be so stupid?"

Rose shook her head. "No. No apologies, remember?"

She touched Vash's arm to reassure her, noticing as she did so that her hands weren't shaking any more. Deep inside, she was relieved that the waiting was over.

Sakas coughed. "I've no argument with you, Munro. We're very alike, I think, both warriors at heart. This woman is not worthy of you. Leave now. Let me do what's necessary, and you get to live."

"And what do you believe is necessary, Sakas?" Vash asked calmly. She moved between Rose and Sakas.

Sakas' eyes flickered; she knew Vash's intention.

"Really, Munro? Do you need me to spell it out?"

"Yeah, I think you do. Sadass or whatever you're called. Seems to me you've got everything you want. Her royal madness has gone. The ship's in your hands. Why are you here? Why is there a man lying dead up there? Can't you just leave us alone?"

Sakas sighed but her gun didn't waver for second. "Because this traitor has something of value, something she stole from us. Queen Penthesilea failed in her duty to return it to the House of Aximendes. I'm not as weak as she was. I won't make the same mistake."

If Vash was scared, she didn't show it. "Well, the way I see it, this band thing's a bad news story for everyone. I did some research myself, and it looks like being around it is a dangerous profession. You might be better off without it."

"You may be right, Munro. Nevertheless, it is our property. Please stand aside."

"What, so you can kidnap Rose again? No way, I only just got her back. She ain't going nowhere, Sakbag."

Sakas' expression didn't flicker at Vash's crude play on her name. "My name, Munro, is Sakas. Your poor attempts at distracting me aren't going to work. And no, I do not intend to kidnap Rose. I intend to kill her. When she's dead, the band will return to its inert form, and I'll be able to retrieve it safely."

Rose felt Vash stiffen in front of her, her hand tightening around her own.

"That's not going to happen, Sakas. You'll have to kill me first." Vash pushed Rose back further.

Sakas sighed. "So melodramatic, Munro. You disappoint me." She changed her stance slightly and locked her arms out.

The air in the tunnel thickened and a steel chain wrapped excruciatingly around Rose's chest. Her head pounded and lights flickered at the edge of her eyes. She could feel the band again, throbbing against her skin and stirring up a hurricane in her brain. Its message was so sweet and inviting. *Let me in, let me help*. It made no attempt to mask its desires. Rose could have killed the guard in Vash's brig. It'd taken more energy to dissuade the band from doing so, to resist its dread offer. All the people who had already died: the thousands up in space, and Jakub's cooling body on the surface just above. She didn't want to become a killer. The terrible consequences of following that dark path could be seen plainly in Sakas' dead and dispassionate eyes. All her life, Rose had tried to do good and care about people. Maybe the truth was that it was better to be dead than give that up. She tugged her hand out of Vash's, stepped to the side and screamed in frustration. "No!"

Vash turned towards her, and Sakas squeezed the trigger, her gun still pointed at Vash. Rose confronted another truth, a more undeniable one. When faced with seeing the woman she loved die, she'd do whatever was necessary to protect her. She relaxed the last of her mental guards and reached out to the band, offering all of herself to it and praying that it would be enough.

Time stopped.

The inner Rose hung easily in the eye of the storm raging inside her head. Tendrils of light flowed from her inner self to the swirling dark clouds, and she watched flickers of electricity searing across them randomly, as the band welcomed her.

Back in the tunnel, she moved out from behind Vash in a daze, seeing everything around her clearly as if she was at the centre of an enormous holographic display, one in which she was everywhere and nowhere at the same time. Above the planet, the Aximendes VI orbited serenely in space. The band took her there. The emotions of her people, awaiting the return of their new leader, were now a visible spectrum in a cloud of orange anxiety. The ship's walls were opaque to her, and she hung there for a while watching life on board: the ship's doctor in the sickbay, gently talking to a woman while she delivered her baby; the royal maids removing Penthe's clothing from her wardrobes and packing them neatly into metal boxes for storage; and a troop of marines lined up in a hangar, waiting at attention. This was her family, and she would never see any of them again. All this time she'd been on the run, she had never really admitted to herself that she could never go back. The truth doubled her up in pain. Tears gushed down her face, and she howled into the inky silence for what she had lost.

She might have stayed like that forever, if she had not started to feel the band burning her skin again. Rose let it take her back to the surface. Jakub's body lying where he had fallen. How cruel of the band to bring her here. It must know her guilt at his death was a dark hole inside her. She hadn't had the decency to check on him before going to look at the Aximendes VI. She dropped to her knees and contemplated giving the band its final order.

LOOK CLOSER, BEARER. NOT DEAD, BUT CLOSE.

The words shocked her out of her daze. Yes, there were the faintest signs of life, how could she have missed them. *Help me*. There was a brief pain on her arm and an energy tendril flicked out of her body towards his. It played over and through the skin, healing as it went. The blood seeping from his chest dried up and the puckered bullet hole smoothed out. Inside, another white finger caressed his heart, making the minute adjustments needed to get it back into the proper life-giving rhythm. Jakub reared up from the ground and sucked in the air with a loud gasp. Then he lay back again, breathing normally, his eyes flickering open, and the colour returning to his cheeks. She felt a glimmer of hope in herself again, a hope that she could make things right again.

In the space she inhabited between the seconds, every dust mote hung in the air like a faint blizzard. One of Sakas' eyes was mid-blink and Vash's mouth partway to opening wide. Did she intend to speak or to scream? The sound was trapped in time as well.

She looked at the shell, floating mid-air only inches from the barrel of the gun. It visibly quivered, its pent-up energy still seeking motion. If she touched it, she would free it again. Instead, she gave it a wide berth and focused on Sakas. A terrible darkness filled her mind again. Sakas had nearly killed the two people Rose held most dear. She brought her hand to her mouth. Stars, if she had a mirror right now, her own eyes might betray the same lack of mercy.

She gritted her teeth, a part of her still resisting killing another person. After all, Sakas was another victim of the Akmonian system, wasn't she? But no, that wasn't right. Penthe had killed others only after cycles of abuse had caused a terrible psychosis. In the medical bay, Rose had seen her fight to be better. Sakas was different. She had been trained to kill, that was true. But she enjoyed it. Rose could still see her smile as Jakub lay dying. Sakas had chosen to deal in death rather than life. She would never stop hunting and killing. If it was just Rose at risk, she might still have let her go, but she couldn't risk the lives of those she loved.

"I'm so sorry, Sakas, but I can't let you take Vash. Go well." She spoke softly but firmly to the band, and a small orb of light broke out of her chest and crossed the short distance to Sakas. It penetrated her clothing and disappeared with no clue to its dread purpose.

Rose reached out tentatively, unsure of what had happened. But as she made contact, time returned to Sakas' body, and she fell heavily to the ground in a heap at her feet. The fire in Sakas' eyes had finally been extinguished; another life had departed for good. She knelt and offered the traditional Akmonian respects. "May the gods have mercy upon you, my sister."

The words sounded so hollow. Why should the gods be merciful when she hadn't been? She closed Sakas' eyes and stood up unsteadily, thinking desperately for the best thing, the right thing, to do.

It came to her.

On her orders, the band dissolved the body into a mist of particles which rose through the ceiling of the tunnel. On the Aximendes VI above, in the command hub, it would reassemble. Sakas would be home, at the same time taking with her a compelling message that it was time for them to leave.

There was no time to rejoice. A great storm raged inside her, and Rose stood on the edge of a precipice. She'd stepped over a line in her soul, and there could be no return. Her brain was under siege by the twin forces of shame and disgust, and no amount of rational excuse could hold them back. Matters weren't helped by the band. It didn't wait for her next order but reduced the shell to a pile of fine dust on the rocky floor. Newly emboldened by its actions, it craved even more power, and Rose was buffeted by the energy intensifying in the band's dark clouds.

LET ME PUNISH THEM ALL. LET ME KILL THEM ALL. THEY DESERVE IT!

It was ravenous for death and destruction and sensed her vulnerability whilst misunderstanding her intentions. It was all she could do to stand firm as it circled her with maddened shrieks for blood-ridden justice. Desperately, she dredged up the last remaining reserves of mental strength in herself and stood firm. *No, I'm not Sakas. I will not kill. I will not destroy. Obey me.* Just as she feared she had nothing left, the voice went silent. With a barely disguised mental pout, the storm clouds dissipated, and the band released her. Sagging exhausted against the wall, she exhaled heavily.

Time returned.

"Rose."

Vash's mouth completed its journey to a shout, though the message changed as she took in her surroundings.

Rose froze, anticipating her reaction.

"What the fuck just happened?"

The wary expression on Vash's face cut Rose in two. The hint of fear in her lover's eyes brought her crashing back down. The band could erase her memories, but she loved Vash too much to do that. She would face the consequences of her actions. Vash looking at her, saying nothing, her face asking the hardest question to which Rose couldn't answer with a lie. She nodded her head and lowered her gaze, waiting to hear Vash walking away. But her hand cupped Rose's chin and lifted it. Where she had expected to see disgust, there was only a sad understanding. She was enveloped in those strong arms and collapsed into them as Vash held her tight.

***

It was dark when she awoke and reached out absentmindedly for Vash. It was a few moments before she remembered that she wasn't on board the Bellerophon, but in Jakub's shack. Lying in the gloom, quiet movements in the room beyond filtered through the walls, but the voices were too low for her to make out what was being said. Reluctant to leave the safety of the heavy blanket that covered her, she tugged it up higher like a shield. Once she got up, the questions would start, and she didn't know how to answer them.

The door creaked open, and Vash poked her head in. "I wondered if you might be awake." She sat down on the side of the bed and stroked her head. "You gonna get up and have something to eat? Might make you feel better."

She wasn't sure anything was going to make her feel better, now or in the future. She'd killed someone, and she couldn't get that moment out of her head. One moment Sakas had been alive, the next she was lying crumpled at her feet, her lifeless eyes looking up accusingly. Thinking about it made her stomach churn and any appetite vanished in a backwash of acid.

"You've got to stop going over it, Rose." Vash's gentle voice brought her back to the present.

"I can't, Vash, I just can't. I know she was going to kill us both. I know it was her or us. It just doesn't make any difference."

"It shouldn't either. Killing another person should never be taken lightly," Jakub said.

He stood in the doorway, just visible over Vash's shoulder. Vash made a shooing motion. Rose grabbed her hand. "It's okay." She motioned to Jakub to come in.

He shuffled around the other side of the bed and sat down gingerly as if worried about crushing her feet and brought his hand to his chest. "You saved my life, thank you."

"Well, the band did. I thought you were dead." She shook her head. His thanks were the last thing she wanted. An image of Sakas' eyes, staring sightlessly, filled her mind.

"That thing can give life or take it away. It's the person who bears it who decides whether to let it, who has to be strong enough to resist."

The room began to break up into a kaleidoscope of blues and greys. "I had no choice, Jakub. If it'd just been me…please, you must believe me. I'm not a killer." She clutched his arm, feeling the muscles bunched under the thin shirt.

"Don't you think you're being unfair, Jakub? Rose saved your life. Sakas was the one trying to kill people." Vash stood up and pointed to the door. "Maybe you should leave."

"You're right. Rose saved my life. I just don't want to see you fall onto a path of darkness, Rose. You're too pure for that."

Rose hung her head for a moment, then looked him in the eye again. "I won't ever kill again, Jakub, I promise. I swear on everything… everyone I love, I'll never use the band like that again. It's like a part of me died at the same time."

Jakub's eyes were as warm as his smile. "I know, Rose. That's why, if I could, I would have stopped you, even it had meant I'd died as a result." He reached out and grasped her shoulder. "Bearing the band for the rest of your life is going to be more a curse than a blessing, and it will test you constantly. I wish I could bear it for you, take the weight from your shoulders, but you know I'll always be here for you when you need me."

He pulled her into a tight hug, and she cried as she had never cried before. Safe in his embrace, she cried for her family, for Penthe, and herself. Vash joined them and they sat holding each other.

CHAPTER THIRTY

As her ship descended slowly through the atmosphere, Penthe rued again its lack of speed. She arrived in orbit just in time to see the Aximendes VI depart. The vessel fired its huge engines and moved majestically away on a trajectory that would take it out of the system.

She trained the sensors on the surface of the planet below. They showed Sakas' fighter was still on the surface. She checked the readouts several times. Some of the tension left her body, but she was still uneasy. If Sakas hadn't returned, why was the Aximendes VI leaving? The sensible part of her told her firmly to let it go. *Leave it there, Penthe. Go on your way.* Like she'd ever listened to the good side of her brain.

She landed her ship a little way from the mine. With only a handgun and a few shells, it was stupid to go rushing into the situation. It was so bitterly cold though, even with a thick padded jacket on, and the wind was against her. Dusk was falling hard by the time she reached the settlement.

Sakas' ship sat forlornly in the darkness, completely powered down. Further on, the muted beam from her jacket light picked up scuff marks on the ground. Only one of the settlement's habpods had a light burning. She stood for a while, arms tingling with adrenaline as she tried to decide what to do. Sheer stubbornness drove her forward again. There was no point leaving without knowing the truth.

Voices carried on the wind as she got closer, but there was no way of telling who they might belong to. A loud laugh rang out. She tensed again and fought an unfamiliar impulse to flee. Prudence dictated going around the back to see if she could find out more before she did anything else. As she rounded the corner, a great noise went up from some kennels she hadn't seen in the dark, as the guardbeasts caught her scent for the first time.

Penthe backed off rapidly, swearing under her breath, but it was too late. A door opened, flooding the area where she stood with light, and a man strode out.

"What's all this racket, the wind spooked you?" He stopped when he saw her. "And who are you?" His eyes drifted down to the gun in her hand and narrowed.

There didn't seem much point in threatening him. She threw it at his feet and showed her empty hands. "I don't mean you any harm."

"Like hole, you don't!" Munro stepped around the man. "Jakub, this is that psycho queen we told you about. The one that's been hunting for Rose."

Penthe didn't know what to say, it wasn't like it wasn't true. The man's frown had deepened, and she kept her hands where they could see them. "I know you won't believe me, but I'm just here because I wanted to know Rose is safe."

Munro threw back her head and laughed. "You're right. I don't believe you." She advanced, hand over her own holster. "Sakas, and now you. Why won't you all just leave her alone?"

"Where's Sakas?" Was she also in the habpod? Penthe tensed.

"She's dead. She wanted the band, and now she's dead." Vash's hand hovered over her holster. "And if you don't want to die as well, you'll leave right now. Last chance."

"What's going on?"

Jakub and Vash both turned their heads at the sound of Rose's voice. Her heart threatened to burst out of her chest at the sound of it. Rose was still alive.

"Penthe? Is that you?" Rose caught sight of her for the first time, and her eyes widened.

"Yes, it's me. I'm so…that is to say, I just wanted to…" Penthe really didn't know what to say. What could she say to someone that she'd hurt so much? She looked instead at Munro and nodded. "I'll be on my way, Captain Munro." She turned to head back into the darkness but halted when Munro shouted. Then someone tugged at her arm to pull her around: Rose.

"Don't go, Penthe."

Her face was so earnest, so full of kindness and understanding, that Penthe had to choke back tears. "I can't stay, Rose. Munro is right, I shouldn't be here."

Rose looked around and shook her head. "I can't see your ship. I guess you'd probably be okay to get back to it in the dark and cold but humour me. At least stay with us until morning and it's light again."

Penthe looked over at Munro, who didn't look happy with the direction things had taken. "Are you sure that's okay with everyone else?"

Rose took her hand. "No, but we have to start somewhere, don't we?"

Again, she was struck by Rose's strength. Her boundless generosity of spirit made her feel so small. "You're right, as always. I wish I'd listened to you all those cycles ago." The tears were flowing down her face now, and she couldn't stop them. The small, concerned glances between Rose and Munro and the clear, unspoken love between them was a painful reminder of what she had thrown away. She felt genuine joy for Rose but at the same time, a deep ache inside. What she would give for just a taste of what they had. "All those wasted cycles."

Rose squeezed her hand. "Come in the warm now. We need to talk about the future."

***

The atmosphere in the habpod was strained. Vash slouched against the wall with her arms tightly crossed. Her expression was stony, but there wasn't much Rose could do about that right now.

Penthe sat at the table, a hunched and pathetic figure. She should hate her for everything she had done. Vash certainly wanted her to, but she just couldn't. She simply didn't have the capacity for the negative emotion. She sat opposite and pushed a cracked mug of hot caffrush across the table. "Here, drink this, it'll warm you up."

Penthe looked up and smiled. "You never stop looking after me, do you? Why, Rose? Why do you care?"

"Yeah, Rose. Why do you care?" Vash asked. "I wouldn't mind knowing the answer to that little conundrum."

Rose blinked slowly and took a deep breath, allowing her inner peace to spread throughout her soul. "I think the better question is, why shouldn't I?"

Jakub put a hand on Vash's shoulder, but Vash shrugged it off and clenched her jaw.

"Look, I know you don't understand, but at some point, someone has to end this circle of hatred and violence and do the right thing," Rose said.

Penthe and Vash looked confused now, but Jakub smiled at her encouragingly.

"I told you I lost this arm in an accident, didn't I?" He pulled up a chair. "That wasn't entirely the truth. Matter of fact, I lost it because of another man's incompetence." He sighed deeply. "He cost me the best job I had ever had and the best means for providing for my family."

"That must have made you feel bitter," Rose said. Family was so important for him.

"When I found out he wasn't going to lose his job, I was dark with anger. Every part of me wanted him to answer for what he'd done. I waited for him to go on leave, and I hunted him down."

"I hope you taught him a lesson." Vash sniffed, obviously outraged on his behalf.

"I was the one who got taught a lesson," he said. "I caught up with him in a bar. He'd been in there a while according to the barman, 'drinking something away.' As soon as I saw him, I realised it was because of me. That haunted look in his eyes when he saw me, well, it was like looking into a black pit."

"So, what did you do?" Rose wrapped her fingers around his hand.

"I thought to myself, so you've lost an arm, Jakub. He's lost his life and his peace of mind. He had guilt nibbling away at his soul. Kicking him around wasn't going to fix anything for either of us." Jakub squeezed her hand back. "So, I told him to buy me a drink, and we talked for a bit. Turned out he'd things going on at home, things none of us knew about."

"Sounds like an excuse to me." Vash pulled up a chair and glared at Penthe.

"Maybe it was, but it didn't seem so at the time. He was a troubled man who'd made a mistake. I had a choice. I was angry, angry as a bunch of caged solflies. It would have been simple to just let the hate win and kill or maim him. But he'd already lost everything. Death would have meant nothing to him, and all that revenge would have gained me was time in the cells and the loss of everything I did have left. So, I let it go. Forgave him. I still have my struggles, but in that moment, I reckon I saved myself as much as I saved him."

"That takes a lot of strength." Rose pressed a hand to her chest. At last, someone who understood where she was coming from.

"Well, that may be so. We keep in touch. I put him in contact with some people who could help him, and he set up a fund for my boy to get him educated." Jakub looked into her eyes. "It seems to me that you're making the same kind of decision now. I know it's the right one."

Penthe clutched the mug as if her life depended on it, her gaze fixed on a spot just over Rose's shoulder. She mouthed something to someone or something that Rose couldn't see.

"Who is it, Penthe? Your mother?"

Penthe blinked and looked at her in surprise. "Can you hear her as well? I thought I was the only one who did."

Vash snorted and pushed her chair back. "You really are deranged, aren't you?"

"Please, Vash." Rose shot her a pleading look and turned back to Penthe. "No, I don't hear her. But I remember her, and I remember what she did to you. I think I can guess what she's saying."

"She never stops, Rose. I was never good enough. I killed her to make her go away, but she's still here."

Rose sucked in her breath. Over the cycles, she'd thought about the events, but to hear Penthe admit to matricide was still terrible. No wonder she had slid further and faster into the psychosis. Living with having killed her mother and unable to tell anyone. But she'd lived with the horrible woman and her abuse for cycles, so what had made her finally do it? "Why did you kill her?"

"Mother said she was going to pass over me because I wasn't good enough to succeed her. She was going to canvas the senior officers and find another. I would have to leave."

"I didn't know she could do that." Rose looked over at Vash, who was shaking her head.

"She was right though; I wasn't good enough." Penthe brought her hands up and raked her nails down her cheeks, drawing blood.

"Fates, no." Rose grabbed at Penthe's hands to stop her hurting herself any further.

"Nova!" Vash got up and grabbed the first aid kit from the wall.

She passed some wipes, and Rose gently wiped the blood from Penthe's face.

Jakub appeared at Penthe's side with a hypospray. He pressed it to her arm, and it softly hissed. Penthe's eyes glazed over, and he caught her as she collapsed to one side.

"Vash, help me get her to the bed," he said.

Penthe's face was peaceful, almost childlike, as they laid her down and pulled a cover over. The bloodied wipes still lay stacked in the middle of the table and leeched pink onto the nearby surface. Rose gathered them up and tossed them into the waste disposal unit.

"We keep some knockout shots just in case. It's not safe if someone gets agitated somewhere isolated like this." Jakub ran his hand through his hair. "She's in a bad place, Rose."

Rose nodded, and Vash looked thoughtful.

"She'll kill herself at this rate." Vash chewed her lip. "Perhaps I should've done as she asked back on the ship. It might have been a kindness."

"No." Rose reached out and stroked the back of Vash's head. "I'm sorry, but after everything that's happened, you must see that isn't the answer."

Vash closed her eyes and sighed. "I know, I know. But what are we going to do with her?"

Jakub poured himself another caffrush. "It seems to me we have two choices."

"I can't hand her back to them, Jakub. I know I should, but she's as much a victim as I am." Rose thumped the table and made Vash jump. "I'm sorry, but you didn't see her, see the cuts and bruises every day. Watching the light steadily fading from her eyes, and all of that at the hands of her own mother. No one helped her. This is a chance to put that right."

"Well, there's only one other choice. But are you prepared to make it?" Jakub tilted his head to the side.

"Someone mind filling me in?" Vash looked more confused than ever.

"What he's trying to say is that I'll need to keep her with me for now. We need to get help for her."

Vash's face paled. "You're joking, right? She's a danger to us as much as to herself."

Rose slid from her chair and hunkered down next to Vash. "I know this is a lot to ask, too much to ask really. I need to do this. It's like Jakub said, saving Penthe is saving myself and putting right a wrong." She stroked Vash's face. "You've done so much for me already. I love you too much to make you come on this journey with me if you don't want to."

"It's not that I don't want to, Rose. It's just that I don't know if I can."

Vash exhaled and cupped Rose's face in her hands. "I love you. I love you more than I thought possible. I'll do everything I can to keep you safe. I just don't know if I can do that if Penthe is with us."

Jakub coughed. "I have a suggestion. You don't have to agree, of course." He dragged his nail along a crack in the table.

"Any suggestion is welcome at the moment." Vash crossed her arms.

"Well, it's like this. The company have already made it clear they aren't keen on keeping me on.

"Yeah, that Tyler guy described you as an 'eccentric'. Just how bad have things been with them?" Rose said.

Jakub grimaced. "They never much liked my style of working, and I didn't appreciate their lack of concern for my health and safety. Anyhow, this mine is about to give up, and I didn't fancy signing on with them again. I was going to look for something else. Then I remembered what you said not so long ago—"

"You mean when she told you she'd give you a job?" The words were out before Rose could stop them.

Vash stared, mouth open. "Did you hear everything I said?"

"I wasn't spying, Vash. I was making us a drink, and I must have dozed off. When I came round, you were talking to Jakub. I didn't want to…that is… I'm really sorry, you must believe me." Rose swallowed hard, too ashamed to meet Vash's gaze. How could she ever have put herself in that position?

Vash leaned over and kissed the tip of her nose. "It's not like I can judge. I should have talked to you about it. I was just so embarrassed."

Rose threw herself at Vash and enveloped her in the biggest hug she could muster. Vash lifted her onto her lap and turned to Jakub.

"So, Mr Wolcuk, would you like to sign up to my crew?"

"I did wonder, Captain Munro, if you could do with a spare hand, especially considering these difficult circumstances." Jakub waved his good hand, with a cheerful smile. "I'm good with most things mechanical, and I'm a quick study."

Rose tapped Vash on the top of her head. "You know that we can make this work with him on board."

"Okay, okay. Don't damage the bodywork! Welcome aboard, Jakub." Vash offered her hand and Jakub shook it. "Or should I say, Chief Wolcuk?"

Jakub grinned. "Aye, ay, captain. Here's to the Bellerophon and all that sail the celestial seas in her."

Rose smiled. She may have lost her natural family, but she had found a chosen family now. Wherever she went now, whatever happened, they were going to be there to support her.

CHAPTER THIRTY-ONE

Penthe woke with a start, and sat up, disorientated. Where was she? There was movement on the other side of the bed. A man? His face was familiar. Jakub. The name popped into her mind. He was reading a tattered book. She tried to speak, but all that came out was a croak. Jakub looked over and smiled. He got up and propped her up on a couple of pillows. He slipped out of the door, leaving it ajar. She should get out of bed, but her limbs were strangely leaden. Jakub returned and handed her some water, holding the cup for her while she sipped at it.

"Where are they?" she asked.

"Vash and Rose? They've gone back to your ship to see what they can scavenge. We've got a long trip ahead of us," he said softly.

"I see." Her heart was heavy, but she couldn't blame them. "I don't suppose it will be long before the authorities get here."

Jakub frowned. Then shook his head. "I think you've misunderstood me, miss. I meant you as well. You're coming with us."

"I'm coming with you?"

"Unless you fancy explaining yourself to the system authorities. I assume you don't want to do that."

"But what about Munro?" She didn't remember everything from the previous evening, but Munro hadn't wanted her to stay. That stood out clearly.

"Captain Munro is happy to have you onboard. Mind, you'll have to work for your passage. Rose was very concerned for you, and Captain Munro wants to see that you're all right too." Jakub's poker face gave nothing away.

Penthe wasn't sure that she entirely believed him. However, the door opened before she could ask any more. Rose came in, carrying a bowl of broth.

"Penthe? Jakub said you were awake. How are you feeling?"

"Confused. Jakub said that I was coming with you." She searched

Rose's face, still sure that this was all a trick. Rose just looked back at her, guilelessly.

"I know it must seem strange, but it just feels like the right thing to do. We've both got a long road ahead of us, and I think we can help each other. Are you happy to do that?"

Shock robbed her temporarily of speech. While she was mulling it over, Vash came into the room and looked down at her with a not completely unfriendly expression.

"So, the sleeper awakes. Well, I hope you've got some energy back. We're going to need your help to get off this hunk of rock sooner rather than later. Help her get dressed, Rose, we need to get going." Then she was gone, striding from the room.

The next few hours were a whirlwind, helping to load the Bellerophon with supplies. No time to think or ask questions. Finally, she was shown to a remarkably cramped cabin. She looked to her right as she stepped through the hatch, expecting to see more space or another room. There was only a bulkhead and a mirror on the wall.

Jakub carried her bags in and put them by the bed. "I'll leave you to settle in."

She'd already grown to like his quiet, steady presence. She hadn't been around many men in her life, and most of them had been either violent, egotistical, or both. Jakub was none of these things, and his presence calmed her.

When he was gone, she sat alone, looking at the bulkhead. With no warning, thoughts crowded in, filling her brain with a tsunami of emotions. Overwhelmed, her vision started to blur. Old familiar harsh voices were shrieking in her ears, louder and louder, and shadows started to move in the corner of the room. She clutched her head and started to shake.

"How are you doing?" Jakub was stood at the door peering in.

"I'm…help me, Jakub. Please." She reached out if she was drowning. He took her hand and knelt in front of her.

"Look at me." He gazed at her intently. "Only me. I'm the only real thing here. Everything else is just an illusion. Understand? So, *look* at me. Breathe deeply and stay with me, Penthe."

She stared at him: at his craggy face, covered in deep creases; at his brown eyes and grey stubble; and at the sewn-up arm of his shirt, with a chewed pen sticking out of the pocket. Slowly the shadows stopped moving, and the voices went quiet. All she could hear was the thrum of the ship's engines and Jakub's steady breathing. "I'm sorry, Jakub. I don't know what happened." Penthe looked at the floor, embarrassed to meet his eye.

"You aren't well, Penthe, and I shouldn't have left you so long." He sat down next to her. "Now listen. I'm going to be sticking close to you for the time being, okay? I've got some meds that will help you sleep, and when you're awake you'll stay with me where I can keep an eye on you."

"I don't have a choice, do I?" Fatigue was fighting with despondency for control. Every part of her body was leaden, as if the gravity controls had gone into overdrive.

"Yes, of course you do. We'll stop before long, to refuel. If you want to leave, you can go and make your own way. You'll understand that in the meantime, you'll be kept under close watch. For your safety as much as ours."

The truth in his voice was undeniable. A second chance. Was she really going to throw it away? "Will I get better?"

"I believe so, and so does Rose."

Her heart lightened just at the mention of her name. Perhaps there was hope if Rose believed. But she needed to ask something else, something more important.

"There is one thing, Jakub. Something that I'm afraid of. Will you make me a promise?"

"Depends on what you ask." He frowned slightly.

"If I ever go bad." She shrugged. "If I ever *return* to being bad, if I ever try and hurt Rose, will you do what is needed?"

The silence lasted a while. With each passing second, her pulse pounded faster behind her eyes. Eventually, he looked up at her, sadness in his eyes.

"What you're asking isn't easy for me. Ask Vash…no, that's unfair, she's changed a fair bit too." He scratched at his chin. "But I know what you're asking and why. It takes strength to do that, and I reckon that if you've the strength to face that possibility, you've got the strength to overcome all of this."

"Promise me, Jakub." She couldn't leave this to chance.

"I promise, Penthe. I'll never let you hurt her. Even if that means killing you." He looked away. "Well, let's hope that day never comes."

Penthe took his hand and squeezed it, unable to speak, unable to thank him or tell him that, for the first time in her life, she felt truly safe.

CHAPTER THIRTY-TWO

THE BAND WAS LARGELY invisible on her arm now. Rose traced a finger over her skin and could only feel the smallest bit of friction beneath the surface. She closed her eyes and sought it deep within. It wasn't hard to find now. She followed the soft beating pulse behind her eyes until she found it: a small cluster of lights, bobbing and dancing like fireflies. Nothing like the raging electrical storms she had withstood the day before.

"Hey, gorgeous? Maybe you should go to sleep if you're tired."

She opened her eyes and blinked. "I'm not tired."

Vash raised an eyebrow. "Well, the dark circles around your eyes tell a different story."

"I must concur with the captain, Rose. You are extremely fatigued." Bel sounded concerned.

She closed her eyes again. Everyone meant well, but they just didn't understand. Her hand was busy on the arm of chair, drawing random patterns. Vash sat down and the warmth of her hand stayed its movement.

"Why don't you tell me what is going on in that head of yours? Maybe I can help."

"I'm not sure anyone can." She opened her eyes. Vash looked crestfallen. "It's just I don't know how to explain. It all feels such a mess."

"Is it about what happened yesterday?"

"Yes, but it's more than that. This thing…" Rose touched the faint markings on her arm. "It's part of me now, Vash. I can't get rid of it."

"Do you wish you could?"

"Yes. No. I mean, I don't know half of what it can do, and it scares me. But if I did remove it, it would just move on. Perhaps the next person—"

"Would be like Princess Nutter next door?" Vash slapped her forehead. "Sorry, that was bad."

"No, it was honest. I know this is really difficult."

Vash let out a deep breath. "Listen, I can't pretend I understand why she's here exactly, but if it's important to you, that's enough for me."

"I just feel responsible."

Vash snorted. "How can you be responsible for anything she has done?" She took her hand back and stood, legs astride and hands on hips. "And you're sure, right? Because I'd happily push her out of the airlock, you just give the word."

She smiled. Her warrior, ready to take on the galaxy to protect her. It was a good feeling. Vash raised an eyebrow, and Rose quickly shook her head. "We both need to heal and part of my healing is to see her get to a better place. I don't feel responsible for her actions, Vash, but she's family. My natural one, that is." Her lip hurt where she kept on biting it. She could see from Vash's frown that she wasn't doing a good job of explaining herself.

"Aren't I family? Or Jakub? Aren't we enough?"

Vash looked genuinely hurt, and Rose kicked herself for being so clumsy. She got to her feet and wrapped her arms around her. After a pause, Vash reciprocated.

"You are family, and you know it. Same goes for Jakub. You're an even more special family because you both chose it, and you chose me." A warmth spread through her body as she spoke the wonderful words.

She drew circles on Vash's back, just where she always liked it. This time, the tension didn't release. Instead, Vash stepped back.

"So, what do you mean?" Her gaze was intent and serious.

Rose paused for a moment, her brain buzzing as she searched for the right words.

"You know how you reacted when I told you I was an Ak?"

Vash flushed. "Well, yes, but you're different, Rose. Not like the others."

"No, that's the point. I'm not. The Akmonians you hear about, they're all at the top of the shop. Heads of Houses, ruling their fiefdoms through fear and violence. *Most* Akmonians are exactly like me."

Vash chewed her lip. "Still doesn't explain why you want to keep Penthe around. I would've thought you'd want to be a million lightyears away from her."

"Penthe wasn't born like this. She was nurtured by an unforgiving, violent system. A system we all bought into and celebrated at times." Rose was the one with the hot face now. "I saw how she was treated by her mother, and you wouldn't do it to an animal. And everyone just stood by and let it happen." She thumped the arm of the chair. "I let it happen."

In the ensuing silence, all she could hear was the irregular clicking of the life-support systems on the bridge. Even Bel didn't have anything to say.

"Yeah, well, loads of people have a tough upbringing." Vash scratched behind her ear.

"The thing is, I have a chance now to show her the other side of who we are. If I abandoned her now, she'd never know. She's never been loved; how can I let her die without ever knowing how that feels?"

Vash turned away and fiddled with a display.

Rose sank back into the chair. There was no point saying any more. If this wasn't enough, it was never going to be. Eventually Vash turned and knelt in front of her. Rose swallowed hard at the sight of her red and swollen eyes. She brushed the tears lightly from Vash's cheek with her thumb. "Why?"

Vash let her head rest in Rose's hand. "Sometimes I'm reminded of how lucky I am."

"Lucky?"

"You know how special you are, Rose?"

Rose hadn't expected this. "You're the special one, Vash. You're the woman who accepted me for who I was. The one who fought for me and came back for me."

Vash laughed softly and shook her head as she pulled away. "Nope. I'm just an adventurer. You're twice the woman I'll ever be. You're good, you're good in here." She poked a finger gently into Rose's midriff.

"But…I killed someone yesterday."

"No, you stopped someone killing hundreds and perhaps thousands more. Because she wouldn't have stopped at Jakub and me. She would've carried on."

"She's still dead. Like Jakub said, I let the band do that. It's going to take a while for me to come to terms with that. I never thought I was capable of killing anyone; I get teary when I squash a biter."

"Yes, and that's the difference. You're sorry about it. It's eating you at your core. She wouldn't have lost any sleep."

Rose could see some veracity in what Vash was saying. "But what if it happens again? How can I get on with life knowing what I can do, what the band can do?"

"By remembering it every day," Jakub said. He came onto the bridge and sat beside her. "You'll remember what happened, and you'll remember how it made you feel after. The minute you forget, that's when the band will be a danger again." He rested his hand on her shoulder. "Listen, Vash is right. You ain't no monster, Rose. It's not going to be easy, but we'll be here to help however we can."

She rubbed the bridge of her nose. Did they understand how their love made her feel, how it made her glow inside? It was so powerful, to be loved without question and so sincerely that it gave her the strength she needed at her lowest ebb.

She leaned over and gave Jakub a peck on the cheek, making him blush slightly. "Thanks, I appreciate that, really I do. How's Penthe?"

Jakub's expression was serious. "Sleeping. I found her hallucinating again, but she's okay now. It's going to be a long road."

Vash got to her feet and stretched her back. "Well, she's with us now." She looked down at Rose. "We'll look after her."

There was a lump in her throat again, but before she could say anything, Bel's soft voice came over the speakers.

"Captain?"

"Yeah, Bel? Everything okay?" Vash rolled her eyes.

"I thoroughly checked all systems before we left the planet's gravity well."

"Of course you did. So?"

"I was wondering if you'd decided yet on a destination. We're coming up on the edge of the system."

Vash wrinkled her nose. "Yeah, well about that, the thing is—"

"The Helion Nebula." The words flooded out before Rose had a chance to stop them.

Vash looked at her quizzically. "The Helion what? Is that something to do with your band?"

She stared at her feet. "Sorry, I was going to talk it over. It was just that Bel told me that there was a nebula called Helion, and I wondered if they were connected."

"And you want to find out more about it?" Vash lifted her chin, excitement in her eyes. "I think that's a great idea. Bel, how long will it take us to get there?"

"At our standard cruising speed, I calculate an ETA of…three standard cycles and fourteen days."

Vash swallowed hard. "Not nearby then?"

"It's on the far side of the galaxy, captain."

"Three cycles!" Jakub guffawed loudly and clutched his stomach. "No wonder you hadn't told her."

"I was trying to find the right moment." Now her face was really burning. She looked at Vash, dreading her answer, but Vash just gave her a wry smile.

"Well, I always wanted to see a bit of life. We'll have to do a bit of trading on the way though, fuel doesn't buy—"

She threw herself at Vash, wrapped her arms around her neck and planted a big kiss. "I love you, Vash Munro!"

Vash grinned. "Bel, set course for the Helion Nebula, please."

"Yes, captain, course is set."

"Oh, there is just one more thing I need to ask." She was being naughty but couldn't resist.

Vash's eyes narrowed slightly. "Yes?"

"I think I'm a bit tired now. Would you mind taking me to bed?"

Jakub's laughter followed them as they walked hand in hand down the corridor. Rose squeezed Vash's hand, and Vash looked at her.

"You okay?"

"Couldn't be better." The truth of her words warmed Rose inside. She felt safe and loved. She'd finally come home.

GLOSSARY

Term	Description
agribots	Robots used on agrifarms
agrilab	Industrial laboratory dedicated to growing food for consumption
agrifarm	Agricultural industrial building
antiploi	Equivalent to commander
anthypoploi	Equivalent to sub-lieutenant
archiploi	Equivalent to commodore, chief of staff
avatoids	Artificial representative (usually humanoid) of artificial intelligence running a spaceship
basilinna	Akmonian word for queen
bilgepiss	Epithet
bilgeslime	Epithet
bilgeslug	Epithet
bilgesucker	Epithet
biomesh	Sub-cutaneous electronic device
caffrush	Non-alcoholic, caffeinated drink, usually served hot
citriflush	Non-alcoholic citrus drink
coleoidea	Grouping of cephalopods which includes octopus, squid and cuttlefish
cotbed	Bed found onboard ship
cotroom	Ship cabin
cryofood	Food kept at sub-zero temperatures for transportation
cycle	Locally defined period, during which a planet or orbital completes its orbit of a star
docvid	Documentary style footage
electrocomb	Tool for arranging hair
fabplant	Fabrication plant
fates	Exclamation
gelech	Game involving bat and ball
guardbeast	Canine-like mammal bred purely for guarding premises
hab	Slang for accommodation
habpod	Habitation pod, usually temporary
habroach	Cockroach-like creature found
habroom	Living space
Headvid	Kit worn on head which provides video or VR display
hotshake	Non-alcoholic drink – often herbal or fruit based
kelefstis	Equivalent to petty officer

Term	Description
kidbin	Small transport for young children
kras	Alcoholic drink, traditionally made from grapes
leafroll	Addictive smokable stimulant
matronbot	Robot designed to take care of young children
medibed	Bed found in Medical Units
medichair	Patient transport equipment, can be self-propelling, motorised or autonomous
mouthbead	Over-ear mounted microphone
naftoi	Equivalent to seaman/marine
nova	Exclamation
oil wool	Heavy, oiled material, natural or synthetic. Used for its thermal properties
orbon	Alcoholic drink, traditionally made from vegetables or fruit
parbird	Type of bird, found on tropical planets, often garishly coloured
plasticups	Drinking vessels
plastiglas	Building material made from durable material
plastiknife	Knife made from durable material
plastimetal	Building material made from durable material
plastitile	Building material made from durable material
ploiarchos	Equivalent to captain
podcar	Autonomous vehicle
quickneedle	Injection equipment, usually sold complete with pharmaceutical
sexden	Brothel
shackle	Bracelet which records activities of mining operatives
snowhound	Canine breed
sol	Star at the centre of a solar system
solfly	Type of common insect, capable of producing its own light
sollight	Sunlight
solrise	Sunrise
solspot	Sunspot
standard cycle	standard period, created by Galactic authorities to facilitate trade and diplomacy between planets operating on radically different cycles
standard day	Standard diurnal period used largely onboard ships and by computing networks, created by Galactic authorities to facilitate trade and diplomacy. Planets and orbitals are

Term	Description
	free to set their own localised diurnal period if required, however these are not recognised at a galactic level. Standard period created by Galactic authorities to facilitate trade and diplomacy.
standard year	Standard diurnal period used largely onboard ships, created by Galactic authorities to facilitate trade and diplomacy. Planets and orbitals are free to set their own localised diurnal period, however these are not recognised at a galactic level.
stars	Exclamation
sysgeld	Standard galactic currency
T-Suite	Torture suite
tac-glove	Glove with built-in sensors, enabling its virtual use alongside holographic displays
tanskin	Material made from the skin of an animal
tech	Slang for engineers
thumbscan	Form of personalised identification
trakhener	Type of mammal, usually four-legged, used as pack animal
twistleaf	Mildly hallucinogenic natural product – can be smoked or chewed
twistpoly	Synthetic material, often used for clothing
twistrug	Rug made from natural materials
unitape	Like gaffer tape
vidrecorder	Equipment used to record vid
vidscreen	Screen on which recorded or live feed can be viewed
ypoploi	Equivalent to lieutenant

Other Great Butterworth Books

Dead Pretty by Robyn Nyx
An FBI agent, a TV star, and a serial killer. Love hurts.
Available on Amazon (ISBN 9781915009128)

Scripted Love by Helena Harte
What good is a romance writer who doesn't believe in happy ever after?
Available from Amazon August 2021 (ASIN B0993QFLNN)

Caribbean Dreams by Karen Klyne
When love sails into your life, do you climb aboard?
Available from Amazon (ASIN B09M41PYM9)

Nero by Valden Bush
Banished. Abandoned. Lost. Will her destiny reunite her with the love of her life?
Available from Amazon (ASIN B09BXN8VTZ)

Warm Pearls and Paper Cranes by E.V. Bancroft
A family torn apart. The only way forward is love.
Available from Amazon (ISBN 9781915009029)

That Boy of Yours Wants Looking At by Simon Smalley
A gloriously colourful and heart-rending memoir.
Available from Amazon (ASIN B09HSN9NM8)

Judge Me, Judge Me Not by James Merrick
A memoir of one gay man's battle against the world and himself.
Available from Amazon (ASIN B09CLK91N5)

LesFic Eclectic Volume Three edited by Robyn Nyx
A little something for all tastes.
Available free via BookFunnel (ISBN 9781915009135)

When I'm Gone by Lee Haven
When your second chance with the love of your life literally means giving a piece of yourself away, is there really any choice?
Coming soon

What's Your Story?

Global Wordsmiths, CIC, provides an all-encompassing service for all writers, ranging from basic proofreading and cover design to development editing, typesetting, and eBook services. A major part of our work is charity and community focused, delivering writing projects to under-served and under-represented groups across Nottinghamshire, giving voice to the voiceless and visibility to the unseen.

To learn more about what we offer, visit: www.globalwords.co.uk

A selection of books by Global Words Press:
Desire, Love, Identity: with the National Justice Museum
Aventuras en México: Farmilo Primary School
Life's Whispers: Journeys to the Hospice
Times Past: with The Workhouse, National Trust
Times Past: Young at Heart with AGE UK
In Different Shoes: Stories of Trans Lives
From Surviving to Thriving: Reclaiming Our Voices
Don't Look Back, You're Not Going That Way

Self-published authors working with Global Wordsmiths:
E.V. Bancroft
Addison M. Conley
AJ Mason
Ally McGuire
Emma Nichols
Helena Harte
Iona Kane
James Merrick
Karen Klyne
Robyn Nyx
John Edward Parsons
Simon Smalley
Valden Bush

Lightning Source UK Ltd.
Milton Keynes UK
UKHW020133290422
402191UK00007B/75